ZODL

Conrad Jo...

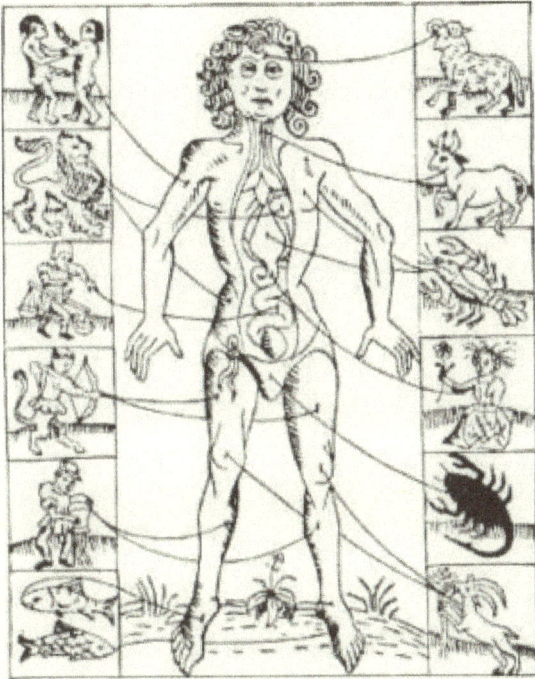

Zodiac Man

The Detective Alec Ramsay Series
The Child Taker
Slow Burn
Criminally Insane
Frozen Betrayal
Concrete Evidence
Desolate Sands
Three
The Inspector Braddick Books (follows on from Ramsay)
Brick
Shadows
Guilty
Deliver us from Evil
The Anglesey Murders (runs alongside Braddick)
Unholy Island
A Visit from the Devil
Nearly Dead
A Child from the Devil
Dark Angel
What Happened to Rachel?
Good, Bad and Pure Evil
Circus of Nightmares
Unravelling
A Disturbing Thing Happened Today
Soft Target Series (feature Tank from The Child Taker)
Soft Target
Tank
Jerusalem
18th Brigade
Blister
The Journey Series
The Journey
The Journey Back
The Journey Home
The Magic Dragons of Anglesey
The Rock Goblins
The Pirate's Treasure
Standalone
Zodiac
The Curious Haunting at 44 Brick St

Red Dragon Publishing LTD

ISBN: 978-1-7394066-8-4

This book is a work of fiction. Any resemblance between these fictional characters and actual persons, living or dead, is purely coincidental.

RED DRAGON BOOKS

The 12 Zodiac Signs

EACH SIGN CORRESPONDS to a specific date range and has distinct characteristics:

1. **Aries (March 21 - April 19)**: Represented by the ram, Aries are known for being energetic, assertive, and pioneering.

2. **Taurus (April 20 - May 20)**: Symbolized by the bull, Taureans are often seen as reliable, practical, and patient.

3. **Gemini (May 21 - June 20)**: Represented by the twins, Geminis are adaptable, curious, and sociable.

4. **Cancer (June 21 - July 22)**: Symbolized by the crab, Cancers are intuitive, sensitive, and nurturing.

5. **Leo (July 23 - August 22)**: Represented by the lion, Leos are known for their confidence, creativity, and leadership.

6. **Virgo (August 23 - September 22)**: Symbolized by the maiden, Virgos are analytical, meticulous, and helpful.

7. **Libra (September 23 - October 22)**: Represented by the scales, Libras are diplomatic, charming, and value harmony.

8. **Scorpio (October 23 - November 21)**: Symbolized by the scorpion, Scorpios are intense, passionate, and resourceful.

9. **Sagittarius (November 22 - December 21)**: Represented by the archer, Sagittarians are adventurous, optimistic, and philosophical.

10. **Capricorn (December 22 - January 19)**: Symbolized by the goat, Capricorns are disciplined, ambitious, and pragmatic.

11. **Aquarius (January 20 - February 18)**: Represented by the water bearer, Aquarians are innovative, independent, and humanitarian.

12. **Pisces (February 19 - March 20)**: Symbolized by the fish, Pisces are empathetic, artistic, and dreamy.

Chapter 1

4-years earlier

It was late at night, but she didn't know how late. She'd been blindfolded for hours, and time had merged into a terrifying blur. Her lips were swollen and cracked by dehydration and a series of hard backhanders, received when she had struggled. She hadn't had anything but a few sips of water since she was taken from that room, and she was weak with hunger and exhaustion. Fear and pain had warped her mind, and she was blaming herself for her situation.

She had trusted him, and he had used that to abduct her. Her mother had warned her to trust no one, especially men but she had let her guard down for a moment and a moment was all it had taken; like a moth to a flame. He had kept her in a room which had been warm and dry and at first, she thought he might not hurt her. She had been wrong, very wrong. The first assault had been prolonged and brutal, and she thought he was going to kill her, but then she sensed others had arrived, and something arrived with them. Things went from bad to worse to indescribable. She had felt the evil from the onset, and she had wished for death to take her.

The assaults were brutal and relentless, and the incantations echoed in her mind and chilled her to the bone. It was like the worst nightmare anyone could imagine and then some more. Her mind had drifted away to some dark places and her dreams had been darker still, haunted by devils and demons and entities that she had no words to describe. The gulf between reality and imaginary had merged. There was no peace to be found, just terror and debilitating anxiety that she wasn't going to survive the ordeal.

Her family were front of mind every second and she yearned to be back in the safety of her home with mum, dad, annoying brothers and sisters and her adoring grandparents. She wished she could tell them how much she loved them.

She had been relieved when finally, he had dressed her and put her into the boot of a vehicle, but her relief was short lived as realisation hit home. She was covered in bites and scratches and there would be DNA inside her. He couldn't let her go.

Her captor had been quiet since he took her from the vehicle and forced her to walk, barefoot through a forest. She knew it was a forest because she could feel pine needles piercing the skin of her feet, the blood trickling between her toes. The unmistakable smell of pine trees filled the air, and she could hear the peaceful gurgling of a stream in the distance. The occasional hoot of an owl pierced the night, and the scurrying of nocturnal mammals and insects were coming to her from all directions.

Her hands were bound behind her, the rough hemp of the rope biting into her wrists. The blindfold was tight, pressing against her eyelids and plunging her world into darkness so deep, her brain could not comprehend it. She stumbled over the uneven ground, guided—or rather driven—by the man whose grip on her arm was unyielding.

'Where are you taking me?' Her voice trembled as much as her legs. 'Please let me go!'

'Silence!' The word wasn't just spoken; it was spit out like a curse which echoed through her mind. The incantations drifted to her again. The Latin was fluid, the words unfamiliar but unmistakably ancient, resonating with an eerie authority that made her skin crawl.

'Please,' she whispered, the plea barely leaving her lips before the sound was swallowed by the forest around them.

The man didn't respond. Instead, he began to chant in a rhythmic cadence, the Latin flowing faster from his tongue, quietly like a whisper. She felt the hairs on the back of her neck rise. There was something deeply unsettling about the tone of his voice, a fervency that suggested this was no mere recitation but a prayer to something unseen.

As they walked, the earthy scent of the forest filled her nostrils, damp and heavy. Leaves crunched underfoot, twigs snapped, and somewhere above, a branch creaked ominously. Fear knotted in her stomach, each step forward tightening the coil.

'Exaudi nos, o Dea tenebrarum,' the man intoned. His grip on her arm slackened as he stopped abruptly. She nearly collided with him but caught herself at the last moment.

'Stand still,' he whispered. 'Listen. Can you hear her?'

She obeyed, her breath shallow. Whispering voices floated on the breeze, almost angelic in tone. The chanting continued, growing more frantic, urgent. Then, the sound of digging reached her. The scrape of metal against soil, rhythmic and determined. The man was burying something—or someone.

'What are you doing?' she dared to ask. He didn't reply. The sound of a shovel moving earth continued. His chanting continued, merging with the other voices. Their harmonies like an acoustic choir. Other voices joined in the chant, swirling around her. Male, female—they seemed to come from all directions, some clear and near, others so faint she could barely make them out. They sounded ethereal, ghostly, as if the singers were not of this world.

'Who are they?' she asked. 'What do they want?'

'They want your silence,' he warned, his own voice melding into the chorus of chants. 'Listen and be still.'

She strained her ears, trying to decipher the meaning hidden within the cacophony of voices. Each syllable seemed to throb in the air, vibrating with power. She pictured the forest around her, imagined the trees bending inward, their branches reaching out as if to witness—or partake—in whatever unholy ceremony she had been brought to.

'Libera nos,' the voices pleaded together, a haunting litany. 'Release us,' the man whispered. 'Forgive us.'

'I'll forgive you if you let me go,' her voice was a whisper, fear mingling with terror. She needed to understand, to find some logic in this madness but she could find none.

'Your forgiveness means nothing to me. Do you think you can release me from oblivion, from all eternity?' the man beside her said softly, almost kindly. 'Can you save me from the abyss where forgotten things dwell?'

'Will my family ever know what happened to me?' Her voice cracked with the weight of her dread. 'I want my mum...please let me go. I want my mummy...'

'Perhaps, they will know,' he murmured, the chant ebbing away as he spoke. 'Or perhaps you will be remembered forever as a girl who was lost and never returned.'

'Please, let me go,' she begged, desperation seeping into her voice. But there was no mercy in the thrumming voices that filled the air, no compassion in the cold grip of the man who held her fate in his hands. 'What is happening to me?'

'Patience,' he chided her. 'Soon, all will be revealed.'

The chanting grew louder once more, the voices overlapping until it was impossible to distinguish one from another. She felt dizzy, the darkness behind her blindfold spinning. The ground beneath her feet seemed to pulse with the rhythm of the chant, and for a moment, she wondered if the very earth was alive, responding to the summons of these strange acolytes.

'Why me?' she asked, her voice barely audible over the din. 'Why are you doing this to me?'

'Because you were there at the right time,' the man answered simply, as if that explained everything. 'You chose yourself.'

'But why me, why was I chosen?'

'Does it matter?'

'To me, it does. I need to know what I did wrong.'

'Then believe whatever will give you the most peace?' he said, a note of finality in his voice. 'You made yourself an easy choice.'

She sobbed harder than she had ever before, to the point she thought she might choke. The chanting reached a fever pitch, the voices desperate, pleading for something she could not comprehend. She felt tears stinging at the corners of her eyes, their warmth incongruous with the chill of fear that enveloped her.

'I want my mum...' She stood at the edge of understanding, teetering between the known and the unknowable.

'Finished,' the man announced suddenly, and silence crashed down like a wave.

Her heart froze in her chest, waiting for what would come next. But there was only the soft rustle of leaves and the distant cry of a night bird.

'Are you going to kill me?' The question hung in the air, fragile as glass.

'Life and death,' he said cryptically, 'are merely threads in the tapestry of existence. The universe is life and death and energy. Tonight, we weave with those threads.'

A chill ran down her spine as she realized that whatever purpose she had been brought here for was inexorable, woven into the fabric of this night by forces she could neither see nor understand. Whether victim or vessel, she was part of something ancient and terrifyingly larger than herself. And as the forest held its breath, she waited for the next verse of the chant, the next turn of the spade, the next revelation in the dark symphony that had claimed her. He forced her to walk on, deeper into the trees.

It felt like hours before he grabbed her and threw her to the floor. That was when she heard the sound of a spade again cutting through soil, dead twigs, and tree roots. She knew he was digging her grave.

The cold ground beneath her was unforgiving, the jagged earth pressing into her side where he had thrown her. Her breaths came in short, sharp gasps, terror constricting her chest like a vice.

'Please,' she whispered. The darkness seemed to press harder, suffocating her. She was lost, blind in her world of terror. 'Why are you doing this?'

Her captor didn't answer, the only sound was the relentless thud and scrape of metal against the earth. She could almost feel each shovelful of soil being lifted and tossed aside, a grave growing deeper with every moment that passed.

'Talk to me,' she tried again, her voice cracking with desperation. 'I won't tell anyone what you've done, I swear.'

Still, no response. Just the rhythmic digging, an eerie lullaby that seemed to mock her pleas for mercy. The smell of pine was thick in the air, mixing with the metallic scent of her own blood as it seeped from the cuts on her feet.

'Stop, please!' she cried out, her words devolving into sobs. She shifted, trying to find some position that would offer comfort, but the forest floor was relentless in its harshness.

Suddenly, the digging ceased. She held her breath, straining her ears for any sign of what would come next. There was a rustling sound, then footsteps approaching. He held her chin and felt her jawbone and scalp with his fingers.

'Your time here is over,' said a chillingly calm voice right above her. 'You'll soon be part of something truly beautiful. The universe will welcome your energy, embrace it.'

A sob tore from her throat, the reality of her situation crashing down on her with the weight of the dark sky above. This was it—the end. And yet, as her tears soaked through the blindfold, she couldn't stop the last sliver of hope from whispering through her mind, begging for a miracle in the stillness of the night. The images of her parents, grandparents, brothers and sisters flashed by, extinguished by a single blow from the axe.

He took out his phone and pressed pause and the incantations stopped. The forest fell silent again. He knelt and sniffed at the perfume he had sprayed on her. It was musky and mingled with the coppery smell of blood, it made his head spin. There would be time to be with her again while she was still warm before he put her in the ground...

Chapter 2.

The Whitehouse

The morning that Gary White saw a dead body for the first time, was a cold damp Monday in November. He turned off his alarm and reluctantly climbed out of bed, pulled on his socks and opened the curtains. He could see his own breath as he yawned and rubbed the sleep from his eyes. Condensation ran down the window and the ever-present smell of damp lingered in the air. Black mould stained the wallpaper beneath the windowsill where moisture pooled and dripped down the wall. His dad said he was going to fix the problem, but it was probably way down his endless list of things he never fixed.

Gary reached into the wardrobe for his school uniform. His shirt collar was a little grimy, but it would have to do for another few days until his mother did the washing, which was piling up as usual. His clothes felt cold and uncomfortable but that was nothing new to him. Warm fresh clothing was never available in the White House, the name the family gave their home. His father, Bill called himself the president and his mother, Hayley the first lady, which he found hilarious, but Gary seldom saw the funny side of anything his father said. He loved his dad, no doubt about it but he wasn't much of a role model, drank too much, smoked weed, didn't work regularly and as a result financially, the family struggled. Bill struggled with his mental health, as did his late parents, brother Ted who committed suicide and sister Janine. His side of the family had been plagued with debilitating mental issues.

Every now and again, his father would come into some money, and they would live well until it was all spent. He would never say where the money had come from, and Gary didn't care. His mother had three jobs on the side, so they could claim benefits, but they hardly paid her enough to cover the gap between their habits and the bills.

Gary yawned again and dressed, fastened his trainers and fumbled with the zipper of his faded winter jacket; his fingers clumsy in the chill of the morning. At least it felt warm, which was a good thing. One of his old favourite toys caught his eye. Gary knelt on the carpet, his fingers tracing the spine of a plastic Tyrannosaurus rex before setting it aside with a sigh. Once his pride and joy, the dinosaur joined the ranks of neglected toy soldiers lined against the wall, their miniature battles now perpetually on pause. His gaze lingered on the train set which ran beneath his bed, its tracks cold and lifeless, the imaginary thunderous chug of the engine now a distant memory. Online gaming and football were now his focus. He shivered again.

His slender frame felt the cold, nothing a bowl of hot porridge couldn't fix but there was more chance of winning the lottery than getting breakfast in the Whitehouse. He tiptoed along the landing and padded down the stairs as quietly as he could, which was difficult on bare floorboards and stairs. His dad had promised his mum a carpet when Gary was born, twelve years ago but it never materialised. His mum moaned every day until the floorboards were varnished by a friend as a favour for Bill; they looked okay but were cold. Bill White was full of promises and big ideas, which were never delivered. Everyone on the estate called his dad a dick, which was embarrassing.

In the kitchen, Gary flicked the light switch, but only a dim bulb above the sink sputtered to life, casting long shadows across the kitchen's stained surfaces. He moved through the clutter with a practised step, avoiding a minefield of empty tins around the overflowing bin. His parents had had friends over the night before, who brought an Indian takeaway with them. The smell of curry hung heavy on the air. Crusted dishes and scattered cartons covered the countertops. Rice had spilled onto the worktop, looking like maggots in the dull light.

'Jesus, what a mess, and they say I'm untidy,' he muttered, his voice disappearing into the gloom. 'Every time they have a takeaway; the place is a shit tip.'

The stench was palpable—a mix of days-old rubbish and something sour that he couldn't quite place. Something deep inside the bin was rotten. Gary's hand instinctively went up to cover his nose, but he dropped it immediately, knowing the gesture was futile against the pervasive odour. It wasn't right to hold your nose in your own home. He glanced toward the living room, where the detritus of his parents' latest party lay testament to their neglect. Empty bottles formed an uneven obstacle course on the floor, a few rolling listlessly as he kicked them accidentally. The ashtrays on the coffee table had long since given up on containing their contents; mounds of cigarette butts spilled onto the threadbare carpet.

'Fucking hell, they can't even clean up after themselves,' Gary grumbled, kicking a bottle aside. It clinked hollowly against another, the sound echoing mockingly in the dingy space. 'If I leave a bowl in the sink unrinsed, I'm a lazy pig.'

His eyes narrowed at the haze that lingered in the air, the unmistakable scent of weed mingling with the other foul odours. The smell brought back memories—none of them fond—as he recalled the countless times, he'd come home to find his parents passed out, lost in their own chemical escapes. The fact they had children seemed to be a second thought to them. Gary was growing up and growing resentful. He wanted more from them than they were capable of giving. It was like living with the lunatics in charge of the asylum. No one was in charge at all. No one took responsibility, no one cared.

'Gary! Are you ready for school?' his sister shouted. 'I can hear you muttering down there. What's up?'

'Every single time they have a takeaway, the place is like a fucking bombsite, and they leave fuck all for us to eat.'

Don't worry, son, we'll put some aside for you to ding in the morning.

'Never happens. Greedy twats,' he said under his breath, the edge in his tone cutting through the silence.

'Stop moaning. Are you ready?'

'Yes, I'm ready.'

He made his way through the living room, careful not to disturb the fragile ecosystem of crap. It was a landscape he knew all too well, one that fuelled his determination to never follow in their footsteps—to be different, to be better and not to be poor and hungry.

None of his friends at school had to put up with this shit. Yes, some of them were short of expendable income and didn't have the newest brand clothing, but they weren't hungry. His friend Trent from next door invited him for tea a few times a week. His mum was Jamaican, and their kitchen was a hive of activity, constantly producing the most amazing stews and casseroles. The spices and chillies made his eyes water but the meals he'd tried were like a taste explosion. She loved to feed her family and their friends. Gary's mum struggled to get off the settee for a piss.

'There's no way out of here anytime soon, Gary,' he muttered to himself. 'But I'm not living like this until I'm old enough to leave, at sixteen,' he promised himself quietly, 'just hang on a bit longer and something will change. It has to. They have to.'

With each step, Gary felt the weight of his resolve harden. This wasn't just a messy house—it was the embodiment of every reason he had to succeed in life, to pull himself out of the circle of unemployment; the benefit trap. And nothing, not the dirt, the darkness, nor the despair, would keep him rooted in that place any longer than necessary. He loved his parents but despised who they were. It was a difficult conflict to manage at such a tender age.

He went back into the kitchen, glanced at the empty shelves inside the fridge with a resigned sigh, the familiar pang of hunger gnawing at his insides. His sister Rosie came into the room, accompanied by the scent of fake Chanel. At thirteen, she was a year older than Gary but physically and mentally, she was much more mature than him. She was very protective of her younger brother and in a constant battle with her parents about their lifestyle and the effect it had on them. They smoked, drank and sniffed their money to the detriment of their children, and she called them out daily and demanded shopping was done or food delivered when they hadn't eaten. Gary idolised her. She was his hero.

'Are you hungry?' she asked, checking her hair in the mirror. She was pretty with long dark hair and hazel eyes. Gary shared her dark features and eye colour. 'Of course you are. There's fuck all in to eat as usual but I have some money on me.' She winked.

'How come you always have money?' Gary asked. 'I never have any money.'

'I've told you before, I do a bit of part-time work sometimes,' she said, tapping her nose with her forefinger. 'Don't worry where it came from. We'll get a bacon butty from the van on the high street. Can't have you starving to death. Come on, Gaz,' his sister said softly, her voice a gentle nudge against his low mood. 'We'll be late for registration, but we'll be full up.'

He smiled and nodded, casting one last, forlorn look towards the barren kitchen before following her out of the house. The air outside was crisp, whispering promises of a day he wasn't quite ready to face. They walked in silence as she texted at frightening speed without bumping into a lamppost or traffic sign. It was a skill she had mastered. It was still only half-light and a mist hovered around the streetlights, forming halos around them. There was something eerie about this time of day. His sister's presence was a comfort against the day's bleak beginning.

'Hey Gary,' a voice called.

'Dinosaur boy,' another voice called. 'Come on, Gary, you're not still playing with those baby toys, are you?' The voice echoed from beyond the garden wall next door, followed by the appearance of Gary's friends, their grins teasing.

I don't play with baby toys, you prick,' Gary said, shaking his head.

'I'll ask your sister.'

'Shut up, Mike,' Gary muttered, feeling a flush of embarrassment creep up his neck.

'I'm just joking,' Mike said with a wink. He pushed his blond curls from his face. 'Nothing wrong with dinosaurs, when you're six.'

'Whatever.' Gary kicked at a tin can. It clattered down the street. 'It's just stuff I played with when I was a kid. We all have old stuff.'

'Yes. Stuff for kids,' another friend called Pete, chimed in. 'Stick them on eBay.'

'You can shut up, Peter Blackwell,' Rosie interrupted. 'I've been to your house, and you used to play dollies with your sister, so don't take the piss out of my brother or I'll let everyone on the school bus know.'

'Did you play dollies with your sister?' Mike laughed. His chubby cheeks were reddened by the cold. Pete blushed and walked away. 'Which was your favourite dolly, Pete?' Mike called after him.

'Fuck off, Mike, you fat knobhead.'

Gary laughed, relieved to be out of the firing line. Rosie to the rescue again. She smiled at him and walked ahead, saying hello to some other boys wearing the same school uniform. They stared at her chest too long.

'Hey. You know what we were talking about yesterday?' Mike whispered. 'Jenny Simons.'

'Jenny Simons,' Gary repeated, the name feeling foreign, yet familiar on his lips. 'My sister's friend with red hair?'

'Yep, rumours are she's runaway with some guy from Toxteth,' Mike said, nudging Gary's shoulder. 'Apparently, she's been with a few older lads. She's got a decent rack, mate, but like, the not too big kind, you know?'

'Ugh, don't be saying stuff like that around Rosie,' Gary protested, but curiosity flickered within him. Girls had always been as alien to him as the lost world of his dinosaurs. A 'Missing' poster jumped out at him, wrapped around a lamppost. Another was pasted to a phone mast nearby. Jennifer Simmons, missing since the previous Saturday. That was over two weeks ago. 'Her posters are everywhere,' Gary said. 'I bet her mum and dad are going bananas.'

'No doubt about it. She'll be grounded until she's a hundred when they find her. Hey, speaking of girls,' Mike said, nodding towards Gary's older sister. She was walking past a group of boys from school, some of them trailing behind her like eager puppies. 'Looks like your sister has got herself an entire pack of admirers.'

'Leave her out of this,' Gary snapped, more protective than he wanted to admit.

'Chill out, mate,' Mike said, hands raised in mock surrender. 'Just saying, she's popular. Maybe she can give you some tips.'

'Shut up,' Gary mumbled, but his eyes couldn't help following his sister's confident stride, a stark contrast to his own awkward shuffle. Rosie glowed with energy and people gravitated to her.

'Anyway,' Mike said, clapping Gary on the back, 'I had better move on. My bus will be here in a minute.'

'Yeah, see you later,' Gary agreed, a part of him yearning to join his friends, but they went to a different school.

'Later, T-Rex Gary,' Mike called over his shoulder as they exited, laughter trailing behind them like the tail of a comet. 'See you after school.'

'You're a knob. Later,' Gary whispered to the empty space where his friends had been, feeling the pangs of hunger. Three girls from the year above him walked by and smelled gorgeous. They were pretty too. Very pretty. Females were becoming the focus, and he wasn't sure that was a good thing.

At the bus stop, there were more posters. 'Jennifer Simmons, missing.' Gary shuffled his feet, the cold seeping through the worn soles of his Nike trainers. They were a year old now and already too small for his growing feet. He shifted from foot to foot, the chill of the rain seeping into his bones. He glanced at Rosie; her small hands buried deep in the pockets of her white padded jacket. It was a fashion copy of a much more expensive brand with a logo on the left sleeve, but she looked good in it. She looked good in anything.

'The bus should've been here by now,' he muttered, scanning the grey street for the familiar green shape of the double-decker that would carry them to school.

Rosie nodded, her teeth chattering. She hugged his arm. 'It's freezing, Gary.'

'You should've worn the hat nan knitted,' he said with a half-smile, trying to lighten the mood. 'That was so funny.' He chuckled at the memory of Rosie's expression when she saw the hat. Horrified was the word. 'I thought you were going to cry.'

'It wasn't funny!'

A sudden screech cut through the drizzle, and both siblings snapped their heads up. A teenager on an electric scooter swerved wildly, trying to avoid a sleek black motorcycle that had appeared seemingly out of nowhere. Metal clashed against metal, and the scooter skidded across the saturated pavement, the rider thrown to the ground with a thud. People ran to him, trying to help.

'My leg!' the boy cried.

'Did you see that, Rosie? His leg is bent the wrong way,' Gary exclaimed, his heart racing. She nodded; her eyes wide with shock. The traffic slowed to a crawl as drivers skirted the accident. The rain intensified, making it cold and uncomfortable.

'Is he okay?' she asked. 'Stay here,' she said firmly, taking charge as her instinct to help kicked in. She jogged over to the scene. The motorcycle had come to a stop, its rider dismounted and crouching beside the teenager who lay motionless on the wet asphalt.

'Hey, are you hurt?' a woman asked.

The motorcyclist looked up, his helmet masking any expression. 'The stupid fucker shouldn't be on the road on a scooter. Call an ambulance,' he said gruffly. Gary pulled out his phone, fingers fumbling slightly as he dialled 9-9-9 but the man next to him was much quicker and he listened as he relayed the details quickly, his gaze never leaving the still form of the teenager. He had gone quiet. There was no movement from him now. His face was pale and drawn, eyes open and staring. He recognised him as a kid from their estate, who lived in the next street. Gary thought he was dead.

'Help is on the way,' someone assured the motorcyclist. 'Don't worry, it was an accident. We all saw what happened.'

'I'm not worried. I couldn't care less, to be honest. He shouldn't be on the road, stupid fucker.'

The motorcyclist picked up his machine and restarted the engine. The onlookers were shocked when he climbed onto his bike and drove away at speed, leaving nothing but muddy spray and the spell of exhaust fumes behind him. He disappeared into the traffic in seconds. Rosie walked away from the victim, leaving it to the adults. She stood next to Gary.

'He looks dead to me,' Gary said, whispering.

'Me too,' Rosie said. 'Come on. Let's move up the road. We need to be able to get on the bus when it gets here.'

The sound of sirens approaching drifted to them. The bus appeared from around the corner, navigated the traffic created by the accident and came to a halt fifty yards further on past the bus stop. A police car arrived, followed swiftly by an ambulance. Gary and his sister waited patiently in the queue as passengers slowly boarded. There was an eclectic mixture of school kids, work commuters, shoppers and mums with toddlers. They reached the door and stood on the step, half in the bus and half out. The rain was bouncing from the pavement as they waited.

'Hey, look who it is—little Gary White and his fit sister!' a taunting voice cut through the bustle as the bus filled up. It was an older kid sitting in the front seat. He was always a knobhead and picked on Gary. 'Gary White, smells of shite!'

'Shut your face,' Rosie snapped at him. The boy wasn't sure how to respond. 'Unless you want me to slap your head in front of all your sad little friends and make you look like a prick?'

'Calm down, Rosie, only joking,' the boy said, blushing.

'I'll calm down when you wind your neck in, little gobshite,' Rosie said, glaring at him. He sat back in his seat and folded his arms. Rosie White was a well-respected and popular girl and friendly with the toughest kids in the big school. 'Leave my brother alone. He's twelve, understand?' she said, leaning towards him and lowering her voice. 'I said, do you understand?' The boy nodded.

'Hurry up and shut the door, knobhead!' a voice called from the back. 'It's fucking freezing in here.'

'Don't use that language on my bus or you can get off and walk, you little wanker!' the driver counted. Jeers and cheering filled the air. The driver looked at the offender in his mirror. 'I know who you are. One more word out of you, Darrel Stevens and you're off!'

Gary's eyes darted up, meeting the smirking faces of the local bullies who lounged across the back seats like they owned them. His heart sank further as he climbed aboard behind his sister, the interior of the bus offering no refuge. It was noisy and intimidating, standing room only at the front. The atmosphere felt charged with bad energy. It was nearly full, the windows steamed up and the deafening chatter of rowdy teenagers filled the space around him.

There was no peace to be had on the school time buses. The older passengers looked suitably pissed off with their plight. They would have to endure the noise until the bus reached the schools along the route, which could take between twenty-minutes and an hour at peak time.

'Nice coat. Did your grandad pass it on to you?' one of the bullies sneered, plucking at the threadbare fabric on Gary's coat sleeve, where a badge had once lived, long since fallen off.

'Leave him alone,' Rosie snapped, her voice carrying a protective edge. But her words seemed to bounce off them, ineffective. Gary felt the entire bus was laughing at him, his sister the only protective voice in his world.

'His coat looks like it's from a charity shop,' the bully laughed. 'You have to admit, it's shit.'

'Who made you the fashion police?' Rosie snorted. 'You can't talk, you scruffy little twat.'

'Aw, does little Gary need his big sis to defend him?' another bully chimed in, laughter bubbling among them. 'We're only having a laugh, Rosie.'

'Well, you're not funny. Leave him alone.'

They moved along the bus. Gary kept his gaze fixed on the floor, trying to become invisible as he edged past the rowdy group on their left. They found a double seat and slid into it; Gary next to the window. He wiped the condensation away with his hand, making a circle he could look through. Whispers and sniggers followed him like dark shadows, making him paranoid that everything being said was a jibe at him. He longed to be big enough and old enough to protect himself. Being smaller and weaker than the rest of the world was a frightening place to be. He knew most of it was banter, jibes and jokes but sometimes, it became overwhelming. He could take the stick and ignore it, but the sight of small packets exchanging hands made his stomach churn with unease. He knew that they contained drugs and drugs were really bad. People went to jail for having them. It seemed to be happening more and more on the way to school, as if it was just normal. An older kid in front of him caught him looking. He grinned and winked. He nudged the kid next to him.

'Oi, you want some candy, Gary?' one bully offered, dangling a small baggie in front of him. 'This stuff makes school go by in a flash,' he grinned.

'No thanks,' Gary muttered, looking away.

'Your loss, gay boy,' the bully shrugged, turning back to his noisy friends.

'Not taking drugs doesn't make him gay,' Rosie said, interfering. 'He's twelve, you prick!'

'I've heard you've had a dabble,' the boy said, winking. Rosie blushed and glared at him. He giggled and winked again. 'My brother is mates with Imran at Top Kebab.' He grinned. 'Don't worry. Your secret is safe with me and your little brother here. Isn't it, Gary?' Gary shrugged and blushed. 'Don't tell your dad what I just said.'

'Fuck you, Milner,' Rosie hissed, sticking her middle finger up to him.

'Not right now, but thanks for the offer,' he said, smiling. 'Maybe on the way home?'

Gary pretended he was looking out of the window but was shocked that Rosie may have tried drugs. That was the insinuation.

He decided not to mention it unless she ever did. Steven Milner was an arrogant bastard because he was related to one of the older kids, who always sat upstairs on the way to school, someone with a bad reputation – Jordan Milner. The surname Milner was synonymous with trouble. Gangsters. Though upstairs and unseen today, his reputation was well-known, an insidious warning that squashed any thoughts of standing up to the family. He was nasty and violent, and it was rumoured his family worked for some real heavy gangsters. A powerful OCG, renowned across the city. They were known as the Diddy Men gang because they originated from a place called Knotty Ash, a suburb of Liverpool. The area was renowned for Alder Hey Children's hospital and the comedian Ken Dodd, who created the Diddy Men and had his own children's television show with them in the seventies. Gary had watched them on YouTube and thought it was childish shit but apparently, the gang using their name was scary.

Milner turned around when another kid tapped him on the shoulder. They looked back at Gary, warning him to look away. Gary turned back to the window and wiped his view hole wider to look at the grey rainy world outside, but he listened to what they were whispering.

'We've run out of Ket,' the kid whispered to Milner, his voice tinged with a mix of fear and admiration. 'I've sold the fucking lot. There's nothing left!'

'I told you the kids are mad for it. There will be more later. Jordan has everything under control, don't worry,' Milner murmured, just loud enough for Gary to hear. 'He'll be buzzing that it's all gone.'

'What shall I do with the cash?'

'Keep hold of it until we get to school,' Milner said. 'Jordan's dad, my uncle will be outside to collect it all before we go through the gates. We can't risk it being confiscated by teachers and the Dibble if there's an inspection.'

Gary tried to shut the noise out and rested his forehead against the cool window, the world outside blurring as the bus rumbled along the road. He felt small, insignificant, and trapped in a cycle that seemed destined to repeat day after day, leaving him hungry for more than just food. It was monotonous and not much fun. Was this the way life would be until he could leave school?

'I'm so hungry, I might have a sausage on mine as well as double bacon,' he whispered to Rosie. He nudged his sister, and she smiled and punched his arm playfully.

'Greedy bugger,' she laughed.

'I can almost taste the brown sauce on my butty.'

Five minutes on, the bus stopped and a group of teenage boys from St Edmund's Comprehensive boarded, looking wet and bedraggled. They were rivals of Roby High and Prescot Grammar, all three schools serviced by the Number 10. The new passengers glared aggressively along the bus, almost provoking abuse. They weren't disappointed by the response to their arrival.

'Look out, the Eddie's bummers are getting on the bus. Jordan is upstairs, waiting for you.'

'Wankers,' someone shouted, pretending to cough. 'Keyboard warriors, we'll see how hard you are today...'

'Tossers!'

'Arse bandits!'

'You're all going to get striped, fucking wankers!'

'You're the wanker, mate!' One of the new arrivals stuck his fingers up to the kids at the back of the bus. 'We're not scared of Milner or anybody else.'

'Thick twats,' someone shouted. 'Don't stand up or you'll get bummed by the St Eddie's queens.'

'Fuck you!'

'See, I told you, he wants to fuck me.'

The bus erupted in raucous laughter and jeers. The teenagers went up the stairs, scowling; it had gone very quiet up there. The school bus, usually a cacophony of laughter and mischief, had transformed into something sinister as it pulled into the traffic. The windows were misted with condensation and the floors wet with footprints. The atmosphere was damp and charged with nervous anticipation. Gary thought it felt odd, almost too quiet.

Suddenly, a noise began to drift downstairs to them. Heavy footsteps running along the top deck. Voices, angry and aggressive. There was an exchange of abuse. Gary heard the words, 'cunt, liar, thief,' and then someone shouted, 'Knife....'

The lower deck of the bus buzzed with questions about what was happening upstairs. Noisy chatter filled the air. A fight broke out on the stairs. It started as a rumble, then escalated into shouting and then screams that pierced through the chatter. The bottom deck fell deathly silent as everyone listened to what was happening upstairs. The school bus jolted over a pothole, the windows shuddering in their frames as shouts and jeers erupted from the back seats. Gary, clutching his school bag tightly to his chest, cast a worried glance toward his sister.

'Did you hear that?' Gary whispered. 'Someone upstairs has a knife.'

'If there is a knife, leave them to it. We do not get involved, understand?' Gary nodded. 'Stay sitting down, Gaz,' Rosie said, looking around. Her protective gaze sweeping over the bus like. 'Do not move unless I tell you to.'

'Prescot cunts!' they heard one of the older kids from the rival school shouting. He spat venomously, and the insult was met with a chorus of agreement from his friends. One of them ran downstairs, his nose bleeding.

'If any of you Prescot twats get involved, I'll batter you,' a tall boy from Eddie's shouted, standing unsteadily amid the swaying motion of the bus. Two of the boys from Prescot stood up and approached him. 'I'm fucking warning you!'

Like oil meeting flame, his words ignited a scuffle, and suddenly punches were flying, school ties yanked askew, blazers twisted in the tight grip of teenage angst. The three boys were swinging at each other, like human windmills in a gale. An elderly woman shouted for them to stop but no one listened. A boy was punched in the mouth and a tooth went flying, blood and saliva spattered a window.

'Stop the bus!' another woman shouted.

'Rosie, I'm scared,' whispered Gary, ducking as a haversack whizzed past, narrowly missing his head. It bounced off the window and landed on a young mum with a pram. She brushed it away, angrily and it slid along the bus.

'Don't worry. It's going to be okay. Just stay close to me,' she whispered back, her arm snaking protectively around Gary's shoulders. 'The driver will stop the bus if they carry on.'

In the chaos, an elderly woman clutched her shopping bag close, but it was no match for the flailing limbs. The bag burst, unleashing a cascade of tinned food that rolled across the floor, clanging and spinning dangerously. A tin of baked beans collided with someone's ankle, eliciting a curse that was almost drowned out by the general cacophony.

Then came a high-pitched gasp, a sound so chilling that even the most embroiled of fighters paused.

'I've been stabbed...'

A thin, gleaming blade slipped from a trembling hand, skittering across the floor of the bus as time seemed to slow. With a sickening realisation, all eyes followed the knife until it slid beneath the seats, hidden by passenger's legs. It came to a stop by Gary's scuffed shoes. He looked down at the marbled handle, the blade smeared with blood. He wanted to reach for it.

'Gary don't—' Rosie began, her voice strangled by fear, but it was too late.

Acting on instinct, Gary reached out and grabbed the knife, its metal cold against his palm. He couldn't leave it there, couldn't let someone pick it up. There was blood on the blade. Someone else could get hurt. With shaking hands, he pressed the button and closed the blade and slid it into his bag amidst his homework and reading books.

'I'll give it to the driver,' Gary whispered.

'You'll give it to nobody,' Rosie whispered. 'Nobody, understand?'

'Okay. No one saw me.'

'You shouldn't have touched it in the first place!' she hissed, barely above a whisper. 'We'll get rid of it when we get home. Until then, you tell no one.'

'Help me. Someone's been stabbed!' cried a voice from near the stairs, breaking through the stunned silence that had enveloped the bus. A teenager was lying on the floor, trying to stand but failing. His hands were covered in blood as he tried to stem the flow, unsuccessfully.

'Move! Let me through!' A stern woman with a ponytail of greying hair pushed her way forward, her nurse's uniform partially visible beneath her coat. 'I'm a nurse!' she announced, dropping to her knees beside the teenager who lay crumpled on the floor, blood seeping through his fingers.

'I can't believe a kid has been stabbed on the bus,' Gary muttered. 'Is he going to die?'

'I don't know,' Rosie said, shaking her head. 'There's a lot of blood.'

'The human body has ten pints of blood in it,' Gary whispered. His wide eyes were locked on the scene unfolding before him. 'I reckon there's at least three on the floor.' He craned his neck to get a better view. 'How much do you think you can lose before you bleed to death?'

'Quiet, Gary,' Rosie murmured, her own face pale. She pulled her brother closer, shielding his view as much as she could. 'Stop asking stupid questions.'

'He's stopped breathing. Give me some space!' The nurse ordered, her voice steady and commanding. She tilted the boy's head back and checked his airway before beginning chest compressions, counting aloud with each push against his ribcage. 'One, two, three, four...'

The bus driver, having pulled over in a panic, dialled emergency services, his voice cracking as he relayed their location and the situation. He stepped out of his seat and slipped in some blood, falling and banging his head against the bulkhead. His body was still as chaos reignited.

'Stay with me, son,' the nurse coaxed, her hands moving rhythmically as she administered CPR. 'Come on.'

'Shouldn't we do something?' Gary asked quietly, his small frame trembling with the enormity of what was happening. 'There might be a first aid box or something, but the driver has slipped over.'

'Right now, the best thing we can do is stay out of the way,' Rosie replied, though her eyes were wet with unshed tears. She held Gary tighter, wishing she could do more, wishing she could make this nightmare disappear. 'It's not safe. Stay right where you are.'

'Hey, kid,' called a lanky boy from Prescot, his lip split and bleeding. Rosie recognised him from year 13. He was a dick. 'A knife dropped on the floor. It went under the seats near you, right?'

'No, it didn't. It slid under there,' Rosie said, pointing across the bus. 'Leave him alone!' Rosie warned, her stare fierce enough to warn the older boy. People were taking pictures and videos of him and he suddenly realised he was being captured on camera. 'You shouldn't be carrying a knife, you prick,' she added. 'I know who you are. You're Liam Walsh.'

'It's not mine. I was going to hand it in,' he muttered, looking away. 'It wasn't mine anyway. I wouldn't carry a blade to school.' It was clear that the adrenaline was fading, replaced by the dawning terror of consequences yet to come.

'Did you stab this boy?' the nurse shouted at him.

'No, I didn't.' He pressed the emergency button, and the middle doors opened with a hiss. Liam Walsh ran from the bus and sprinted away.

'I hope plenty of you have his photograph on your phones.'

'I do,' several people replied.

'Me too.'

'This girl said his name is Liam Walsh,' a young mum said, pointing to Rosie. 'Do you know him?'

'He goes to the same school as we do,' Rosie said. 'I don't know him, but I know who he is.'

'You need to tell the police. That boy could die.'

'Keep breathing,' the nurse urged the injured boy, her resolve unbroken despite the beads of sweat on her brow. She looked concerned by his lack of response. 'Help is on the way.'

'Is he...' Gary couldn't finish his sentence, the weight of the word 'dead' too heavy for his young tongue.

'Shh, no, he's not,' Rosie assured him, though she couldn't be sure herself. All she knew was that she needed to be strong for Gary, to keep him safe in a world that had once again shown its darkest side. They had witnessed fights on the school bus may times but nothing on this scale. 'The nurse knows what she's doing.'

'Stop it!' A shout from upstairs. It was clear the battle had continued on the top deck. 'He's had enough.'

'Leave him alone!'

The shouts from the upper deck were muffled but frantic, sprouting seeds of panic among the already terrified passengers downstairs. Gary's gaze shot upward as a shadow stumbled down the stairs—a boy, no older than fourteen, clutching his side where scarlet bloomed across his shirt like a gruesome flower. He staggered and fell, leaving smears of his bloody distress on the walls and handrails. His face was a mask of pain and panic. The sight of his own blood mesmerising him.

'Help me!' he asked, no one. No one moved. No one dared. 'I've been stabbed!'

'Fucking move out of my way!' a voice boomed from the stairwell. 'You think you can rip me off, you little twat?'

The venom in the voice was unmistakable. Jordan Milner, known to all as related to the local dealers, an unwelcome predator in the area. His face was twisted in anger as he chased the injured boy, who was clearly one of his unfortunate customers, turned victim. Jordan was holding a zombie knife in his right hand, like something from the Walking Dead. It was black and bright blue with jagged teeth, blood dripped from the blade.

'Hey, get that knife off my bus! What's going on in your head, stupid kid?' The bus driver, mumbled, coming around. He craned his neck to catch a glimpse of the chaos unfolding behind him. Seeing the bloodied teenager staggering down the bus, his eyes widened. 'What the fucking hell is going on?' he shouted, shocked and confused, trying to stand. 'Get off my bus!'

'Milner stabbed me! Let me out, let me out!' cried the injured boy, his plea drowned by the sound of the bus front doors flinging open with a hiss. Jordan jumped down the last few steps and closed the gap. The injured boy jumped off the bus and sprawled onto the pavement. He struggled to his feet but was clearly unsteady.

More bodies spilled down the stairs, punching, kicking and stabbing at each other. Two kids trapped in battle, one in a headlock toppled over and a third jumped from the steps on top of them, crushing one of the combatant's hands against a seat. Cries of pain and anger reached deafening levels. A mother grabbed her toddler and pushchair and jumped from the step, landing in a heap on the soaking pavement. An elderly woman followed suit, misjudging the drop. She staggered a few steps before her knees gave way and she crumpled to the ground. Concerned passersby tried to help. Gary sat transfixed by the scene.

The rear doors hissed open, and the chase spilled onto the street, Jordan Milner hot on the heels of the terrified victim, whose pale face was a stark contrast to the crimson that soaked his clothes. Onlookers gasped, some reaching for their phones—this was a scene that would flood social media within minutes.

'Everyone off the bus!' The command snapped Gary out of his reverie, and he realised it was the driver ushering people off the bus at the rear exit.

On the stairs, a tangle of teenagers, embroiled in their own battles stumbled down in a disorganized mass brawl, fists flying and tempers flaring. Gary saw another knife being wielded. He saw blood splattering the ceiling and windows.

'Keep moving, kids! Off the bus, quickly now!' the driver's voice held a note of urgency that met no argument. 'Get away from the people fighting. Do it right now!'

'Move Gary,' Rosie shouted, dragging him from his seat. She shoved him towards the door, and he tripped on the step. They poured onto the pavement like a spill of marbles, some of the kids with tear-streaked faces, others shouting and pointing at the running figures of Jordan and his quarry as they ran into the road. Horns blared and brakes squealed. Gary stood up on the curb, his small frame trembling—not just from fear, but from the adrenaline rush of witnessing something far removed from the mundane safety of his daily routine. This was mental. 'Are you okay?' Rosie asked.

'I think so,' Gary said. 'Are you?'

There was a screech of brakes, a cry of fear and then a sickening thump. A body was flung into the air, twisting as it travelled. The victim landed with a splat on the pavement, jaw shattered and hanging loose, eyes staring wide into space, blood pumping from the nose, ears and mouth. Jordan Milner's corpse was within touching distance of Gary, the third dead kid he had seen that morning, and it wasn't nine o'clock yet.

Chapter 3

2 -years 8 months earlier

Allison was sitting at the small kitchen table, another purchase from Ikea. The house was like a show home for the Swedish furniture giant. She was pushing her breakfast around her plate, feeling hot and hormonal. Through the window, the harshness of winter was obvious. Rain and fog drifted across the garden of her foster home, blurring the view beyond. It was torrential rain again, and deep puddles had formed along the rough track which led to the main road. The house had once belonged to a farm, long gone, replaced by new build houses built by the council. It was a nice home as far as care homes go. The kitchen was always stocked with food and drinks and the trendy linoleum floor gleamed, freshly mopped. Her foster mum, Linda never stopped cleaning and mopping, baking and cooking soups and stews. Allison always joked that the mop was glued to one hand and a wooden spoon to another.

Although it was comfortable, it wasn't home. Everything felt false. Her real parents were dead, killed in a car crash three years ago and none of her living relatives were alive or in a position to bring her up. Adoption had been explored but no one suitable was found, so foster care was the only solution. It was a substitute home, substitute parents, substitute childhood. Nothing was real. She missed her old life, so much it dominated her thoughts and emotions. Two of the other children thumped down the stairs, chattering and laughing about something she couldn't hear. They shouted goodbye and slammed the door on the way to get their bus to school.

The old farmhouse echoed with the memories of a hundred hasty breakfasts, eaten by a succession of children in need of a home. Allison yearned for the love of her real parents and the safety and security of her old life. Her life had been so happy and full of love and then in the blink of an eye, everything she knew was gone. This was her life now and it was shit in comparison, but it was all she had left.

The kitchen was filled with the smell of burnt toast and bacon. She looked out of the window again, dreading the walk to school and the rain-soaked despair it would bring. Her foster mother, Linda, moved with the efficiency of a woman who had never grown tired of holding the roles of chef, cleaner and enthusiastic caretaker. She was like a human dynamo, always fussing. 'What is wrong with you?' Linda asked, mop in hand. 'Are you not hungry?'

'I'm not eating this,' Allison said, pushing the plate away with a clatter. The toast had the texture of cardboard, and the scrambled eggs looked like a yellowish pulp—nothing like a real breakfast that her mum used to make. 'I don't like your scrambled eggs.'

Linda shook her head, the lines etched in her forehead deepening with irritation. 'Allison, you have to eat something. You can't just sit there and starve yourself and, I'll have you know that everyone else likes my scrambled eggs.'

'No, they don't,' Allison said. 'They feed it to the dog when you're not looking.' Allison was due to have her period, and she felt the heat creeping up her neck and she was agitated.

'No, they don't, do they?'

'Yes, they do.'

'I don't believe you,' she argued. 'Eat your eggs. You can't starve yourself.'

'I'm not starving myself, Linda. I'm just not eating this shite...'

'Don't you dare use that language at me, young lady!' Linda's eyes narrowed, a flicker of the authority she wielded as if it were a deterrent against abusive teenagers, but it seldom worked. 'I've given you a roof over your head, food on your plate and a clean bedroom. I don't deserve to be spoken to like that.' Linda put the mop down and moved Allison's plate, dumping it in the sink with a clatter. 'It's time you started appreciating it.'

Allison's hormones were raging, and her stomach cramped, the familiar pulse of anxiety knitting tight in her chest. 'Maybe I'd be better off somewhere else. Maybe I'll just fuck off and vanish.' The words flew out before she could reel them back, bitter truths tasting worse than the scrambled egg did.

'Run away?' Linda's laughter was harsh and mocking, ringing out against the dreary morning like a witch's cackle. Allison hated her laugh; it grated on her nerves.

'You say that every week but you're still here.'

'I say it because I mean it.'

'And where exactly would you go?'

'Anywhere I can get a decent breakfast,' Allison grinned sarcastically. With a defiant thrust of her chin, Allison stood up, the wooden chair scraping loudly against the floor as she shot out of the kitchen in a huff.

'Cheeky madam,' Linda shouted after her. 'Steak and kidney pie for your tea,' she added as the door slammed. 'It's your favourite.'

'Stick it up your fat arse!'

Allison grabbed her schoolbag and left the house, the heavy rain slapping against her skin like Mother Nature's own reprimand for her cheeky behaviour. She walked along the pitted track to the main road avoiding the deepest puddles. The world was dreary, dull—just shades of grey and a relentless downpour that turned the track to a mire. She pulled her coat tighter around her, but it offered little comfort against the biting wind. The rain pounded the ground, masking the sound of her footsteps as she moved toward school, each step feeling heavier than the last. It was a fifteen-minute walk, which felt like hours in the winter, especially in the rain. More so when it was absolutely pissing down, and she was cold.

But there was something more than the cold weather gnawing at her. A prickle beneath her skin—an instinctual dread that someone was watching her. She looked around but the pavements were empty. There was a huddle of other schoolkids at the bus stop across the road and a jogger heading towards her. The sensation rippled down her spine, causing her to glance over her shoulder in the other direction. The street was empty, save for the shimmering puddles that formed on the concrete, reflecting the headlights of passing vehicles. She couldn't shake the anxiety that she was feeling.

As she trudged along, her feet squelching in her shoes, the uneasy feeling gnawed deeper. The world felt too quiet, the kind of quiet where the shadows held their breath as if something sinister lurked just beyond sight. Every shadow held a demon or devil. She felt frightened for no particular reason.

Suddenly, a car pulled up alongside her, the engine humming softly beneath the noisy deluge. It was a sleek, dark Volvo, gleaming even in the dismal light, and the window slid down to reveal a vaguely familiar man with tousled hair and a smile that didn't quite reach his blue eyes. The warmth from inside the car poured out into the cold rain, a tempting embrace that tugged at her resolve.

'Hey there, you look cold and wet,' he called out, his voice deep and local. 'You look like you could use a lift. Want to jump in?'

'No thanks,' Allison said, desperately wanting to get in.

'Don't be silly. The car's nice and warm.' His smile had gone, and his eyes were piercing.

Allison walked on, her heart beating faster—not from exertion, but with a surge of instinctive warning. She scanned his face, searching for something—a flicker of malice or sincerity. Instead, she found the unsettling neutrality of a shark's eyes, yet he was familiar, but she couldn't place him.

'No, thanks,' she managed, her voice trembling slightly as she took a step back, the rain mixing with the fear coursing through her veins.

The man leaned closer to the window, the smile stretching wider as if he were savouring the moment. 'Come on, Allison. It's really coming down out here. You shouldn't be walking alone in a storm like this. Your school is just up ahead—we could get there in no time, and it's much warmer in here.'

'How do you know my name?' she asked, suddenly curious and terrified. A shiver crept up her spine, and she backed away further, her head aching with tension. 'Whoever you are, I'm okay. Really.'

The man's smile slowly faded, turning predatory, the interest in his gaze turning into something darker. 'Suit yourself.'

With that, he rolled up the window and the car glided away, leaving Allison standing there—breathing hard, drenched to the skin, feeling an invisible weight pressing down as she battled the storm both outside and within. She picked up her pace, pushing through the clinging dread and heavy rain, each step towards the school becoming a small victory against the shadows that lurked. The fear never left her, wrapping around her like the bitter chill of a winter morning—Allison never arrived at school that morning.

Chapter 4

4-years earlier

It had been a shit day in a string of shit days, at the end of one shit month after another, which had gone on for as long as he could remember. Year after year of total shit. Go to work, take shit from your employers and the people you try to help, then go home, eat, shit, sleep and do it all again. Day, after day, after day, after day... the life of a mundane human. They deserved to be fucked and slaughtered; sacrificed to the universe, their energy released from their chubby little bodies, he was doing them a favour. The fear and pain he inflicted on them were the most intense feelings they would experience on this planet before they left it, and he had given those moments to them. The agony and terror they endured was nothing like anything they had experienced before or would again. Unforgettable moments seared into their souls; moments he would savour until it was his time to leave. Agony and terror were his gifts to the dying. Their souls his gifts to the universe.

Human beings frustrated the life from him, literally. Their weakness turned his stomach, always moaning and whinging and needing help from the rest of society to survive. Some didn't appreciate the help; others didn't want it in the first instance. Few could live a solitary existence, the state brought them into the world as babies, and the state treated them when they were ill and needed a doctor or a hospital and the state burned their bodies when they passed.

Civilisation.

Society.

Sheeple.

And he was a shepherd, tending the flock but he took the odd one here and there for his own pleasure. He played with them for his own pleasure and then released them from their miserable lives for their own benefit. They became something so much more than human.

Most of them lived such a pointless existence, they may as well have never lived at all. Dross, parasites, human detritus. They were sheep to be tended until it was time to slaughter them to feed the energy of the universe. He was building his connection to the universe, a bridge he could cross whenever he wanted to, and their souls were his currency.

Only the strong thrived on this planet, predators and prey. He was living proof that ridding the world of the spineless mundane fuckers was the way things should be; his mission to be become a powerful being was well underway. He was transforming, achieving something outside of the norm with his life. Most achieved a big fat zero.

The humans preached their inane bullshit, night and day. Be kind, be beautiful, be mindful of others and their feelings.

Fuck off.

What they really mean is my feelings matter more than yours. Cunts. Don't be racists, sexist or encourage genderphobia, and do not judge. Judgement will come from God.

Really?

Which God?

Islam, Judaism and Christianity are the 3 big boys on the block but what about the other couple of thousand gods? Who will do the judging and what will they judge? The scriptures tell of creation, man and woman. Adam and Eve, not Adam and Steve but they were written by men to control other men, so what they preach is irrelevant. He couldn't listen to the snowflakes debating gender and sexuality.

Why did God not stop him killing the sheeple? Because he's as powerful as the tooth fairy and Santa Claus because none of them exist. That's why.

Humans are full of shit. Offended by this and offended by that and offended by the other.

Fuck off.

Their whining made his blood boil, so spilling theirs evened the field. Humans spout shit, day and night. The world's leaders mince around pretending to be the protectors of humanity, yet they do nothing to protect the weak and innocent. Religion has caused the slaughter of millions throughout history. More recently, thousands of women and children have been blown to kingdom come in revenge for the dreadful murder of other women and children. Humans slaughtering humans. The wheel never stops turning and the World watches. Putin does what the fuck he wants to and what does the rest of the World do? Nothing, but the universe watches and energy, both good and bad can never be destroyed, only altered. What drives the wholesale slaughter of other humans?

Revenge.

Religion.

Money.

Power.

Control.

And what do the sheeple do to help the weak and vulnerable people around the planet? Fuck all. They chat shit about how bad it is but in reality, do zilch.

They watch and do nothing. Nothing at all. Killers allowed free rein to kill on an industrial scale without consequence. What he was doing paled into insignificance in the grand scheme of things, yet it had meaning, fuelling the darkness. The twelve sections of the universe, the zodiac held everything together. He was becoming part of the zodiac, at one with the twelve, his energy, and their energy bound together.

The predators prey on the weak. That's the way of the world, always was, always will be. He was a predator, and he was just beginning to find his true calling. Each kill made him feel stronger, more powerful than those around him and less visible to the mundane. He was surrounded by potential victims who had no idea what he had done or what he was planning to do next. Inches away from a serial killer. They did not know who he was or what he was becoming, the living embodiment of evil. People laughed and joked, cried and grieved in his presence and they could not sense who he was. What he was. They were blind to him; evil was his shield.

He was in his lair, working on the zodiac wheel; the most beautiful piece of art ever created. His handmade table, painstakingly constructed from twelve different types of wood, stained with twelve natural resins, the symbols of each star sign intricately carved into it. The scales, the crab, the scorpion, the lion, the bull and all the others chiselled into the timber, sanded and polished to a glass-like sheen. At the centre of each section would sit the skull of his victims, boiled clean, preserved and varnished so they would last forever. There were four spaces remaining and his altar to the universe would be finished. It would soon be complete and then his bridge to the universe would be complete.

He was polishing the latest skull to be added, applying another layer of varnish. In his lair. The room where he killed some of them. The air was thick with the musk of incense and disinfectant, tainted with varnish, old leather, vomit and excrement and death. His family had owned and operated a successful slaughterhouse, started by his great grandfather and passed down the generations until September 1985 when bovine spongiform encephalopathy arrived, and cow herds were slaughtered and burned. Mad cow disease was the death knell for the family business, although they kept the properties. Diseased land is impossible to sell, and its value plummeted.

The old slaughterhouse was attached to the family home in a forgotten corner of a once-bustling farming area on a green belt called Tarbock Green. Its weathered walls, stained with the memories of happy days long past. His father had worked within these walls, which echoed the haunting silence of abandonment. His family and the cattle were long gone but the atmosphere hung heavy with the lingering stench of dead animals, a persistent reminder of the life that once filled this space. The passing of time had done nothing to dull the stink. He revelled in it.

From the high ceilings dangled rusty chains and hooks, swaying slightly when disturbed by the faintest draft as if caught in a phantom wind. They creaked sometimes especially when he hung a live one from them. Watching them twist and writhe on the hooks was fascinating but sadly didn't last long. These remnants, now coated in layers of grime, tell stories of the countless animals that met their fate here. The hooks, sturdy but corroded, hint at the brutality that occurred within these walls. He had brought his own brand of brutality to those stories. A brutality beyond the imagination of most normal human beings.

The floor was a cold, unforgiving expanse of concrete, cracked and stained. The surface bears the marks of years of use, with the stains and dark rivulets of dried blood now just a memory of their former vibrant red colour. A central drain, lined with rust and dust, remained in the floor, an unyielding dark hole designed to whisk away the remnants of mortality. Yet, despite decades of disuse, the drain had retained the essence of its grisly purpose. The lifeblood of his victims trickled down into the sewers.

Moonlight filtered through the filthy windows, revealing motes of dust that danced in the air, swirling lazily around the desolation. The once haunting sounds of terrified animals had faded into a deafening silence, occasionally pierced by the terrible screams of his victims. He lived for that sound. It was the most beautiful thing he had ever heard.

Tonight, he was a solitary figure sitting hunched over his table. The wall behind was covered with bookshelves. Books of astrology, astronomy, the occult, Wicca, tarot, Ouija and a myriad of subjects. He had finished The Magnus by Francis Barrett the day before. He read one book after another, learning, absorbing the knowledge from the pages, becoming knowledge himself. He wanted to look at the night sky and understand everything there was to understand about the universe. Where did it end?

The flicker of candles cast elongated shadows against the cracked plaster walls, where more iron chains hung. In one corner of the room lay a mattress, stained with blotches of dark crimson that told tales of violence and despair. Its presence held a memory of each one, a reminder of the sacrifices made, and the rituals performed in the pursuit of power that twisted his soul.

He was twisted and he'd known from an early age how twisted he was. His mother had bought him a magnifying glass when he was six years old, and he had spent hours playing with it. She thought he was studying leaves and the bark on trees, but he had spent a wonderful summer holiday frazzling insects with it. He loved ants because there were so many to incinerate, but his favourite were caterpillars because they wriggled in agony before exploding. That was so much fun.

As he grew older, he experimented with torture and torment. Local pets in the area had a habit of disappearing and he was interviewed by the police about an accusation made by the daughter of a neighbour that he had offered her money to do things that she wouldn't disclose. Because she was so scared, she didn't speak out and the charges were never filed. It had been a happy childhood for him, different but happy.

His computer screen flickered, casting shadows. He glanced up at the image on the screen. He was fucking Allison from behind and from the expression on her face, she wasn't enjoying it as much as he was. The television screen bathed the room in a cold, blue glow, a stark contrast to the warm candlelight. On the screen, a chant played on loop, the guttural syllables of an arcane language spoken by a voice that seemed to crawl from the depths of the earth itself. As the man's lips moved in sync with the incantation, not a word escaped into the stillness; his recitation was silent, internal, as if he feared someone may hear him. One day, the power would be unleashed, and the words be given voice.

The film showed his back was turned to the viewer, revealing a large, intricate tattoo of the zodiac emblazoned across his flesh—a symbol of all he had pledged allegiance to. Each line of ink pulsed with the promise of forbidden knowledge and the lure of darkness. Evil oozed from each painful line of ink. As the man continued his silent incantation, the air around him grew colder, denser. He could feel something shifting, an awakening in the fabric of reality, as though his very breath were drawing forth spectres from the other side. His heart raced with anticipation and dread, for even he did not fully comprehend the forces he was attempting to invoke. Yet he did not stop. The thirst for knowledge, for control over the unseen realms, drove him deeper into the spell. Each whispered verse from the screen resonated with the beating of his own heart, binding him ever tighter to the path he had chosen—a path from which there was no return. It wasn't about Satan. It was about him choosing bad over good and feeding it like an animal.

Evil over innocence.

A bang on the ceiling at the far side of the room brought him back into the real world. He opened the door and listened.

'Can you hear me?'

'Yes, Nan,' he shouted, shaking his head. She was in her eighties and wheelchair bound. 'What's up?'

'You said you had work in the morning, so I've made you one of those pies that you love.'

'Steak and kidney?'

'They're still warm, so come and get it before they get cold.'

'Thank you, Nan,' he said, smiling. 'I'm coming up now.' He turned off the lights and the computer and closed the huge metal door, locking it with a clunk. 'Can I have one of those liver pate toast slices with it?'

'I've put two on a plate for you,' she said. 'I know you like them.'

'Thanks Nan,' he said as he climbed from the slaughterhouse into the family home attached, like leaving one world and entering another, a short corridor and staircase between them. 'What would I do without you?'

'Heaven, forbid you have to find out,' she joked. 'Not tonight anyway.'

'No Nan, not tonight.'

Chapter 5

The Mere-3-years earlier

The forest was almost silent as he reached the fork in the path, which he had walked many times on his disposal missions. Disposal was the hardest part of murdering humans and getting it wrong was simple. It was how most killers get caught. He changed his methods as often as possible, using different methods and dump sites. It made sense forensically and kept things exciting. There was an amazing sense of accomplishment when a mission was completed successfully. The pieces of the wheel were fitting together.

The trees were dark witnesses to the grim task ahead and he could feel their lifeforce. Energy flowed from them and the earth from which they had grown. The air was filled with their scent. Earth, water, air, and fire all elements of the building blocks of the universe. They towered above him, blocking the light from the sun, which was struggling to make an appearance yet. It was too early in the morning. The path ahead was shrouded in a thick mist that seemed to swallow the sound of his footsteps. The crunch of dead leaves and twigs didn't carry far in the eerie atmosphere of the pine forest. It hadn't stopped raining all night and each raindrop against his skin was an icy pinprick, jolting him with the reality of his perilous undertaking.

From a human perspective, there was no rational explanation for what he was doing, except that he was a psychopathic, narcissistic, murdering paedophile. The danger of disposal was as arousing as the rest of the insidious process. His senses were heightened by the fear of being caught in the act. He was acutely aware of the parcel's weight beneath his overcoat, its contents evidence of his morbid obsession with death, sex and the destruction of the human shell to release the energy within back into the universe—a secret that could have him sentenced to a lifetime behind bars with no chance of parole. They would never understand his task and they would lock the door and throw away the key.

Best not to think about those things. It was a half mile further on to the mere, a sinister body of water whose depths were as unforgiving as the world he operated within. The dark, acidic waters caused by the rotting pines, promised the perfect concealment, ensuring that the evidence he carried would be swallowed whole and decompose quickly, never to resurface in the light of day. DNA would be broken down completely. Ashes to ashes, dust to dust, nature devouring everything, absorbing the nutrients so that something else could grow.

Fastening his heavy overcoat against the cold morning air, he felt a wave of nausea as the stench of decay seeped from the plastic-wrapped burden hidden beneath. He was getting a waft of decomposition each time he moved. It was a sickening smell that stirred an unsettling arousal within him. In his twisted reality, the line between carnal desire and the finality of death had long since blurred into a singular, perverse thrill. Death and sex intrinsically linked. He had been obsessed with the likes of Ed Gein, Ed Kemper, Dennis Nilsen, Jeffery Dahmer, Gary Ridgeway, and Ted Bundy, all nefarious killers who had sex with their victims after death. They took the lives of others to enhance their own. They were engraved into notorious legend by their hunger for sex with the dead, but no one truly understood what drove them. Energy.

The law of conservation says that energy cannot be destroyed or created, only transformed and that is what they did. That is what he was doing. Reading their cases made him feel less unusual. He had embraced his desires as they had. Society abhorred such dark desires but fuck them. Literally.

His heart skipped a beat at the sound of twigs snapping nearby and a scurrying noise drifted to him. Instantly on alert, he halted in his tracks, eyes darting into the darkest depths of the shadows beneath the tree canopy. Was it an animal drawn towards him by curiosity or something far more threatening? Hunger. Or it could be the police, searching for missing persons.

Every nerve ending screamed for him to remain unseen, to reach the mere without incident or encountering other humans. He could not afford discovery—not here, not now, no witnesses.

Taking a deep breath, he steadied himself against the gnawing fear, acutely aware of the stakes. With a cautious step, he resumed his journey, senses straining against the oppressive silence of the forest, every echo a potential harbinger of his potential downfall, arrest and incarceration. The damp earth squished under his boots, a rhythm that matched the blood pounding in his ears.

He had been walking through the forest unhindered for nearly an hour, the weight of the illicit parcel pushing heavily against his ribs beneath his coat. He was close now, close to his destination where he could rid himself of the burden that smelled of death. Rotting flesh. The last bits of her.

Suddenly, a burst of movement shattered the silence. A dog, large and unkempt, bounded from the thickets, its eyes wild with energy, saliva hanging from its jowls. It was some kind of mastiff, a big one. The man's heart lurched as the animal circled him, nose twitching, homing in on the scent of the concealed flesh.

'Fuck off,' he hissed at the animal. It barked and lowered its chest to the floor, ready to pounce. 'Shoo! Fuck off, hssssssss!' He poked a boot in its direction, kicking forest debris in its face. The animal barked in response. 'Get away, you twat...'

Before he could react further, the dog launched itself at him, paws scraping against the fabric of his coat, jowls snapping inches from his hands, which were clutching his coat closed. The animal's claws raked the material. The man kicked the dog, catching it in the back leg and it whelped in pain. A man emerged from the trees.

'Did you just kick my dog?' a man shouted. 'How dare you?'

'I'll kick its fucking head in if you don't get it away from me, right now!' the man growled. 'Fuck off,' he hissed at the dog. The dog was wary, fear in its eyes. 'Get away!'

'Down, Dill! Down!' the owner's voice cut through the growling and snarling. He closed the gap between himself and his pet. From the shadows emerged the owner's partner, her features obscured by the dim light filtering through the canopy.

'What on earth is going on?' she shouted.

Her partner lunged forward, attempting to grasp the dog's collar, which seemed to only encourage the canine's frenzy.

'Get your fucking dog under control!' the man spat out, anger lacing his words as he tried to fend off the dog without making it obvious, he was protecting more than just himself. 'Before I kick its teeth out...'

His mind raced with the fear of being discovered, images flashing of the consequences if this disobedient mutt unveiled his macabre secret, witnessed by two people, who had seen his face.

'Don't you kick my dog again!' The owner yanked at the leash, but Dill was relentless, driven mad by the scent of death that clung to the man like a second skin.

'Did he kick Dill?' the woman asked, angrily. 'How dare you attack my dog!'

'Shut up, you stupid bitch.'

'Do not kick my dog!'

'I'm going to kill the fucking thing, if you don't get it away from me!'

'Dill, come here!'

With every jump and snap of teeth, the man felt the thin thread of control slipping. He couldn't afford to be exposed, not when he was so close to finishing what he'd started. With a swift movement born of desperation, he delivered a sharp kick to the dog's ribs and then another which caught it in the penis. The animal squealed and growled, a sound that cut through the patter of rain. He aimed another at its genitals and connected. The dog's reaction was instant and unsettling. It was a terrible high-pitched whine that seemed to pierce the ears.

'You've hurt him!' the woman shouted. 'You bastard. I'll have you arrested, you bastard.'

'I'll have your animal put down,' the man shouted. 'It attacked me.' He kicked it again and it howled and scampered away, its tail between its legs, the owners cursing as they swore at him, and they disappeared in pursuit of their pet.

The man listened until they were far away before continuing his task. Alone once more, the man allowed himself a single shuddering breath before continuing down the path, rain baptizing him in cold judgment. He walked until the trees parted ways to reveal the mere—a dark mirror reflecting nothing but the void of the murky morning.

Without ceremony, he withdrew the package and peeled off the wrapping. The stench was sickening but he savoured it. A hand and lower arm, severed at the elbow. He sniffed at the fingers, enjoying seeing her red nails again. Flashes of her capture came to him, the fear in her eyes, the tears, her screams, music to his ears. Fuel to the flames. Energy becoming something else. He felt her skin, sticky and moist and savoured the intoxicating odour.

He closed his eyes and hurled it into the mere, watching as the black water swallowed it whole. Ripples echoed outward, each concentric circle a whisper of what had been done. A life snuffed out early, but her body would be consumed by the inhabitants of the mere. She would feed them becoming part of new things. Transforming into something different. He closed his eyes and felt hot tears flowing down his cheeks. It was such a wonderful experience.

He was not alone for long.

A woman materialised from the obscurity of the trees; her approach silent but for the crunch of wet leaves beneath her boots. Her eyes met his, shared knowledge flickering within their depths like the ghostly dance of fireflies. Wordlessly, she too revealed her burden—a parcel akin to his own—and she opened it to reveal the matching hand and arm. The opposite side of the same victim. She let him look for long seconds before she dispatched it into the waiting arms of the mere.

Together, they stood sentinel over the still surface, the trees their only confessors, as the ripples grew wider and slowly faded into the darkness of the water. They embraced and kissed, and he pushed her against a tree and pulled her hair. She put her hands inside his coat, seeking the flesh beneath his clothes. Her nails raked his skin, drawing blood and causing him to wince. He choked her and pulled harder on her hair as the rain intensified.

The sex was always electric when they were in the forest and their victim had been disposed of but this time, it was epic.

Chapter 6

The Cuckoo

Janine White's hands trembled as she rifled through the duffel bag, the heavy fabric smelling faintly of chemicals and sweat. It had been a sports bag at some time, the smell unmistakeable but that was in its previous life. She was in her own flat yet felt anxious and scared of being caught doing something naughty; something she knew she shouldn't be doing. Janine tried very hard not to be naughty because naughty was bad, and she tried to be good as much as possible. She was fifty-five but had always been in trouble for doing the wrong thing at the most inappropriate time without realising. 'It was the only skill she had,' she would tell people when she was nervous and waffling. 'If anyone is going to fuck it up, that's me.'

Her flat was silent except for the sound of Homes Under the Hammer on the television in her living room and her shallow breaths. The soft rustle of plastic wrapping against her eager fingers was deafening because she shouldn't be searching their stuff. She knew that she shouldn't be doing what she was doing, but desperation made her reckless. Her mind, clouded by alcohol and the dull ache for a smoke of weed, barely registered the risk. It was her home, she told herself, but it didn't make her feel any safer. Needs must. She had shared a litre of vodka with her friend and needed something to take the edge off the approaching hangover.

'Here. You have a look in this holdall,' Janine said to her best friend Gilbert. She handed him a bag from the wardrobe. It was heavy. Gilbert was older than her and much more vulnerable, if that was possible. He had hardly any teeth left in his mouth and refused to wear his dentures because they hurt his gums. His brown eyes were watery and sad, even when he was laughing. Janine and Gilbert laughed a lot when they were together. They were both functioning alcoholics with cannabis and junk food issues and their mutual addictions meant that they enabled each other to abuse all three. They also shared a liking for Slazenger tracksuits. Janine dressed in pastels, pink today; Gilbert favoured greys, a light shade this week, which unfortunately showed the wee stains when he dribbled. They would become more prevalent as the days went by. He seldom changed his clothes. 'There must be some weed in here somewhere. I'm sure one of these bags must have something to smoke inside them.'

'Won't they be pissed off if we take their stuff?' Gilbert asked, whispering. 'The Diddy Men are dangerous. I don't want any trouble from that lot. They're all nuts.'

'Don't worry. They won't know,' Janine said, shaking her head. The knot in her stomach told her different. 'This is my home and I'm doing them a favour and they promised to keep me supplied with weed if I looked after their stuff, so they owe me.'

'It still feels dangerous to me,' Gilbert chuckled. 'I feel like a naughty schoolboy.'

'It'll be alright,' Janine laughed nervously. 'Although, I feel like I'm being really wicked.'

She pretended to be unconcerned about what they were doing but she was struggling with her anxiety. They had warned her not to touch anything that they had left in her spare bedroom, but they would never know, and she was only looking for a little bit of puff. There were kilo bricks of powder of all kinds in there, but she had never so much as touched one of them. It was their fault that she was beginning to feel anxious, and they couldn't deny that. They had said they would keep her supplied with cannabis if she did as they asked and stored their stuff, but no one had been since the day before yesterday, and she had run out. That was mostly because she had shared her supply with Gilbert, but he was her friend and sharing is caring. Gilbert said she was a good person because she always shared her alcohol and weed with him. He said that if he ever had any of his own, he would share it with her. That's what friends do, he said.

She had to smoke to maintain her sanity and control her anxiety. She had told them when she was running out, and they had ignored her text messages. She didn't want to piss them off, but needs must. She needed a smoke and was desperate. They had stacked over one-hundred sealed parcels, the size of a brick, all containing white powder under her double bed and in a wardrobe and a locked cabinet they had installed. She reckoned they were kilo parcels, so that was a shitload of drugs, and she was allowing them to come and go as they needed.

They had also left four haversacks and the duffle bag in her wardrobe, and she was curious if they had left any resin or skunk buds in them. She searched the bag closest to the wardrobe door, without moving it too far. Gilbert had the other bag and there were three more to search. There must be something to smoke in them.

'Please, please, please. Come on, there has to be something that we can smoke,' she muttered under her breath, her voice hoarse from too many cigarettes and not enough water. 'It took five guys to bring all this stuff in here. One of you must smoke weed. Please, please, have left a bit in your bag for me and Gilbert.'

'Please, please, please,' Gilbert agreed. 'Give us a bit of puff.'

Her spare bedroom was now a storage unit for some of the Diddy Men's illicit inventory. Her brother Bill had introduced her to them and said she could earn some easy money. Janine was aware it was a bad idea to get involved with them, but the promise of regular cash and a regular free high had lured her in. They had been nice to her, groomed her and then they closed the trap and took advantage of her loneliness, her need for some kind of connection to the outside world. She struggled to make decisions and her capacity to stand up for herself was minimal. She could be coerced and bullied easily. And she let them because it was either that or face the desolate silence of her existence day in and day out alone. Always alone. She had been alone most of her adult life because she was different.

She knew she was different; she always had known. The doctors spotted it when she was seven and labelled her special. Special needs amongst other things. Educationally challenged, disabled, mentally handicapped, intellectually limited, emotionally vulnerable and so on and so on. She had been given more labels than a supermarket, none of them changed anything or the way other humans acted around her. People had called her names since she was a little girl, and they had been very cruel. Thick, dumb, stupid, spastic, mong, Joey, empty head, biff and many, many more.

She thought back to the day in school, which had changed everything. In the eighties, for kids with challenges, the classroom was a battlefield, and Janine felt like a soldier without armour. She was a constant target. The cacophony of mockery bounced off the walls, fellow pupils aiming arrows of ridicule at her, Monday to Friday. The cruel labels tossed around like grenades, exploded against Janine's self-esteem with every snicker and sneer, slowly chipping away at her. Days, months and years merged into one long nightmare, which was the symphony of her youth. That fateful day was the rotten cherry on the shit cake.

'HEY, JANINE!' A BOY called out from the back of the room, his voice laced with a taunt that was all too familiar. 'What's two plus two? Bet you can't get it even if we give you all day! Thicko.'

Her cheeks burning with humiliation, Janine tried to focus on the numbers scribbled on her paper, but the digits danced before her eyes, jumbling and tumbling into nonsense. She could hear the laughter growing, feeding off her discomfort.

'Leave me alone, Tyler,' she muttered, her words barely audible.

'What was that?' he prodded, leaning forward, his cronies egging him on. 'Speak up, genius!'

'Stop it,' she said, louder this time. Her hand gripped the pencil so tightly she thought it might snap. 'I'm not playing your game.'

'Ooooh, she's not playing!' another voice chimed in, followed by a chorus of laughter. 'Can you remember the question, thicko?'

'Enough!' Mrs. Callahan's sharp voice sliced through the torment, silencing the class. 'Tyler, that's your third warning this week. I will not tolerate your bullying. Go to the headmaster's office, now.'

As the offender slunk away, the amusement fading from his face, Mrs. Callahan offered Janine a sympathetic glance. But pity was a double-edged sword—it protected and cut deep at the same time, confirming there was something worth pitying.

'Janine, why don't you come sit up front? I can help you with the questions,' the teacher suggested gently.

'No, thanks,' Janine replied quietly, not wanting to draw more attention to herself.

'Are you sure, dear?'

'Y-yeah.'

'Alright then. Class, let's continue with the lesson.' Mrs. Callahan turned back to the board, and normalcy attempted to reassert itself.

Later on, Janine tried to shake off the sting of embarrassment as she walked home, the words still echoing in her head. It wasn't just school where she fought daily battles; home—or rather, the succession of homes—were no sanctuary either. Her parents couldn't cope with her, so they put her into care, which was devastating. She missed her younger brother Bill. He was the only person who didn't laugh at her.

Her earliest memories were fragmented, like shards of glass reflecting images she'd rather forget. Harsh voices raised in anger, a feeling of abandonment, and hands that should have been gentle but weren't. These memories were the monsters under her bed, the shadows in her closet. They haunted her in the silence of night, when the darkness seemed to press against her like an unwelcome blanket.

'Janine, you're late for dinner,' Ms. Baxter, her current foster mother, announced as she stepped through the door.

'Sorry,' Janine replied, her voice flat, trying to mask the dread she felt. At the table, the food was a bland mash of colours and textures. She ate mechanically, knowing that being difficult would only make things worse.

'Did you do your homework?' Ms. Baxter asked, eyeing her with a mix of concern and frustration.

'Most of it,' Janine answered truthfully.

'Make sure you finish before bed. You need good grades if you want to get anywhere in life.'

'Okay,' Janine repeated, the word tasting like ash in her mouth. 'Okay' had become her shield, her way of deflecting further scrutiny. It was easier than explaining the tangled thoughts that resisted unravelling, the lessons that slipped through her grasp like water through cupped hands.

Nighttime brought its own set of challenges—the whispers of the house, the creaks and groans of settling wood that sounded like ghosts roaming the halls. It reminded her of all the other places she'd been, each one supposed to be a fresh start, yet somehow always ending up the same.

'Janine,' Ms. Baxter's voice came again, softer now, at the threshold of her room. 'You know, I'm here if you need to talk about anything, right?'

'Thanks,' Janine murmured, offering a faint, weary smile. It wasn't that Ms. Baxter was unkind—quite the contrary—but how could Janine explain the labyrinth within her mind? How could she articulate the fear that she wouldn't just be left behind, but that maybe she already was?

'Goodnight, Janine.'

'Night.'

Sleep was elusive, as it often was. Janine lay in bed, staring at the ceiling, tracing the patterns of shadow and light cast by the streetlamp outside. Her thoughts drifted back to school, the faces of those who found her pain amusing, and the teachers who tried to help but couldn't quite reach her.

'Tomorrow will be better,' she whispered to herself, not quite believing it. But hope was a stubborn thing, and it clung to her despite the evidence to the contrary.

The sun rose, indifferent to the turmoil of the previous day, casting its golden glow over the world. Janine gathered her books, squared her shoulders, and prepared to face the gauntlet once again. Each step was an act of defiance against the doubts that gnawed at her resolve, against the hurtful words that tried to define her.

'Today, I'll try again,' she promised herself as she joined the stream of students heading to school. It was a small victory, but victories—no matter how small—were the milestones on her path.

'Hey, Janine,' a voice called out, not in mockery this time, but in a tentative offer of friendship. It was Molly, a girl from her English class.

'Hi,' Janine replied, surprised.

'Mind if I walk with you? I could use some company.'

'Sure,' Janine said, and for the first time in what felt like forever, she smiled genuinely.

'See, not everyone is against you,' she told herself silently. And with that thought, she took another step, another breath, and moved forward into the day.

'Follow me. I'm meeting some friends, who want to meet you.' Molly had taken her to a quiet clearing in the woods behind the school where two of her older friends were waiting. Both of them raped Janine while Molly watched and held their coats. They frightened Janine with threats to her life, which she believed. They weren't at her school and so she never told a soul, but it changed her dramatically. She blamed herself for everything shit that ever happened to her throughout her life. Never once did she think she was special in a good way. She was a dunce, who people abused and laughed at and raped, and she deserved everything she got.

School had failed to protect her from the bullies, social services had failed to protect her from her abusive father until it was too late, and now society pretended she didn't exist. They gave her somewhere to live, paid her benefits and hoped she would be okay until she died, when no one would notice she had even been here. When death came for her, she would embrace it with open arms. Life on Earth as Janine was shit and she had no desire to continue any longer than she had to. She couldn't end it herself because she was a coward, so she would have to wait until her time came and hope it was sooner rather than later.

'I ONLY WANT SOME WEED. It's not stealing, stupid, stupid, thicko,' she chastised herself as she dug deeper, past the little sealed bags of cocaine, ketamine, and amphetamine. They were twenty-pound bags, she knew that but there was no weed. Her heart hammered against her chest, her diabetic body protesting the exertion and the constant neglect of nutrition. 'Why can't there be any weed here?'

'There must be something in here,' Gilbert said, smiling and scratching his testicles. 'Nothing's ever easy, is it?'

'Never.' she grumbled, frustration mounting. That's when her hand brushed against cold metal. It wasn't the familiar shape of a drug packet—it was too solid, too ominous.

'Jesus!' she exclaimed, jerking her hand back as if scalded. She looked inside. Her eyes widened in shock at the sight of the handgun lying amongst the drugs. Its dark barrel stared at her; an unblinking eye full of malice. Next to it, more terrifying still, was a grenade—a metal pineapple, its pin intact but looking far too fragile for comfort.

'God, oh God, why on earth would they leave them in my house?' Janine whispered, stumbling backward, her legs hitting the edge of the bed. She collapsed onto the mattress, her vision swimming. Alcohol fumes mixed with the icy tendrils of panic rising in her throat. She wasn't cut out for this; she was just Janine, who struggled to make sense of the world on a good day, who fought her own demons each night with a bottle and a joint in her hand.

'What is it?' Gilbert asked, shocked.

'A gun,' Janine whispered. 'And a fucking grenade!'

'A grenade?'

'Yes.'

'Like on a war film?' Gilbert asked.

'Exactly like that,' Janine said, nodding. 'Okay, okay, think,' she coached herself, trying to slow her rapid breathing. 'What do I do with this?'

She couldn't call the police; The Diddy Men would know it was her. They had eyes everywhere, and they'd made it clear that snitches didn't get second chances. But leaving weapons like these in her flat? That was crossing a line she hadn't even realised was there until now. She shouldn't have looked but that line was crossed.

'What are you going to do?' Gilbert asked. He took a small metal tin from the holdall he was searching. 'This bag has these tins inside it.' He turned it over in his hands, silver in colour with a high shine finish. 'This looks like a shoe polish tin. Someone has sanded the branding from it and made it shiny. My friend had one just like this and he kept his tobacco and weed in it!'

'Really?' Janine stared at the tin. She could see the threads around the sides which held the lid in place. 'Is there anything in it?'

Gilbert shook it next to his ear. 'It's heavy but it's not rattling. Shall we open it?'

'I don't know anymore,' Janine said, shaking her head. 'This stuff shouldn't be in my home. I don't want to complain about what is in this bag. They will hurt me if I complain because I shouldn't have looked in the bag. I'm in over my head,' she admitted aloud, her voice breaking. The realisation was a punch to the gut, a sobering slap to the face. She'd been so focused on getting through each day, on numbing the pain and the emptiness, that she hadn't stopped to consider the depth of the hole she was digging for herself. 'I should never have looked in here. We need to put it all back and pretend we never found it.'

'I'll do whatever you think we should do,' Gilbert said, disappointed. 'But I think there is tobacco and weed in this tin.'

'Maybe we could just take a look and pretend we've never been in here?' Janine said. 'I'm good at pretending.'

Who are you kidding, Janine? She thought. You can't handle this. Tears pricked at the corners of her eyes, the saltiness mingling with the sweat on her flushed skin. Janine glanced at the gun again, her stomach churning. She thought about the weight of it in her hand, the power it represented. Power, she didn't want. And then there was the grenade—an object so out of place in her dingy little flat that it seemed surreal. It belonged in war zones, in action movies, not nestled between her spare linens and the empty pillowcases. She had been tricked with promises of an easier life and allowed evil into her home.

'Maybe... maybe I can put it back,' she reasoned, her voice barely audible. 'They'll never know I saw them.'

But even as she said it, she knew it was a lie. The holdall had been disturbed, the contents shifted. The Diddy Men weren't fools; they'd notice.

'Fuck it!' she swore, slamming her fist against the bed. Each option led to a dead end; every thought circled back to the same conclusion: she was trapped. 'Think! There's got to be a way out,' she berated herself, wiping away the tears with the back of her hand. She had to be smart about this, smarter than she'd ever been. She had to protect herself without tipping off the gang to her discovery. 'Hide it back where it was,' she decided suddenly, a spark of clarity cutting through the fog of her panic. 'Yeah, hide the damn things until I can work this out. If they notice it's moved, deny everything.'

With trembling hands, Janine covered the gun and the grenade beneath the twenty-pound bags. She closed the duffle bag carefully and shoved them deep into the recesses of her closet, behind boxes of forgotten trinkets and clothes she no longer wore, where they wouldn't be seen without searching. If she could just keep them out of sight, perhaps she could buy herself some time to come up with a plan to ask them to move them.

'Please don't let them find out that I looked,' she prayed to a god she wasn't sure was listening. Janine couldn't afford to lose the fragile thread of control she had left. Her very survival depended on it. 'Be normal,' she told herself, practicing her most nonchalant expression in the mirror. 'Just be Janine. They won't suspect a thing. Thicko. Pretend to be thicker than you already are.'

'Everything will be okay,' Gilbert said, shaking the tin again. 'There are four of these tins in this bag. I reckon they're tobacco and weed tins. Definitely.'

'Are you sure?' Janine asked.

'What else would they put in them?' Gilbert gave a toothless smile. 'Shall I open this and see what's in it?'

'Have a look but don't take anything out of it, just in case,' Janine said. 'I need a wee and a drink.'

'Me too,' Gilbert said. 'I'll have a wine. Sharing is caring.'

'Sharing is caring,' Janine agreed. Taking a deep breath, she left the spare room, carefully closing the door behind her. The click of the latch sounded like a judge's gavel—final, condemning. She would have to tread carefully now, every step a potential misstep, every word a possible betrayal.

'Keep it together, thicko,' she whispered as she poured herself and Gilbert a glass of cheap red wine, the liquid's ruby colour mirroring the pulsing veins beneath the skin on her cheeks. 'Just keep it together, Janine.'

Her phone rang and she looked at the screen. It was Bobby Allen, one of the Diddy Men. He was one of the older members and a complete psycho. Her heart froze in fear. She wanted to ignore it but couldn't. She answered the call.

'Hello Bobby,' Janine said, trying to sound normal.

'Why are you rummaging around through our stuff, Janine?'

'I wasn't,' she whispered, shocked.

'Don't lie to me.'

'How do you know?'

'A little bird told me,' Bobby said.

'There are no little birds in my flat.'

'We have motion sensors in the bags, Janine. I told you never to touch the stuff we left with you to look after, didn't I?'

'Yes.'

'Then why are you fucking around with our bags?'

'I was looking for some weed,' she said, confused. How did they know, thicko? What is a motion sensor? 'I've run out and my anxiety is going through the roof. I haven't stolen anything...'

'I'll send someone around with some smoke for you but you're going to have to be disciplined, Janine. You've broken the rules.'

'I'm sorry,' Janine said. 'Are you going to hurt me?'

'I'm afraid so...'

A deafening explosion ripped through the flat. The sound of glass shattering filled her head. Silence settled like an icy blanket.

'What the fuck?' Billy growled. 'Tell me you haven't touched the holdalls, Janine,' he shouted. Janine was too shocked to answer. 'Janine, you fucking idiot! Tell me you didn't touch the holdalls.'

'My friend did,' she muttered. 'He found a tin and thought there might be some weed in it...' Billy didn't reply.

The call ended and Janine sat staring at the blank screen, the stench of exploded ordinance and burnt flesh reached her and smoke filled the air.

Chapter 7

3-years earlier

The room was like a time capsule from the sixties, decorated in deep reds and furnished with dark wood tables and chairs. It was dimly lit, the orange glow spreading from a solitary church candle perched precariously on the edge of Shelly's mantlepiece. A log burned in the fireplace, shadows danced around the walls, twisting and contorting, much like the unease that coiled in the pit of her stomach. Her client, Jon had a dark aura around him; he oozed evil, but she was too frightened to tell him to leave. There was an eerie silence, save for the sound of her own heartbeat echoing in her ears. Cold sweat trickled down her spine and her sense of foreboding was overwhelming.

In the heart of the living room on a walnut table, lay an antique Ouija board, its surface worn smooth by the touch of countless hands—a relic of the past. Once a common parlour game, a plaything of the rich, it was now Shelly's workplace. She traded on the desperation of other humans who wanted to talk to loved ones passed over. She exploited their hopes for the future, and the trepidation of what it held. The rich mahogany wood gleamed with a warmth that belied its chilling purpose. It was not the kind of piece that belonged to just anyone; it had a presence, a story veiled in whispered tales and haunted places. Shelly had inherited it from her grandmother, who was also a seer. Her grandmother had spotted the gift in her when she was a young girl. She taught her to read palms and tealeaves, and she picked them up quickly. By the time Shelly was a teenager, she could use the Ouija board like her grandmother and was almost as convincing. It was a special board, beautifully crafted.

The planchette, a small, heart-shaped piece of polished wood, sat on the board, its brass pointer dulled by time yet still pleasant on the eye. People often asked if they could touch it. The crescent moon and star decorations, delicately etched into the wood, glimmered faintly in the candlelight. The grain in the wood was highlighted by the highly polished surface. Each letter, each number and symbol, seemed to pulse with a life of its own, the markings carved into the wood holding decades of mystique. The board had been her tool to make money but tonight, it felt malevolent. Her client stared at it, fascinated by its carvings and decorations but his eyes kept shifting to her, lingering too long.

'So, this is your connection to the universe?' Jon asked. Shelly nodded and smiled nervously. 'It's truly beautiful,' he added. 'Do you mind if I ask where you got it?'

'It belonged to my grandmother,' Shelly said. Her memory made her glow inside and she felt a little safer when she thought about her. Just a little. Her intuition was screaming at her to get rid of the client. 'She had the gift, and she recognised it in me when I was a young girl.'

'Fascinating,' Jon said. 'May I touch it?'

'Yes,' Shelly said. She watched as he ran his fingers across the letters, the carvings and symbols. 'It was carved by a true craftsman.'

'Really?'

'My grandfather made it for her,' Shelly said. 'He was a cabinet maker by trade.'

'He was a very talented man,' Jon said, moving the planchette. 'Do you talk to your grandparents through this?'

'No,' Shelly said. 'They have never come through and I have never asked them to. It's an unwritten rule never to contact your own loved ones.'

'Why not?' Jon asked. He tilted his head to listen to her answer. 'You must be tempted?'

'When my grandfather passed over, I asked my grandmother if we could talk to him on the other side, but she said no, despite being heartbroken.' Shelly smiled at the memory. 'She said reaching into the darkness to contact your own loved ones leaves you vulnerable to evil spirits, who can masquerade as others.'

'Do you believe that?' Jon asked, smiling. 'In evil, I mean?'

'Of course,' Shelly said. 'Not everyone that has passed was good. Good and evil exist in equal measure.'

'I'm so glad you believe that,' Jon said.

'I do,' she said, nodding.

Shelly had always been a believer in the unseen—a medium, a conduit through which spirits could speak, or at least, that's how she liked to brand herself. Some branded her a charlatan, but that was because she charged her clients money to participate in her seances. Shelly didn't leave much to chance and she researched her clients in depth using social media. She could gather a plethora of information in a short space of time, which meant she could tell her clients things that would make them think she was communicating with the dead. It was a simple trick, like sleight of hand for a magician but impressive to the clients. The research provided those, 'How could she know that?' moments.

The truth was the spirits didn't always come through and she didn't do refunds. The Ouija board was her ritualistic tool, its alphabet-tiled surface a portal to the beyond but sometimes it was simply a chunk of wood. Tonight, however, was different; tonight felt wrong, a crack in the fabric of her reality. She felt evil energy all around her and it was emanating from her client.

She studied him. A man who was good looking, piercing blue eyes, tousled dark hair—it was unsettling how attractive he was. But something about the way he was sitting, with an unnerving stillness and an unsettling grin that lingered just a split second too long, made her skin crawl. It was as if he was excited but trying to keep a lid on his excitement. She felt like a moth fluttering too close to a flame, drawn in despite the instinctive warning that told her to turn back. Get him out, her instincts screamed.

'Are you ready, Shelly?' he asked, his voice smooth as silk yet laced with something sinister that sent a shiver racing down her spine. 'I'm keen to get started.'

She nodded, her hands trembling slightly as she placed them on the planchette, the delicate wooden heart that had seen enough paranormal encounters to fill a library of ghost stories, some true, most made up, creations of her financial exploitation of vulnerable clients.

'Let's begin,' she said, attempting to sound confident. Closing her eyes momentarily, she inhaled sharply, as if bracing herself against a sudden tide of dread. She felt the air shift, the room growing heavier as shadows pooled around them. Her breathing was shallow.

'Is there anyone here with us?' she asked softly, her eyes snapping open to meet Jon's expectant gaze. He raised his eyebrows and grinned. 'Does anyone want to join us today?'

'Reluctant ghosts,' he whispered.

'Spirits,' she corrected.

He remained silent, a smile lingering at the corners of his mouth as she pressed on, the familiar yet uneasy rhythm of the séance beginning to take shape. The planchette twitched under her fingers, a soft movement that felt more like a warning today. Don't invite him in...

Jon leaned forward, his eyes glinting in the candlelight like shards of black ice.

'I want you to contact Allison,' he said, his tone sharpening, the nonchalance in his voice gone. It was more of a demand than a request. 'She was so beautiful, so young, so innocent...so frightened...'

'When did she pass?'

'Not long ago. She suffered terribly.'

'That's awful. I'm sorry for your loss.' Shelly swallowed hard, tilting her head to the side. 'Was she your daughter?' she asked, her heart thudding heavily in her chest.

'You could say she's one of my children,' he said. 'Not biologically but she's mine. She always will be.'

'If Allison is listening, could you give us a sign?' Shelly asked. The planchette remained still. There was a chill in the air and she felt a shiver run down her spine. 'Allison, are you there?'

'She's probably still angry with me. She was very angry at the end.' His smile broadened, exposing perfect pearly whites that seemed far too white for the darkness around them. 'What about Belinda?'

'Belinda?'

'Ask if she's here.'

'Belinda are you able to talk to us?' Shelly asked. 'Allison, can you?'

'I don't think they want to talk to you,' Jon said. 'Maybe you're having an off night.'

'The spirits can be unpredictable.'

'I imagine they are.' He grinned. 'They were both murdered, but I'm sure you know that?'

'Why would I know that?' Shelly asked. The colour drained from her face.

'Because you talk to the dead, don't you?'

The words hung in the air like a chilling fog, their weight suffocating. The shadows seemed to deepen in response, clustering closer like silent witnesses to something unspeakable. Shelly recoiled slightly, her stomach twisting violently. This wasn't what she had signed up for; this was beyond her understanding.

'They may not want to speak because both of them were murdered?' she stammered, battling the urge to flee, to extinguish the candle and throw open the door into the night. 'You can't ask me to contact spirits ripped from this realm before their time.'

He leaned back in his chair, the light flickering in tandem with her heartbeat. 'Oh, but I can ask. I want to talk to them. They had good reasons to leave this world.'

'What reason could they have to be murdered?'

'To become part of something truly awesome,' Jon explained. 'I've seen glimpses of the power and energy around us both good and bad. Some things cannot be unseen, Shelly. Some things... must be seen to be believed.' He nodded. 'Try again...'

'Is there anybody here right now?'

With a trembling hand, she forced herself to slide the planchette to 'YES,' unsure if she were really asking the board or merely giving in to the wildness spinning in her mind. A visceral dread flooded her veins as she stared at Jon. He smiled as the planchette moved, a man who should have been nothing more than a stranger, yet felt like a dark thread woven into the fabric of her own fate. The universe had brought them together, she thought but she knew the thought wasn't her own. It was shared but she didn't know who by.

'A messenger is here,' Shelly lied. 'She can pass on a message to them. What do you wish to say to them?' She could barely form the question, but the inquiry spilled out before her brain could stop it.

'Tell them...what I did was my gift to them. I released them,' he replied languidly, as if recounting a grand and twisted story. 'Or they would still be here, struggling to survive.'

Shelly felt the walls of reality contract, the air tightening around her throat. A malevolence emanated from him, a potency that wrapped itself tightly around her, daring her to breathe again. All her training told her to keep asking questions, to probe deeper into the spirit world, but all she could think of was how to escape.

'Is there a specific one you'd like to pass the message onto first?' She barely recognised the tremble in her voice.

He leaned forward, his eyes boring into hers, glittering with a macabre hunger. 'Allison,' he said, whispering the name like a prayer. 'She was so beautiful...But beauty comes with an expiration date, doesn't it? I want her to know why she had to go.'

As Jon spoke, the candle flickered violently, almost as if in protest. An unseen wind began to swirl around them. Shelly could feel the frigid breath of the departed creatures, their anger and resentment churning at the edge of her perception. She clutched the planchette harder, her palms slick with sweat, eyes darting around the perimeter of the room, seeking an escape but only finding darkness creeping deeper. Shelly knew better than to play with forces she didn't understand, and Jon was no ordinary man. He was an enigma wrapped in wickedness, and she was about to uncover threads of horrors she could never have imagined.

'Why are you really here?' Shelly asked him.

'Why, Shelly?' Jon asked, his voice mildewed and dripping with regret. 'Why do you look frightened?'

'Because I am frightened,' she said. He smiled and nodded. Because I know the truth now, she thought, the words racing through her mind like poison. You murdered them.

'You can join them, soon,' Jon said, standing. He took a large knife from his pocket. 'But first I have some gifts for you...'

Chapter 8

The Eyewitnesses

The police car's engine made a low, almost comforting growl as it came to a stop in front of a rundown semi-detached house in Huyton. It was scruffy in comparison to the rest of the estate, which was well-maintained with nice cars parked on the driveways. Once a council estate, it was now mostly privately owned. The garden was neglected and littered with takeaway, pizza boxes and fast-food wrappers, discarded by inconsiderate neighbours and passersby. It was clearly a build up over months, never picked up by the owners. It stood out because the surrounding gardens were tidy and well groomed.

Gary White, his fingers picking at the sleeve of his jacket, peered out of the rear passenger window at his home, his eyes tracing the familiar cracks in the render beneath the window frames. The remaining panels of the rotting fence were leaning at an unnatural angle, the wood disintegrated in places. A couple of panels had been stolen for bonfire night and never replaced. It was embarrassing. His dad called it the Whitehouse, but his friends called it the shite house.

'Your parents aren't keen gardeners, are they?' PC Martins muttered to himself. He surveyed the scene before him with a practised eye, making assumptions about the people who lived there. As a police officer, he could tell a lot about the people he was about to encounter from the condition of their property. Noting the overgrown weeds that vied for dominance in what once might have been a nice garden, he decided the owners were lazy twats. A rusty set of swings creaked mournfully as a breeze picked up, its chains groaning under the weight.

Gary and his sister had used the swings when they were younger, back when their parents could be arsed playing with them. They seemed to have more energy back then. More zest for life. Everything seemed to be a struggle nowadays.

'They're not big into DIY either, are they?' Martins asked.

Gary and Rosie exchange glances but didn't reply. It was obvious the police officer wasn't impressed with their home.

'Dad has got some paint but he's waiting to borrow some ladders,' Rosie lied. Gary frowned, wondering where the paint was. An elbow in the ribs stopped him asking the question.

'Looks like nobody's painted anything for a while,' Martins muttered to himself, his voice barely audible, above the engine and radio. 'Do they own the house?' Martins asked.

'Yes,' Rosie said, nodding. 'It was my grandmother's house, but she died, and my mum inherited it.'

'That figures,' Martins said, looking at Rosie in the mirror. She looked away, embarrassed. 'I can tell it was well looked after once upon a time.'

The house itself seemed to sag under the burden of years of disregard; paint flaked away from the woodwork like dead skin, and several windows were boarded up, while others boasted cracks that ran deep into the render. The roofline appeared uneven, as if the very bones of the building had given up on standing straight. The front door, its once vibrant colour now faded to an indistinguishable hue of green.

'That front door needs replacing,' Martins said, pointing. 'A hard swift kick would open it.'

'We don't get many burglaries around here,' Rosie said.

'Community spirit?' Martins asked.

'No. They get their legs broken if they get caught,' Rosie answered, grinning. 'We don't hear about break-ins on the estate very often.'

Martins smiled but he thought it was a burglar's dream, no need to break any glass. Not that any self-respecting thief would bother to break in. There was clearly nothing of value in there.

'What happened to the windows at the side of the house?' PC Martins asked.

'My dad had a row with a local headcase over some money, so he bricked our windows,' Rosie explained, matter-of-factly. 'My dad isn't a fighter, so he called the police. You lot didn't do anything about it, so my dad is still fighting for compensation to fix the damage. He refuses to pay for the glass.'

'A row over some money, you say?' PC Ellis repeated, frowning. 'Was it anything to do with drugs?'

'Probably,' Gary said, nodding. 'He smokes weed a lot.'

'Gary!' Rosie hissed.

'What?'

'Shut up!'

'I'm just saying it probably was to do with drugs.'

'Shut up, Gary,' Rosie said.

'I'm just saying,' Gary protested. 'It wasn't his fault the windows were bricked, and my dad isn't great at DIY,' Gary pointed out, sensing the police officer's surprise at his honesty. 'He doesn't have much money, and he hasn't been well.'

Gary shrugged. People were always telling him to shut up. His dad promised the windows would be repaired and the house would be repainted before summer but hadn't specified which summer. Another job on his never ending, never dwindling, never to be completed list.

'Take no notice of my brother and you shouldn't be asking him stuff like that anyway,' Rosie said, angrily. 'He's twelve years old.'

'We're not here to judge your parents, Rosie. We're here to make sure you get home safely, alright?' PC Martins said, unconvincingly. Gary nodded, knowing that he was in fact judging them and had already made up his mind.

PC Martins smiled, casting a glance at the rearview mirror where Rosie met his gaze with a nod. She looked away quickly, uncomfortable under his gaze. Martins was in his late twenties, handsome, tattooed and muscular with sculptured black hair, shaved to a fade above the ears and nape of the neck. His teeth were too white to be the originals. 'Let's get you inside and explain to your parents why you're not in school.'

'I don't think they'll be arsed,' Gary said.

'Gary!' Rosie warned.

'What?'

'Shut up...'

'Don't worry about it. How are you feeling?' PC Ellis asked, turning around. She was black and very pretty, Gary was smitten. She looked like Rhianna but younger. 'Fit as fuck,' his friend Dave would have said. He smiled and shrugged, too tongue-tied to speak. 'A lot has happened this morning and it's been a shock for you. Tell your parents if you feel upset or frightened, okay. It's okay not to be okay.'

PC Martins was out of the vehicle first. The rear door clicked open and Gary hesitated, the lingering image of the school bus chaos flashing behind his eyelids. Rosie reached over, her hand briefly squeezing his shoulder before she slid out of the car. He followed, the weight of the day pressing down on him like an anchor. Dead kids, dead eyes, blood on the blade. The knife in his bag...

Why had he picked it up? He asked himself. Knobhead.

'The curtains are closed. Is it always this quiet here?' PC Ellis asked. She frowned and winked. 'Or are they vampires?'

'That would be cool if they were vamps but unfortunately not, they're still in bed because they're sleeping off a late night,' Rosie said.

'At this time?' Ellis asked, checking her watch.

'They're not morning people.' Rosie shrugged. 'They stay up late, and sleep in.'

'Who gets you ready for school?' Martins asked, shaking his head.

'We do,' Rosie mumbled. 'We're capable of getting dressed.'

'Do you make your own breakfast?' Martins pushed.

'We're not big on breakfast,' Rosie said.

'I am but there's never any food in,' Gary said. Rosie nudged him hard. 'What?'

'Shut up.'

'I'm just saying.'

'Your parents don't work, do they?' Ellis asked, her voice carrying a note of concern as they approached the front door.

'Mum works sometimes, Dad has mental health problems,' Gary explained. Rosie glared at him again. 'What?' he muttered, rolling his eyes. 'What have I said now?'

'Too much information,' Rosie whispered. 'They don't need to know about dad.'

'I'm just saying...' Gary muttered.

'It's like my partner said earlier, we're not here to judge anyone,' PC Ellis said, shaking her head. 'I'm just asking why there's no sign of life.'

'It's always quiet when mum and dad are sleeping off the night before,' Rosie replied curtly, her lips pressed into a thin line. 'They had friends around last night, so it was a big one.'

'Sleeping off the night before?' PC Ellis echoed, her eyebrows knitting together. Martins smiled and nudged her in the back so that the kids couldn't see. 'That doesn't sound good.'

'Drinking, she means,' Gary clarified, his voice barely above a whisper. He caught the constable's eye and saw the flicker of understanding there. 'They're always rough if they're on it the night before.'

'Right. I understand.' She cleared her throat, her professionalism masking the worry that had crept into her eyes. Her expression hardened.

Rosie fumbled with the keys for a moment before the tumblers gave way and the door swung inward. The smell of stale beer and cigarette smoke wafted out tinged with the pungent tang of weed, and Gary's face scrunched up in response. The officers exchanged a glance, which registered cannabis had been smoked in the property. Recently.

'Mum, Dad, are you awake?' Rosie called out, but the silence that greeted them was thick, unyielding. She waited a few seconds before trying again. 'Mum! Dad, wake up!'

'We're trying to have a lie in,' Bill White shouted, his voice thick with sleep. 'What the fuck are you doing here?'

'Get out of bed!'

'Why would I do that?'

'Because the police are here,' Rosie called upstairs. 'They need to talk to you.'

'Check if social services are involved here with the children,' Ellis whispered to Martins. Martins nodded.

'They are,' Gary said, earwigging. Both officers looked at him. 'We're on a children in need plan.' Rosie glared at him again. 'What?' he sighed. 'I'm just saying. They're going to find out anyway.'

'Too much information, Gaz! Stay here and I'll get them up,' Rosie said, as she advanced up the stairs, Gary following closely behind, sheepishly. 'My dad walks around in his billies, you don't need to see that, honestly, you don't.'

Gary jogged up the stairs and the officers watched him disappear around the corner before he turned into his bedroom. He closed the door and went to his drawers, opening the bottom one. He took out a black cotton vest and opened his school bag. Carefully, he lifted the knife and wrapped it in the vest, hiding it at the back of the drawer beneath his winter jumpers, the ones he didn't wear anymore. His mother rarely went into his room and the chances of her putting clean clothes into his drawers was zero. But the police were here and they might search his room. Gary changed his mind, removed the wrapped weapon and went to his wardrobe. The storage box full of dinosaurs was a safer option. He plunged the illicit package into the box, beneath the hundreds of prehistoric monsters that had been such an important part of his childhood but were now just plastic shapes with no meaning. It would be safe there.

He checked his hands to make sure there was no blood. They were clean but he wiped them on his trousers anyway. Relieved to be rid of the murder weapon, he took off his coat and went to speak to his parents. Rosie was already in their bedroom doorway, explaining why they needed to get out of bed, in her own special way.

'Get up, you lazy twats!'

'Charming. Are you sure she's, my daughter?' Bill asked. Hayley shrugged.

'I can't remember, to be honest,' she said. 'There's been so many men and so little time.'

'Mum!' Rosie moaned. 'That's disgusting.'

'Did you shag the milkman while I was out?' Bill asked.

'I've done a few milkmen, window cleaners, the coalmen,' Hayley said, seriously. 'There were three coalmen, all brothers. She looks like the eldest brother, to be honest.'

'You're so fucking embarrassing!' Rosie hissed, trying to keep her voice down. 'There are two police officers downstairs, waiting to talk to you. The house is a shithole and stinks of weed.'

'What is her problem?' Bill moaned. 'I need to sleep. Tell them to fuck off.'

'The police are here, and they want to talk to you!' Rosie hissed, trying to be quiet. 'And neither me aged thirteen or your son, who is twelve are going to tell the police to fuck off. So, be an adult for a change and speak to them.'

'The police are actually inside the house?' Bill suddenly understood.

'Yes. Two of them.'

'Just to be sure I'm not dreaming. There are two police officers in our house?' Bill asked, his voice still thick with alcohol.

'Yes.'

'That's one each, love,' he joked with Hayley. 'What do they want?'

'They want to talk to you about why we're not in school,' Rosie said, irritated. 'Get out of bed and come and talk to them!'

'Wait a minute!' Bill said, sitting up. 'Hayley. Our kids are not in school. Someone call the police!'

'No need, they're already here, apparently,' Hayley said, chuckling.

'Oh, my God, you're like a couple of kids,' Rosie shouted. 'You are so embarrassing.'

'I'm your father,' Bill said, yawning. 'I'm supposed to be embarrassing. That's my role in life.'

'Fuck off, Dad,' Rosie said. 'This is not funny.'

'Don't tell your dad to fuck off,' Hayley said, yawning in sympathy. 'He can't because the house is in joint names.'

'You can fuck off too if that's your attitude,' Hayley said, folding her arms. 'Aren't you worried that the neighbours will think we've done something wrong.'

'Why would they think that?'

'Because there's a police car outside and two uniformed officers on the doorstep,' Rosie snapped. 'And Gary has told them we're on a CIN plan with social services.'

'Why has he told them that?' Bill asked, frowning. 'Fucking hell, son. Some things are best kept secret.'

'They're police officers,' Gary said. 'They find things out for a living. I didn't think it would be a secret for very long.'

'Good point,' Bill said, nodding. 'He's smarter than he looks.'

'Why are the police here, anyway?' Hayley asked, yawning again. 'And why are you not in school?'

'There was a fight on the bus, two people were stabbed, one died, and another one was runover and he died too,' Rosie explained. 'We saw everything.'

'There was a fight on the bus?' Bill asked.

'Yes.'

'Did you stab anyone?' Bill asked.

'No!'

'Did Gary stab anyone?'

'No, of course not!'

'Then why are the police in my house?' Bill asked, climbing out of bed. He put his hands into his boxershorts and rearranged things. 'What do they want to talk to me for?'

'Because your children have witnessed a murder and they're concerned about our welfare,' Rosie said, shaking her head. 'It's not rocket science.'

'Is everything alright up there?' PC Ellis called up the stairs.

'Yes. I'm just waking our parents up, won't be long,' Rosie called back. 'Get up. Hurry up, for fuck's sake!' she hissed.

'We need to have a word with them, please,' Ellis added, sounding annoyed. 'And we don't have time to hang around.' She purposely increased the volume to make sure the adults could hear her. 'So, if you would be so kind as to make yourselves presentable, please and come downstairs...'

'Fucking hell,' Bill whispered. 'She sounds like a real Nazi.' He pulled on a pair of tracksuit bottoms and slid a black vest over his head. 'I suppose we'll have to talk to them, or social services will be here in a flash. The last thing I need today is them mithering me about what a shite parent I am.'

'Social services are here to help us. Maybe you should try listening to what they say,' Rosie said, sighing. 'Being a parent isn't rocket science but you make out it is.'

'Why don't you go and make the nazis a cup of tea while your parents get dressed?' Bill said, angrily. 'She's doing my fucking head in,' he added, pointing at Rosie. 'I can't wait until she grows up and fucks off.'

'The feeling is mutual,' Rosie said, storming down the stairs. 'The truth hurts. They tell you you're a shite parent because you are a shite parent!'

'You're a shite child,' Bill retorted. 'I'd rather have a dog!'

'There's no milk to make them a cup of tea,' Gary said.

'What?' Bill glared at him and his mother blushed, embarrassed. 'What are you talking about?'

'You said, make the nazis a cup of tea but there's no milk or teabags.'

'Shut up, Gary,' Bill snapped. 'You're doing my fucking head in, as well.'

'Don't swear at him, he's sensitive,' Hayley said.

'I'm certain you shagged the milkman twice,' Bill said, combing his hair with his fingers. 'I don't think they're my kids. They're too thick to be mine.'

'I'm not thick. I'm just saying there's fuck all in the kitchen.'

'Shut up, Gary,' Bill snapped. 'Go and bore the nazis because you're boring the shit out of me.'

'I was just saying.'

'Go downstairs, Gary!'

Gary felt like everyone told him to shut up. He followed his sister downstairs, impressed with her ability to tell their parents what she thought, without beating around the bush. He wouldn't dare speak to his dad like that. His dad was more than happy to give Gary a slap around the head if he was cheeky or didn't do as he was asked but he never laid a finger on Rosie. Rosie was not the type of person to tolerate corporal punishment. The last time his dad grabbed her, she bit him so hard, the wound didn't stop bleeding for days and it became infected. Bill had to go to the doctor for antibiotics, which meant explaining the bite wound. Another bad mark in the social worker's file. He hadn't touched her since.

'They're getting dressed, but don't hold your breath,' Rosie said, skipping past the police officers, who were standing inside the hallway with the front door still open. 'I would offer you a cup of tea, but there's no milk. In fact, there's fuck all in the kitchen again.' She went into the kitchen and came back with a roll of binbags and a damp cloth. 'Give me two minutes and I'll clear up a bit.'

Rosie opened the blinds and stuffed empty bottles and cans into a bag, tipping two full ashtrays away, followed by three takeaway cartons. Rosie's fingers worked deftly, sweeping squashed chips and crumpled napkins into her palms. The stench of stale beer rose from the carpet as she scrubbed at a dark stain that had no intention of leaving. Gary, came into the living room and was diligently collecting empty glasses, stacking them with a precision that belied his age. He glanced at the doorway; the police officers had stepped further into the house and watched impatiently.

'Rosie,' he whispered urgently, nudging her with his foot, 'the police are watching.'

She glanced over her shoulder where the two officers stood by the door, hats in hands, their eyes scanning the room with practised detachment. Rosie straightened up, her back protesting slightly, and gave Gary a nod.

'Keep going,' she said under her breath, tucking a loose strand of hair behind her ear.

'Shouldn't Mum and Dad come down and talk to them?' Gary asked innocently, dropping another handful of plastic into the rubbish bag that was already bulging.

'They're not exactly... presentable yet,' Rosie muttered, surveying the living room once more. Empty bottles formed colonies on every surface, and the air was thick with the scent of overindulgence.

'Are they in trouble?' Gary's voice quivered just enough to betray his worry. 'I bet social services will come around again, won't they?'

'I don't know, Gaz. Let's just clean this up quick.' She forced a smile, trying to be the rock he needed right now. She always was. 'They're due a visit soon anyway.'

PC Ellis caught her eye and offered a small, sympathetic nod. Rosie returned it with a tight-lipped smile and turned away, her heart sinking in shame.

'Maybe we should offer them black coffee or something,' Gary suggested, always the one wanting to help.

'There's no coffee, so unless they want hot water, we have nothing to offer,' Rosie said, shaking her head. 'Let's just focus on this mess.'

'Can you have black tea?' Gary asked.

'There's no tea,' Rosie replied, hastily wrapping her arm around a cluster of beer bottles and making for the kitchen.

The clink of glass trailed behind her as she moved, a conspicuous soundtrack to the morning-after chaos. The officers' silent vigil spoke volumes, their presence heavy in the already stifling atmosphere. PC Ellis looked around the cramped living room, her keen eyes taking in the details that would most likely go unnoticed by the untrained eye. The media wall, an ambitious installation for such a modest dwelling, was a chaotic amalgamation of screens, wires, and dusty speakers, all centred around a television that hadn't seen a software update since its inception.

'Seen better days, huh?' Ellis muttered to herself, walking past the settee that sagged despondently under the weight of time and neglect. Its once vibrant fabric now bore the muted testimony of countless spilled meals and drunken afternoons; frayed at the edges, it seemed to sigh with exhaustion.

'Hasn't it just,' Martins agreed. 'It stinks of skunk in here.'

Casting her gaze across the room, Ellis noticed the armchairs, their cushions so deeply indented it was as though the ghosts of previous occupants still lingered, weighing them down. One stood out with a particularly deep crease, the favourite seat of someone who had spent endless hours there. The windows—coated in grime both inside and out—scattered the weak sunlight into fractured beams that danced lazily across the room.

'Could use a window cleaner,' she whispered, although the state of the windows did little to obscure her vision of the life that unfolded within these four walls—a life punctuated by long drinking sessions and a complete disregard of the world outside.

'Think they'll wait around much longer?' Gary asked, peeking out from the doorframe.

'Doesn't look like they have a choice, or they would have gone by now,' Rosie answered, forcing a note of cheerfulness into her voice. 'We've got this, though. Teamwork, remember?'

'Teamwork,' Gary echoed, his smile fleeting but genuine as he followed her lead, picking up speed with the cleanup. 'Teamwork makes the dream work.'

'That's shite,' Rosie chuckled. 'Don't say that...'

'I was just saying...' Gary mumbled.

'Only knobheads say stuff like that,' Rosie explained. 'Don't say knobhead things.'

They heard footsteps on the stairs and looked at each other, smiling. Their parents were out of bed and about to make an appearance.

'Good morning, officers,' Bill said, from the stairs. 'Apologies for keeping you waiting, we were having a lie in.' He poked his head into the living room and smiled to reveal nicotine-stained teeth. His hair was a throwback to his obsession with Oasis, brushed forward above the ears and parted in the middle. He was greying fast. 'I see the kids have started clearing up. They never clear up, so it must be because we have guests. You're making a good impression, thanks kids.' Bill's smile was forced. 'Sorry to keep you waiting. How can we help you, officers?'

'We need a chat about an incident this morning,' PC Ellis said. 'Why don't we take a seat. This won't take long.'

Bill and Hayley walked into their living room, heads bowed, eyes searching nervously for incriminating evidence of their cannabis use. Rosie had thrown the contents of the ashtrays, sparing them the embarrassment. They sat on the settee like naughty school children waiting to be scolded by their headmaster. Hayley pushed her hair off her face, nervously making an effort to look decent. She had struggled into a black tracksuit but the pants were inside out, disclosing the rush with which she had dressed.

'Can you sit down too, please,' Ellis said to the children. 'It won't take long.' She gestured toward the empty chairs. 'We need to talk about what happened today, and how you're feeling about it.'

'Scared,' Gary admitted, sinking into a chair that had seen better days. 'And kind of sick.'

'Understandable,' Ellis replied, taking out a notepad. 'You've been through a traumatic event.'

'Before you start, do you think you should explain to us why you're in our home with our children, when they should be in school?' Bill said, irritated. The police officers looked uncomfortable, which he enjoyed. 'Unfortunately, we're not psychic, so we haven't got a Scooby doo what the fuck is going on.'

PC Martins blushed red, angry at Bill's attitude. He looked like he was going to punch him. Ellis took the lead to avoid an argument.

'Apologies. We should have done that first.' Ellis nodded and held out her hands, in a calming gesture as she spoke. 'There was an altercation on the school bus this morning and a number of people were stabbed,' Ellis explained. 'Unfortunately, one child died from his wounds at the scene, and another was killed when the fight spilled onto the road.' Gary looked down at his feet and Rosie studied her nails. 'Rosie and Gary witnessed both deaths, hence we've brought them home, so that we can ask them some basic questions without going through the stress of going to the station.'

Bill shrugged, yawned and sighed, unimpressed. 'I'm sure they see worse on Netflix every day. The youngest is a real horror fan. Hostel, Saw, Paranormal Activity, Evil Dead, you name it, he's watched them ten times over.'

'That's not the point,' Martins said, shaking his head. 'We need your permission to ask them questions about what they saw,' Martins added, glaring at Bill. 'Hence, we're here, getting you out of bed, so apologies for the inconvenience but it needs to be done.'

'I understand you have rules to follow, although I think they're bollocks,' Bill said. Martins was going to reply but his partner nudged him. Bill smirked. 'Ask your questions. They're tougher than they look.'

'As I said, we just want to know what they saw,' Ellis began. 'Detectives will be around later this afternoon to take a full statement from them, if they deem it necessary. It will depend on what they tell us.'

'Okay,' Bill said, shrugging. 'Is that it?'

'Yes.'

'All this fuss over fuck all,' Bill sighed, yawning. 'Teenagers get stabbed all the time these days.'

'Two young boys lost their lives,' Martins said, calmly but with steel in his voice. 'This is not a fuss or fuck all, it's a murder investigation.'

'My kids didn't murder anyone and they're unlikely to have seen anything,' Bill said, shaking his head. He tapped a finger to his temple. 'People around here don't see anything and if they do, they don't tell the police. My kids know better than most.'

'I think you'll find that the majority of the community are happy to help when a child has been murdered,' Martins argued. PC Ellis could see Bill White was being awkward for the sake of it and her partner was being suckered into a pissing contest with a skunk. She interrupted them.

'Let's not get drawn into the semantics of society and lose focus on why we're here.' She glanced at Martins, and he understood. Bill White looked disappointed that the argument had stalled. 'We have a responsibility to make sure witnesses are treated with due care and attention, especially children.'

'I get the message,' Bill said. 'Can we get on with it.'

'Rosie and Gary have witnessed a violent murder, in a situation where they were in danger themselves. The victim bled out on the bus in front of them.' She paused to let the seriousness of the situation sink in, but the White parents didn't look concerned. 'Shock is often delayed, especially in the young. They can suffer nightmares, panic attacks and the like,' Ellis cautioned. 'Don't take this lightly, trauma is common in these cases.'

'Trauma seems to be our family's middle name,' Rosie muttered, nudging her brother. 'Dad gets trauma every time they go shopping. That's why there's fuck all in the kitchen cupboards.'

Gary laughed and his parents glared at him. He tried to stop but couldn't.

'You can see that there's nothing wrong with her,' Bill snapped. 'Tough as old boots and twice as thick.'

'Remind us how many qualifications you left school with again,' Rosie said, smiling coldly. 'That will be a big fat zero and you say I'm thick?'

'Rosie,' her mum chided softly, her eyes darting toward the officers. 'That's not helpful, darling.'

'Truth hurts,' she shot back, folding her arms over her chest. 'I'm not as thick as old boots. I have a job and earn more money than him and I'm still at school.'

'You call hanging around the Paki shops on the Parade, shaking your ass for the perverts a job?' Bill white sneered. Rosie looked shocked. Gary looked more shocked. 'Oh, you don't think we know where you're hanging about at night, smart arse?'

'Bill, now is not the time,' Hayley said, grabbing his arm. 'We can talk about it another time.'

'She brought the subject up and I think you lot should be doing something about those paedophiles who run those shops,' Bill said, pointing to the officers. 'The only reason they're encouraging silly bitches like Rosie to hang around is try and fuck them.'

'Dad!'

'What?' Bill snapped. 'Can't you understand that the only thing they want from you is your fanny but you're too arrogant and too stupid to realise that.' The room went quiet. Rosie looked stunned. 'Everyone knows the old paedo who owns those shops, is a wrong 'un. The young girls call him Uncle for fuck's sake!' Bill snorted. 'Uncle paedo, more like.'

The police officers exchanged glances. Bill picked up on it straightaway.

'I can tell by your face you know who I'm talking about,' Bill said, grinning but there was no mirth in it. 'From what I'm hearing, Jennifer Simmons was hanging around there too and look what's happened to her.'

'Mr White...'

'Mr White what?' Bill waved her off. 'She is someone's daughter and now she's nothing more than a Facebook page, a missing poster on a bus stop. Do you suspect them, I bet you do?'

'We can't comment on an ongoing case, but Rosie shouldn't be hanging around there at night,' PC Martins said, shrugging. He looked Rosie in the eyes. 'Don't go near those shops alone. That would be my advice.'

'You see, paedos, every one of them,' Bill gloated. He stabbed a finger towards Rosie. 'And you have a job working for the paedos, do you?'

'That is so much bullshit!' Rosie's voice quivered with teenage indignation as she slammed her palm against the table, causing the legs to clatter in protest. 'They pay me to take deliveries nearby, because it's cheaper than sending a driver. I'm sick of having no money because you're a waster, so I earn my own.'

'You're a cheeky madam and I'm not having any more of your lip,' Bill said, standing up, his face a mask of anger and frustration. 'That's enough!'

'Sit down, right now, Mr White!' Martins ordered. Bill thought about arguing but decided against it. 'I won't ask you again.' Bill sat down. 'Thank you.'

'What are you going to do, Dad, hit me?' Rosie teased. 'The last time you did that, it didn't go very well for you.' She folded her arms. 'Come near me and Social Services will be all over you like a tramp on chips.'

'Rosie, stop winding him up. You're not helping the situation,' Hayley said, trying to calm her family. 'Your dad is worried about you being around those men for a good reason,' Hayley reached out and touched her daughter's knee. 'He's protecting his little girl, because he loves you.'

Rosie looked embarrassed. 'I can look after myself,' she said, blushing. 'You don't understand—'

'I don't understand?' Her mother's voice was a mix of exasperation and concern, cutting through the tension like a knife. 'You don't understand that we don't want you to hang around that place at night?' Hayley shrugged. 'You're thirteen and some men will try to take advantage of young girls. Those men shouldn't be encouraging teenage girls to hang around their businesses and plying them with booze. They only want one thing from teenage girls, that's obvious. Rosie, it's not safe!'

'Everyone goes there, Mum! They're not trying to shag us all,' Rosie's cheeks reddened as she shot back, her dark eyes sparking with defiance. 'No one has tried anything on with me.'

'They wait and watch and identify the vulnerable ones,' PC Martins said, nodding. 'They will lull you into a false sense of security and pretend to be your friends. Be very careful, Rosie.'

'Listen to the officer. I told you all this,' Bill said, nudging Hayley. 'Fucking paedophiles and they're all related. The off-licence, the kebab shop, the taxis, the mobile phone shop, the fucking lot of them on that arcade. You need look no further for that young girl, Jennifer Simmons, she's probably tied to a bed in the back of one of those shops!'

'Don't be ridiculous, Dad,' Rosie huffed. 'They're nice guys and they're businessmen. As if they have her held captive in the back of the kebab shop. Really?'

'My colleague is not saying anyone from those businesses is a criminal,' Ellis said, backpedalling. 'He's generalising how grooming works.'

From his chair in the corner of the room, Gary watched silently, his small frame almost disappearing into the shadows. He hugged his knees tighter to his chest, sensing the unease in the air. Rosie was getting upset and he felt the need to defend her but didn't know how.

'Rosie, love,' her father said in a calmer tone, attempting to bridge the gap of misunderstanding, 'it's not about us trusting you.

It's about them. We don't trust them. We've heard...stories about those shops and the men in them.'

'Stories are just stories!' Rosie tossed her dark hair, refusing to back down. 'They're just rumours!'

The two police officers, who had been quietly observing the family dynamic, exchanged a glance. Martins watched with sharp eyes. 'Your parents aren't the only ones worried, Rosie. We've had reports we can't ignore.'

'Reports?' Rosie's voice cracked, a hint of uncertainty creeping into her bold front. 'What reports?'

'Sexual assaults,' Martins said. 'I can't say any more than that.'

'They're allegations,' Ellis added.

'People are racist,' Rosie argued. 'They get abuse all the time.'

Gary shifted uncomfortably in his chair, the weight of unspoken knowledge heavy on his young shoulders.

'Look, we're not here to scare you, but you shouldn't be hanging around the shops at your age,' Ellis said with a sympathetic frown, trying to reassure her. 'But we need to be cautious what we say, for everyone's sake and we need to get back to the reason why we're here. Can we do that?'

'Okay, I've had enough of this anyway,' Rosie said, nodding. 'Ask me your questions.'

Bill and Hayley appeared to relax although Bill didn't look happy. They sat back and listened.

'Can you tell me exactly what you saw on the bus?' Ellis asked. Neither of the children answered but they looked at each other. 'Did you see the boy who died, John Dean being stabbed?' she pressed gently. 'Apparently, it was near the bottom of the stairs, near where you were sitting?'

'Everything just happened so fast,' Gary started, his hands shaking as he recalled the blur of fists and the flash of a blade. 'One minute we were going to school, the next...'

'Someone was lying on the ground, bleeding,' Rosie finished his sentence, her voice hollow. 'And then the bus stopped... and the driver was shouting for everyone to get off and then we were in the back of your car.'

'Did you see the fight start?' Martins asked, sitting down. Ellis sat next to him, the coffee table between the children and them. 'Think carefully.'

'It started upstairs, so we couldn't see what happened,' Rosie said. 'Then it spilled over and people fell down the stairs, still fighting and the boy was stabbed. A nurse tried to help him but he stopped breathing.' Rosie fidgeted with her sleeve, trying to ignore the way her heart rate increased. Across from her, PC Ellis leaned forward, a notepad in her hand. Beside her, Martins surveyed the children with sharp eyes that missed nothing. He seemed to be analysing everything they said. Rosie felt his eyes on her, looking at more than just her behaviour.

'Rosie,' Ellis began, her voice gentle yet laced with authority, 'we need you to tell us the details of everything you remember about what happened on the bus not a summary, details. Do you understand?'

'Yes.'

Gary, perched on the edge of his chair next to Rosie, reached out and gave her hand a quick squeeze. She drew in a deep breath, grateful for her brother's silent support.

'So...I...it was all so fast,' Rosie stammered, meeting Ellis's gaze. 'One minute, everyone was laughing, looking at their phones, then the bus stopped and some boys from St Eddie's got on and there was some abuse thrown around and they went upstairs.'

'What was the abuse?' Martins asked.

'Bummers,' Gary answered. Everyone looked at him. 'They always call them bummers when they get on the bus.'

'Thanks Gary,' Martins smiled.

'Carry on, Rosie.'

'A few minutes later, there was shouting from upstairs.' Her words came out in a tumble, images flashing through her mind like a disjointed film reel. 'The fight started. We could hear it happening. It was like seconds, then boom, it was over, and the lad was on the floor.'

'One step at a time, did you see who had the knife?' Martins interjected, his tone direct.

Rosie bit her lip, shaking her head slowly. 'No, but... but I heard people saying it might be someone from our school.'

'Who said that?' Ellis asked.

'I can't remember.'

'Rumours can be dangerous, Rosie,' Ellis said. 'We need facts. Did you recognise any voices?'

'Jordan Milner,' Rosie said. Gary nodded.

'He is the boy who was run over,' Martins said. Rosie nodded.

'Yes.'

'Did you actually hear him yourself?' Martins asked.

'No,' Rosie said. 'There were lots of voices, lots of shouting.' She shook her head. 'I couldn't actually say I heard him specifically.'

'We know he had a knife. Did any part of the altercation stand out?' Ellis asked.

Rosie hesitated. The weight of the officers' expectant looks pressing down on her. 'There was just the one voice downstairs,' she finally whispered. 'Loud, angry—I think I've heard it before, at school maybe, but I couldn't see his face.'

'Anything else, even if it seems small or unimportant?' Martins encouraged.

'Someone shouted 'Stop it!' right before the bus driver pulled over,' Gary chimed in, his brow furrowed with concern. 'But it was so mad, I don't know who it was.'

'Okay, that's good to know, Gary, thank you,' Ellis nodded, scribbling her notes. She turned her attention back to Rosie. 'Let's finish with you first. You're doing great, Rosie. We just want to catch whoever did this, keep it from happening again.'

'Will we be safe?' Rosie's voice held a tremor as she looked up at the officers, her eyes clouded with the fear that had taken root in her since the incident. 'Snitches get stitches around here.'

'Snitches end up in ditches,' Gary added, nodding knowingly. Bill rolled his eyes skywards. 'Snitches are bitches around here. Stitches, bitches, ditches.'

'Okay, Gary, we get the message,' Bill said. 'When did you become mafioso?'

'I'm just saying,' Gary muttered.

'What are you worried about?' Martins asked.

'Being a witness,' Rosie said. She shrugged. 'There were lots of witnesses,' Rosie said. 'Do you think he'll try and threaten people not to testify?'

'We won't allow that. Your safety is our top priority,' Martins assured her, offering a faint smile that didn't quite reach his eyes. 'We're going to increase patrols around the school and the estate and talk to other students, who were on the bus too. If we had a name, we could arrest him, and everyone would be safe.'

Rosie nodded, feeling a tiny flicker of relief as Gary squeezed her hand again. She didn't give them all the answers they wanted, but she hoped her vague piece of the puzzle would help bring the perpetrator to justice, without her having to make a statement. Snitches get stitches.

Gary looked at her, a concerned expression on his face. The boy hesitated, his loyalty to his sister warring with the fear that gripped him. After a moment, resolve hardened his features, and he nodded.

'Do you think the guy who did the stabbing could be dangerous to Rosie if she tells you his name?' Gary asked. The officers exchanged glances and nodded.

'He's going to be charged with murder, so witnesses are potential targets. Unless we can get him off the streets,' Martins said, sensing the boy was hiding something. Something that was bothering him. 'Everyone is in danger while there is a murderer on the loose but if we lock him up, he can't hurt anyone.'

'It was Liam Walsh who stabbed him,' Gary blurted out. 'That's his name. Liam Walsh.'

'Gary!' Rosie put her head in her hands and shook her head. 'You're such a knob, sometimes.'

'Let him speak,' PC Martins said, curtly. 'Go on, Gary.'

'His name is Liam Walsh. He was looking for his knife on the floor and people started filming him, so he pressed the emergency button and ran off.' Everyone in the room looked stunned. Bill White went pale and shook his head. Rosie stared at him, open-mouthed. 'What have I done wrong now?' No one answered. 'I'm just saying what happened.'

'What happened to snitches get stitches, Gary?' Bill muttered.

'Are you absolutely sure, Gary?' Martins asked, excitedly. 'It was Liam Walsh. You must be certain.'

'I'm positive.'

'How can you be so positive?'

'I've got his knife upstairs,' Gary added. 'I picked it up on the bus.'

Silence fell across the room as his words sunk in.

Chapter 9

19 months earlier- Capricorn
Candy sat in the corner booth of the fast-food restaurant, a bright red plastic chair sticking to the back of her legs through her fishnet stockings. The smell of kebabs, chips and fried chicken wafted around her, blending with laughter and the music from the kid's birthday party in another section of the restaurant; it erupted in shrieks and corny pop songs. Balloons bobbed cheerily against the ceiling, a stark contrast to the anxiety in her chest. She was clucking and needed some Ket and would do pretty much anything for the money to buy some.

Across from her, a man in a dark leather jacket leaned forward, his steel-blue eyes boring into her. Sitting beside him, the woman—a petite figure with long, dark hair—sipped a coke, her expression unreadable. She seemed to be studying her as if she was a lower species, beneath her. Candy felt their eyes crawl over her skin, but she met them with practised indifference. She met every kind of pervert and freak, time and time again.

'Are you feeling alright, sweetheart?' the woman asked, her voice dripping with a sugary concern that sounded foreign on the ear. 'You look like you're struggling.'

'I'm fine,' Candy replied, a half-smile on her lips. 'I need some sugar. Can you buy me another coke please.'

'No problem,' the man said. He went to the counter and ordered one. It seemed a while until he came back. She took the coke and slurped half of it down quickly. The sugar helped pick her up slightly. 'That's better.'

'Have you got a place to go?' She could feel the heat of their stares, a scrutiny that made her skin itch.

'Yes,' he said. 'It's not far away.' Couples often paid her for sex, a threesome fantasy explored. Preferable to an affair in most cases.

'It's a hundred per hour, okay?' Candy slurred. She was surprised by her own voice.

'That's fine. My car is outside.'

'Let's go,' Candy said, feeling odd. She stood up but the world around them began to blur, their faces distorted. Children in party hats danced clumsily, their movements exaggerated in Candy's vision like a film playing in slow motion. Her grip on reality had slipped. She felt drowsy, dizzy and nauseous. Happiness wrapped itself around the birthday girl, each giggle a sharp pain that reminded her of lost moments from her own childhood. Candy sat down and leaned back, her head spinning as she struggled to keep her eyes open.

Suddenly, she felt heavy, the booth turning into a cocoon. The vibrant colours of the restaurant melded into a dizzying whirl. Voices faded in and out like radio static, the laughter of children growing distant as shadows from the corner of her eye stretched toward her.

'Candy?' The man's voice broke through the haze, jagged and urgent. She blinked, trying to focus—and that's when everything started to slip away. 'Come on, darling. Let's get you home.'

The next thing she knew, she was being lifted to her feet. Hands gripped her arms with a firmness that contrasted the gentleness of the party around them. The woman's voice was low, almost soothing, but it sent ice through her veins.

'Let's get you some fresh air.'

They guided her outside, the chill of the evening air snapping at her like a whip. She heard the door swing shut behind them, the muffled clamour of the restaurant fading away. The world spun dangerously, and she felt her knees buckle.

'Did you drug me?' she asked.

'Yes,' the man said.

'Why are you doing this?' Candy slurred, her tongue thick in her mouth.

'Because I'm going to hurt you badly before you die and it's easier if you are drugged,' he answered.

Her heart nearly exploded with panic, but she couldn't resist. The man was at her side, a rush of adrenaline coursing through her as he half-dragged her toward a waiting vehicle. Through the blurred edges of her vision, she saw its dark, unmarked surface gleaming under the streetlight. Before she could protest, the woman shoved her inside. The leather seats swallowed her, warmth mixing with the cool prickling in her veins. The woman slid in next to her, an imposing presence that drowned out the distant sounds of the party.

'Stay with us, Candy. Just a little longer and we'll be home then we can have some fun,' she said, her tone betraying a hint of impatience. As Candy's consciousness began to flicker like a dying bulb, she felt cold metal wrap around her wrists. Handcuffs, what the fuck?

Panic ignited within her, but it was quickly snuffed out by darkness. The world faded to black as the woman secured the handcuffs. In her last conscious thought, she wondered if the laughter still echoed from the party, or if she had plunged too far into the silence to hear it.

Chapter 10

C anning Place

    The rain-lashed at the windows of the top floor office at Canning Place, the police headquarters on the River Mersey. They framed a grim view of the Albert Docks, the huge white Ferris wheel turning slowly, the Liver Buildings on the Pier Head and the river beyond. The water was choppy and the colour of dull steel, mirroring the sombre mood inside the operations room. The clouds parted briefly, and sunlight glinted off the River Mersey, casting a dance of light across the walls of the briefing room where Steff Cain stood, her gaze momentarily lingering on the restless waters before snapping back to the task at hand. She shuffled through the case files in her hands, each page a testament to the tragedy they were grappling with: the murder of a local teenager and multiple stabbings on a school bus.

'Anything new come in?' a detective called Riggs asked from across the table, his fingers drumming on the wooden surface, a rhythm born of impatience and caffeine.

'We're still combing through the victim's social media,' Cain replied, her eyes not leaving the papers. 'But nothing's jumping out yet. If the conflict started online, we'll find it.'

The room hummed with an undercurrent of tension, as if charged by the collective focus of the detectives gathered within. Maps pinned to cork boards showed a spiderweb of streets around the crime scene, red pins marking key locations, while photographs of the victims smiled sadly down at them, frozen in happier times.

'There were a lot of knives on that bus at the same time,' she said. 'That tells us the altercation was planned or at the very least, anticipated.'

'I agree. It was planned.'

'Let's tick off the basics. Forensics confirm the time of death?' Cain said, leaning back in her chair with a furrowed brow. 'Between 8 a.m. and 8.30, at the scene, prior to the paramedics arriving,' she confirmed, her voice steady despite the weight of the information. 'They're still processing evidence from the scene. We should have more to go on soon.'

The faint murmur of conversations faded as the door swung open, and all eyes turned toward the entrance. Chief Inspector Genesis stepped into the room, his reputation and presence immediately commanding silence. He carried himself with an air of authority that demanded attention, his years of experience etched in the deep lines of his face. His complexion was craggy and tanned.

'Morning,' he greeted them, his voice cutting through the quiet with the sharpness of a knife. 'Let's get started.'

Detectives straightened in their seats, papers shuffling as everyone prepared for the briefing. The Chief Inspector surveyed the room, his gaze pausing just a fraction longer on Cain, who met his eyes with a determined look. They had indulged in a brief encounter which had lasted for just a few weeks before both of them realised their marriages were in jeopardy. Cain had no regrets and she was ready to dive back into the depths of the investigation, to chase down leads and piece together the puzzle until justice was served. George Genesis behaved like it had never happened.

Outside, the river continued its flow, indifferent to the gravity within the room, as the detectives braced themselves for the road ahead. They were here to investigate the death of teenage school children, which was always a difficult task. Knife crime in the inner cities was on a disturbing rise and dealing with dead children and their families was draining.

Detective Chief Inspector George Genesis sat down and leaned forward, hands splayed on the desk, his gaze fixed on the team assembled before him. He was late forties, six feet tall and unfit with short dark hair and chiselled cheekbones but his face was lived in, and he looked ten years older. His nose was misshapen from boxing for Merseyside Police Force when he was young and fearless.

As he scanned his team, the Matrix Unit's finest stared back at him, their expressions a mix of determination and concern. They were joined by members of the PVPU (protecting vulnerable persons unit), selected murder detectives and drug squad officers drafted in for their experience.

'Okay everyone, thank you for being prompt,' Genesis began, voice cutting through the silence like a serrated blade. His voice had been deepened by smoking twenty a day for twenty years. 'We've got a situation that's sensitive, ugly and about to get uglier. On the face of it, a fight on a school bus which escalated quickly into a multiple stabbing, murder and fatal RTA.' He paused. 'Knives have come to the fore yet again. Two dead schoolboys—one stabbed, one hit by a van—and four others in Whiston hospital with stab wounds and we don't have a single weapon in evidence.' He shrugged. 'It does not get more fucked up than that.' He paused to allow the details to impact on the team. 'Two of the four victims are critical and may not survive their injuries.'

The room remained silent, the weight of the information settling on each officer's shoulders.

'You may be asking why are Matrix leading this investigation and why are so many Drug Squad detectives here?' he asked the room. 'This is not simply a teenage fight gone mad. All our victims had drugs on their person. We've recovered Ketamine and cocaine in twenty-pound wraps, but the real game changer is the death of,

Jordan Milner.' An image came on the screen. It showed Jordan posing for a school photograph; he looked like a schoolboy. The image changed to a Tik Tok post. Jordan was posing with a large zombie knife and a scarf around his face, and he looked anything but an innocent schoolboy. Coolio was singing 'gangsters' paradise,' in the background. 'Jordan Milner is the kid who was hit and killed by a van, and is Jack Milner's son.' He let the name hang in the air, knowing the reputation that came with it. 'Jack Milner is known to most of you, and he is not just any local gangster; he is a tier one criminal. He's one of the leaders of the Diddy Men, a man feared for his propensity for violence and his son is in the morgue. You can see where this could go.' A collective murmur rippled through the team.

'Our second fatality, John Dean, died on the scene from stab wounds despite being given CPR by a nurse who was on the bus. He is the son of Richard 'Dixie' Dean, known associate of Jack Milner.' He paused. 'From what witnesses are saying, Jordan Milner was dealing on the bus most days. This may have been the cause of the fight, we don't know yet but whatever the reasons, these two men have lost their sons, and we have a potential flash point waiting to go off.' He paused again. 'Our priority has to be the murder. We don't have the murder weapon, or any of the other knives used and as you can imagine, the witnesses—school kids—are scared out of their minds.'

'Sir,' said a seasoned detective, her brow furrowed, 'have we got anything off the CCTV or phone footage yet?'

'Analysis is ongoing, but both decks of the bus are covered by CCTV, so we should have a clearer picture soon,' Genesis replied, pressing a button on the remote in his hand. The screen behind him flickered to life, showing still images from the bus. The top deck appeared; every seat taken. 'This is the top deck before the fight started and it's only a matter of time before we piece together what happened from the footage, but time is what we don't have.'

Genesis pointed to the image. 'We need two teams working together to identify and interview everyone who was on that bus. That's our starting point. Jackie and Rob, can you get moving on this please with your teams.'

'Yes boss.'

'On it, boss.'

'Thank you.'

'Any leads on the weapons used?' another detective asked, jotting down notes.

'None. They could be anywhere by now, but we have to assume the owners have disposed of them, hopefully in a panic without thinking it through. So, I want bins, drains, and gardens along the route the bus would have taken searched. Get uniform involved and leave no stone unturned.'

'Understood, sir.'

'Here's how we're going to play this,' Genesis paused, surveying the room, making sure he had everyone's full attention. 'We canvas the area, talk to every shop owner and resident, and get more eyes on that bus route footage. We need to know if anyone saw anything unusual around the time of the incident as people were leaving the bus.'

'Sorry to interrupt, Boss,' interjected another officer, his finger tracing over the map spread out on the table, 'I have a PC Ellis on the telephone and she's at an address in Huyton, where a twelve-year-old boy has the murder weapon in his wardrobe.' The room fell silent.

'Are you fucking kidding me?' Genesis asked, shaking his head.

'The PC says she's seen it. Apparently, he was on the bus with his sister, and he picked up the weapon when the killer dropped it on the bus.'

'Has he touched the knife?' Genesis asked, open mouthed.

'Not the handle, apparently.'

'Get a forensic vehicle there ASAP,' Genesis said. 'Does he know who the knife belongs to?'

'An older kid from his school. Liam Walsh,' the detective said. 'The constables have sent all the information through. I have it here.'

'Do we have an address?'

'We will have in five minutes.'

'I want those children brought in here with their parents, immediately!'

'Run Liam Walsh and his parents through the system.' Genesis paused. 'We already have the Milners, and the Deans involved in this. Let's hope Walsh is nothing to do with them.'

'Do you think the fight is linked to the parents?'

'I think it's drug related for sure,' Genesis said, nodding. 'Keeping their families out of this is going to be impossible unless we're focused on their business.'

'Milner was run over,' a detective said. 'Technically an accident.'

'Do you think Jack Milner is going to see his son's death as, technically an accident?' No one replied but there were several shakes of the head. 'You're right, it was an accident, but that doesn't mean he won't retaliate, though. We need to keep an eye on his movements.'

'Retaliation could escalate things quickly,' the detective pointed out.

'Exactly. And that's why we need to solve this fast and keep it clean. No mistakes, people. The last thing we need is a gang war on our streets.'

'What about protection for the witnesses, sir?' queried a younger detective, looking up from his laptop. 'They're going to be children, aren't they?'

'Definitely, we need to get it arranged quickly. Family liaison officers are with the families we have identified already. Interviewing them will be tricky. But we need to remember, these are kids. They might not understand the importance of what they've seen, or they might be too afraid to speak up. We approach this with care.'

'Sir, given the sensitivity with everything surrounding the Milner family and ongoing investigations, should we consider bringing in extra resources?' a seasoned detective asked.

'Good point. I'll have a word upstairs about getting additional support. For now, stay sharp and focused on the task at hand.'

'Are we assuming the trigger was a targeted attack, then?' a voice chimed in from the back. 'Instigated by Jordan Milner on the top deck?'

'Too early to say,' Genesis admitted. 'Could be an unfortunate consequence of a brawl between rival teenagers, but we can't rule out a deliberate attack on an individual. Especially given the connection to Jack Milner. Witnesses say they heard accusations being made before the attack began. We have to focus on the drug angle.'

'School kids don't usually pack knives for a fight,' someone else remarked. 'The number of knives used tells me they knew there was going to be a fight.'

'Which is exactly why we need to dig deep on this one. Go over the mobile footage frame by frame, interview the injured lads once they're able to speak, and keep pressing for any scrap of info.' Genesis said, nodding. 'We need all their mobile phones information dumped, tablets, laptops the works. There will be text messages, Facebook conversations, WhatsApp, Tik Tok in the build-up to today.'

'Sir, if Jordan's death was an accident, could John Dean have been the real target?' offered the young detective, keen to prove his worth.

'Possibly. We can't discount any theories at this stage. Let's also get background checks on all the other victims. See if there's any prior beef between them. Might give us a clearer motive.'

'Are we prepared for media attention, sir?' another detective inquired, well aware of the frenzy that would ensue once the story broke. 'The families involved in this are going to create local interest.'

'The press office is drafting statements as we speak but we all know that leaks will occur when uniform are involved.' A ripple of laughter spread through the room. 'We blame them, and they blame us, so all I can say is keep tight-lipped about details till we release official info.'

'Understood, sir.'

'Alright, team, let's get to it,' Genesis concluded, the urgency in his voice reflected in the swift movements of his unit as they dispersed to their respective tasks.

'Remember,' he called out, as the detectives readied, 'speed is of the essence, but so is empathy. I don't want accusations being slung around without evidence. You all know that shit sticks. We owe it to those boys and their families to get this right.'

Acknowledging nods were his answer as the team filed out, leaving Genesis alone with the weight of command heavy on his shoulders. He turned back to the window, where the docks below seemed to churn with the same restless energy that now coursed through the investigation. The world outside continued to turn, shoppers and tourists going about their day, unaware of the grieving parents who said goodbye to their children when they left for school and never returned.

Chapter 11

6-months earlier-Tarot

The room exuded an air of mystique, its walls adorned with tapestries of long-forgotten stories and cheap prints from Asia and the Middle East. An ornate rug hung next to a dreamcatcher, both clearly reproduction and cheap ones at that. A swirling incense embraced a concoction of sandalwood and jasmine, attempting to seduce the senses into believing that the ethereal resided within these four walls. Amelia, the self-proclaimed seer, sat at a small table draped in velvet, her tarot cards fanned out like a peacock's tail. They were colourful and well illustrated, enticing the viewer to touch them.

Amelia had long red nails and huge false eyelashes that framed her almond green eyes. Her eyes looked wrong but coloured contact lenses were cheap enough. She looked as fake as her rug.

The door creaked open, and in walked a woman who seemed to embody elegance itself. She had striking features, with hair cascading like a waterfall and blue eyes that shimmered with unspent energy and an inquisitive glint. Yet, oddly enough, there was a veil of distraction that clouded her beauty, as if she were trapped on the other side of a glass wall, peering in but unable to fully engage. Nervous maybe.

'Welcome to my humble home, dear one,' Amelia said, gesturing for the woman to take a seat. 'What may I call you?'

'Alice,' the woman said, looking around the room. 'What a wonderful place to work in. It has such an atmosphere...'

'Thank you. I like my clients to feel relaxed.' Alice didn't respond but her eyes locked on Amelia. 'Do you feel relaxed?'

'Yes.'

'What do you seek today?'

'Sorry?'

'What are you hoping to find today?' Amelia asked. 'Do you want to know about your health, or wealth, love or conflicts?'

'I'm not sure I have an agenda in mind,' Alice replied, her voice barely above a whisper, yet it carried a hint of uncertainty. Uncertainty or scepticism. 'I was curious about your advert, perhaps...it enticed me to investigate your powers and see what it's all about?'

'Powers,' Amelia smiled, the practised tilt of her lips hiding the glimmer of apprehension that danced within her. This client was cold, not easy to read. Some come with an open mind, desperate for positive predictions, others looking for clues of what life holds for them in the future. This one was unusual. 'I prefer to call my skills, my gifts.'

'Ah, gifts?' Alice said, nodding. 'I like that.' Her smile vanished. 'Where did your gifts come from?'

'I beg your pardon?'

'Did they develop with training or were you born with them?' Alice asked. 'Your gifts, that is.'

'That is a question I cannot answer,' Amelia said, curtly. 'We are what we are, nothing more, nothing less.'

'Indeed,' Alice smiled but there was no warmth in it. 'And what will be will be and all that twatwaffle...' Amelia looked shocked. 'Let's get started, shall we, I'm excited to hear what you have to reveal, with your gifts...'

'Erm...absolutely,' Amelia said, disturbed. 'I usually begin by reading the tarot cards.'

'How exciting,' Alice rubbed her hands together. 'I want to know what you can see coming...'

'Let's shuffle, deal and reveal,' Amelia said.

'I love that,' Alice said, grinning. 'Shuffle, deal and reveal.'

Amelia dealt her tarot deck face down. As she began to flip the cards, she noticed Alice's brow furrow further with each turn.

'Have you had heartbreak in your life recently?'

'No,' Alice said, shaking her head.

'I see here a great conflict that will be healed,' Amelia said, blushing, her fingers hovering over the Three of Swords. 'Heartache resolved... a rekindling of lust and love—'

'Wait,' Alice interrupted, her tone sharp. 'That's not how the Three of Swords is interpreted. I—'

'Are you familiar with reading the cards?' Amelia stammered, irritation prickling at her.

'Yes, and the three of swords represents heartbreak, sorrow, resentment...'

'Every reader has their own interpretation...'

'No, I don't pretend to be an expert but yours appears flawed—' Alice said, smiling. 'Incorrect, in fact.'

'I beg to differ,' Amelia argued, her face flushed with embarrassment. 'Perhaps you should trust my interpretation of my deck and make up your mind at the end?' Amelia continued, forcing a laugh. The air felt taut, electric with an unspoken tension.

But Alice shook her head, resolute. 'I want you to reshuffle. This isn't right.'

'I'll start again for you.' A bead of sweat trickled down Amelia's temple. She feigned confidence as she collected the cards and began to shuffle, her fingers fumbling slightly under the relentless gaze of her client. 'Please keep an open mind and be aware that each reader interprets their own deck differently.'

'I have to disagree with you,' Alice said. 'The cards are designed to be read in a specific fashion, and their meanings are clear and well documented.' Amelia blushed again. 'If you make it up, it's like having a map and changing the town names.' She shook her head. 'Using the energy of the universe is a science, not make believe.'

'Maybe we should agree to disagree?' Amelia put the deck down and closed her eyes. She breathed in and out deeply.

'Is everything okay?' Alice asked, her voice softer now but underscored by anger. 'You seem unsettled?'

'I just need a moment,' Amelia finally said, standing up.

'Would you... like some water?' Alice asked. 'I could get you some while you reset?'

'I'll get it, thank you,' Amelia said. 'Would you like some?'

'Sure,' Alice replied, her gaze still locked onto Amelia's face.

Amelia retreated to the small kitchen, filling two glasses with water. She took a moment to compose herself. Her client was clearly versed in the cards and Amelia wanted her gone, quickly, but her reputation was on the line. As she returned to her parlour with the water, she felt a cold draft in the air.

'Excuse me a moment,' Amelia said. 'I think the front door may have opened. Did you close it behind you?'

'I'm not sure,' Alice smiled. She took the water and sipped it.

Amelia rolled her eyes internally, knowing she had a difficult audience to appease.

'I'll go and check it. Excuse me, one moment,' she said, slipping out of the room, careful to maintain a show of professionalism.

Moments stretched unbearably as she paced along the hallway. The door was ajar. She looked outside, checking the garden path both ways. It was raining and dark but there was no one there. She thought she could smell aftershave, maybe Aramis. Closing the door, she turned and took a deep breath to compose herself. She noticed wet footprints on the tiles. Maybe Alice hadn't wiped her feet. She was a dislikable character. Amelia returned, sitting down. She drank from her glass and smiled.

'Was the door open?' Alice asked. She drained her water. 'I can feel a chill in the air.'

'Yes,' Amelia said nodding. She finished her water and crossed her legs, picking up the deck of cards. 'Shall we try again?'

But something was off; her throat felt thick and clogged, her limbs suddenly heavy. Drowsiness wrapped around her like a cloak, and she fought to keep her gaze focused. The room spun, shadows deepening, and nausea churned in her stomach—an ominous tide rising to claim her. Just as the edges of her world blurred, the door swung open.

A man walked in, evil radiating from every step he took. He had an aura of darkness that confused her—the last fragments of her consciousness were slipping away, lost among the threads of confusion, deception, and an unsettling sense of fate—an indistinguishable cycle, masterfully woven by the unseeing hands of destiny.

Unseen.

The irony of her predicament hit her.

'You didn't see this coming, did you?' Alice asked, smiling. She stood and walked around the table. Alice and the man lifted her by her arms and turned her around, forcing her to bend over the table, squashing the deck of tarot cards, bending them and creasing the images. The water glasses toppled and rolled onto the floor, smashing. Her skirt was lifted, and her tights torn off. She tried to protest but her voice was lost.

'Wait, what are you doing?' she managed to croak, her senses wresting control, but the room spun further into twilight.

'Relax, this is going to hurt,' the man said. 'I have some gifts for you before you go...'

She turned her head and looked over her shoulder. The man was undressing, a cold smile on his face and the bluest eyes she had ever seen...

Chapter 12

Janine
The sirens wailed, slicing through the morning calm as Fire Engine Delta-4 screeched to a halt outside an aging brick building in Toxteth. Plumes of smoke curled from an upper window; the glass blown out over the street. It was a scene of chaos with its acrid tendrils climbing higher.

'Control, this is Delta-4, on scene, at Parkview,' barked the engine chief into his radio, opening the door and stepping out into the cool air. 'No sign of conflagration here. There's glass and debris everywhere. Something exploded.'

'Copy that, Delta-4. What are you thinking?'

'I'm not sure but we know there's no mains gas, so if there's no gas bottles here, we may have to think about HME.'

'Homemade explosives?'

'There's considerable damage,' the chief said, looking at the smoke drifting higher. 'It was a big bang.'

'Proceed with caution. Explosives Unit has been alerted.'

'Roger that. Will do.'

Janine White stood on the pavement, a coat clutched around her, eyes darting nervously. The firemen prepared themselves to enter the building. She looked nervous and guilty as sin. The bedroom windows behind her gaped, jagged black holes against the sky.

'Are you the occupant, lovely?' the fireman asked, studying her expression and body language. She was clearly shaken and frightened,

'Yes.'

'What's your name?'

'Janine White.'

'Hello Janine,' the chief said, identifying that she was a vulnerable person. 'There was an explosion?' He approached, noting the distress in her stance. 'Can you tell me what exploded?'

'Explosion? No, no explosion here,' Janine's voice cracked, unconvincing. 'The radiator has been faulty for a while.'

'Your windows are blown out,' he pointed out, firm yet gentle, understanding her fragile state. 'The radiator didn't do that, did it?' he said, shaking his head.

'I—I must've turned up the heat too high,' she stammered, a poor lie that hung awkwardly between them. 'The boiler is electric. I've never liked it.'

'There's no gas in there,' the chief said. 'Do you have any gas bottles in there, a portable fire or something?'

'No.'

'There was an explosion,' another lady said. She was wearing a pink tracksuit and Ugg slippers. Large rollers were pinned into her hair. 'I'm Betty from next door. There was a hell of a bang, and the windows blew out of the front bedroom, and I knocked on the door to see if Janine was okay.' She lowered her voice. 'She's not all there, you see. I keep my eye on her when I can.' She led the fireman away from Janine. 'It smells of burning meat in there and she's being really squirrelly. She wouldn't let me look around.'

'Burnt meat doesn't sound good, okay, thank you,' the chief said. 'Let's take a look inside.' He signalled to his team, concern etching his features. Two teams suited up ready to check the building. 'Homemade explosives could be in play, be careful.'

The first three firemen filed in, heavy boots on, each step taken with practised care. The living room was a mess but not caused by an explosion, just an untidy resident.

'The area is all electric, so there's no gas feed to the building,' Officer Davies said, his voice muffled by the mouthpiece of his respirator as he readied his equipment. His eyes, visible through the visor, were focused and sharp, betraying his years of experience in the face of danger. He was the member of the team with previous Explosive Unit experience. 'If there's no gas, what the fuck has blown the windows out?'

'Looks like HME to me,' replied Officer Jenkins, adjusting his helmet. 'Keep your guard up, though. Could be chemical.'

'Right.' Davies gave Jenkins a firm nod. They had been partners long enough to communicate volumes with just a look. Together, they approached the main entrance. The door was open, their colleagues already inside. They entered and caught up with the first team. The bedroom door, blasted off its hinges, lay amidst the debris on the floor at the end of the hallway.

'Clear!' called out Jenkins, after a quick survey of the front room, its walls painted pink, and the furniture red.

'Kitchen is clear,' Davies responded from the adjacent space. 'No signs of a meth lab or anything that could have caused this.'

'Let's check the bedroom,' Jenkins said, leading the way down the hall. Each step was a calculated risk, but it was part of the job—a job where hesitation could cost lives.

Reaching the wrecked doorway, Jenkins studied the room before entering, seeing nothing but the remnants of a life interrupted—a half-melted photograph here, a scorched book there. He moved back into the hallway. 'I'm going in.' Jenkins stepped inside and took in the scene. 'You better take a look at this.'

The urgency in his partner's voice spurred Davies forward. He stepped into the bedroom and stopped dead in his tracks. Amidst the destruction, the mutilated body was stark against the soot-covered walls—possibly a male, judging by the size and shape, clearly killed by the explosion. The force had been brutal, scattering evidence of the man's last moments like a macabre jigsaw puzzle. His forearms were missing, and his face was gone. The ceiling was splattered with flesh and brain matter. Three teeth were lodged in the plaster next to the ceiling rose. In the epicentre of the destruction was the body, contorted and lifeless; it was in a sitting position. No hands, no face; just an anonymous shell of what was once a person. The chest, a macabre jigsaw of wounds and burns, shrapnel glinted in the flash.

'Fucking hell,' Jenkins muttered, shaking his head slowly. 'What the hell happened here?'

'Looks like we've got more than meets the eye on our hands,' Davies said grimly, already reaching for his radio to inform the Incident Commander. 'It's not obvious what exploded but there's a sports bag on the floor in front of the body.' He peered into the bag from a distance. 'There are several small metal tins, polished, circular like shoe polish tins. They look innocent enough apart from being covered in intestines. Something is not right with them.'

'Have you seen anything like them before?'

'I have,' Davies said. 'There was an outfit in Albania, using polish tins to manufacture limpet mines. They put a strong magnet inside, so they can be fitted underneath vehicles. You twist the top to arm them but if you twist it too far...'

'Boom?'

'Boom indeed,' Davies said. 'They are cheap to make but extremely unstable. I think the victim may have tried to open one of them, maybe?'

'I agree. The victim's hands and forearms are missing and his jaw and face are gone. The splatter indicates the explosion was omnidirectional but ignited below the head. I'm guessing he was holding whatever exploded when it went off. The blast went up and out,' he added, gesturing to the ceiling where daylight peeked through a fresh wound in the building's fabric, and to the cast iron radiator, now a grotesque sculpture with a dent that spoke of phenomenal violence.

'What would do that, grenade, IED, HME?' Jenkins asked, though it sounded more like a statement than a question.

'Has to be. No accidental explosion does this,' Davies replied, his gaze not leaving the gruesome scene before them. His eyes focused on the holdall. 'My guess is that those tins aren't as innocent as they look.'

'Alright, let's secure the area. No one gets in until the bomb squad has had a look,' Jenkins ordered, his mind already racing with the implications of their grim discovery. 'There are several bags that I can see but I can't see the contents. This room is unsafe until we can rule out more explosives.'

'Copy that,' Davies acknowledged, moving to stand guard by the door. 'Keep your distance! We don't know if there are more devices,' the chief ordered, his voice cutting through the tense silence. 'Everyone out!' He spun on his heel, signalling evacuation with urgency. 'Control, we have a fatality. The scene is not secure. Suspect secondary devices.'

'Understood, Delta-4. Proceed with caution.'

Outside, Janine's gaze followed the firemen as they retreated, her posture sagging with a burden heavier than she could handle. The lies, the confusion, all woven into a tapestry of fear and secrets that the flashing lights could not dispel. The police had arrived and were erecting a cordon at the end of the street. Residents were being evacuated from their homes, most reluctantly. Arguments were occurring up and down the street as residents refused to leave their homes.

'Wallis, over here!' Sergeant Wrench's voice cut through the cacophony of sirens and shouted commands as he beckoned his partner to the edge of the taped-off zone where the fire brigade had set up their control point. Toxteth's mid-morning calm had been shattered by the explosion that now had them walking cautiously into a scene of organised chaos.

'There's no fire.' Wallis screwed up her face, confused. 'An explosion without fire is not good. Another day in paradise,' Wallis muttered under her breath, joining Wrench on the fringes of the devastation. Her eyes quickly assessed the damage: shattered windows, smoke escaping from what used to be a flat's facade, and the grim dance of emergency responders weaving through debris. 'Who lives in the flat?'

'Janine White, the owner, she's over there,' Wrench pointed towards an ambulance where paramedics were attending to a dishevelled woman. Janine's eyes darted around wildly, her hands fidgeting with a blanket wrapped around her shoulders. The police officers approached the ambulance. 'The firemen said she's a vulnerable adult. Take it easy.'

'Ms. White, I'm Sergeant Wallis, and this is Sergeant Wrench. Can you tell us what happened?' Wallis asked, her tone a practised blend of empathy and authority. 'Your neighbour reported an explosion.'

'I don't know what happened. I went to the kitchen to check the stove... I was cooking...and we needed more wine,' Janine stammered, glancing away, her voice a trembling thread of inconsistencies.

'You don't know what exploded?'

'No, no... maybe the heater in the bedroom. I was so scared. One minute I was pouring wine...It just went boom!' Janine was shaking. Tears ran down her cheeks. 'I didn't touch anything.'

'Okay, Janine, it's alright, no need to get upset,' Wallis soothed, though her eyes met Wrench's with a silent signal that they were both thinking the same thing: something didn't add up here. The woman was a vulnerable adult and a terrible liar.

Wrench crouched down beside Janine, trying to maintain eye contact. 'We're here to help, but we need the truth. Was anyone else with you in your flat?'

'Gilbert was with me! I'm usually alone...but we were having a drink. We were minding our own business.' She shook her head, almost convincing if not for the quiver of deceit that laced her words. 'He was in the bedroom when I went to get some wine but he didn't touch anything.'

'Like what, Janine?' Wrench asked. She looked confused. 'What didn't Gilbert touch?'

'We have one fatality,' the radio crackled. Janine watched and wiped the tears from her eyes. 'Is that Gilbert, Janine?' Wallis queried, nodding toward the flat. 'Is that Gilbert they're talking about or was there anyone else in there?'

'Male, unidentified, looks like he took the brunt of it,' one of the firefighters reported, his face smeared with soot. 'Never stood a chance.'

'Any ID?' Wrench asked, standing back up.

'Nothing yet. We'll know more once the boys from the Explosive Unit get a look at the place.'

'Keep the area clear!' another firefighter barked suddenly. 'We've got indications of more devices inside. This isn't over.'

'Christ,' Wallis exhaled, peering towards the blackened skeleton of the bedroom. 'Evacuate the surrounding flats. We can't risk anyone else getting hurt.'

'They're already on it,' Wrench confirmed, pulling out his radio. 'Control, this is Wrench. We need full evacuation of adjacent buildings on Larch Street as well as Parkview. Potential secondary devices on site.' He clipped the radio back to his belt, his seasoned gaze taking in the scene with a mix of frustration and resolve.

'Let's step back, give them room,' Wallis suggested, signalling to Janine that they would return to question her further once she had received medical attention. They retreated to a safer distance, watching as the controlled urgency of the fire brigade continued amidst the aftermath of unexpected violence.

'Back to square one,' Wrench remarked grimly. 'But we'll unravel it, Wallis. We always do.'

'Starting with Ms. White's little web of lies,' Wallis affirmed, already racing ahead to the interviews, evidence collection, and painstaking puzzle-solving that lay before them. 'We're going to need social services involved in questioning her. Let's get a call in to them.'

Chapter 13

18 -months earlier
  Nigel pulled the frayed edges of his blanket tighter around his shoulders as the wind whipped through the park, rustling the leaves above him. The grey skyline of Liverpool loomed in the distance. It reminded him of home, like a distant memory of stability, as he found himself drifting from one park to another, always dodging the glare of disapproving passersby and the scrutiny of the police. Each night echoed his estrangement from his father, a man whose love had morphed into an oppressive weight since Nigel had come out of the closet at the age of fifteen. He said if he was gay, he had to leave his house, as if the ultimatum could change his sexuality. His mother knew already, she always had but his father was a homophobe. Life on the streets was hard but preferable to being in care. There was no way he was going into a home.

The tent he called home was a tattered affair, displaying patches of various colours where previous owners had mended it before donating it to a charity shop. It was waterproof and would do the job for now. It was parked under a small cluster of trees opposite the shops on Tarbock road, where even the most curious eyes would struggle to penetrate. His heart ached with a combination of sadness, pride and resentment. He was living his truth, his way, yet the fight for acceptance as a gay male became a relentless struggle that woke him in cold sweats. Some days he wished he had remained in the closet until he was in a position to fend for himself financially.

Today had been brutal. The rain had come in buckets, soaking everything in sight and he had stayed inside to keep dry. A kind-hearted woman, who had brought him hot drinks before was walking towards his tent. She was a pretty lady, perhaps in her forties, and she had stayed and chatted to him a few times. It lifted his spirits to see her again.

'Are you hiding in there?' she asked, from beneath her umbrella.

'Hello Alice,' Nigel said. 'I'd invite you in out of the rain but there's not a lot of room.'

'I'm fine but you look like you could use some warm food and drink,' she said softly, placing a paper cup filled with steaming coffee in his hands. She gave him a paper bag with a bacon sandwich inside. He had flirted with vegetarianism for a while but being on the streets meant he couldn't be choosy. 'Brown sauce, right?'

Her smile filled him with a fleeting sense of hope—a reminder that kindness still existed in the world. He sipped gratefully, the warmth spreading through him, offering a momentary respite from the cold of the streets.

'You're very kind, thank you,' Nigel had said. He bit into the sandwich and slurped the coffee. 'That is so good.'

'Enjoy them, Nigel,' she said. 'I can't hang around today. I have somewhere to be.'

'I can't thank you enough,' Nigel said with a mouthful of food. The sandwich was gone in a few minutes, and he swilled it down with the coffee and the world felt like a better place.

But as the rain continued to pour outside, Nigel began to feel strangely light-headed, the coffee swirling in his mind like the summer clouds he used to watch as a child. The peacefulness he was seeking slipped away, replaced by a growing heaviness in his limbs. As a drowsiness began to cloak him like shadows, his vision blurred and pricked at the edges with darkness.

He heard footsteps approaching, the rustle of fabric mixing with the patter of rain. A silhouette emerged above him, a man seeming to loom against the dreary afternoon. Nigel struggled to focus, but his eyelids felt like lead.

'You shouldn't have to suffer alone, you know,' the man said, his voice smooth and soft. There was a gentleness to his words that both comforted and unnerved Nigel. 'Let me release you from all this shit.'

'What...?' Nigel's voice trembled, slipping into the void that tasted like fear and confusion.

'I have some gifts for you, but I'll have to hurt you first...'

He wanted desperately to ask who this man was, what gifts he meant, but there was only the sensation of being pulled deep inside the tent, the man's features fading into the enveloping darkness. He heard the tent zip being closed and felt his pants being pulled down, as the world around him melted away...

Chapter 14

The Whitehouse

Bill White stood at the window, peering through the slats of the blinds, waiting for the detectives to arrive. Gary had shocked him to the core with his admission that he had picked up a murder weapon and named its owner. That boy just didn't know when to shut his mouth.

A marked interceptor arrived, the blue and red lights flashed intermittently, casting eerie shadows across the street. Two uniformed officers exited the vehicle. Another siren could be heard approaching. The sound grew louder, closer, until finally, the vehicle arrived, and two detectives stepped out of an unmarked car and made their way up the garden path. The uniformed officers went outside to speak to them, away from the White family. It was an unusual situation. Hayley watched them talking until the detectives had been briefed and approached the front door.

'Bill,' Hayley whispered, her voice laced with worry, 'they're here. I'm worried. Social services are already on our backs.'

'Don't panic. No one has done anything wrong.' He turned to face her, attempting a reassuring smile that didn't quite reach his eyes. 'Let them in, love. It'll be alright.'

Hayley nodded, smoothing down her jumper before she opened the door. Gary sat rigid on the sofa, a blanket around his shoulders, his sister Rosie beside him clutching his hand. His eyes were wide, still haunted by the morning's chaos and his shocking confession.

'Mr. and Mrs. White?' asked Detective Steff Cain as she entered, flashing a badge. Beside her, Detective Parsons remained silent, her gaze sweeping the room, settling on Gary.

'That's us, welcome to the Whitehouse,' Bill confirmed, stepping forward to shake hands, his grip firm despite the tremor in his voice. 'Come in, come in. I'm sorry about all this but boys will be boys.' The detectives nodded but looked serious. 'Our Gary isn't a bad kid, not like some of the little twats around here!' The detectives didn't reply.

'May we ask your children a few questions?' Cain asked, gesturing towards the living room. She looked focused on anything but Bill White and his jokes.

'Of course,' Hayley said, motioning to the couch opposite Gary and Rosie. 'Can I get you anything? Tea?'

'Thank you, no,' Parsons declined politely, her eyes never leaving Gary. 'Gary, I'm Detective Parsons and this is Detective Cain. We're here about the incident this morning on the school bus.' She paused. 'Nothing to worry about but we need to clarify a few things, okay?'

'Okay.' Gary shivered, and Rosie tightened her grip on his hand. Bill sat beside his son, protective, while Hayley perched on the armrest, her maternal concern palpable. 'I made sure I didn't touch the handle of the knife,' he blurted. 'I watch CSI, so I know not to contaminate evidence.'

'That's a good thing. Let's start at the beginning,' Cain said, nodding.

'Okay.'

'Gary, can you tell us what happened before you picked up the knife?' Cain began, her tone gentle.

Gary swallowed hard. 'I was just going to school, like normal. Then these two guys started arguing upstairs on the top deck. I heard someone shout that one of them had a knife.' His voice broke on the last word, and he took a shaky breath before continuing. 'We could hear the fight starting, couldn't we, sis?' he said, turning to Rosie. She nodded. 'They fell down the stairs, fighting and then one of them was ...stabbed and the knife fell on the floor. It slid down the bus.' He shrugged. 'It was under my feet, so I just picked it up. I didn't really think what I was doing, and I didn't know it was a murder weapon because no one was dead. Not at that point anyway.' Gary looked from one detective to the other to see if they agreed with his logic. 'Do you know what I mean?'

'I understand. Carry on,' Cain said, listening intently. Soft creases wrinkled her forehead, and a smile touched her lips. 'What happened next.'

'One lad was on the floor, the other guy stepped along the bus and asked where his knife was. Everyone was screaming, and people were filming him. He must have realised it had all been recorded. The driver was shouting and people were crying. It was deafening. He ran off the bus when it stopped. I saw the knife on the floor, and I didn't think—I just picked it up.'

'Where is the knife now, Gary?' Parsons interjected, her eyes keen.

'In my dinosaur box in my wardrobe,' Gary replied, pointing to the ceiling. 'Upstairs, of course.'

'How did you carry it home?' Cain asked.

'In my rucksack,' Gary said.

'I'll get it,' Bill said, standing up swiftly.

'No, no, no. Please, don't,' Parsons said, stopping him with a raised hand. 'A forensic team is en route. Is that the bag?'

'Yes.'

She walked over to the backpack and carefully pulled out a forensic glove; she then placed the bag inside an evidence bag.

'Did anyone see you pick up the knife, Gary?' Cain asked, scribbling notes onto a small pad.

Gary shook his head. 'I don't know. I don't think so. I was scared.'

'Understandable,' Cain said, offering a sympathetic nod. 'And you did the right thing by telling the officers and your parents.'

'Is he in trouble?' Hayley's voice quivered as she asked the question that had been haunting her since Gary came home with a sheepish look on his face. The boy couldn't tell a lie to his mother without her spotting it a mile away.

'Your son is a witness and a minor, Mrs. White. We'll need to take a formal statement and eliminate his DNA, but he's not under arrest,' Parsons reassured her.

'Rosie, were you with Gary this morning?' Parsons turned her attention to the silent girl.

'Yes. We go to the same school. I was sitting next to him,' Rosie answered quietly, her gaze flickering between the detectives and her brother.

'Did you know he had picked up the knife?'

'Yes.'

'And you've identified the boy who asked where the knife was?' Cain asked, frowning. 'Liam Walsh?'

'Yes,' Rosie and Gary replied at the same time. They smiled at each other.

'Did you see him stab John Dean?' Cain asked. 'I mean actually see him do it?'

'No,' Rosie said. 'They were wrestling and punching and then John Dean stopped fighting and the knife clattered across the floor. That's when Gary picked it up and put it in his bag.'

'Gary?'

'No. Like Rosie said, I saw the knife on the floor but not in anyone's hand,' Gary agreed.

'Have either of you noticed anything unusual this morning, any strangers in the area or someone watching the house?' Cain asked the parents, her questions methodical.

'Nothing. It's been normal apart from a house full of police officers,' Bill said, exchanging a look with Hayley. 'This is a quiet neighbourhood.'

'Alright. We'll need Gary to come to the station to give us his prints and make a formal statement. We can arrange for a victim support counsellor to be present,' Cain explained.

'Can I go with him?' Rosie blurted out, her voice betraying her fear of being separated from her brother.

'Of course, and your mum can come too,' Cain assured her with a faint smile. 'We'll take good care of both of them.'

'Okay, thank you,' Hayley said, nodding.

'Will this be over soon?' Gary asked, his voice barely above a whisper.

'We're doing everything we can to catch the person responsible,' Cain promised. 'You've been a great help, Gary.'

'Thank you, detectives,' Bill said, leading them to the door. 'We appreciate everything you're doing.'

'The forensic team is here,' Cain said. 'Can we take them up to the bedroom with Gary, please?'

'Yes, of course.'

The front door opened, and PC Martins ushered in the CSI team. Gary went upstairs with the detectives. As the door closed behind them, the Whites remained together in the living room, the silence heavy with unsaid fears and unanswered questions. The tension was electric.

Rosie waited at the bottom of the stairs, waiting for Gary.

'Are you okay, Rosie?' PC Martins asked. Rosie shrugged and blushed. 'You don't need to worry about anything. Gary will be fine.'

'I told him not to pick it up, but it happened so fast,' she said, her voice hushed. 'I love the bones of him but he's such a knobhead sometimes.'

'Little brothers usually are,' Martins smiled. His teeth were nice and she could smell his aftershave. It was Creed. Some of the older kids at school had the cheap copies. 'My little brother is in jail.' Martins whispered. 'Imagine my parents' reaction, one son a police officer and the other in jail.'

'No way!' Rosie said, smiling. 'What did he do?'

'I'll tell you when you're twenty-one,' Martins joked. He winked at her and grinned.

'That's something my dad would say and he's a knob,' Rosie frowned. 'Don't be a knob. Tell me what he did.'

'I'll tell you if you promise not to hang around the shops at night anymore?' Martins said, lowering his voice. Rosie frowned. 'I know they give you money but that's part of the grooming process. They're not nice men.'

'They're nice to me and I need the money,' Rosie said, folding her arms. 'I don't believe the rumours.'

'How many young boys work for them?' Martins asked. Rosie shrugged. 'None. Listen to me. I do a lot of work with social services,' he said. 'I'm one of only a few officers trained to do welfare checks on CIN, like you and Gary. I'll keep my eyes on you two and make sure you're doing okay. But you need to stay away from those men. They're rapist paedophiles but don't tell your dad that I admitted that.'

'Really?'

'Really.'

'I'll be careful,' Rosie said. Martins raised his eyebrows and shook his head. 'Okay, okay. I'll stay away.'

'Is everything okay?' Hayley asked from the living room

'Everything is fine,' Rosie said. Martins winked again and Rosie smiled. Rosie went back into the living room.

'Everything's going to be okay, lovely,' Hayley said, though her voice lacked conviction. She hugged Rosie.

'Yeah, Mum. What do you think, Dad?' Rosie looked up at her father, searching for the certainty she needed, challenging him. Gary came back into the room. He looked worried.

'Sorry,' Gary said.

'Everything's going to be fine, son,' Bill said, wrapping an arm around Gary's shoulder. Gary felt awkward. Rosie pulled a funny face, and he laughed.

'We're going to get through this together, as a family but I don't want either of you hanging around at the shops, understand?' Bill said.

'Promise.' Rosie whispered, her eyes reflecting the vulnerability they all felt. I won't do anything for them again.'

'Promise?' Bill echoed, pulling both children into a hug. 'It's not safe. They're paedos.'

The Whites remained sitting together, drawing strength from one another, as another fading siren sound outside marked the passage of events in a world that, for them, had irrevocably changed.

Chapter 15

The Forest

The smell of wet soil and pine trees was heavy on the air of Delamere Forest as Andrea Dent entered the familiar trails that she walked daily. She varied which paths she took, the forest was crisscrossed with countless walks and full of memories of her late husband, Dave. They had been together since school, partners for life, lovers and best friends. Dave had died behind the wheel of his van, taken by a sudden but fatal heart attack two years prior. Life had been lonely since, brightened by her canine companions, Hugo and Henry and their walks in the forest.

It was strangely quiet today, even the birds were muted in comparison to their usual volume. There was an odd atmosphere, unfamiliar and unpleasant, and unwelcoming. A shiver ran down her spine. She felt uneasy, almost frightened; it was completely irrational, but the feeling was unshakeable. The twin leash in her hand twitched with life, connected to her golden retrievers, their tails swished with uncontainable excitement. They were behaving as if they sensed something amiss too. Their noses searched the air, twitching and sniffing invisible tendrils of scent. They were tugging at the leash, agitated and eager to be released. The shadows beneath the trees appeared to shift, sinister and threatening. This wasn't the usual relaxing experience it had always been. Her nerves were jangling, and a chill spread through her bones.

'Easy there, you two. We've got all morning,' Andrea said, her breath misting in the cool air. She usually loved these walks—just her, the dogs, and the symphony of nature. It was their ritual, a sacred time when the rest of the world fell away but today was different.

Henry's nose was exploring excitedly; it led from one scent to the next, his paws crunching over a carpet of fallen leaves, sniffing for hedgehogs, voles, moles and rats. But today, his attention snagged on something different, something that sent a sharp tug through the leash and into Andrea's palm. Her arthritis was painful and she released her grip, gasping at the pain.

'Henry, what is it?' Andrea asked, trying to peer ahead but the shadows between the trees were dark and shifting. Before she could tighten her grip, Henry bolted and Hugo followed, the leash slipping through Andrea's fingers, leaving a painful slice like a papercut. The dogs sprinted into the forest barking their excitement.

'Henry, get back here!' Andrea called after the sprinting silhouettes, her voice swallowed by thick foliage. 'Hugo, you little bugger!' Panic knotted in her stomach. She dashed into the trees, desperate to keep up, her own steps muffled by the verdant underbrush. 'Come here...you little...'

The dogs were gone, driven by something she couldn't comprehend. Their senses far sharper than a human, they were homing in on something.

'Henry, come back!' Her calls echoed amongst the ancient trunks, each one a silent witness to her distress. 'You little fuckers,' she muttered under her breath. 'One word from me and you do what the hell you want to!'

Branches clawed at Andrea's jacket, snagging fabric and pulling at her hair. She ducked beneath a particularly low-hanging limb, her heart pounding with every step.

'Bad dogs,' she muttered under her breath, though worry for them bled through her frustration. 'You little buggers...wait until you want a treat...'

Andrea stumbled into a clearing, panting, and scanned the area desperately. 'Hugo!' Her voice cracked, betraying her growing fear. Then, a distant rustling drew her gaze to the right—a patch of earth disturbed, a dark contrast against the surrounding green. They were well away from the beaten tracks. She didn't recognise the area.

She pushed forward, ignoring the sting of scratches on her cheeks. As she neared, the rustling grew more frantic, more urgent. It was her dogs, digging with wild abandon, their paws flurrying dirt into the air.

'What the fuck are you doing, Henry?' she shouted. 'Stop that!' Andrea approached, reaching out to yank the dog away from whatever had caught his interest. But Henry was relentless, driven by a scent or curiosity that Andrea couldn't fathom. Hugo was growling as he scratched at the ground. Both animals ignored her commands.

'Come on, you two, let's—' Andrea froze, her voice catching in her throat. There, among the flying clods of earth, a human hand emerged, pale and delicate, fingers splayed as if reaching for salvation.

'Jesus Christ!' Andrea's heartbeat increased dramatically, her mind reeling with shock. A human hand, here, in their forest. Was it attached to a body? Her eyes darted around the clearing, half-expecting some malevolent figure to emerge from behind the trees.

'Henry, leave it!' she shouted, but the dog was undeterred. With a final determined tug, Henry pulled the limb free, dragging it a few feet before dropping it at Andrea's feet. The arm had been severed by a sharp blade. She could see the cut was clean not ragged.

'Good God...' Andrea murmured, her hands trembling. She needed to call the police, to report this gruesome discovery. But her phone was back at home, charging on the kitchen counter.

'Stay, Henry. Stay Hugo. Stay with me,' Andrea instructed, her voice barely above a whisper. She needed to think, to act, but her thoughts swirled like leaves in a storm.

'Okay, okay,' she muttered to herself. She took a deep breath, willing her racing heart to calm. The first priority was to secure the dogs; she couldn't have them disturbing a potential crime scene any further. Andrea reached down, her hands still shaking, and grabbed the leash and made sure it was clipped onto Henry's collar.

'Good boy, you little fucker,' she murmured, though her praise felt hollow against the weight of the situation. She did the same with Hugo, who sat obediently, his head tilted, sensing the shift in his owner's demeanour.

'Let's mark the spot. We'll find a big stick or something,' Andrea said, more to herself than to the dogs. She spotted a large broken branch nearby and dragged it over to the hole they had dug. Placing it upright in the ground, she hoped it would be enough for the authorities to locate the site.

'Come on. We need to get help.' Andrea's command was firm, yet her legs felt rubbery as she turned back toward the path they'd come from. Each step seemed to echo in her ears, the forest now a place of secrets and shadows. As they retraced their route, Andrea's mind raced with questions. Who did the hand belong to? How did it end up here? And most importantly, where was the rest of the body?

'Almost there. Just a bit further,' Andrea coaxed, pushing through the last stretch of dense underbrush. She emerged onto the main trail, the openness feeling both welcome and vulnerable after the claustrophobic chase through the trees.

'Good boys, you did good,' Andrea said, though her voice was strained. She glanced down at the dogs, who looked back with innocent brown eyes, unaware of the gravity their discovery carried.

The walk back to her cottage was the longest Andrea had ever experienced. Each snap of a twig, each rustle of leaves, set her on edge. When they finally reached the safety of her home, Andrea didn't hesitate. She locked the door behind them, ensured the dogs had fresh water, and picked up the landline.

'Police, please,' she said when the operator answered. Her voice was steady now, the urgency of the situation propelling her into action. 'I've found something in Delamere Forest. Something terrible.'

The operator's calm voice guided her through the necessary details, and Andrea provided them with precision, her training as a lawyer surfacing even in this harrowing moment.

'Thank you, Mrs Dent. An officer will be with you shortly. Please, stay inside and keep your dogs with you,' the operator advised before ending the call.

Andrea sank into a chair, her gaze drifting to Henry. The golden retriever lay by her feet, the picture of serenity amidst the chaos.

'Who did you find? What have we stumbled upon?' Andrea whispered, more to herself than to the dogs. Her mind was already piecing together scenarios, but she pushed them aside. Answers would come in time, and for now, she had done her part.

Chapter 16

Janine
    The room was small and no place for a comfortable chat. Janine sat at the steel table, her hands trembling slightly as she clutched a flimsy paper cup filled with lukewarm tea. Across from her, Detective Harris's gaze was unyielding, despite the fact she was clearly a vulnerable adult – Janine couldn't maintain eye contact with him. She knew it was a silent challenge to spill the truth and the truth was dangerous. Harris was mid-forties, overweight, overbearing, and angry with the world. His unruly ginger hair framed a chubby ruddy face with a complexion caused by alcohol and smoking cigarettes. He didn't want to be there; it felt pointless. She was a vulnerable adult and virtually untouchable, no matter what she had been involved in. She was flanked by social service muppets, who had more power and influence than he had.

    'Janine, I'm not happy with your version of events,' Harris began, his voice even but tinged with frustration, 'let's go over it again.'

    'Is that really necessary?' Phil Moult asked. 'Janine is clearly in shock, and I want to get her out of here.'

    'I've got a job to do too,' Harris said without looking at him. 'I'll be as quick as I can.' He sat back and looked Janine in the eyes. 'Let's go over it again.'

    'Over what?' Janine moaned. 'I've told you what happened. Gilbert found some tins in a sports bag in the spare room and one of them exploded.'

    'Okay. Back to the beginning. How well did you know Gilbert?' Harris asked.

She swallowed hard, her eyes darting around the sterile interrogation room before settling on the detective.

'He... he was my best friend. He helped me with shopping and fixing things sometimes. We have been friends for longer than I can remember.' Her voice was a whisper, fragile as the body it emanated from. 'I can't believe he's dead.'

'Did he know about the contents of your spare bedroom?' Harris pressed on. 'About the stuff you 'looked after' for Billy Allen?'

'He knew that I keep some stuff for Billy, but not that stuff...' Janine cried and wiped tears from her cheeks. 'I didn't know what else they had in there.'

'Like a bag full of grenades in your wardrobe?' Harris sighed. 'Who would have thought that...'

'I don't think that's helpful,' the social worker said. 'Janine had no knowledge of what was in those bags.'

'So, she says,' Harris muttered beneath his breath. 'How could she not know?'

'I didn't know they were there!' she exclaimed, a hint of desperation creeping in. 'We were looking for weed and he found what he thought was a tobacco tin. But it wasn't a tobacco tin.' Janine pointed her finger at the detective. 'I didn't know it wasn't a tobacco tin.'

'No, it was a homemade grenade, and it blew up in your friend's face.'

'Detective Harris...' the appropriate adult intervened. 'I must insist we move on.'

'But I didn't know it was there,' Janine insisted. 'How would I know? He found the tin by accident.'

'I think we've established that, Janine,' the social worker said, calming her. 'Can we move on, please?'

'Of course,' Harris frowned. He sighed and sat forward. 'The firemen have seen large packets of white powder in the sports bag,

Janine. That's not personal use. That's distribution level,' Harris said, leaning forward, hands folded on the table. 'You knew that was there?'

'Yes.'

'And there is a locked metal cabinet against the wall,' Harris said. 'What's in it?'

'That's their cabinet, not mine.'

'Is it full of drugs?'

'I don't know. Probably.'

'We've established that Janine was groomed to allow her flat to be a storage facility,' Phil Moult, a senior social worker interrupted. 'She's a vulnerable adult and she's been cuckooed.'

The detective sat back and folded his arms, shaking his head. He was frustrated that Janine couldn't be held accountable for the drugs or the explosives.

'Bobby Allen and those men,' Janine started whispering, a shiver running through her frame, 'He said they'd hurt me if I didn't help them. I had no choice.'

'We know Bobby Allen but who are these other men, that you refer to?' Harris asked, his pen poised above his notebook, ready to jot down any lead she might provide.

'I don't know their names. They're just always around, watching.' She hugged herself, as if the memory of their presence could still touch her. 'One of them is called Jono and one is called Davy.'

'Jono and Davy,' the detective repeated, smiling coldly. 'Watching? What do you mean?' The detective's eyes narrowed, sensing more to her story.

'Everywhere I go, there's someone on a corner, outside the shop. It's like they're reminding me they're there,' Janine explained, her voice barely above a whisper, the weight of paranoia evident in her tone.

'Janine, we need something concrete. Descriptions, places they hang out, anything,' Harris urged, trying to coax out the smallest detail that might lead to a break in the case.

'They're all big guys, tattoos, mean faces,' she offered, though her description was vague, generic. 'They meet at the abandoned casino down Jamaica Street by the river sometimes. I've seen cars go there late at night. They say there is illegal fighting in there.'

'Who says?'

'What?'

'You said, 'they' say there is illegal fighting. Who are they?'

'I don't know,' Janine said. 'People say that, just people around where I live.'

'Okay. Good. That's a start.' Harris nodded, scribbling notes. Beside him, Carol, the social worker assigned to Janine's case, watched the exchange with a furrowed brow, her compassion battling the necessity of hard facts.

'Janine,' Carol interjected gently, 'you're safe here. We want to help you, but you need to trust us.'

'Safe?' Janine scoffed, a bitter laugh escaping her lips. 'Gilbert thought he was safe too, and now he's dead because of those things in my flat. They are called the Diddy Men from Knotty Ash, and no one messes with them.'

Carol reached out, placing a comforting hand over Janine's own. 'We're going to get you out of this environment, find you somewhere new to live, away from those who have been exploiting you.'

'Can you really do that, Phil?' she asked Carol's boss. Phil nodded. Janine's eyes were wide, a glimmer of hope surfacing amidst the fear. 'Thanks Phil.'

'We can, and we will,' Carol assured her firmly. 'But we need your cooperation to put these people away.'

'Okay,' Janine breathed out, nodding slowly. 'I'll try. I'll do my best.'

'Let's talk about the drugs,' Harris cut back in, focusing on the pressing issue at hand. 'How did they end up in your flat?'

'They told me it was just temporary, that I wouldn't be involved.' Janine's hands wrung the hem of her shirt, her nervous tic betraying her angst. 'We'll put some stuff in your spare bedroom. Just storage, they said.'

'Did they pay you for this 'storage'?' Harris inquired, his tone sceptical.

'Sometimes... a little. But mostly, they just promised they would give me some weed and wouldn't hurt me,' Janine admitted, shame colouring her cheeks.

'Janine, you understand that you're looking at serious charges here, but if you work with us, we can offer protection, maybe even some leniency considering the circumstances,' Harris explained, laying out the stakes plainly.

'I don't think Janine is going to be charged with anything,' Phil said, sternly. He shook his head, warning the detective. 'She's a vulnerable adult and making her anxious isn't helping things.'

'I'm just talking generally,' Harris said, blushing. 'I'm explaining that we can protect her.'

'You can offer me protection?' Janine echoed, doubt clouding her features. 'From men like that?'

'Yes. We can protect you.'

'Would I have to go to court?'

'No. You could give evidence remotely.'

'But I would have to say that Bobby Allen put drugs and grenades in my bedroom?'

'Yes.'

'So, he would know it was me, anyway, even if I'm not there.'

'Witness protection is an option,' Carol added, squeezing her hand reassuringly. 'We take this very seriously.'

'Alright,' Janine said finally, her voice steadier than before. 'What do you need from me?'

'Everything you know. Times, dates, how they contacted you, how often they came by,' Harris listed methodically.

'Mostly at night, once or twice a week. Always different guys, so I wouldn't be able to tell you anything, I think,' Janine recounted. 'They would say Billy sent them and ask to see the dog I'm looking after. They always called their stuff the dog.' The details pouring out as the dam of her silence broke.

'Did they threaten you directly, or was it implied?' Carol asked, her social worker instincts kicking in, assessing Janine's mental state.

'Both,' Janine replied, a shudder passing through her. 'Said things would get bad for me if I messed up. After a while, didn't have to say it anymore. I just knew.'

'Janine, you did the right thing coming out with the truth to us,' Carol reassured her, though the path ahead was fraught with uncertainty.

'I don't like telling lies,' Janine said. 'Will I be allowed to go home?'

'It's not safe for you there.'

'So, I can't go back?'

'No. It's better for you if we get you away from the Diddy Men.'

'I can't believe this happened.' She sighed and wiped a tear away. 'Is it really over?' Janine asked, the longing in her voice palpable.

'It's the beginning of the end for you and having them in your life,' Harris said confidently. 'And a new start for you.'

'Thank you,' Janine murmured, her gaze finally lifting to meet theirs, a flicker of resolve shining through the fear. 'Thank you, Phil.'

As the interview wound down, Harris and Carol exchanged a look of quiet understanding. They had their work cut out for them, but for Janine, perhaps there was a chance at a peaceful existence after all.

'Where will I go?' Janine asked.

'We don't know yet.'

'Can I call my brother Bill?'

'Yes. You can talk to him, but not today,' Phil said. 'I'll call at his house on the way back to the office and explain what's happened and you talk to him tomorrow.'

'I want to see him today,' Janine said, her face darkening. Phil shook his head.

'I need to see my brother.'

'Not today, Janine.'

'I want to see Bill, right now!'

'You can't,' Harris snapped. 'Why are you pussyfooting around her. She might be vulnerable, but her friend just blew his own face off because of what she's been doing for a bit of weed!'

Janine started screaming at the top of her voice and she banged her head against the table. Carol and Phil tried to stop her from hurting herself, but she was stronger than she looked. Within seconds, her face was a bloody mess.

Chapter 17

The Diddy Men

Dixie Dean stared out of the tinted glass window of his penthouse apartment overlooking the river, his eyes fixed on the sprawling city across the water. The towers of both cathedrals and the St. John's Beacon reached towards the grey clouds. The lights were already twinkling from the West Tower, Liverpool's tallest building, where his favourite restaurant Panoramic 34 towered over the city.

Liverpool was magnificent in its splendour when viewed from the Birkenhead shore. He had chosen the Wirral as his main residence because he wanted to look at the city in its entirety, especially at night. He had bought the apartment off- plan before they had started building it and it was perfect. His sanctuary. The waterfront was stunning, and he loved his city. At nighttime, the neon lights blurred, reflecting from the water into a mesmerising river of colours which he stared at for hours. Today, it was a dull cloudy afternoon, and his mind was far from the vibrant scene before him. His eldest son was dead. Murdered with a knife. Another victim of the epidemic eating into society like a cancer.

His son had been stabbed and bled to death on the school bus. *The fucking school bus!*

How do you get stabbed on the way to school? He thought back to his childhood and his biggest fear back then was not having done his homework. The thought of being stabbed didn't exist in those halcyon days. Being dumped by Jackie Hayes at the school disco was the most painful thing he could remember. He had cried for days. She had been the prettiest girl in the school, and everyone fancied her. They had dated for three months and then she dumped him for an older lad called Sergie, who had left school and drove a 3-litre Capri. What a twat he was.

Dixie had left school, and he didn't give her a second thought, although the pain of being dumped lingered. It made him insecure and jealous as he floundered from one relationship to another. He had bumped into Jackie a few years back in a pub in the city centre, The Vines, he remembered. She approached him and began talking and he hadn't recognised her until she mentioned school. She weighed about twenty stones and hadn't aged well. Dixie had asked her if she was married, and she was. She had married Sergie and had five children to him. That had made him feel better for some reason; at least she had dumped him for the man she was to marry. Things were different back then.

The world had changed, and he accepted that, but children should be safe on the school bus, surely that was the least a parent could expect. No one that age should be carrying a blade but how do you make sure of that; it's impossible to police. No one on the bus should have been armed, but there were multiple people carrying weapons. His son had told him that he sometimes carried a knife for protection at night when he went out with his mates and Dixie had gone apeshit. He told him, if you carry a blade, you had better be prepared to go to jail or go to a funeral, maybe your own. The lecture he had delivered was epic and John was stunned by his father's anger and concern.

Dixie had been up to his neck in violence since being a teenager and he didn't want his son to travel down the same roads he had. John had been contrite and apologetic and promised never to carry a weapon again but now he was dead. Stabbed with a knife.

How ironic.

Had he listened to what his father had said at all?

Dixie had not been allowed to see his body. The police wouldn't let him see him because his slut, bitch, cunt of an ex-wife had taken a restraining order out on him years before. Dixie had forfeited his parental rights because the courts deemed his 'significant domestic abuse' made him a danger to his children. All of them. He still saw them, but it was always covertly.

The police and social services knew he was a senior figure in an Organised Crime Gang and that made him unfit to be a parent and a danger to his family. Of course, his ex-wife revelled in it.

Slut.

He had caught her fucking her personal trainer at her gym; a guy called Jim, which was ironic. When she said she was doing the gym, she was actually doing Jim. He had suspected she was playing away and put a tracker on her Jeep and followed her to his home. He had waited outside Jim's house until she left and then knocked on his door.

Poor Jim had written a suicide note that afternoon and then jumped underneath the 19.10pm to Euston. Of course, his family and friends hadn't seen it coming, neither had Jim. The note was written while a knife was being held to his penis, and then he was taken from his home, dangled upside down and dropped from the footbridge begging for mercy but there was no mercy given. Parts of him were found three miles up the track, most of him was never recovered.

Dixie's wife never came home again, and she took the kids from him. She was shagging around yet he lost his family. That didn't sit right with him. It was her fault, but she could never admit that and take responsibility for what happened. Slut.

Standing next to him, his long-term associate and equally bad parent, Jack Milner poured himself a glass of whiskey, the amber liquid reflecting the dim light of the winter sun. To look at them, they could have been brothers. They both stood above six feet and were gym built, wide at the shoulders and narrow at the hip, although their forty plus years on the planet were etched into their craggy faces and grey hair had overrun the dark of their youth. They both brushed their hair back from their face and kept it cropped short at the sides and back. Thick gold chains hung around their bull-necks and sovereign rings adorned most of their fingers, displaying wealth, poor taste, their age, and acting as permanent knuckledusters. Many a rival had lost their teeth to those rings; others had the scars where they had been stitched back together in the Accident and Emergency department. They were both tanned all year round, their teeth were bought in Turkey and they were extensively covered in ink.

They had both lost children that day and there were pregnant silences between them, neither wanting to tip the other over the edge of grief into anger. Both were prone to anger issues. Supporting each other had come naturally most of their lives, now was no different. They were broken yet determined to maintain the facades built over a lifetime. Hard men, almost indestructible. Dixie's phone rang and he answered it.

'Hello Billy.'

'Alright Dixie. Just checking in.'

'Have you heard anything new?' Dixie's voice was low and gravelly, weighed down by grief and anger.

'More of the same, boss. Like I said earlier, Liam Walsh is who witnesses are saying fought with John,' Billy Allen said. 'A contact at Canning Place is saying the same name, so the police definitely have him in the frame.'

'Liam Walsh. That's the name the police have?' Dixie asked, nodding. Jack Milner nodded in agreement. His sources were saying the same name.

'Definitely, Liam Walsh,' Billy said. 'I've got Suzie running a search online, parents, grandparents, siblings, pets, the fucking works. We'll have everything within the hour. Apparently, Liam sells weed to his mates.'

'Could be what the fight was about?' Dixie said.

'Probably.'

'How old is he?' Dixie asked.

'Fourteen.'

'Fucking hell,' Dixie muttered.

'I should have all his info soon.'

'Good. Keep me posted, Billy,' Dixie said. 'Has anyone said exactly what happened, yet?'

'No. There are conflicting versions,' Billy said. 'Some are saying Walsh didn't have the knife, others that he did.'

'I need to know which it is, Billy,' Dixie said. He closed his eyes and shook his head. 'If my lad pulled that blade out, it changes everything, understand?'

'Absolutely.' Billy lowered his voice. 'About the other thing...'

'Do you mean a hundred kilos of sniff with the Dibble all over it at Janine White's flat, Billy?' Dixie growled.

'Yes.'

'What about it?'

'The fire service has evacuated Janine's gaff,' he said. 'The entire street is being emptied.'

'Thats because there are grenades in her bedroom, you fucking idiot!' Dixie snapped. 'No wonder they're evacuating the street...'

'I've said sorry, Dixie,' Billy said, his voice quivering. 'I didn't think for one minute that she would be fucking around with the gear.'

'It's a hundred kilos. We want that gear back, Billy,' Dixie said, calmly. 'Get ghost on it. It's going dark and the Dibble will be back in the morning with the bomb squad and once the all clear is given, the stuff will be seized and that will be the end of that.'

'I've already called him,' Billy said. 'He's on his way.'

'Good,' Dixie said. 'Is she going to name you to the Dibble, Billy?'

'I'll make sure she doesn't,' Billy said. 'I'll shut her up. I won't let you down again.'

'Don't fuck this up, Billy. This is on you.'

'I'm on it like a car bonnet, boss.'

'Keep me posted.' Dixie ended the call and looked at his friend. Jack shook his head, a bitter twist to his lips. 'They are evacuating Janine's street. Billy has contacted Ghost.'

'It's Billy's fault the White woman had grenades in her wardrobe, the fucking retard,' Jack scowled. 'They should have been locked away or better still, not there at all. He's a fucking idiot sometimes.'

'Most of the time,' Dixie agreed. 'If we lose that stash, he's going for a long swim.'

'I think we should sink him either way,' Jack said. 'Once the dust settles, we need to have a conversation about him.'

'Let's see if he can rescue the situation.'

'We can't do anything while the police are focused on us,' Jack said. 'I was followed here all the way from home. They weren't even trying to be covert.'

'They want us to know they're keeping an eye on things. I don't know why they haven't sat down with us yet. It's like they're keeping us in the dark on purpose, to piss us off.'

Dixie clenched his fists, his knuckles white. 'I think they're waiting until they have something concrete to share,' he said. 'They won't be in a rush to talk to us. John's mother will be telling the police that I'm estranged and don't give a fuck about my son.'

Jack's eyes narrowed as he took a sip of his drink. 'And what about this Gary White kid? Rumour has it he picked up the murder weapon on the bus.'

'He's a twelve-year-old kid, probably scared to death,' Dixie said. 'Until the police tell me exactly what happened, I'm not going to stress about it or speculate. It's driving me insane. I can't focus my anger on anyone, they're just kids for fuck's sake.'

A tense silence settled between them, the weight of their losses threatening to suffocate them. Dixie spoke, his voice barely above a whisper.

'Here's to John and Jordan. Rest in peace, boys.'

Jack nodded in agreement, a fire igniting in his eyes.

'We'll get to the bottom of this and if anyone has crossed the line, we'll sort it out.'

As they clinked their glasses together in a silent toast, the city across the river continued to pulse with life, unaware of the storm brewing in the hearts of two of its most powerful inhabitants. The hunt for answers had only just begun, and blood would be spilled if the wrong answers came along.

Sitting in the kitchen, listening to them was Amber Dean, Dixie's daughter. She was sixteen going on thirty-six and she was distraught that her kid brother was dead. She had loved John very much and she wanted to know what had happened. Her fingers were skimming over the screen on her phone, searching for news and chatting to her friends on social media. Rumours were rife about what had happened, but everyone was talking about a brother and sister who witnessed the incident. Rosie and Gary White.

Chapter 18

4 -months earlier.

JENNIFER SIMMONS WAS in her school uniform waiting for the man who had groomed her for over a year. She was fifteen and he was nearly twice her age, married with three children and a practicing religious man, which complicated things further.

The biting wind swept through the streets of Liverpool, sending flurries of fallen leaves spiralling into the air. Jennifer Simmons huddled at the bus stop, her heart pounding with excitement, the chill forcing her to push her hands deeper into her coat pockets. She pulled her scarf tightly around her neck as she waited, glancing anxiously at her phone's screen. It was her special phone given to her by Ahmed. He said it was to communicate with him alone, but she used all his credit talking to her friends too. When her credit ran out, he topped it up without questioning her usage. Ahmed was late but he was always late. The only time he came early was when they had sex.

He had promised her that they would meet early and go to the flat above the kebab shop before lunch, 'a secret moment away from the prying eyes of the world,' he said. That meant he wanted a shag.

Jennifer was only fifteen, but she felt so much older when she was with him. She loved being in his company. The way he looked at her, the way he made her laugh—he filled the voids in her ordinary teenage life. He was so much more interesting than boys her own age. She knew it was a crazy teenage crush, but she loved him.

She had skipped lessons, knowing the consequences, but that didn't matter; she was willing to risk everything for him. Her attendance at school had been checkered over the years and social services had been involved at one point. Her parents were fined on several occasions, which put pressure on them financially, but things had settled down until she met Ahmed. It was spinning out of control again, but she was nearly old enough to do as she pleased. Nearly but not quite.

Not that she understood the full extent of what being with him in a relationship would mean. He had told her that he would leave his wife and children when she was old enough to be in a relationship without him being locked up as a paedophile. She believed him and dreamed about them living together and having a family of their own. Deep inside, she knew it was an impossible dream but for now, it filled her thoughts with hope for the future.

The wind howled again, and she huddled further into her coat, stealing glances up and down the street, looking for his car. The mobile phone shop loomed just a few hundred yards away, its bright neon sign flickering warmly against the dull grey sky. The row of shops was owned by his uncle and cousins, who all ran businesses from there. It was Ahmed's world, but it felt like hers too. The place where her and her teenage friends hung out at night and drank cider and vodka for free, knowing their parents would flip if they knew; a dangerous blend of fascination and fear. Yes, the men there were sex pests but some of the girls liked the attention, most hated it. The older guys were fat and sweaty, disgusting perverts, always offering the girls money for a wank or a blow job. A couple of the girls were willing if the price was right, and they were pissed. Jennifer hated the other men, but Ahmed was different; he only had eyes for her.

'Hey there,' a voice interrupted her thoughts. A police officer stood before her, eyebrows furrowed, his breath visible in the frigid air. He was young and handsome with nice tattoos. 'What are you doing here at this time of the morning?'

'It's a bus stop,' Jennifer said, shrugging. 'Have a guess.'

'So, you're waiting for a bus?' he asked. 'To school...'

'I can see why you're a policeman,' Jennifer smiled. He stopped smiling. 'I overslept and I'm running late. The bus will be here soon, so feel free to go and catch some criminals.'

'You shouldn't be here at this time, especially not when you're supposed to be at school.' The police officer smiled and shook his head. His blue eyes were bright and full of energy. 'I have a social responsibility to ask you why you're not in school.' He pointed his finger at her. 'So, make sure you get on the next bus, please.'

'I will,' Jennifer said, nodding.

'What's your name?' the officer asked.

'Jennifer.'

'Jennifer what?' he asked taking out a notebook and pencil.

'Jennifer Simmons.'

'Where do you live, Jennifer Simmons?'

'On Huyton Lane.'

'What number?'

'Why do you need to know that?'

'So, I can ask your parents if you got to school on time,' he answered with a wink. Jennifer opened her mouth to protest. 'I'm joking. I won't tell your parents that you're not where you are supposed to be, if you give me your address.'

'Sixty-six,' Jennifer muttered.

'How old are you?'

'Fifteen,' Jennifer blushed. 'Why?'

'Do you have a mobile phone?' the officer smiled again. It was a different smile this time, like a cheeky grin.

'Erm, yes,' she said nodding. He was very good looking, and she was getting vibes from him which felt more like he was hitting on her than interrogating her.

'What is your number?' he asked with a wink. He smiled again. 'So, I can check if you got to school later...'

'I'm not giving you my number,' she said, laughing. She blushed red. He frowned.

'I have your parents' address,' he reminded her. She gave him her number and he put it into his phone and called her phone. 'Now you have mine. Text me when you get to school.'

'Okay,' she said. 'What's your name?'

'George,' he said, smiling. His teeth were straight and white. 'Text me later.'

'I will,' she said, smiling.

A car slowed as it approached the bus stop, and she saw Ahmed driving his Mercedes. He saw the police officer and picked up speed, accelerating into the traffic. George had spotted the vehicle.

'That was odd.'

'What was?'

'You're not waiting for Ahmed Shah, are you?'

'I've never heard of him?' Jennifer lied and looked at her shoes. 'I don't know what you are talking about?'

'Ahmed Shah, the guy who runs the mobile phone shop on the roundabout,' George gestured towards the shops. 'He was driving his Mercedes, and he looked like he was going to stop in the bus stop until he saw me?'

'I don't know him...' Jennifer shrugged and blushed.

'Please tell me you're not letting him fuck you?' George said, staring into her eyes.

'OMG!' Jennifer was shocked. 'How dare you say that...'

'Don't play all innocent as if butter doesn't melt in your mouth. He's married with kids and is a serial philanderer with a preference for teenage girls.'

'Sounds like a pervert to me.' Jennifer shrugged and felt her eyes fill with tears. 'Never heard of him.'

'I can tell you're lying and I can see you're upset,' the officer shook his head. 'You need to stay away from the men who run those businesses. They're no good.'

'Sounds a bit racist to me.'

'I'm not a racist, I'm warning you about a grooming gang, doesn't matter what colour they are. Paedophiles come in many different packages but they're still paedophiles,' George lowered his voice. 'Ahmed Shah is being investigated because a girl who worked in the kebab shop is pregnant.' He looked around. 'Debbie Barry, she's fourteen, know her?'

Jennifer nodded. She did know her, and she knew that she was pregnant, but she didn't know by whom. A call came through on George's comms and he turned and walked away. He mouthed 'text me later' and went out of sight behind the bus stop. Jennifer felt empty inside as if she had been punched in her guts and all her insides had been knocked out.

Ahmed was the father of Debbie Barry's baby.

The absolute lying, cheating bastard. He was cheating on his wife; the mother of his kids so why was she so surprised? Because he had told her he loved her, and she had been stupid enough to believe him. Bastard.

Jennifer felt sick. A sense of panic surged within her. She knew the entire relationship was built on lies and cheating and that the stakes were high but didn't expect this. Ahmed was everything that she had desired—exciting, forbidden—but the reality of the situation began to become clear as day. Bastard.

Minutes turned into what felt like hours as she continued to glance up and down the street, the rain beginning to fall more heavily on the ground. Surely, he would come back for her, where was Ahmed?

Another bus arrived, a few passengers exited and went about their day. Each passing bus felt like a mocking reminder of her choice to be here instead of where she should be, in her nice warm classroom. She checked her phone again, no messages. Her excitement faded, turning into dread. What if he wasn't coming? What if he had decided that their little rendezvous wasn't worth the trouble? She fought back tears of frustration, feeling silly for having let a man who was supposed to love her take the piss out her like this. As the rain fell heavier, the noise of the busy main road dulled to a relentless splashing sound, leaving her in a world wrapped in cold bitterness and heartache. Panic clawed at her chest with each minute that ticked by, and then... a gut-wrenching realisation hit her: she had placed her life in the hands of a man who didn't love her the way she thought he did. A liar, a cheat, a complete cunt.

With no sign of Ahmed, fear began to creep in. She stood up, ready to head toward the shop when the world around her seemed to change in an instant. A cold breeze picked up, and she shivered, suddenly very aware of how isolated she felt, alone in the falling rain.

She heard footsteps and then felt a sickening blow to her head. It sent her spinning, and then, everything went dark.

A few minutes later, Ahmed Shah drove passed the bus stop for the fourth time but there was no sign of Jennifer...

Chapter 19

The ghost

It had been dark for hours and the street was void of people. The evacuation had been thorough and widened to the surrounding streets. Two shadowy figures moved from doorway to doorway with practised ease, almost invisible in their dark clothing and balaclavas. The men were ex-special forces and sold their talents to the highest bidder. This mission was a simple recovery but it needed to be carried out immediately. The price was a premium and there were no negotiations. If it needs to be done now, you pay the asking price, full stop. Ghost and Adolf had been members of an SBS unit, who had been deployed all over the globe. Their work now was much less dangerous and far more lucrative.

Ghost's breath was shallow and rapid, dampening the inside of his mask as he surveyed the evacuated flat, which backed up to Janine's. The front door would be easy to access, and they had no nosey neighbours to worry about. He heard an engine approaching. A police car crept past; the officers focused on the front of the building. All the other buildings were in darkness. The faint scent of smoke and plaster dust tickled his nostrils.

'Adolf, have you got the plans on your phone?' he whispered, his voice barely audible even in the silence that hugged the abandoned streets.

'Right here,' Adolf responded, pulling an image up. The light from the screen illuminated the doorway.

'Okay, let's get in there,' Ghost said. They crossed the road, bent low and Adolf drilled the lock in seconds. The door opened and they climbed up the stairs in silence. The flat was clean and tidy and smelled of spaghetti bolognaise and garlic bread. 'The explosion was in the back bedroom. That one backs onto it. Check the plan.'

They looked at the plan and happy they were in the right place; Ghost drilled a hole through the wall. He slid a snake camera through the hole, so they could see into Janine's bedroom. He looked at the image on a tablet screen. The light flickered against the walls.

'Keep it down,' Ghost hissed, glancing nervously at the sports holdall they had been warned about. It sat innocuously on the bedroom floor, its contents a lethal mystery only the bombmaker could make sense of. The police had access to a military unit, explosive experts, but they wouldn't be there until tomorrow. Informers inside the police force had told them as much.

The charred body of the man who had inadvertently triggered a grenade was still in situ, sitting like a ghastly statue in the midst of the carnage.

'They haven't moved the body yet,' Adolph said. 'That's creepy.'

'He can't hurt you now,' Ghost said.

'I know that, smart arse. Let's get to work,' Adolf muttered, picking up a sledgehammer. Together, they positioned themselves against the wall. With a nod from Ghost, Adolf swung the heavy tool with practised precision, creating a spider web of cracks in the plaster.

Each blow sent a jolt of adrenaline through Ghost's veins. They couldn't afford mistakes—not with the stakes this high. The police were outside but it was pissing down with rain and they were inside their vehicles at the end of the street. No one could hear them. After several more impactful swings, a section of the wall gave in, revealing the dimly lit interior of Janine's bedroom space.

'We're in.'

'Smooth sailing now,' Adolf said, wiping sweat from his brow as they stepped through the jagged opening.

Ghost's eyes darted around the room, finally resting on the metal cabinet that stood like a sentinel against the far wall. He approached it with reverence, his fingers tracing the cool surface before finding the lock. He inserted the key, swinging the doors open.

'Jackpot,' he breathed out, marvelling at the neat rows of cocaine bundles, each a ticket to wealth that most could only dream of.

'Start loading up,' Ghost commanded. They worked quickly, transferring the one kilo packets into their duffel bags. The weight of the drugs settled comfortably on Ghost's shoulders—a valuable burden he was all too eager to bear.

'They want this stuff gone before the bomb squad get chance to inspect it,' Ghost said. 'We're not going to risk moving that homemade shit.'

'Amen to that,' Adolph said. 'It looks like they've been put together by a four-year-old.'

'Three and a half, I reckon.'

'Fire time?' Adolf asked once the last packet was stowed away.

'Fire time,' Ghost confirmed, his mind already racing with their route out of there. 'This one will end with a big fucking bang.'

They doused the flat with lighter fluid, the pungent smell overpowering the dust and decay, making sure each room would be engulfed. In the bedroom next to where the explosion had struck, Ghost struck a match, watching the flame dance at the end of the wood before tossing it onto a soaked mattress.

The fire took hold instantly, greedily consuming fabric and foam. Ghost and Adolf didn't stay to watch. They knew what came next—the heat reaching the holdall next door, igniting the homemade grenades. They needed to be well clear when it happened.

'Move!' Ghost barked. They sprinted back through the gap in the wall, through the empty flat next door and down the stairs. Ghost paused for a second at the front door to be sure the street was clear. The rain was bouncing off the pavement when they jogged across the road, heavy bags fastened to their backs. They were two streets away as the first muffled boom echoed behind them. The sound echoed from the buildings, a storm of fire and debris shot skyward, unleashed by their actions. The grenades exploded in a series of deafening blasts, destroying any evidence and Janine's home.

Outside, the night air was sharp against Ghost's flushed skin. The weight of the bag was beginning to tell. They stepped out of an alleyway onto a main road, which headed towards the river and the Baltic Triangle. The pavements were busier, tourists and revellers enjoying themselves, unaware of the source of the muffled explosions in the nearby streets. A group of drunk Scottish men fell out of a doorway, the sound of music followed them until the door closed.

'Which way are all the birds?' one of them asked Ghost. 'That was a fucking sausage festival in there. Nay women to be seen.'

'Follow the road down the hill to the river and turn right.'

'Come for a dram with us, pal.'

'Another time, mate,' Adolf said, squeezing between them.

'Is it cause we're Scottish, you'll nay have a drink with us?'

'No, mate,' Ghost said. 'It's because you're a cunt.'

'What did he say?' the Scottish man growled.

'He just called you a cunt...'

'He's right,' another man said. 'You are a cunt.'

The two mercs crossed the road away from a potential flashpoint and carried on their way. The Scottish men shouted abuse at each other and headed off in the direction of the river.

Sirens wailed in the distance, growing louder with every second. Police cars and a fire engine screamed past them followed by three ambulances heading in the direction of the explosions. The two men were invisible on the busy streets, backpackers exploring the city. They reached their van, stored the load in the back and climbed in. The engine started, almost silent as it merged into the light traffic and they vanished into the shadows, two phantoms swallowed by the chaos they had caused.

Chapter 20

The farm

THE FLUORESCENT LIGHTS flickered ominously, their buzz echoing in the cavernous space of the old slaughterhouse. Shadows danced on the walls and a thick, coppery scent hung in the air.

Blood.

It was an unmistakable odour. He scrubbed hard at the blood-stained metal table, his muscles straining under the effort. Beside him, Alice cleaned a meat cleaver with equal vigour, the blade glinting as she wiped it clean, crimson pooling beneath her feet. They put the body parts into a chest freezer. There were four of them in a row against the wall. Bodies were so much easier to handle and dissect when they were frozen.

As they worked, he was watching the news headlines on his computer screen which was set up on his desk at the far side of the room. The headlines flashed that human remains had been found in Delamere Forest and the police had begun a massive search of the area.

'That's not good.'

'Oh my God,' Alice inhaled sharply. Her face drained of colour. 'They'll find the bodies...'

'They will, no doubt about it. We need to go and see what is going on.' He gestured to the screen. 'That's not good at all.'

'It would be madness to go there.' She shook her head. 'They will be all over the place. We can't go there.'

'We need to know what they have found and where, before we decide what to do about it.' He shrugged and shook his head. 'The more information we can get, the better for us. We need to know what they know.'

'Okay, I'm not sure you're right but I'll do whatever you think we should do.'

'Good. How far are you willing to go, though?' he questioned, rinsing a hacksaw in the bloody basin. A stream of water swept away the remnants of their grim task, redirecting the gruesome waste toward a central drain hole. Washing the last remnants of blood from the table, he gripped the nozzle of the hose and aimed it down toward the drain. The chill of the water contrasted sharply against the heat of their conversation. Alice was starting to unravel. He could feel her prickling, turning against him. Left to fester, self-preservation would devour her. 'I want to see what they're doing, and they're not going to release information to the press, so we'll need to see for ourselves, which part of the forest they are searching. We might be worrying unnecessarily.'

A surge of adrenaline coursed through him at the thought of watching the search unfold, both thrilling and terrifying. The mundane cunts had uncovered his handywork and once they realised the scale of his accomplishments, it would be news all over the planet. He would become an international legend, talked about for hundreds of years, studied by experts for decades. He lowered the hose, letting the water flow idly as he gazed into the drain.

'You understand that this could spiral out of control very quickly?' he asked. 'It's unlikely to end well.'

'Of course, I understand the risk.' She stepped back, wiping her hands on her apron. 'I've always known the risks of being with you.'

He sighed, his mind racing. Each drop of blood that drained away felt like a moment stolen from the innocent victims they had transformed—a testament to the immensity of his achievements.

He thought about the faces of the victims, those fleeting moments of them smiling just before everything changed and they started screaming. Such a beautiful sound. He wasn't ready for it to end just yet.

'I'm going to the forest. Are you sure you're coming with me?'

'Of course,' she said. But her eyes said something different. Her hand was shaking as she spoke.

'Alright,' he said, resolve hardening in his chest. 'Let's do it. We'll go and see where they are looking. But we need to be smart. We have to cover our tracks.'

'Agreed.' The corner of her mouth hinted at a smile, a flicker of agreement that brought a sense of camaraderie in their shared commitment. But inside she wanted to turn and run away as fast as she could. The dangers had always been there, always hanging over her like a dark foreboding cloud. It had been so exciting at first, but regret and guilt began to grow and then the nightmares started. She couldn't remember the last time she had slept through the night without waking up in a cold sweat, frightened and hysterical. She wanted out but this wasn't something she could walk away from. How could she? 'Let's finish up and go...'

Together, they doused the tools one last time in the stream of cold water, systematically cleaning each tool until they gleamed. The pressure of consequence weighed on them, but in this moment, they found a sense of loyalty, a purpose in the grim business of murder. As they wiped the last droplets from the surface, their eyes met, unspoken promises passed between them. The chill of the air couldn't suppress the fire igniting within; their sex had always been electric. Tonight, they would do what they needed to do first but then he would want her. She could see it in his eyes. Those eyes.

She believed in the fine balance of the universe, good and evil, ying and yang and for every voice they had silenced, for every nightmare perpetuated, there would be the reckoning. Maybe this was it. With a final sweep of the hose, the last of the evidence washed away, draining into the abyss of drains below. Together, they stepped back, the gravity of their decision looming over them, each with their own thoughts but the path ahead was clear. They had to go back to the forest.

HE LEANED AGAINST THE damp bark of a gnarled oak, watching the rain cascade down in torrents. It had been weeks since the weather had turned against them, but the last few days had been a deluge, turning the forest into a quagmire, and washing away the topsoil. Alice was drenched and shivering, her brown hair clinging to her forehead like rats' tails. She looked up at him, concern etched deep across her features. He could smell fear emanating from her, like a radiator giving off heat. She didn't want to be there, and he knew it.

'We can't go any further,' she said. 'The news report said they found body parts near Blakemere Moss. That's less than a mile from here,' she said, her voice shaky, barely cutting through the sound of the relentless downpour. 'What if they start searching other areas, this area?'

'They will use the dogs,' he said. 'The dogs don't miss a trick. They will lead them here.'

His heart raced at the prospect, but he masked it with a calm demeanour. He turned to face her, the shadows of the forest changing her complexion, covering her in gloom. She was becoming less attractive by the minute. He held her and felt her body stiffen in revulsion. The smell of her perfume made his head spin. He whispered in her ear.

'Don't panic, darling.'

'I'm frightened.'

'It's okay to be frightened. We both know how they work. It's just a matter of time now before they search here, and the rest of the forest,' he replied evenly. 'With this rain, the ground will give up its secrets easily. Our secrets.' He forced a nervous smile. 'They will uncover them all and there's nothing we can do about it. It's our time to shine.'

'I don't want to shine.'

'What we want is irrelevant. An investigation is in motion and there's no stopping it until it's done. You know how it works.'

'If you're trying to frighten me, you're going about it the right way.' Alice wrung her hands, anxiety emanating off her. 'We need to get rid of the remains. Right now, while we still can.'

'Get rid of what remains?' he murmured, his mind a whirlpool of calculated risks and options, none of them good. He had always intended for this partnership to be a means to an end, but recently Alice had become more of a liability than an ally. He liked fucking her but even that was losing its shine. The police involvement, the risks piling up—it all made her a ticking time bomb. She was cracking at the seams, weak at heart, and if they questioned her, she would spill her guts to save her own skin. 'You're not making sense.'

'I mean what is left in the freezers and the bits in the forest that they haven't found yet.'

'Are you mad?'

'No.'

'You're suggesting we start digging up the forest while the police are here searching?'

'We have to do something.'

'What we need to do is keep calm' he said. 'If we panic, we will make mistakes.'

The rain grew heavier, a drumming sound that seemed to orchestrate the chaos swirling inside him. The rain. The fucking relentless rain had washed away his hiding places and exposed his secrets.

'We need to do whatever we can, urgently. Think of something.'

'You're right,' he said, his voice deceptively smooth. 'We should act urgently. Let's get out of here.'

Alice looked at him, uncertainty casting shadows across her face. Her features seemed to distort in the darkness, making her ugly. 'What do you mean?'

'Let's go back to your car,' he said.

'I'm not going to argue with that, this rain is driving me insane, and I'm starting to realise how much shit we're in,' Alice moaned. 'I wish...'

'What, Alice?' he stopped and grabbed her arms, squeezing hard. She tried to break away, but he was too strong. 'What do you wish?'

'You're hurting me!'

'Stop whining and get a grip.'

He let go of her and walked away. The rain fell in sheets, drenching the muddy path leading through Delamere Forest. She was on edge and longed for the safety and warmth of her bed. Moonlight broke through the shifting clouds sporadically, casting ghostly shadows that danced on the skeletal branches. With each step closer to her vehicle, her heart raced, pumping her blood through her veins at an unhealthy rate. The pulsing storm above seemed to intensify; she felt as if Mother Nature knew what she had done and was punishing her. The weight of what she had done hung heavily on her shoulders. The lives they had taken so easily, lurking in the back of her mind. She imagined her parents and nanna and how dumbfounded they would be if she was caught, and it appeared online and all over the television. Imagine the devastation that the news would bring and the impact of a trial on her wider family. They would be so ashamed, so shocked, so disgusted. It made her feel sick with worry.

Beside her, he kept pace, his presence once a source of comfort was now frightening. She felt darkness oozing from him, threatening to engulf her. His evilness was attractive at first but now it was just terrifying.

'I want to get into my car, drive and never stop.'

'Calm down. Just breathe, Alice. We're almost there,' he urged, attempting to project calmness that neither he nor she felt. But even his steady voice sounded different and distant, drowned by the patter of rain and the chaos in her mind. 'Stop panicking.'

'Easier said than done.'

'Calm down.'

'Stop telling me to calm down!'

A low droning echoed in the distance—a siren, perhaps, slicing through the night like a knife. Panic surged through her, and she quickened her steps. 'That sounds like it's coming closer. What if they find us?' she whispered, her voice trembling. 'What if they already know it was us?'

He glanced around, his eyes narrowing as if scrutinising the trees that loomed over them.

'They don't know anything yet. They have only just begun digging. If anyone sees us and asks us questions, we're just walking in the woods, remember?' Alice nodded. 'We like to come here for sex, simple and they can't question it.'

'I can't believe they have found the bodies, it's just such a shock,' she panted. 'Blakemere is just a stone's throw away!' Her voice grew louder, frustration tangling with fear. She stumbled on a root that jutted from the ground, adrenaline surging through her veins and she fell to her knees. She let out a high-pitched shriek.

'Shut up for fuck's sake!'

'I'm sorry,' she gasped.

'Alice, look at me,' he hissed, gripping her arm tighter than necessary. 'Focus! You're losing it. We need to get to the car and get the hell out of here—now but you need to calm down!'

His urgency was palpable, yet it barely penetrated the haze creeping through her thoughts. Her mind was a maelstrom of pain and regret. She wished she could turn back the clock and erase the things she had done. Erase him from her body and soul. He had no soul.

The trees swayed ominously, thick with the scent of damp pine and soil, as the shadows seemed to close in around them. She could swear that she could smell the dead bodies on her. Memories of the nights they had killed danced just out of reach, fragmented images of their victims' faces; their agony entrenched in her mind, tangled with guilt. It was crushing her. She could almost hear their voices again, pleading, begging for mercy. They were deafening.

'I can't do this,' she gasped, fighting against the waves of dizziness that threatened to pull her under. 'What if—'

'Stop panicking.'

'Fuck off,' she whispered beneath her breath. 'I'm frightened. I don't want to spend the rest of my life in jail.'

'We won't go to jail, Alice!'

'Why won't we?'

'We did it right!'

His grip on her tightened as they rounded a bend and the faint silhouette of her car appeared in the distance, a beacon of salvation. 'Just keep moving.'

Every step felt heavier, as if the ground itself conspired against her. The rain drummed down, mingling with the sounds of her panicked footsteps—screams, scratches, begging, desperate breaths, echoed around her mind.

'What if we left any evidence?' she asked, her voice a breathless whisper. 'We must have made mistakes along the way.'

He cursed under his breath, his expression a mix of frustration and fear. 'They won't find anything. We were smart about this, remember?'

'Smart?' she echoed, her laughter a brittle, frantic sound. 'We're in the woods at night, running from the police because of all the people we buried here. How fucking smart are we?'

'You need to stop talking like this. You're doing my fucking head in.' He pulled her closer, the warmth of his body grounding her for just a moment, but the chill of reality sank deeper. 'Calm down or I will calm you down,' he whispered in her ear. He slapped her hard and throttled her with one hand. 'Shut the fuck up!'

She froze to the spot, the threat heeded in an instant. Gasping for breath, she thought he was going to kill her right there. A flash of lightning illuminated the forest for the briefest second, casting stark shadows that warped the trees into grotesque figures, and Alice screamed, her voice raw and echoing through the desolation. Each flash seemed to unveil her dread, coaxing it from the depths of her mind into clarity—every sound, every shadow, potential witnesses lurking behind each trunk.

'Alice, shut your mouth!' his voice grew deeper, piercing her dizzying brain. He dragged her by the hair. 'We're almost there, shut your face until we're in the car! Just a few more steps!'

But as they drew closer to the car, Alice's breathing became erratic. She felt as if the forest itself were tightening its grip around her, as if the trees whispered the truth of her actions. They might not find her tonight, but 'what if' hung in the air like the thick fog rolling in off the Blakemere Moss.

In her mind, she could almost see the flashes of police lights splintering through the rain-soaked trees, illuminating her crimes. Her mum, crying, her dad sobbing for his little angel, her nanna so shocked that she couldn't even speak and then there was her husband and children. What would it do to them?'

The jagged edges of her sanity began to fray, unravelling like the threads of a once tightly woven tapestry. It was all slipping away, the love she had felt for him at first, their laughter, the blinding sex, then the excitement, the fear—she was losing her grip on reality, too close to the brink of madness to come back. And in that moment, Alice couldn't help but wonder if the forest was conspiring with the rain to drive her insane, whispering secrets too dangerous to be told. He opened the door and pushed her into the driver's seat. He smiled, though there was no mirth in it.

'You've been very... enjoyable, Alice. But I can't have any loose ends, and you've lost it...'

Before she could comprehend what he meant, he reached for the boxcutter knife he had in his pocket. The blade gleamed malevolently for a second, reflecting the moonlight filtering through the dark clouds above. Alice saw the blade, panic in her eyes.

'Please...'

In a swift motion, he drew the knife across her throat. The sound of slicing flesh mingled with the ongoing symphony of rain. Blood gushed from the wound, arterial spray splattered against the windscreen, dark and vivid against her pale skin, pooling in the footwell. Air gurgled from her windpipe, escaping her lungs as they flooded with blood.

Time seemed to stretch as Alice's eyes widened in both shock and betrayal. Her hands instinctively gripped her neck, trying to stem the flow of life that fled from her, but the blood sprayed through her fingers. She saw Pete, her husband, dressed in his wedding suit, so handsome and happy. Then Carlie and Hugh, her children, twins, sobbing for their dead mother, the murderer. Her heart broke for them...

He stepped back, watching, a chilling calm washing over him. He took a deep breath, feeling the weight lift from his shoulders as the light faded from her eyes. He reached into her handbag and took out her lighter and her perfume, slipping the bottle into his pocket. The backseat was full of discarded paperwork, newspapers and fast-food cartons. He wiped the handle of the knife and put it into her hand, bending her fingers around the handle. He stuffed flammable rubbish around her seat and set fire to it, closing the door behind him. He watched the flames dance and grow and engulf her. She began to twitch, then she was shaking violently. Still alive, he thought, a smile touched his lips. Her long hair caught fire and burned with the most beautiful pink, yellow and blue flames. It was a pleasure to watch. He lingered too long, until she had stopped twitching, but it was a memory he would treasure forever and a day.

With that, he turned away, the forest swallowing him whole as he vanished into the rain-soaked shadows, leaving behind a legacy buried beneath the dark soil of Delamere Forest, waiting to be revealed.

Chapter 21

The Forest the next day

DETECTIVE OLIVIA MANN was at the east side of Delamere Forest, her gaze fixed on the flurry of activity before her. The forest road was a hive of methodical chaos, lined with marked police cars, minibuses, CSI vans and a mortuary vehicle. The search had been started the day before and she had a feeling they were going to need more than one mortuary for this case. She watched as several dog walkers were turned around from the cordon and sent in the opposite direction; a few of the drivers were abusive, not unusual nowadays, she thought. Uniformed officers manned the cordoned area while cadaver dogs were released from their cages, eager and alert, straining against their leashes, sniffing the air and the soil around them.

A swathe of topsoil covered the asphalt to her right, a hundred metres or so wide. She couldn't see the road beneath it. There had been torrential rain for three days, a month's worth of rainfall had fallen in a few hours. It was obvious that the runoff had taken soil from the forest floor, like a black river and deposited it across the road. The force of the water had probably uncovered the grisly find made by the dog walker and her animals.

The severed hand which had been found was at the epicentre of the search and it would spread out from there. It was several hundred yards into the trees to the east. Over forty detectives had been allocated to the investigation so far, but no SIO had been appointed yet. Chief Inspector Knowles was heading up the search with Olivia Mann as the superintendent in charge. Searching a forest was not the norm for an officer of her ranking but this was one search that she wanted to see for herself. It was set to hit the headlines, and she needed to see for herself. Her enthusiasm for cutting edge detective work had not waned.

Olivia had been drafted in from another murder investigation on the island of Anglesey, where she had been seconded for a year. The case was concluding, and the detectives were being reassigned to their respective forces. Her return to Merseyside had been welcomed by most but, not all her peers. Some sinical colleagues put her meteoric rise through the ranks down to more than her investigative abilities and conviction rates.

'She blew a few pink trumpets to get where she is...'
'Polished a few police helmets along the way...'
'Bent over a few desks for that promotion...'

She had heard them all and worse and the biggest culprits were other female officers. Olivia was blonde, with hypnotising features and a brain as sharp as a razor. Men were intimidated by her beauty and wary of her cutting wit and woman envied her attractiveness and natural likeability. She looked like a film star but talked like a barrister and was an expert on firearms and munitions. Her ability to retain information was uncanny. She had no tolerance for fools and no patience for drama, hence she had been single for years. There were no knights in shining armour around anymore, just twats in Under Armour and she would rather be alone than be with a twat. It was simpler that way and she liked uncomplicated.

She walked along the path to a clearing. DCI Knowles was briefing a gaggle of detectives and waved at her, gesturing her to join them. She was about to respond when a CSI approached from a shaded path, removed her mask and smiled.

'Hello Annie,' Olivia said, returning her smile. 'Nice to see you again.'

'And you,' Annie said. 'I heard they were dragging you back for this one.'

'DCI Knowles is acting SIO but I'm overseeing it for now, in case it's connected to the Jennifer Simmons case.'

'Is that one yours?'

'Unfortunately, yes.'

'I see. There's no link to this search yet?'

'Not yet.'

'How was Anglesey?'

'So beautiful but I was ready to be back in the big city, if I'm honest,' Olivia smiled. She shrugged. 'Anglesey is stunning, but I was isolated, and I couldn't face another winter there. It's the windiest place on the planet.'

'I went there in a caravan a few years ago and I remember thinking it was going to take off.'

'I lost three recycling trolleys in November,' Olivia joked. 'Never did find them.'

'Well, it's good to have you back. We must have a catch up,' Annie said. Olivia nodded and smiled. 'Getting down to business, we've finished processing the area around the hand. There's nothing nearby, it was buried in isolation.'

DCI Knowles had finished his briefing and approached. He was a tall man, slim build, wearing a dark suit and Dr Martins shoes. His black hair and glasses gave him a look of Buddy Holly.

'Good to have you back, Olivia,' he said, shaking her hand. 'We have some good people working on this. I'll go through the teams with you back at the station.'

'Good to see you,' Olivia said. 'Have you been told if you're the SIO yet?'

'Not yet. There's a lot going on in town at the moment.'

'I sensed a bit of panic when I spoke to the ACC. What's got them rattled?'

'In a nutshell, a teenager was stabbed on a school bus and his father is a known OCG leader. I think the top brass are shitting their pants in case it blows up in their faces,' Knowles grinned and shook his head. 'I'm sure you remember the politics?'

'I do. Can't say I missed it,' Olivia said. She turned her attention back to the CSI. 'Annie has finished processing the area around the arm.'

'It's been buried in isolation, I'm afraid,' Annie explained. 'The dogs have been over the area twice. It's clean.'

'Could the hand belong to Jennifer Simmons?' Knowles asked.

'No. The victim is wearing a ring on the third finger, so it looks like she was married and, in her forties, or fifties at my best guess, and she's been in the ground too long to be Jennifer,' the CSI explained. 'The rest of her is missing, so that's all I have for now.'

'She's out here somewhere,' Olivia said, shivering. 'I can sense it.'

'I've had the shivers all morning,' Annie said, shaking her head. 'I feel like we're being watched all the time.'

'There are fifty police officers here searching,' Olivia said. 'And I still feel anxious. I've never been a fan of forests. I blame Red Riding Hood and the big bad wolf as a child.'

'The Evil Dead traumatised me as a teenager,' Knowles agreed.

'Blair Witch did it for me,' Annie added.

'I'm looking for Detective Knowles or Detective Mann?' A young officer approached, interrupting their conversation. He looked at Olivia. His eyes widened and he stuttered. 'Is...is that you, boss?'

'That's me.' Olivia turned towards him. He looked like a deer in the headlights. 'What is it you have to report?' she asked, her eyes scanning the treeline as if Jennifer might emerge from the shadows at any moment. She pushed her hands deep into her pockets. Her long-padded coat was keeping the wind out, but her face and neck were exposed. She wished she had grabbed her scarf and gloves on the way out of the house, but it had been a rush that morning and she still had clothes in cases. 'This is DCI Knowles and he's in charge. You need to talk to him.'

'Hello sir,' he said, nodding. 'The dogs have picked up a scent.'

'Okay, where?'

'A few hundred yards to the west but it's confusing.' The officer's voice wavered with an undercurrent of trepidation.

'Why is it confusing?'

'Because we have multiple hits. The dogs want to move on, which means they've detected something else.'

'Show us where,' Olivia said, following him past the fluttering yellow tape into the heart of the forest. The smell of pine filled the air. 'It's so peaceful. You wouldn't expect to find bodies here.'

'No boss, definitely not.' He ducked beneath a branch. 'Especially not dismembered bodies.'

'Especially not dismembered bodies,' Olivia repeated. She smiled. 'Double unpleasant when they are cut up, as opposed to being in one piece.'

'Sorry,' the young officer blushed. 'I meant that finding a dog walker who had had a heart attack might be more...'

'Pleasant?'

'That sounds silly, sorry!'

'Don't apologise,' Olivia smiled. 'I understand what you mean.'

The officer relaxed and walked on. The damp earth muffled their footsteps as they navigated through the dense trees. The shrill barking of the dogs punctuated the silence, guiding them deeper into the woods. Olivia's thoughts were laser-focused on Jennifer Simmons, the teenager whose disappearance had sparked an exhaustive search, which had come nowhere near this forest so far.

She had vanished into thin air and left nothing behind to indicate where she went to. So far.

The discovery of the arm changed everything. They had to rule Jennifer out of the equation. Every second had mattered when she was reported missing and there was still hope she was alive but as time ticked by, it becomes less crucial. The golden hour had gone; it was the critical time following an incident, when missing children are usually recovered. The chances of recovering them fades as time passes. In Jennifer's case, the weeks had gone by with no sign of her. Time was less important now, and discovering every clue was vital. As the clock ticked by, it was more likely that Jennifer was dead, and it would become a full-blown murder investigation.

They came upon a small clearing where a German Shepherd was sitting down next to two markers. Its handler was patting him, to maintain control as the animal wanted to move on. Olivia's pulse quickened; she knew that kind of behaviour meant only one thing. There were more bodies.

'We have two markers, fifteen metres apart and Leo is desperate to search over in that direction,' the handler said pointing west. 'He's made very clear indications in both cases.'

'Thank you, Leo,' Olivia said to the dog. 'He's a beauty.'

'He is. Leo is never wrong. There are human remains here.'

'Okay, I'm convinced. Can we start to excavate?' Knowles asked, cleaning his glasses on his tie.

'Yes.'

'Let's investigate both markers please,' he said, nodding to the CSI nearby who hurried over with their equipment. There were three officers on each marker.

The metallic sound of spades biting into soil filled the air, each scoop a morbid sample to be examined. Officers stopped what they were doing and watched. The atmosphere was tense with anticipation. Within minutes, the silent anticipation changed, replaced by an ominous stillness as the earth yielded its grim treasure.

'Christ...' muttered one of the uniformed men as the first decomposing body part emerged - a human hand, its skin pallid and lifeless, the nails blackened and hooked.

'It's female, roughly in her forties to fifties,' the technician said. 'The limb was severed with a heavy weapon, probably an axe, maybe a meat cleaver or similar.'

'A match for the first find?' Olivia asked. The CSI nodded. 'Okay. Let's bag her and carry on.' Olivia ordered, her voice steady despite the churn of her stomach. This was not what they had hoped to find, but it was an important find—a dark and twisted one. 'Burying limbs separately tells me our killer has plenty of time on his hands and the victims are kept somewhere remote and secure while he plans the dumps.'

'He definitely has forensic knowledge too, although who doesn't nowadays?' Knowles said. 'A few months with a Netflix account are an education in itself.'

'Detective Knowles?' an officer called out from the second newly uncovered site a few yards away. 'You need to see this.'

'We're going to be busy,' Knowles said. 'Shall we?'

'Let's go,' Olivia said, sighing. She strode over, her boots sinking slightly into the soft earth. The officer gestured towards another set of remains, just below the surface. They were wrapped in tattered clothing – a denim jacket, pink tee-shirt, black bra, the remnants of a life once lived.

'Both arms are still attached, but the head has been removed.' The CSI pointed to the neck with a laser. 'The cut is ragged, probably a saw of some kind done postmortem.'

'Thank heavens,' Knowles muttered.

'The lower limbs are buried but intact to the knees as far as we can see. We'll uncover the lower sections next.'

Olivia knelt to take a closer look, feeling the damp reaching her knees, her mind constructing profiles and patterns from the evidence, eyes searching for clues.

'Her clothing has rotted,' she said. 'She's been here a while.'

'She was buried earlier than the first victim.' The CSI said, shaking her head. 'I have a feeling there are more victims in these woods.'

'Agreed,' Knowles said, holding his nose.

'I agree,' Olivia said, removing a small pot of Tiger balm. She handed it to Knowles, and he dabbed a blob below his nose. 'Whoever has done this is organised, meticulous, and has been using Delamere Forest as a dumping ground for far too long.' She looked around and wondered where the missing pieces of the women were. It made her stomach sink, heavy with sadness. 'The severed arms were most probably brought from the murder scene but what about the more complete bodies?'

'Likely they were killed here.' Knowles nodded. 'They're too far into the trees to have been dragged and would be too risky. Being seen by walkers would be difficult to avoid.'

Olivia weighed up the odds. Had the killer made them walk to their graves or had he killed them elsewhere? She shook the thought from her mind.

'Detective Knowles?' Another CSI officer approached, holding a small, muddy piece of fabric in an evidence bag. 'We have remains further to the east and we've recovered this. I thought you should see it immediately.'

'What is it?' Olivia asked, taking the bag and putting on her glasses. She frowned, examining the contents closely.

'I think it's a crest,' the CSI said. 'From a school blazer.'

She peered closely at the fabric, and her heart skipped a beat. It was a fragment of a school blazer – navy blue with a distinctive crest. It matched the uniform of the school Jennifer Simmons attended.

'Jennifer, is that you?' Olivia whispered, a mixture of hope and dread knotting in her gut. 'What condition is she in, this looks like it's been buried a long time?'

'Too early to say, but we'll check it against her other belongings,' the CSI assured her. 'There's a satchel, and pencil case. We're processing them now.'

Knowles summoned a detective constable. 'I need to know if there are any other girls on the missing list, who were pupils at The Liverpool Blue Coat School.'

'How far back?'

'Say, five years for now.'

'I'm on it,' the detective said. She took out her phone, noting the flicker of emotion on Knowles' normally stoic face. 'Put me through to Misper.'

'Detective Knowles,' the young dog handler returned, looking embarrassed to interrupt. 'Leo has identified more sites.'

'How many more?' Knowles asked.

'Four, so far.'

'Jesus,' Olivia muttered. 'We're going to need more men and more mortuary vehicles.'

'This has turned into a monster already and we're just beginning,' Knowles said, sighing. 'When the press gets hold of this, the shit will fly.'

'I think they could help us if we're smart with what we release,' Olivia said. Knowles looked confused. 'We're finding victims that we weren't looking for. Missing women and girls who are not in the news for whatever reasons, but someone out there knows who they were.'

'That makes sense but I'm not a fan of the press.'

'Nor am I but they could save us hundreds of man hours searching through missing persons cases, but it's too early at this stage. We need to know how many victims we have first.' She took out her phone. 'I'll call the Chief Constable and put her in the picture. She's going to have a fucking melt down.'

'Rather you than me,' Knowles muttered, following the dog handler into the trees. 'I spoke to her this morning, and she had a wasp up her arse...'

'I'm about to shove a few more up there,' Olivia said. She made her call.

As the morning dragged on, more uniformed officers arrived, the excavation became a grotesque reflection of the mind of a serial killer, who had been honing his craft for years. More dismembered limbs surfaced, some skeletal, others not so decomposed, painting a macabre picture of violence and death. They couldn't be sure what order they had been dispatched. Olivia felt a chill snake down her spine with each discovery; Delamere Forest was not just a crime scene; it was a killer's playground. He had buried women and girls across the forest with carefree abandon, but the torrential rains had uncovered his conquests, all headless.

'How many are you thinking we have so far,' Mann asked. Knowles grimaced and shrugged.

'Seven at a guess?' he said, shaking his head. 'Maybe eight.'

'That's where I am,' Mann said. 'Over a couple of years at least. He's killing three a year that we know of.'

'Assuming this is his only dump site,' Knowles agreed. 'There must be some identification on some of the victims, no one is foolproof. We need to take each body as we find them, rule them out as missing or rule them in as identified.' Knowles wiped sweat from his brow, turning to the CSI supervisor who was carefully bagging a severed finger. 'He must have made some mistakes over the years. Everyone makes mistakes.'

'We haven't found any skulls, so their teeth are not going to help, but their prints and DNA will give us what we need,' she said. 'He's made no attempt to destroy them.' She gestured to the east. 'There are several bodies of water in the forest. Blakemere Moss is that way and is over a kilometre long, then there are Black Lake, Dead Lake and Linmere Moss and that's not counting the bogs.'

'And your point is what?' Knowles frowned.

'He could have burned the bodies or dumped them in the water or a bog and covered them in Lyme,' she said, without stopping what she was doing. 'Hiding their identities and destroying DNA wasn't top of mind in this case.' She put the finger into an evidence bag. 'We have two victims with three tattoos to investigate but give us time and we will have something concrete, Detective Knowles.' She removed her mask and shrugged. 'We'll run prints and DNA through the database as a priority. We're sending the evidence to the lab as we find it. Some of it will be there already. Might take a while though, given the state of decay,' the supervisor added, her face an example of professional detachment. 'I'm confident we'll have results for you soon.'

'Keep me in the loop and updated, please.' Olivia walked away to answer her phone. 'The minute you get something, I want to know.' She sighed, her mind racing. 'Hello,' she said, answering the call.

'Is this Liv?' a male voice asked.

'Who is this?'

'Liv, it's Peter Evans,' he said. 'We met in St George's Hall at the Alder Hey charity event last year.'

'I remember,' Olivia said, nodding. 'You're the pissed-up journalist who asked me if I was single while your wife was in the toilet.' The line went quiet. 'What do you want?'

'I wondered if there was any connection between the Delamere Forest search and Jennifer Simmons?'

'I'll give you the same reply as I gave you the last time you asked me a question. Fuck off, Peter...'

She ended the call and wondered which idiot had given him her mobile number. It wasn't difficult to find numbers nowadays and she knew it wouldn't be long before the press jumped onto the story. Seven headless females in a forest were big news. International news. She couldn't shake the feeling that Jennifer's case was entwined with these gruesome discoveries. It was too much of a coincidence not to be, and coincidences of this scale were rare.

'That was my first call from the press,' Olivia said returning to the dig. 'You had better warn your people to be ready for the onslaught. This one is going to be messy.'

'No problem,' the supervisor said, nodding. 'They know what to expect but I'll put a call into the office.' She looked up at Olivia. 'While I'm on the phone, do you want to expand the area you originally identified for us to search?'

'Yes. As long as the dogs keep finding evidence, we keep digging,' Olivia said, her voice firm.

'I don't like to mither but are there any budget constraints?' Knowles asked.

'No. Every inch of this forest needs to be combed if we have to. We're dealing with a serial killer who has been at it for years, and I'll be damned if they mention their budget.' She wanted to light a cigarette, but she didn't smoke anymore unless she was very drunk and in the company of other smokers. 'Whatever we need, I'll make sure we get it as long as no one takes the piss with overtime recording. I don't want uniform getting giddy.'

'Understood,' came the reply.

'I'm going to find the dogs,' Olivia said. 'Walk with me,' she nodded to Knowles. They took a path to their right, the barking not too far away. 'Are you sure you want this one?'

'Fuck yes,' Knowles said, looking her in the eye. 'Are you sure you want me on it?' Olivia smiled and nodded. 'Good. Because it will come down to you to decide.' Olivia agreed with a narrow grin. 'No one above you will want to touch this. This is too hot to handle, right?'

'Right,' she said. 'We won't come out of this unscathed. We never do.'

As they followed the sound of the dogs, the watery sun casting long shadows across the grisly search, Olivia remained focused, moving from one tragic find to the next. Each body part recovered, each shred of evidence collected, brought her closer to understanding the monster they were hunting. He was clearly a very sick individual.

'Detective Knowles, we've found something else,' an officer called out from a nearby dig site just off the path. Olivia and Knowles made their way over.

'We have unearthed another body, this one more intact than the others,' the CSI said. 'It's a young female, probably in her teens.'

'How long has she been here?' Knowles asked.

'Recently. Weeks, maybe a month.'

Olivia felt sick. She looked at the body and saw a silver necklace glinting against mottled flesh. The head was attached, long brown hair clung to the face of a young girl. It was impossible to see the colour of her eyes, hidden by mud and dried blood. There was a gash through the neck, which ran through the spine and shoulder to just above the left breast.

'She was hit with something heavy and sharp,' the CSI said. 'Probably an axe. A big one, right in the centre of her spine,' he added.

'Jennifer had long hair?' Knowles said. Olivia nodded.

'What is on the chain?' Olivia asked.

'A crucifix.' Olivia closed her eyes.

'Could this be Jennifer Simmons?' the CSI asked, his voice barely above a whisper.

'Yes. She had long hair and wore a silver crucifix. I read the description of her chain given by her mother,' Olivia explained. 'Her cross had a red stone at the centre.'

The CSI wiped the mud away from the crucifix. A tiny red jewel glimmered like an evil eye. Olivia felt winded like she had been punched in the stomach.

'Okay. I think we all know who this is but until we can verify her identity, this information doesn't leave here,' Olivia said. Everyone agreed in silence. 'Can you arrange to notify the family that we may need them to make an identification of the chain and cross,' Olivia said to Knowles.

'Of course,' Knowles said. 'They have a decent relationship with their FLO. She's the best we have.'

'She will need to be,' Olivia nodded. 'At least she still has her head,' she muttered to herself. 'Not much of a positive...' her throat tightening as she spoke. 'There's to be no mention of other bodies, or Jennifer yet, just the necklace, okay?'

'Right away, boss.'

The news of the chain being found fell like a dark curtain across the searchers, bringing with it a deep, unsettling silence. Where the sunlight failed to penetrate the trees, floodlights illuminated the forest, casting an eerie glow on the faces of the officers and forensic technicians who continued their work. Olivia watched them, a silent sentinel amidst the chaos.

'Boss. We have an ID.' It was the DI he had asked to check the school history, her expression grim. 'The young girl with the blazer and satchel. Her name is written in her books.'

'Who is she?' Knowles asked.

'Her name was Allison Cropper..., she was reported missing three years ago. She was an orphan in foster care, went missing on her way to school. She had threatened to run away during an argument over breakfast and never arrived at school.'

'Written off as a runaway, I bet?' Olivia said, nodding.

'More than likely,' Knowles agreed.

'Poor kid. This bastard is just plain evil,' Olivia cursed under her breath. Her search for one missing girl had led her to the ghosts of many others.

'Keep going. We need to find everyone he has buried, and we need to stop this bastard before he takes anyone else,' Knowles ordered, his resolve steeling. 'Jennifer Simmons is the last one that this fucker is putting in the ground.'

Through the trees a lone figure was stood watching them dig. They had found Jennifer before he had removed her head. Mundane cunts.

Chapter 22

The Shops

THE STRIP OF COMMERCE at the Village Roundabout was alive with the usual evening business. It had been called the Village because of the Chinese chippy, which had been there since the seventies. While other businesses had come and gone, it had endured the test of time. People were going in and out of the shops, chatting over the din of the traffic. The kebab shop's door swung open repeatedly as hungry patrons ventured in for food, while next door, the off-licence cashier worked tirelessly ringing up bottles of spirits, wine and packs of cigarettes. It was a busy shop in comparison to the others. A Pizzeria was busy with delivery drivers rushing in and out, their insulated bags slung over their shoulders and a line of mopeds outside. There was a taxi office at the far end and the mobile phone shop and bookmakers in the middle. A layby allowed punters to park, shop and drive away in minutes, convenience the key to the shops' success.

At the front of the shops, a wide strip of grass was dotted with picnic tables, used by workers and young mums by day and frequented by teenagers in the evenings, indulging in underage drinking, smoking cigarettes, weed and anything else they could acquire. There were fewer kids there that night, the school bus stabbings had rattled the community. It was suspected to be a turf war fuelled by insults posted on social media. Parents were hypervigilant as speculation rippled through the city as to what happened and who was responsible.

The impregnation of Debby Barry by one of the shop owners and the resulting investigation into a grooming gang of older married men had further added to the community's unease at allowing their daughters out. Obviously, not all the parents in the area felt the same, he thought. Some parents clearly didn't give a shit.

Amidst the coming and going, a figure moved with calculated nonchalance. His eyes flicked from one storefront to another behind a pair of dark sunglasses despite the descending twilight. Blending in was easy and he kept his hands tucked into the pockets of a weathered Hi-Vis; bright but commonplace. Workwear was like camouflage nowadays.

He watched the teenagers chatting, swearing and smoking, all of them females. Not a teenage boy in sight. An Asian male in his forties walked out of the kebab shop and gave them a carton of chips and a pizza to share and a bottle of cider to wash it down with. The girls cheered and one of them stood up and kissed him on the cheek. He grabbed her head and kissed her on the mouth, one hand on her head the other on her arse. She was fourteen if she was a day.

He looked round at the CCTV cameras and smiled. That kiss and groping would be on camera for sure. There were at least four of them in the area, probably more. Even the police couldn't miss the evidence if they looked hard enough. He stepped out of the shadows and bumped into someone.

'Sorry,' he said, stepping backwards. 'Hey, watch where you're going!' barked a burly man exiting the bookmakers as he nearly collided with him. 'Stupid twat.'

'Stupid twat? Sorry, but you're the one coming out of the bookies, knobhead,' he muttered beneath his breath, stepping aside with feigned meekness. It was essential that he blended in, just another face amongst the crowd. 'There's only one winner in there. Who is the stupid twat?'

'Fuck you,' the man replied.

'Fuck you too,' he said, smiling. His eyes were like glass when he was riled, dull like a shark. He stared through the man, his expression disturbing. The man sensed he was messing with more than he wanted to and walked away.

His gaze settled on another rowdy group of teenage girls gathered outside the off license. They were loud, their laughter piercing the air as they passed around their bargain booze. Strong cider by the look of it. Everyone was looking in their direction. The distraction was perfect. A hundred feet away, a vehicle pulled off the main road and headed for the small car park at the side of the shops. The headlights went out and the door opened. The driver was familiar to him. It was unlit but he could see the driver hop out, stretching his legs before heading towards the kebab shop. He recognised the car too. It was a Mercedes. Ahmed Shah and he looked pissed off. He kicked open the door and marched into the kebab shop like a man on a mission. Swearing and shouting could be heard from inside.

The man walked towards the Mercedes, all the while keeping an eye on the driver who was now arguing over the counter with another Asian male. The door opened and he could hear them shouting at each other in their mother tongue. It was a heated exchange. Shah stormed out of the kebab shop and marched angrily towards the phone shop.

'Isn't that Ahmed Shah?' one of the teenagers shouted. 'He shagged Debby Barry and got her up the duff!'

'Ahmed, you massive paedo!'

'Paedo, paedo, paedo, paedo!' the teenagers chanted. The volume increased as both groups joined in. 'Paedo, paedo, paedo!'

Ahmed turned and glared at them; the anger clear to see. He was embarrassed to his core but there wasn't much he could do to silence them.

'I heard he was seeing Jennifer Simmons before she vanished,' one of the girls shouted. 'Where is Jennifer, you fucking pervert?'

His face turned purple; his shame was a pleasure to see. The man grinned. He turned up his collar against the chill and glanced at the sky. It was a clear night, no rain for a change. The stars glinted, making the most of their opportunity to shine. He knew they were watching everything, overseeing his progress before it was his turn to join them. A crescent moon hung low in the sky, another silent witness to the mission he was on.

He walked towards the ginnel which gave access to the alleyway behind the shops. It was littered with pizza boxes, empty bottles and confectionary wrappers. Scruffy twats, he thought. It was risky, a lone figure creeping behind the row of shops at night with no legitimate reason to be there. The sound of traffic was muffled, only the soft whispers of the motorway drifted to him from the distance. He could hear his own breathing. Adrenaline filled his system. The excitement of the evening wrapped around him like a warm cloak as he set about his purpose. He reached the access road, used by the council refuse wagons and delivery vans and made his way to the back of the mobile phone shop. He approached a recycling bin, its purple colour muted under the weak glow of a yellow streetlight. With no one around to observe what he was doing, he glanced quickly towards the car park. It was quiet. He lifted the wheelie bin lid and reached inside his jacket and took out a plastic bag, without touching it, he tipped a navy-blue jumper into the cardboard and paper waste. Carefully, he placed a flattened cardboard box over it. Next, he took another bag and fished out a training shoe, its laces frayed, and the sole nearly detached. Dark stains covered the instep. He slipped the shoe inside with a soft thumping noise eager to conceal it from prying eyes. He took the matching shoe and slipped it into a carrier bag. He tied it shut with a knot and placed it discreetly beside the bin, its fate to be left to chance and a little luck, which would be heavily influenced by him.

The only fate is the one we make for ourselves. Caroline Conner said that in Terminator, he remembered.

He checked the road was clear and walked silently towards the small, unlit car park tucked away from the bustling thoroughfare. Shadows enveloped his form, cloaking him from any potential onlookers. He felt the smooth concrete beneath his feet, each step deliberate and cautious, at one with the stars and moon above him. They watched him and they knew his mind. A security light flickered on, triggered by his movement. It went off quickly and then came back on again. The sporadic light from above flickered occasionally, but he moved through the darkness like an apparition. No one saw him and he stayed out of sight of the security cameras, which were focused on the back doors of the buildings. There were blind spots and he had mapped them in his mind.

He made his way towards the Mercedes. There was no one in sight, just the faint rustle of litter blowing in the wind and the quiet hum of the nighttime city. He placed the palm of his hand against the glass in the rear passenger window. With a hard pull, he manipulated the window, forcing it down just a few precious millimetres. The squeaky sound of the glass slipping open barely registered in the still air.

Reaching into his pocket, he pulled out a tiny plastic pouch containing a small silver ring, glinting even in the dim light. It felt cold to the touch, and he hesitated for a fleeting moment, perhaps caught in the weight of memories attached to the delicate band. Shaking off the memories, he dropped the ring into the back footwell, letting it disappear among the shadows of the car's interior. He took a small slim mobile from another pocket and dropped it inside the vehicle. The memories of her swamped him momentarily and he closed his eyes and welcomed them.

He made his way to the front of the shops and glanced around. The shops were still busy, the teenagers tipsy and loud and everyone blissfully unaware of who he was and who he would be. As quickly as he had come, he retreated into the depths of the night, merging with the darkness that surrounded him. The city continued to breathe, unaware of the incredible things happening within its folds.

Chapter 23

J anine

THE CLOCK'S SOFT TICKING felt more pronounced at night in the dim light of the office. Caroline Tunbridge, a dedicated social worker, rubbed her temples as she stared at the paperwork cluttering her desk. Reports, reports, reports. If it isn't recorded, it didn't happen. Social Services were under the cosh and the employees were feeling the pressure. The weight of the week had settled heavily upon her shoulders, but she found solace in her quiet routine, knowing that her efforts made meaningful differences in the lives of those she served. It was a vocation, not a job.

However, that solace had been shattered in an instant earlier when her phone had rung and the news that a child in care had been arrested in connection with a county lines operation. They were so vulnerable.

Her phone buzzed and she checked the screen. It was a little past 2am, and the call was from the care facility where she had placed Janine, a vulnerable adult who had endured endless hardships throughout her life. After the recent explosion at her home, Caroline had tried to provide Janine with a stable environment, hoping to foster a sense of security but the steady rhythm of her life had been shattered, replaced with panic.

'Caroline?' A weary voice broke through the tension on the other end of the line. It was Lisa, the night nurse. 'Janine White... she's gone. I can't find her anywhere.'

The words sunk into Caroline's chest like a stone. 'What do you mean, she's gone? How can that be?'

Her voice shook with disbelief, the gravity of the situation weighing equally on her heart.

'I've checked her room, the common area—everywhere. Her window is open, and I swear I saw it was locked when I did the rounds earlier,' Lisa stammered, her breath quickening. 'She must have opened it and climbed out.'

With trembling hands, Caroline glanced at the surveillance footage from earlier that night, her mind racing through the possible scenarios but there was no sign of Janine. Every second felt like an eternity.

'I'm on my way,' she said, determination taking over as she grabbed her coat and keys.

As she drove through the near-empty streets, the yellow glow of streetlights fought against the chilling dread settling in her stomach. She thought about Janine's gentle smile and the soft-spoken woman she had become fond of over the past few years. The woman had suffered abuse most of her life and she had no family, bar a brother who lived in Huyton somewhere. She loved him but rarely saw him or his children.

Caroline had got to know her, and they had shared laughter and tears. Janine was vulnerable and they had tried to put her somewhere safe but if she wanted to run away, it's impossible to stop her. There were thousands of care users who had run away and never been seen again and now there was the grim reality of her disappearance. Janine was a grown woman and free to leave at any time. The police wanted her kept in custody, but it was deemed harmful. The unit where she had been placed was manned and monitored but was far from a secure site.

When Caroline arrived at the facility, the air was thick with anxiety. Phil Moult, her boss, stood near the entrance, his brows knitted with concern.

'What do you have for me?' he asked, meeting her gaze with urgency in his eyes.

'Janine White is missing. We need to call the police,' she responded, her voice steady despite the tempest in her heart. 'The window was open, and Lisa thinks she slipped out during the night.'

Phil nodded, his expression deadpan, refusing to show concerns.

'She was interviewed this afternoon about a very dangerous OCG who had stashed drugs and explosives in her spare bedroom,' he said. 'We can't assume that she left of her own accord.'

'You don't think they've taken her?'

'I don't know but they will want to keep her quiet about the cache in her home.'

'Oh no.'

'We can't rule anything out. Let's not waste time. I'll make the call.'

He pulled out his phone and began relaying the information to the police, his voice low and commanding. Caroline felt the seriousness of the situation loom over them, but she quickly took action, gathering the staff to form a search party.

'We'll check the grounds first—she may still be close by,' she suggested, rallying everyone around.

'No one goes into the grounds alone,' Phil said. 'Everyone partner up.'

As they combed through the facility's garden and surrounding area, Caroline's mind raced with concern. She thought back to their last conversation, the glimmer of fear in Janine's eyes as they discussed her past. Caroline had promised to protect her, to give her a place to call home, yet here they were, out searching in the darkness. Minutes turned into what felt like hours. Phil rejoined them, his expression sombre.

'The police are on their way, and they won't be happy,' he said, his voice laced with an undercurrent of urgency. 'We'll need to file a report and give them all the details we have. I'm going to drive to her brother's house. If she's on the run, she will go there.'

Chapter 24

The Whitehouse

It was early the next morning when Phil Moult parked his car outside the rundown home of the White family, taking a deep breath to steady himself. He had been a social worker long enough to know that every visit brought a mix of emotions, but today felt particularly heavy. As he emerged from the vehicle, he scanned the quiet suburban street. There were uniformed officers on each corner, reassuring the residents that they would not allow the bus stabbings to ignite retaliation. He pulled on his coat, noting the tension that seemed to hang in the air like storm clouds before a downpour.

Knocking on the door, he was greeted by Hayley White, her eyes red from crying.

'Hello Phil, thanks for coming. Please come in,' she said, her voice shaky and strained.

As he stepped inside, he was met with the sight of the two children—Rosie and Gary—sitting on the couch, their faces pale and worried. He offered them a comforting smile, but it felt like a hollow gesture under the circumstances.

'Hi kids. How are you doing?' Phil asked.

'Shit,' Gary said. 'Everyone keeps calling me a grass. Terry Eccles said he's going to cut my tongue out and he's a nutter.'

'Shut up, Gary,' Bill said from the hallway. 'Phil isn't here to listen to you moaning.'

'I'm just saying.'

'And Terry Eccles is right, you are a grass,' Bill added. 'That's what happens when you talk to the police.'

'Bill, stop that, right now!' Hayley shouted.

'The boy needs to learn how things work. There's a big bad world out there.'

'Shut up, Bill.'

'Is there any news about Aunty Janine?' Rosie asked, her voice barely a whisper.

'No, not yet. I came to check if your dad has seen her,' he said, turning to Bill, who had just entered the room looking dishevelled and worn out. 'Or if any of you had heard from her, a call or text message?'

'No,' Bill replied flatly, running a hand through his hair. 'I haven't seen her. I just... I can't believe she's missing.'

The atmosphere in the room was tense and anxious and Hayley sank onto the couch beside Rosie, wrapping an arm around her daughter. Gary sat beside them in a three-person hug. The kids needed reassurance, and Phil sensed his role in the moment was to provide stability amidst confusion, but he wasn't sure how much they were aware of. Before Phil could speak, the sharp ring of the doorbell interrupted the heavy silence. Almost immediately, Hayley and Bill exchanged worried glances. Bill looked through the blinds.

'It's the police,' Bill muttered, and a sense of dread seeped through the room. Bill opened the front door and greeted them. 'Back so soon?' Bill joked. 'Have you come to lock our Gary up for being a knobhead?'

'No, you can keep him for a while longer,' PC Martins said, smiling.

PC Martins was in uniform, and Detective Harris had donned jeans and a tweed jacket. They entered with the rigid professionalism expected of police officers but tempered by the understanding of the situation they were stepping into.

'I'm DS Harris,' the detective said. 'We've come about Janine White, your sister?'

'We know about our Janine,' Bill said, shrugging. 'Phil Moult from social services is already here.'

'Oh, joy,' Harris muttered.

'Is there any sign of her?' Bill asked.

'Not yet.'

'Go through to the living room. I'll put the kettle on.' Bill gestured to Rosie. 'Put the kettle on for us, lovely,' he said with a wink. 'While I deal with the police.' Rosie huffed and went into the kitchen.

'Have you heard anything from your sister?' Harris began. At least he wasn't bringing bad news, but the weight of his words loomed over them all.

'No, nothing,' Bill said. 'She normally calls us if anything happens, good or bad.'

Phil shifted in his seat, nervous. Maybe he was preparing himself for the news he feared. Detective Harris took a step forward, his eyes scanning the room, landing on each family member with empathetic intent.

'We need to ask some pretty awkward questions,' Harris said. 'We can do it here or we can go to the station?'

'Surely, there's no need for that?' Phil said, shaking his head. 'That's a bit heavy handed, isn't it?'

'We've got a job to do,' Harris snapped. 'I suggest you do yours and leave ours to us.' A tense silence lingered for long seconds.

'Ask your questions,' Bill muttered. 'We've got nothing to hide.'

'You're all aware that Janine has been involved with some distasteful individuals... a drug gang?' Harris said.

Rosie came in from the kitchen to listen. Gary looked confused. 'Aunty Janine, what?'

'Aunty Janine was involved in drug dealing?' Gary asked. 'Is that true, dad?'

'Our kids didn't know about the cuckooing,' Bill said, shaking his head. 'It's been a difficult time for them as it is, without our Janine's troubles to think about.'

'Cuckooing?' Gary asked.

'Shut up, Gary.'

'We believe her flat was cuckooed by a man called, Bobby Allen,' Harris looked at Bill. Bill looked uncomfortable. 'You know Bobby, don't you?'

'From a different life,' Bill said, shrugging. 'We went to the same school.'

'Oh, we know that,' Harris smiled. 'You got into a spot of bother with him, didn't you?'

'I was very young and stupid,' Bill blushed. 'My kids don't know anything about it...'

'About what?' Gary asked. 'What did you do, dad?'

'Shut up, Gary.'

'Are you still in touch with Bobby?' Harris asked. 'Because Janine told us that he scares the shit out of her, and she made a call to him following the explosion at her home...'

'I haven't heard from him in years,' Bill said. He looked down at his feet. 'Do you think he's hurt Janine?'

'Do you?' Harris asked. Bill shrugged. 'She had a large amount of white powder in her bedroom, and it was brought to our attention by an explosion, which killed her friend. An accident but Bobby Allen won't be happy, will he?'

'What caused the explosion?' Phil asked.

'HME,' Harris said. 'Some kind of grenade.'

'What's HME?'

'Shut up, Gary.'

'Homemade explosive,' PC Martins whispered. Gary looked shocked.

'Bobby Allen is not at the top of the tree, so he answers to his bosses, and he will blame Janine, won't he?'

'I don't know who he works for.' Bill shrugged. He looked at Hayley and she looked shocked. Rosie looked gobsmacked and Gary looked confused.

'He works for an organised crime gang from Knotty Ash,' Harris sighed. 'But you know that, don't you?'

'The Diddy Men,' Rosie whispered to Gary.

'How do you know that?' Harris asked, frowning.

'Jordan Miller used to talk about his dad all the time, on the school bus,' Rosie explained. 'Everyone knows his dad is a gangster.'

'Bill knows Jack Milner, don't you?' Harris said, smiling. 'You go back a long way.'

'School,' Bill said, shrugging. 'We were never friends and there were a few hundred other kids there at the same time. I wasn't in his social circle then or since.'

'I don't think Bill knows anything about this,' Phil said. 'She was cuckooed by a dangerous gang because she's vulnerable, no other reason.'

'What's cuckooing?' Gary asked.

'An insidious practice where criminals exploit vulnerable individuals for their own gain.' Phil answered.

'What's insidious?' Gary asked.

'Evil,' Bill said. 'You've watched the film by that name.'

'Yes, but I didn't know what it meant.'

'Cuckooing is usually where they force people to store their drugs or let them deal from their property.' Phil glanced at Hayley, who shook her head in disbelief, her hands clenching her daughter's shoulders tighter.

'So, this Bobby Allen character stashed his drugs and explosives in Janine's flat?' Hayley asked. 'And you knew about this?' She looked at Bill. He looked away.

'Yes. But Janine's friend, Gilbert touched something he shouldn't have, and it exploded, killing him,' Harris said. 'The bomb squad evacuated the street but there was another bigger explosion later on, which took the roof off the building.' He shrugged. 'I have to assume the drugs were destroyed in the resulting fire, which means there are some very angry dealers out there and Janine may be the focus of their anger, hence she's missing. They may have kidnapped her.'

'No,' she gasped, her voice breaking. 'Not Janine. She's always been so sweet. They wouldn't hurt her like that, would they?'

'They're a ruthless gang of thugs.' Harris shrugged and Phil nodded in agreement.

'Did you know this had happened to her?' she snapped at her husband. Bill had a sheepish expression on his face. 'Did you know, and you didn't tell me?'

'Bobby had already got to her and put his gear in there. It had already happened when she told me,' Bill said. 'He gave her money and weed, and she spent it and smoked it. She begged me not to tell you...'

'You're such a wanker,' Hayley said, wiping tears from her eyes. 'How could you let them get away with using your own flesh and blood like that?'

'I tried to stop it. I called Bobby,' Bill said, shaking his head. 'I told him to leave Janine alone and get his gear out of her house, but he told me to mind my own business, or you and the kids would get hurt.' He shrugged and put his head in his hands. 'They know where the kids go to school, what busses they take, where they hang out at night, everything...'

'So, you are in touch with Bobby Allen?' Harris asked, frowning.

'I hadn't spoken to him for twenty years before that call,' Bill said. 'And I haven't talked to him since.' Harris was glaring at him. 'Honestly. I haven't heard anything either from our Janine or Bobby Allen.'

'I can't believe you knew all this and didn't tell me!' Hayley stormed out of the room. 'What did you think was going to happen?'

Gary turned to his father, tears brimming in his eyes. 'What does all that mean, Dad? Aunt Janine... she can't be in danger, right?'

Bill stepped forward, rooted to the spot yet desperately wanting to comfort his son. He placed a hand on Gary's shoulder, his face a mask of determination clouded by sorrow. 'We'll find her,' he said, almost more to himself than to the children. 'I promise you, we will.'

Hayley came back in with a glass of water. Phil watched the family's heartbreak, each child holding onto their father like he was an anchor in a stormy sea. PC Martins continued with the information, describing the ongoing investigation, but the details faded into a distant hum for Phil. All he could see was the fragility of the situation, the worry lines etching deeper into Hayley's face and the helplessness bubbling to the surface.

'Is there anything we can do?' Hayley asked, fresh tears streaming down her cheeks.

For a moment, silence enveloped them, broken only by the gentle sobs of Rosie. As the shadows lengthened outside, uncertainty loomed larger than ever.

'No. Just sit and wait,' Harris said. 'And pray she has run away of her own accord because it they have taken her; I dread to think what they'll do.'

The home of Jennifer Simmons

THE SIMMONS FAMILY home was on edge and had been for weeks. Jennifer's parents had hardly slept solidly since the day she had not arrived at school. It was like walking on eggshells, arguments erupted at the slightest provocation. The atmosphere was tainted with an unbearable tension. They were grieving her loss without even knowing if their daughter was dead or not. The wider family had rallied around and conducted their own investigations and rumours were rife that Jennifer had been having a relationship with a married man, who was linked to a grooming gang. Accusations had been made for years but nothing had been done to stamp them out. Tempers were running high, and fingers were being pointed. Racial tensions were at boiling point. Following the recent riots across the country, the police and government were desperate to keep a lid on the situation.

The living room, once filled with laughter and the sound of music and chatter, was now cloaked in a sombre silence. Her mother Carol sat on the edge of a leather sofa, her hands nervously fidgeting with a faux fur cushion. Her father Dennis paced across the room, his brow furrowed with worry and despair. There was no peace or comfort to be found. He couldn't settle and spent hours driving around the city looking for Jennifer. Photos of their teenage daughter lined the walls—her smile frozen in time, illuminating the earlier happier days and emphasising their loss.

Dennis saw an unmarked vehicle arriving; it was their family liaison officer and a detective from the PVPU. They looked nervous and reluctant to approach the house. They knocked on the door and Carol went to open it. Dennis could hear them chatting at the porch as they wiped their feet.

The living room door opened, and Beverley Miles, the family liaison officer, entered the room followed by Carol and the detective, who introduced herself but the name alluded him. Her expression was serious, her posture tense as she surveyed the couple before her. It was clear there was news, but it didn't look good. They had been desperate for news of any kind but now it was here, Dennis didn't want to hear it. The gravity of the moment settled like a lead weight on his shoulders, and Beverley drew in a deep breath to steady herself.

'Sit down, Carol, and you Dennis,' she began, her voice steady but soft.

'I'm okay standing.'

'I'm afraid I have some news and there's no easy way to tell you.'

Carol looked up, her eyes wide, tears flowing down her cheeks but still with a flicker of hope. 'Have you found her?'

Beverley took a step closer, her heart aching for the parents before her.

'Yes, we have found her, but...' She hesitated, searching for the right words, as Dennis stopped pacing, his eyes narrowing with a sudden sense of dread.

'What do you mean 'but'?' he asked, his voice strained. 'Has she run away with that Paki? Where is she? Is she alive?'

It was only seconds while she gathered herself, but it felt like an age. The deafening silence seemed to go on forever as Beverley stuttered. She met their gazes, filled with desperation, fear and love.

'Jennifer was found in Delamere Forest during a wider search. I'm so sorry to tell you this, but she has been... she has been murdered.'

A piercing silence enveloped the room. The words hung heavily in the air, and suddenly everything seemed to spin. Carol's breath hitched in her throat, and as realisation dawned, her body trembled violently. She slid off the settee as if her bones had turned to liquid and screamed.

'No! No, this can't be true!' she cried, her voice cracking as she wrapped her arms around herself, as if trying to hold onto some semblance of hope. 'Jennifer, no, no, no, please no...'

'Dennis staggered back, his hands clenching at his sides. 'What the fuck was she doing in Delamere Forest?' He couldn't accept the information. He was convinced she had run away with her lover. 'Murdered? Who would do this?' His face twisted in anguish as he glanced at the photographs lining the mantle, a life now shattered in an instant. 'My little princess, murdered?'

'Please, you need to know that we are doing everything we can to find her killer. There's a huge investigation underway and we will find them,' Beverley said, her voice breaking slightly. 'But right now, I need you to focus on each other. I'll be here to support you.'

Carol clawed herself up but collapsed into Dennis's arms, her sobs erupting like a dam breaking, each wave of grief crashing over her.

'No, Dennis! Please no, she's not dead, please no!'

He embraced her tightly, his own tears streaming down his face, mingling with her cries of devastation. 'My baby... my little girl...' he managed to choke out, his voice filled with agony. 'No!'

'Who killed her?' Carol screamed. 'Did that Paki kill my daughter?'

'I'll skin that bastard if he touched my girl,' Dennis shouted. 'I'll fucking skin him alive, do you hear me?'

Beverley didn't speak. There were no words to quell such anger and grief.

Time felt frozen in that moment; the world outside continued unaware of their suffering. Beverley stood by, her heart breaking with compassion as she watched the sorrow that enveloped the family. She knew there would be no words that could ease their pain, only the promise of support and the commitment of justice that lay ahead. The echoes of their grief filled the room, a haunting reminder of a love forever lost. Innocence torn from them in the most brutal way.

Chapter 25

The graveyard

THE SEARCH TEAM AT Delamere Forest was hard at work. It had been a long uncomfortable day and night, but the rain had finally let up. Heavy clouds loomed overhead, cloaking the moonlight, offering only narrow slivers of visibility where the torches illuminated the dark underbrush. Olivia Mann stood at the centre of the unfolding nightmare; her hands thrust deep into the pockets of her coat. DCI Knowles was in control of the search, and it was obvious he was a competent SIO.

The shadows danced unsettlingly as the search party continued their grim work, sifting through the mud and roots to uncover victims who should have remained buried but for the rains. The search was spread over a mile square already and growing.

The dogs and CSI officers had done their jobs, and the ground had given up its horrors, revealing the dismembered bodies of seven people for definite but possibly eight, their lives ended in a manner both violent and unthinkable.

The early morning sun struggled to break through the heavy canopy of the forest, dappling the ground with patches of light that flickered like distant memories. The scent of damp earth, mingling with the rotten stench of decomposition floated on the breeze. DCI Knowles walked towards her with two cups of coffee and a frown.

'I've had a very strange call,' Knowles said. He handed one of the cups to Olivia.

'This can't get any stranger than it already is,' Olivia said, sipping her drink. 'But I'm listening.'

'Uniform were called to a burning vehicle on the west side of the forest last night,' he explained. 'The owner was still inside, burnt to cinders but they found the remnants of a carpet knife in what's left of her right hand. It looks like a suicide.' He sipped his coffee and frowned.

'That's horrible but is it relevant to the search?'

'I don't know yet. The victim is a police officer, Alice Walker, married with two children. Works out of Halewood station, ring any bells?'

'No. Her name isn't familiar to me,' Olivia said, shaking her head. 'That is strange.'

'Coincidence?'

'I don't like coincidences. Put one of your team on her and find out what was going on in her life. Leaving her husband and kids behind would have taken a lot of weighing up.'

'Who is going to tell the family?'

'Uniform are on the way.'

'Send a DC with them to do some digging,' Olivia said, with a shiver. 'It feels like it's all wrong to me. The timing and the place...'

'My thoughts exactly,' Knowles said. 'I'll make a few calls.'

'I'm going to head back to the station, and bring the Jennifer Simmons team up to speed,' Olivia said. 'The family has been informed.'

'How did that go?'

'As badly as can be expected,' she said. 'The press are having a field day, as they do. Keep me in the loop.'

'Will do, speak later.'

A FEW HUNDRED METERS away, CSI Caroline Mitchell knelt beside a patch of disturbed soil, her gloved hands expertly brushing aside the detritus of the forest floor. The CSI team moved slowly, methodically, knowing that every inch of this sacred ground was a piece of a puzzle that needed careful unveiling. Behind her, forensic technician Greg Holloway set up the portable tent, a fragile barrier against the world that would soon be crowded with questions. Photographers were lined up along the cordon and three television camera vans were on the edge of the forest. The dogs had indicated the spot held remains and then moved on to the east. They could hear them barking, indicating more victims somewhere nearby.

As the team worked, tension swelled in the air. Each member could feel it, the unspoken weight of what they were about to confront. They spent the next hour methodically removing layers of soil and foliage, their movements synchronised as if they had rehearsed for this moment countless times before.

'Found something,' shouted Caroline, her voice breaking through the quiet. She held a trowel, the edges of which glistened with dark, wet earth. They brushed the soil away, millimetres at a time.

Below the surface, a set of ribs emerged, stark white against the black mud. The discovery spiralled into another dawning horror as they continued to unearth more of the victim. The team had learned over the years that the manner in which they uncovered the remains could speak volumes. Context was everything; the slightest misstep could mean the difference between a conviction and a cold case.

'This one is different,' she said, looking up at Knowles.

'What?'

'It's a male,' Caroline said.

'Are you sure?' Knowles asked, shocked. Caroline glared up at him, offended. 'Sorry. Of course, you're sure. I was thinking out loud, it doesn't fit.'

'No offense taken, but I disagree. It does fit,' Caroline said. 'You're looking for a batshit crazy psychopath.'

'Is that a clinical term?'

'It should be.'

As the last layers of earth were moved, the outline of a young male body began to take shape. Caroline felt her stomach churn as she noticed the neck—what should have been the junction between head and torso had been cleanly severed, as though a surgeon had wielded a blade with precision.

Gaze steady, she instructed Greg to record the details. 'Take images of the cut. It's too clean for typical violence; might suggest someone who knew what they were doing.'

Just then, Jenna spotted something glimmering amidst the remnants of the forest—a chain necklace lying just off to the side, partially buried in the mud. 'What's that?' she asked, her eyes wide.

Caroline moved closer, recognizing the pendant—a small, silver star.

'It could belong to him,' she murmured, carefully requesting Jenna to retrieve it without disturbing the remains. The moment the necklace was free, a chill ran down her spine. It was engraved with initials: J.S.

'Let's finish digging him out,' Caroline said, her voice steady despite the turbulence within. As they worked, a sense of clarity began to dawn. A name, a face, a life lost. This was more than a gruesome discovery; it was the key that would unlock the chain of events leading to this young man's end. Just another victim of a world that often turned dark without warning.

With a collective effort, they finally unearthed the body, exposed to the chill of the morning air. Around them, the forest remained tranquil, vivid greens and browns teeming with life, oblivious to the macabre tableau before them. Birds chirped indistinctly in the trees, as if mocking the silence that hung thick around the crime scene.

Knowles stepped back, taking in the scene before him. Another headless body, a severed connection, and another family that would soon be shattered by the discovery. The day continued in the same vein, each discovery had sent waves of shock through the team, but it was the presence of the three young males that had rocked them to her core. The search had thrown up female victims so far and dictated a predictable demography—this was not it.

Alice Walker's home

THE TRAFFIC DRONED by persistently outside, a dull rhythm of the vehicles on the motorway cars, vans and lorries roaring past. The triple glazing did its job to muffle the worst of the noise inside the modest Walker home.

Inside, the atmosphere was tense with grief and disbelief. Sergeant Norris sat at the edge of the dining table; his hands clasped tightly together. Detective Constable Palmer leaned against the fireplace, arms crossed, observing the broken family gathered around them.

Peter Walker, heart-wrenchingly pale, was sitting in his favourite armchair. His brow was furrowed, eyes red from lack of sleep and endless tears. Alice hadn't come home from work and hadn't answered her phone. He instinctively knew that something terrible had happened to her. He sobbed into a tissue, glancing at photographs on the walls—smiling family moments captured in time, now painful reminders of a family irrevocably torn to pieces.

'I just... I can't believe she's gone, especially like that,' Peter murmured, his voice quaking. 'How am I going to tell Carlie and Hugh? They deserve to know the truth, but how... how do I even begin to tell them their mother set fire to herself and then slit her own throat?'

Norris exchanged a solemn glance with Palmer before speaking.

'We're here to help, Peter. We'll do everything we can to help you. Alice was a serving officer, and we look after our own. You're not alone in this.'

'Funny you should say that because I've been feeling like I'm alone for a very long time.'

'What do you mean?' Palmer asked.

Peter sniffled, swallowing hard, but his gaze remained distant.

'Alice was different these last few months. Working double shifts, making excuses to skip her training at the gym... it was like she was trying to run away from something. We barely talked anymore.'

His voice cracked, filled with a mix of anger and sorrow. 'And the worst part? I think she was having an affair again.'

'An affair?' Palmer raised an eyebrow, intrigued.

'Yes. All the signs were there,' Peter sniffed. 'I caught her at it a few years ago.'

'Do you think it was someone—'

'From the force?' Peter scoffed. 'Of course it was. You lot are an incestuous tribe with the worst divorce rate I know of.' He looked the officers in the eyes but neither of them challenged him. 'PC Martins his name was.' A flare of emotion ignited in Peter's eyes. 'It was happening a few years back. I caught her in a lie, but we got through it—or so I thought. I can't shake the feeling that she was seeing him again... or someone else. It's like she was pushing me away all the time. If she was having sex, it wasn't with me.'

Norris leaned forward, attentively listening. 'Have you noticed any other signs? Friends she was meeting? Changes in her behaviour?'

'Why do you ask that?' Peter asked. 'Is there a chance it wasn't suicide?'

'There has to be a postmortem and thorough investigation before we can be sure so, in the meantime, we'll keep all options on the table.'

'What can I say? She kept things from me,' he answered, running a hand through his dishevelled hair. 'I saw her sending messages on her phone. Thought she was just chatting with colleagues, but looking back... I should have known better.'

'Did you read any of the messages?' Norris asked gently.

'Nope. I would never have looked at her phone, no matter how suspicious I was.' He shrugged. 'If someone is going to cheat, they're going to cheat anyway.'

'Did you argue?' Palmer asked.

'Am I a suspect now?' Peter snapped. 'You have all the subtlety of a brick in the teeth.'

'Your wife has died a violent death, and you've just told us that you suspect she was having an affair. We have to explore all avenues.'

'Of course, you do,' Peter said, flatly. 'There were times she was supposedly at work; I found out she was somewhere else entirely. I confronted her about it, but she just dismissed it as work related and she kicked off and asked me if I wanted to put a tracker on her car. I thought I was being paranoid.'

'You mentioned she was worried about her job?'

'Yeah. The department has been under scrutiny—like everyone's on edge. It felt like she was trying to hide everything from me,' Peter's gaze fell to the floor, the weight of his words heavy and suffocating.

Norris took a measured breath.

'Do you think she felt threatened? Perhaps by anyone related to her work?'

'I don't know. If she was having an affair and things had gone wrong, who knows?'

'Was there anyone she mentioned as not getting on with?'

'Maybe...' Peter started hesitantly, 'Alice had some conflicts with other officers. I didn't think anything of it—just office politics, you know? But... now I'm left wondering if this... this was more. Maybe the pressure was too much.'

Palmer felt an instinctual knot form in his stomach. 'Who specifically? Any names that come to mind?'

Peter hesitated, clearly torn between loyalty to his wife's memory and the nagging chills of suspicion. 'There was talk about a new officer wanting to prove herself... Janice Flannery. Alice didn't like her; said she was overstepping the mark sometimes. Then there was a guy called Meto—he had a thing for her, always dropping by her office for no reason.'

Norris noted the details, mentally piecing together a narrative that could lead to clarity.

'Alice was a strong officer. It's common for ambitious colleagues to feel threatened or uncomfortable around someone like her.'

The weight of sudden realisation struck Peter. 'What if someone... someone wanted to make her disappear? Or what if she felt unsafe and couldn't see anyway out except to kill herself?'

'Let's not jump to conclusions just yet,' Norris cautioned. 'But every detail is important. We will uncover the truth, but you need to focus on your children now. They'll need you.'

Peter's expression twisted in anguish, but slowly, he nodded. 'You're right. I have to figure out how to tell them. Alice was their mother, no matter what she did.'

As the mood in the room shifted from despair to determination, Palmer placed a hand on Peter's shoulder.

'We won't let this go unexplained. We will find out what happened.'

Outside, the world moved on, indifferent, while the weight of loss engulfed the Walker house. In that moment, life was suspended, the search for answers had just begun.

Chapter 26

The Zodiac

Olivia put the phone down to the ACC, who was having a torrid time from the press. All part of the pressure at the top of the tree, she thought. He was pressing her for a progress report, but results were slow in the early stages of any investigation. She didn't have a magic wand, and she couldn't pull forensic evidence from her backside. Deeper excavation had unearthed several items, which had caused excitement and confusion. A set of tarot cards in a velvet pouch were discovered beneath the body of one victim and a wooden and brass planchette beneath another. Some other items had been sent to the lab for identification.

They knew that they had eight victims, five female, three male and not much more except two of them were schoolgirls, Jennifer Simmons and Allison Cropper. Allison was an orphan and had no remaining family to speak of, but Jennifer did, and they were angry and devastated and baying for blood. The Simmons family numbered into the hundreds and some of them were part of the criminal fraternity. Threats had been made online but as there were no definite suspects yet, they were taken with a pinch of salt.

As soon as the phone hit the cradle, it rang again. She needed to pee but didn't want to miss an important call.

'Great. Just fucking great,' Olivia murmured under her breath, her mind racing. 48 hours into the search, and all they'd found were headless corpses and a grizzly puzzle to piece together. 'Superintendent Mann,' she answered.

'Olivia, it's the postmortem surgeon, Dr Henderson. We haven't spoken for a while.'

'Dr Henderson, I've been waiting for your call,' Olivia answered, her heart pounding in her chest. 'The press are clamouring for information, as I'm sure you can appreciate, so are my superiors. What do you have for me?' she asked, trying to keep her voice steady.

'I am sure you are under pressure Olivia, but I think you need to come down to the mortuary and see this for yourself,' Henderson said, urgency etched in her voice. 'I know you're not the SIO but you're in charge of the Jennifer Simmons case, right?'

'They're connected now, so I think the two will merge,' Olivia said. 'I've got a meeting with the ACC and the press officer in thirty minutes and it's going to take most of the day, so I'm stuck in the station today. Can you summarise for me if DCI Knowles is on his way, you can show him in person?'

'Okay.'

'Thank you, it's appreciated.'

'We've conducted initial examinations on the bodies, and there's something you need to see. I'll send you the images now.'

Olivia checked her laptop and opened a zip file. She scrolled through the images. It was a grizzly gallery indeed.

'I can see some type of lettering cut into the victims. What is it?'

'They're not letters, they're symbols.'

'They're familiar.'

'I thought so too. There are symbols carved into the skin of each victim—specifically, the buttocks, chests and back of each victim. They're intricate and I felt they were oddly familiar.'

Olivia's breath caught in her chest. She could see the symbols and they were familiar but she couldn't put her finger on why. 'They are familiar but it's not coming to me.'

'They are the signs of the zodiac.' Henderson hesitated, her voice lowering as if sharing a secret. 'They're actually the Babylonian signs of the zodiac. Each victim bears a different symbol—Leo, Taurus, Pisces and so on. It's not random. There's a pattern.'

'Each victim has a different symbol carved into them?' A chill gripped Olivia.

'Yes.'

'What does that mean?'

'I can't say just yet, so your guess is as good as mine,' the surgeon replied, 'but this isn't just the handiwork of a killer. It's not a fetish or torture, in my opinion; this feels ritualistic.'

Ritualistic. The word echoed ominously in Olivia's mind. This wasn't a random series of murders; this was something darker, possibly a message. Maybe a mission, a twisted mind with a job to complete. Whatever he was doing, they needed to stop him, preferably with a bullet.

'Ritualistic?'

'In my opinion.'

'What type of rituals include the signs of the zodiac?'

'Hundreds, maybe thousands. Some people don't leave their houses in the morning until they've checked their horoscope, but ancient civilisations revered the stars and constellations.'

'It gives us an avenue to follow. Where are you up to with the postmortems?' Olivia asked

'I have four other surgeons here. We're almost done,' Henderson said. 'Give me a few hours. I'll prepare the files and send them to you.'

'Okay, thanks.'

'I'll call you later this afternoon to go over the findings but there is one important thing you should know sooner rather than later.'

'Go on.'

'The heads were removed a long time after death and burial.'

'Really?'

'Yes. Your killer buried them and went back months later to remove the skulls.'

'Why would he do that?'

'He wanted a skull, not a head,' Henderson explained as if it was obvious. 'Heads are messy and full of brains, eyes, tongues, ears etc, all difficult to remove and dispose of but Mother Nature is an excellent cleaner, and human tissue is food for other organisms.' Henderson paused. 'The killer went back and removed the skulls when most of the tissue would have been broken down or eaten. Less mess, easier to handle.'

'That would explain why Jennifer still has hers?'

'Absolutely. What he is doing with them is beyond my thought process but he's clearly creating a collection. He's making his own version of the Zodiac, in my opinion. A victim for each of the twelve signs.'

'And we have found eight,' Olivia said. 'There are four missing.'

'Or four more to come. Heaven forbid.'

'Amen to that. Thank you, that makes sense,' Olivia said. 'I'll talk to you later.' The call ended. She stared at the phone, thinking about what she had been told. 'We've got a fucking nutcase on our hands, Olivia,' she said to herself. 'The press are going to dine out on this for decades.'

Olivia looked out of the window, her gaze swept over the river, the dark waters heading out to sea. The Liver Birds looming like sentinels guarding the macabre secrets of the city below. This was not just a killer killing for the sake of it. Something deeper and more ancient seemed to pulse beneath the surface of this case. The carved symbols evoked images of lost civilizations and forgotten rites—indications that the killer might be tapping into something far older than the city itself. It was chaos but underneath the chaos, there was order—a pattern waiting to be uncovered, a reason these lives had been chosen. The symbols would speak, and she was ready to listen.

THE STREETS OF LIVERPOOL were buzzing with shoppers and commuters, tourists and commercial vehicles. It was a mission that no police officer wants to be on. Talking to parents about the death of their children was never easy. DCI Genesis and DI Steff Cain approached the imposing façade of the tower block building that housed Dixie Dean's flat, overlooking the river and the Albert Docks across the water. The weight of the city's pulse drummed beneath their feet—a blend of murmurs, footsteps, and distant sirens that spoke of the life that thrived in the shadows. Genesis adjusted his collar against the brisk wind that blew in off the river.

'Are you ready for this?' he asked, glancing at his partner.

Steff, dressed in her standard dark trousers and a fitted jacket, nodded with a resolute expression. 'Let's just get it over with. We owe it to the parents.'

They stepped into the building, the interior dimly lit and decorated with an air of modern grandeur. Dixie Dean was a name that loomed large in Liverpool; he was not just a gangster, but a myth wrapped in flesh and bone. Everyone knew he had fingers in many pies, but his reach was reputed to go well beyond mere crime. Genesis knew he was dealing with a dangerous animal, one with huge teeth.

They spoke to a voice on the intercom and were buzzed into the building. They took the lift to the top floor and waited. After a moment's wait in a sparsely furnished hallway, a heavy wooden door swung open.

Dixie Dean appeared, his presence commanding the space. He looked younger than Genesis and Cain had expected, with sharp features framed by cropped hair; his eyes burned with a fierce intensity that suggested he was very much in control. There was anger in them, tinged with sadness.

'Come in and sit down,' he ordered, his voice a low growl. The detectives took their seats across from his desk, exchanging a glance that conveyed both uncertainty and determination. Dixie sat behind his desk in a Chesterfield swivel chair, studded with brass nails. The green leather looked worn and comfortable.

'How are you, Dixie?' Cain asked, her best smile on her face.

'Let's not pretend to be friends, even for a moment. We despise each other with a passion.' He shrugged. 'Why are you here?' Dixie leaned forward, his elbows resting on the desk.

Genesis decided to take the lead. 'Mr. Dean, we need to discuss your son, John and how he died.' There was a beat of silence, and it was as if the air had shifted.

'About fucking time,' Dixie sighed. At the mention of John, a flicker of emotion crossed Dixie's face, but it was quickly masked by his hardened demeanour. 'Obviously, I know the basics but what happened exactly?' he asked, his tone rife with a mixture of dread and defiance.

'CCTV shows there was a fight on the top deck of the bus and John was stabbed,' Cain interjected softly, noting how Dixie's posture stiffened. 'He bled to death despite attempts to save him.'

Genesis took out his tablet and pointed towards the CCTV footage they had collected. 'The footage shows that when the fight broke out, John drew a knife from inside his coat.'

Dixie's expression twisted, the slightest hint of disbelief flashing in his eyes. 'So, he was stabbed with his own blade,' he replied, though the uncertainty in his voice betrayed him. 'I warned him about carrying a blade but kids don't listen, do they?'

'Not always.'

'Witnesses saw him pull out the knife on the top deck. It was chaos and spilled downstairs, Mr. Dean. During the struggle... he was killed with his own weapon.'

Silence fell over the room, thick and suffocating. Dixie leaned back, the tension radiating from him palpable. 'I raised him better than this,' he muttered, more to himself than to the detectives. 'He thought he was a big man, but he was just a kid.'

Genesis seized the moment. 'He got mixed up with the wrong crowd, Mr. Dean. But you need to understand the circumstances are complicated—it was a tragic outcome, and there are so many layers to this.'

Dixie's gaze sharpened, twisting into something harder. 'Tragic? You think I care about tragedy in this city?' He waved a hand dismissively.

Steff leaned forward; it was her turn. 'There are others involved in the dispute, and we believe if we can piece together what led to this, it might help prevent further violence.'

At her words, the anger in Dixie's expression morphed into something far darker. 'You think my boy's death is just another statistic to you? Just a lesson to be learned?' He stood abruptly, fists clenched at his sides.

Genesis maintained his composure, despite the looming threat.

'We know this started with Jordan Milner not your son. We don't want to punish anyone without cause, Mr. Dean. We need information from you; your connections could help us find the truth about that day.'

A tense moment passed between them, the air thick with unspoken animosity. Dixie seemed to wrestle with his options—defend his son at any cost or face the reality of a life cut short by violence. With a long, drawn-out sigh, Dixie sat back down, tension seeping from his shoulders. 'What do you need from me?'

Genesis felt a glimmer of hope. 'We need to know who he was running with, who instigated the fight, and why. Every detail counts.'

'You expect me to grass?' Dixie laughed. 'You want names and numbers of people who clashed with Jordan, and caused this?'

Dixie's gaze fell to the desk, the pain of responsibility pulling at him. Cain felt the shift—a gangster on the edge of revealing truths amidst a sea of regrets.

'We can help you, Mr. Dean. Together, we can make sure the story of what really happened is told.'

'The story is what it is,' Dixie said, shrugging. 'My son left home carrying a knife. If you live by the sword, you may die by the sword. It's the oldest story in the book.' Dixie stood up and poured himself a single malt. 'Show yourselves out...'

Chapter 27

Tipoff-3 days later

The cobbled streets of Liverpool glistened under the early morning drizzle and watery sunshine, that had become a staple of the city's weather lately. DCI Knowles leaned against his desk, the faint aroma of brewed coffee wafting through the air as he stared at the blinking cursor on the computer screen. He had been sifting through forensic reports all night without any sleep. He was tired and weary.

Days had passed since the last body had been processed, and the wait for forensic results was beginning to bite. He watched the Ferris Wheel at the Albert Dock turning slowly and compared it to the investigation. It was moving too slowly for comfort and the top brass were on his case. His phone rang.

'DCI Knowles.'

'Ben Knowles,' came the familiar voice of Mark Lathom, a seasoned journalist from the Liverpool Echo. 'How are you doing?'

'Fucking knackered, to be honest,' Knowles answered, yawning. 'To what do I owe the honour of a call from the mighty Echo?'

'I've got something that might be worth your time investigating.' His tone was urgent, with a hint of hushed excitement. 'I was going to investigate it myself, but this is too big, and I don't want to fuck up your investigation.'

'Which investigation?'

'The Forest Ripper.'

'Oh, fuck off,' Knowles laughed. 'Please tell me you're not running with that tagline?'

'Straight from the editor herself.'

'She's a twat.'

'Can I quote you on that?'

'Absolutely,' Knowles chuckled. 'Tell me what you have.'

'It's about Jennifer Simmons.'

'Sore subject, don't dabble with a story about a murdered schoolgirl unless you are ready for the backlash.'

'No half a story here, just horrible truth, which is far worse.'

'How horrible?'

'Horrible.'

'This sounds expensive.'

'This is a freebie, but I want the first dibs on the story when you've locked the bastard away?'

'Deal. What have you got?' Knowles leaned forward; his curiosity piqued.

'I've been digging through the sewers of local gossip, and it appears Jennifer Simmons had been involved in a relationship with a man called Ahmed Shah, a married man, who runs a mobile phone shop on the Village Roundabout, Huyton.'

'I know the area but haven't heard the name before.'

'Run it through your system, Ben,' Mark said. 'The sleazebag is already being investigated for making a fourteen-year-old pregnant. Debby Barry. Your colleagues are looking into allegations of a grooming gang in the area, all run from that row of shops.'

'Is this kosher?'

'I called the PVPU this morning and they fobbed me off, which means it's verified information and there's more—rumours say it's been going on for months, but his friends and family were turning on him because of the pregnancy investigation shining a spotlight on all of them,' Mark explained. 'She was seen coming out of the backdoor of the kebab shop, where it's claimed the groomers take their victims for sex. Shah was seen acting suspiciously around the recycling bins at the back of his shop.'

'What was he doing?'

'My source saw him with a training shoe in his hand,' Mark said. 'A small one.'

'You're kidding me?' Ben asked, shocked. 'Who is the source?'

'I can't tell you that.'

'This could be the break we need.'

'I knew it would be of interest to you. This bunch of arseholes have been sniffing around young girls for years but every time we think we have a story, it gets squashed upstairs.'

'By who?'

'I can't say but I am sure if I write another article about them, the same thing will happen again. But, you can do something with it...'

'Oh, I will. I can't believe there's a known paedophile group in the area where a young girl has gone missing, and no one has thought to mention it to me?'

'They have now,' Mark said. 'This slimeball was brazen about the relationship. Jennifer has been seen in his Mercedes, several times. There might be DNA, right?'

'I can't get into that, Mark,' Knowles was shocked. 'I need to look into this and get back to you.'

'Okay, do something to stop these perverts, Ben.'

'You can count on it.' He hung up without saying thank you. Knowles dialled his counterpart at the PVPU.

'DCI Stamp.'

'Frank it's Ben Knowles.'

'The man of the moment. How's the Delamere case going?'

'Shit. The press are killing us. They're calling it the forest Ripper case.'

'Fuck's sake.'

'My words almost exactly,' Ben said. 'Do you know the name, Ahmed Shah?'

'Shah? The businessman?' Stamp asked.

'Yes, has a shop on the Village Roundabout.'

'We're about to charge him but I can't say too much yet,' Stamp explained. 'He's impregnated a fourteen-year-old.'

'Has the baby been born?'

'Why do you ask?'

'I'm trying to get a timeline in my head.'

'Debby is twenty-two weeks gone but we can DNA test from ten weeks,' Stamp said. 'Shah is the father. What's your interest?'

'I've had a tip-off that he was having a relationship with Jennifer Simmons,' Knowles dropped the bombshell.

'The missing girl?' Stamp asked, shocked.

'She's not missing anymore.'

'I know she's not missing anymore.' Stamp was stunned. 'Off the record, he's also part of a wider investigation involving a grooming gang, all linked to those businesses on the roundabout. If his name is linked to Jennifer Simmons, it will blow the lid off the operation.'

'You know I have to look into it, don't you?'

'Of course,' Stamp said. 'He's known around town and so is his wife. If this is true and a scandal follows...'

'It's going to get messy but the silly fucker should have thought about that before he started shagging kids.'

'It could blow up in your face. Shah's got connections. His wife is a prominent figure, and Jennifer has had massive press coverage. This will be huge.'

'I'm calling you out of respect,' Knowles sighed. 'I'm going to have to get a warrant and search his properties.'

'I'll make sure we don't interfere in anyway, go and nail the bastard,' Stamp said.

'Will do, thanks.'

Chapter 28

The mobile phone shop search

OLIVIA MANN WAS STANDING at the side of a meeting room at Canning place where DCI Knowles was addressing two search teams, ready to execute warrants against Ahmed Shah. She was cautiously optimistic that they could find evidence to help them with the Jennifer Simmons case. It had to be dealt with in isolation. Each victim found in Delamere Forest had to be taken on their own merit. Their identities, the details of their abductions, injuries, deaths and disposal were all individual to them. The killer could not be charged with murdering them all, en masse, despite it being obvious that the same person buried them all in the forest.

'Quiet please. Listen up,' Knowles said, rallying his officers. 'You're aware that we received a tip-off regarding Jennifer Simmons and an alleged sexual relationship with a local businessman, Ahmed Shah. He runs the mobile phone shop on the Village Roundabout. He's thirty years old and married with children.' A murmur of disapproval rippled through the gathering. 'We're heading to his home and business simultaneously. This could lead us to something substantial about her disappearance.'

'Where is the tip-off from, guv?'

'A reporter at the Liverpool Echo,' Knowles replied. He could see the expressions on his detectives' faces. They didn't trust the press at any level. 'Ordinarily, I would be sceptical, but I crosschecked the information with the PVPU Superintendent, and he confirmed that they are looking into this case from a different angle. It's solid.'

'Are we suspecting he killed her?' a detective asked.

'I'm not suspecting anything, just yet.'

'Whoever put Jennifer in the forest, killed the others too, right?'

'We're keeping an open mind on the entire case,' Knowles said. 'No preconceived ideas until we have cold hard evidence.'

'There's a grooming case in operation on the owners of those shops,' another officer said. 'Is Shah implicated in that?'

'In a word, yes but the same applies,' Knowles said, shrugging. 'We look at this with fresh eyes, no preconceived notions.'

The officers nodded; their faces set in determination. They knew Knowles and respected his decision making.

'Prepare to split into two teams: one for Shah's home and the other for his business. DS Clark will be leading the search of his shop and the flat above the shops nearby and DS Hill will lead on the home warrant. Let's move quickly and discreetly,' he instructed. 'His wife is a very influential businesswoman in the city, so keep the language down and be mindful that everything we do will be scrutinised and that they will play the race card at every opportunity.' He paused. 'Superintendent Mann and I will be overseeing the operation. Any issues, contact one of us immediately. Don't second guess this one, okay?'

'Yes, guv,' the collective reply.

As they filed out of the station, Olivia's mind raced. The potential implications of a scandal like this could rock the community and tip the fine balance, but there was also the possibility of something darker lurking beneath the surface of the grooming gang. Something much darker. Was Shah the killer of multiple victims, obsessed with the Zodiac? It didn't feel right. He was a paedophile but that didn't make him a serial killer. She was on a rollercoaster that had started running and she couldn't get off until the ride was finished. In the meantime, all she could do was hold tight.

DS CLARK ADJUSTED HER coat as she stepped into the mobile phone shop, the bell above the door ringing softly as she entered. The faint smell of plastic and metal mingled with the air-conditioned coolness, creating an oddly sterile atmosphere. The smell of cheap aftershave lingered in the air. Brightly coloured promotional posters adorned the walls, promising the latest gadgets, handsets and unbeatable deals. But today, the shop's cheerful posters didn't match the gravity of her operation. The search team followed her in, and the shop assistant looked terrified.

Ahmed Shah, the owner, was already under scrutiny for allegations that hung ominously over him like storm clouds. The case involving Debby Barry—a teenage girl now facing an uncertain future—had drawn Shah into a world filled with whispers and accusations being made behind his back. His future was precarious at best and deeply unsettling for his wife, children and wider family. Clark and the team hadn't arrived with much sympathy for him.

'Where is Mr Shah?' she asked the assistant.

'He's down there at the rear of the shop.'

As she approached the rear, set against a backdrop of Samsung and Apple devices, she took a breath and prepared to confront the man at the centre of it all. He was stacking a shelf in the rear of the shop.

'Mr. Shah,' she called, her voice steady. Ahmed looked up from behind the counter, his expression shifting from mild surprise to wary recognition. 'We need a word.'

'Are you the police?' he asked, forcing a smile that was strained.

'Yes. I'm DS Clark. I'm here to conduct a search,' she stated firmly, no room for negotiation.

'Why would you search my shop?' he asked, shocked. 'Is this to do with the Barry girl because she's a fucking liar?'

'No. It's to do with the murder of Jennifer Simmons.'

'Her murder?' he scoffed. 'I barely knew her. Why would I murder her?'

'We're just here to search the property, Mr Shah, not to speculate about the case.'

'Is this really necessary?' he asked, though the tremor in his voice betrayed his unease. 'Jennifer was never in this building, not ever.' He shrugged, looking angry. 'This is my business, and she never came in here.'

'Given the circumstances, I believe it is necessary to search all your properties. This is your copy of the warrant.' She gestured for the team to begin their search. 'I need you to unlock any cupboards, doors and the rear exit, please.'

'Okay but I want to call my lawyer.'

'You can call him once we're done here. Right now, I need you to stay where I can see you, please.'

With that, she began her search. DS Clark moved past the rows of sleek smartphones, the shiny casings gleaming under fluorescent lights. She noticed several items that were of no interest—a bin full of discarded receipts, and old chargers—but they seemed far removed from the more pressing concerns that clouded her mind. Everything inside the shop was as it should be. However, as the search progressed, her attention turned toward the yard at the rear and a bank of recycling bins tucked in the corner next to a small storage shed.

One of her officers was checking a bottle bin, noisily moving the contents around. With a glance back to ensure Clark was watching, she pulled the lid off the cardboard bin and peeked inside. She lifted the top layers of cardboard to see what was underneath.

'Boss,' the officer called, raising her hand. Clark approached and looked inside. Her heart skipped a beat as she spotted a school jumper—faded and slightly stained, yet unmistakably belonging to a young person. The logo belonged to the Blue Coat Girls' School.

'Bag it,' Clark said. 'That's the school Jennifer attended.

'Okay, Boss.'

She carefully retrieved it, holding it up for a closer inspection. The name tag, partially ripped but still visible, displayed the name, Jennifer. It was put into a clear evidence bag to preserve evidence and prevent cross-contamination.

'Get Ahmed out here, please,' she ordered. He was hovering inside the back door, looking extremely nervous.

He shuffled through the backdoor like a naughty child, hands together, head down, eyes darting here and there.

'Can you explain why this school jumper, with the nametag, Jennifer sewed into it, is in your recycling bin?' she asked, the question cutting through the silence like a knife through skin.

Ahmed froze, his body rigid, the smile long gone. He looked stunned. 'I... I've never seen that before,' he stammered, eyes darting dangerously toward the exit. 'You've planted that...'

'Don't be ridiculous,' Clark muttered, her face like thunder. She stepped closer to him and held up the evidence bag. 'She was wearing a jumper like this when she left home. What would a school jumper, marked Jennifer be doing in your shop, Mr. Shah?'

'I have no idea...'

'There must be an explanation why it's in your bin,' Clark said. 'You said she's never been here.'

'She hasn't.'

'Did you bring her through the shop when you were taking her upstairs for sex?' Clark asked. She gestured to a metal staircase at the rear of the neighbouring shop. Officers were walking up the stairs with the shop owner, who was glaring at Shah, accusingly. 'That is where you went for sex, isn't it?'

'I never touched her,' Shah said, shaking his head but he looked like he was going to vomit. 'Jennifer and her friends hung around the shops all the time, drinking and causing trouble. The kids always leave things behind on the benches and we have to clean up their mess,' he replied hastily, though she could detect the lie hanging in the air like a thick fog. 'The only way that could have been put into my bin is if my cleaners brushed it up from the front of the shop and binned it.' He shrugged angrily. 'Either that or someone planted it there.'

'We'll need the names of your cleaners.'

'Fine, no problem,' he said.

'Carry on the search, concentrate on the bins and the yard,' Clark ordered. 'Is that storage shed locked?'

'Yes, of course it is,' Shah muttered. 'There's a lot of crime in this area.'

'That's why we're here, Mr Shah,' Clark replied, curtly. 'Open the door please.'

'I don't think you're funny,' Shah snapped. 'I'll be making a complaint to your superiors. This is not a joking matter.'

'Feel free. It wasn't a joke,' Clark said, leaning closer. She whispered into his ear. 'Open the fucking door before I have you cuffed and thrown into the back of a van, where you can wait while we do the search.'

Shah opened the door without argument. 'I'm going to report this to my solicitor. This is outrageous.'

A detective moved one of the wheelie bins to look around behind it. Seconds later, he called out, his face marked with unease, holding up a plastic carrier bag.

'Boss, I found this near the shed behind the bins,' he said, revealing a training shoe inside, worn and tiny. 'Looks like it was hidden.'

'Another piece of the puzzle?' Clark said, eyebrows raised. She stared at Ahmed, whose façade was cracking under the pressure. 'That is identical to the trainers Jennifer's mum described that she was wearing when she disappeared. You have quite a collection of items that don't seem to belong to you, Mr. Shah.'

'I'm just a small businessman with a wife and children, not a killer for fuck's sake!' he protested, though Clark could see the cracks in his bravado. 'I've never raised a finger to a woman in my life, let alone killed anyone.'

'Raised your hand to a woman no, young girls are different to you, though aren't they, Mr Shah?' Clark asked. 'A grown woman wouldn't put up with you for five minutes.'

'How dare you...'

'Give me your car keys, please,' Clark said, abruptly. Shah looked furious as he handed them over. 'Search the Mercedes and take him with you, so he can witness anything we find. I'll follow you over in a minute. I need to tell the boss what we have so far.'

Knowing she needed to expand her search, Clark motioned for more officers to explore the parking area around the vehicle. Early autumn leaves had turned to sludge underfoot as they sifted through the piles of debris along the kerb edges. When they approached Ahmed's Mercedes parked nearby, her heartbeat quickened with anticipation. She had a feeling they were going to find more inside. Just a hunch.

'Let's double-check inside that vehicle,' she instructed, and the officers complied with practised efficiency. As they searched the vehicle, Clark remained on the lookout, her senses heightened. Shah looked extremely agitated. It wasn't long before one of the officers called out to her, excitement and urgency mixed in the officer's tone.

He was holding the rear passenger door open. 'DS Clark, you need to see this.'

Clark hurried over to the car, kneeling to peer inside. There, nestled in the back footwell, lay a tiny silver ring—its elegant design contrasting starkly with the grim situation surrounding its discovery. The gleam of the metal seemed to whisper secrets, begging for an explanation. Knowing it had belonged to a teenage girl, murdered and buried in a forest far away from her home, made her sick with anger for Shah, and empathy for her loved ones.

'Does this belong to you or any of your family, Mr. Shah?' she asked, maintaining her steady gaze on him. He opened his mouth to respond, but no words came out. The fear was palpable, and with it a mixture of anger and desperation. 'Before you tell me another lie, we'll DNA test it and if it was worn by Jennifer, we'll know.'

'I have nothing more to say to you,' Shah complained. 'I want a lawyer.'

'You're going to need one,' Clark said. 'Charge him and take him to the station.'

Chapter 29

The mortuary

Olivia Mann stood in the sterile confines of the mortuary engulfed by the aromas of disinfectant and decomposition. She was keen to work through the victims for as long as it took. There were too many questions and not enough answers. Her gut was telling her the killers was playing games with them, but she didn't know the rules. Dr Henderson methodically examined the body on the cold steel table. The young man's torso was a grisly canvas, the symbol of Leo—a primal circle with a tail—carved deeply into his chest. The wound boasted jagged edges and deep tissue lacerations, remnants of a brutal struggle, which meant the symbols were carved while the victim was alive. A seven-inch slash beneath the ribcage on the right was wide and torn at the edges. The victim, a teenage-something with dark, tousled pubic hair, lay eerily still, the once vibrant life snuffed out too soon. His head was missing and his skin olive coloured, his toenails discoloured from poor hygiene. The smell of decomposition hung heavily in the air. She took a small jar of tiger balm from her pocket and twisted the lid off, dabbing a blob beneath her nose. It helped but didn't stop the stench from clinging to the tissue inside her nostrils.

'You said there are some consistencies, that are bothering you?' Oliva said. 'What do we have, Dr Henderson?'

'All the victims have this incision made below the right ribs,' Dr Henderson said, pointing to the dark rent in the skin. 'The postmortems revealed the liver and right kidney of each victim were removed postmortem. They were removed by someone with a reasonable amount of skill, maybe a butcher or meat processor.'

'That's disturbing,' Olivia said.

'There are some sections of buttock muscle which have been cut away, probably with a scalpel.'

'What are you thinking?'

'The muscle looks like it's been filleted from the body, like a steak,' Dr Henderson said, shrugging. 'The liver and kidney would be edible.' Olivia didn't speak. She couldn't think of the words. 'I think your killer is removing pieces of his victims to eat them.'

'That is quite an assumption.'

'An educated guess, that's all,' Dr Henderson said. 'Your killer is consistent in his modus operandum.'

'All the victims have their organs removed, the liver and right kidney?' Olivia asked, her voice steady despite the bile rising in her throat. She had seen death many times, but the sadism inflicted upon this young man felt different. More personal. It had been an intense and sustained attack, and the victim would have suffered indescribable pain. The final insult was to eat some of him.

Dr Henderson glanced up, her expression grave as she continued her examination. 'Our findings show all the victims were subjected to extensive torture before death, the carving of symbols into their skin and then the dissection and organ removal postmortem. Various abrasions and lacerations indicate prolonged sexual assault and restraint while all this took place.'

'Any ID on him?'

'Nothing. His prints are not in the system, no DNA match. My guess is he's an illegal immigrant, who has been living on the streets. No one reported him missing because no one knew he was there.'

'And that matches the profile of all the other victims except, Jennifer Simmons,' Olivia said. 'We appear to have victims selected because they are off the radar. Runaways, care users, homeless, immigrants, he's smart.'

'He's very smart.' She tugged on his gloves, inspecting a small, circular wound beside the Leo symbol. 'There are also signs of sexual assault, which further complicates the picture. This wasn't just murder; it was a calculated act of power conducted over days, not hours. The organ removal backs that up. A final insult to the memory of the victim.'

'He has somewhere isolated where he can carry this out, unheard and undisturbed,' Olivia said.

'Definitely. He can take his time without having to gag his victims,' Dr Henderson said. 'There are no gag marks on any of the victims, which tells me he wanted to hear them screaming, probably begging for him to stop. He had the ultimate power over pain, suffering, life or death.'

'Power,' Olivia echoed, feeling a chill dance down her spine. She nodded. It all made sense. The lack of gag marks said it all. This sick fucker wanted to hear them scream and beg for their lives and then eat their liver and a human rump steak. The carvings in the flesh were purposeful, echoing the methodical way the killer had chosen his victims. 'And the symbol carving? It's ritualistic?'

'It is,' Henderson murmured, removing a sample from beneath a thin layer of skin, clearly disturbed by the callousness of the act and the implications of the missing liver and kidneys. 'And it bears obvious similarities to the other cases. The five women... all had Zodiac signs carved into their bodies and body parts removed. Each a different astrological symbol marked—Capricorn, Aries, Scorpio, Cancer, Libra and so on. The killer seems to have a specific fixation on astrological signs.'

Olivia pressed her lips together, a thought forming. 'And if he is following the signs of the Zodiac, that leaves the potential for more male victims, especially correlating to the masculine signs. Taurus, Leo, Aries...'

'Exactly,' Henderson agreed, flipping through his notes. 'We might find several more graves in the forest if our assessment holds merit. The patterns allude to the killer having a type of victim to target, but we can't dismiss the psychological aspect either; he may be compensating for some lack of control in his own life, or he may be on a mission. That would probably the most dangerous type of individual, as they're not going to stop until the mission is completed.'

Olivia shuddered as the implications lingered in the air. The symbolism; those carved signs binding the lives of the victims together, extending from the grave to astrological beliefs, all orchestrated by a disturbed mind shrouded in darkness. She had a growing sense that this would spiral deeper—grievously deeper.

'Do we have any information on how far back these killings could have started?' she asked, hoping for a light at the end of the tunnel, against the mounting dread.

'I'm going to say less than five years ago but we can only give an educated guess at this stage,' Henderson replied, shaking her head.

'If this young man aligns with the other victims with a Zodiac motif, it raises the possibility of his murder being one of twelve—murdered as part of a sick game. We have started to examine missing persons' cases and any unsolved murders in the surrounding areas from the last few years.'

'And have you had any success?'

'Yes, Olivia said. 'CSI found a deck of tarot cards beneath one of the female bodies and we found a woman reported missing in suspicious circumstances a few years back. She was a tarot reader, who vanished following a fire at her home.'

'And she wasn't reported missing?'

'She had no family to speak of and there was a fraud case looming, so it was suspected she may have up and run away.'

'Another runaway.'

'Exactly.'

'Let's also check if astrological signs have any significance to the victims,' Henderson suggested, her mind racing with the thousand knots of information untangling. 'Places they visited, history—something that might connect them in a subconscious thread. The killer must have a well thought out method of selection.'

Olivia nodded, 'I think if we can work out how he is selecting them, it will go a long way to identifying him.'

'We're running what results we have with the profiles of the previous victims and aligning them,' Henderson said. 'I'll begin an in-depth analysis, but don't be surprised if we uncover more disturbing details; cannibalism could be the tip of the iceberg. This pattern might outline a larger gallery of crime than we anticipated. We're assuming there are only twelve but there could be many more.'

With a resolute nod, Olivia turned her gaze back to the body, struck by the innocence that had been so savagely silenced. Somewhere in the shadows of the forest, another victim might lie, and it was up to her to unearth the truth before the killer claimed his next 'prize.'

As the grim reality enveloped her, she felt the weight of the case crushing her, a chilling reminder of the darkness lurking not just in the forest—but within the human heart. The killer was the prime example of a dark heart, no empathy, no sympathy, no regret for his actions.

Chapter 30

The search

DS Hill and his team were at the Shah residence—an elegant townhouse with wrought iron railings and manicured hedges. It was in the million-pound bracket and the vehicles parked on the driveway were both new. The Shahs were clearly wealthy and influential, yet the search could put away a murderer, and he felt the instability of the situation.

They exited their vehicles and knocked on the front door. He signalled the team to prepare for the search and they waited nervously. Searching a family home was always a delicate operation but this one was going to be a battle from the start.

'Remember,' he said, 'this is about gathering evidence, not about what we think of Ahmed Shah as an individual.'

The door opened and Ushna Ahmed looked out. She was wearing a traditional dress, bright green in colour, her fingers were covered in gold rings. She was attractive with huge almond shaped eyes and lashes like a camel. She looked at them as if they had taken a shit on the step.

'Yes?'

'I'm DS Hill and we have a search warrant for this property.'

'Are you at the correct address?' she frowned. 'This is the Shah residence.'

'Yes. It's correct. We're here in connection with an investigation involving your husband, Ahmed Shah into the murder of Jennifer Simmons.'

'Who, murder? Don't be ridiculous,' Ushna scoffed but she looked shell-shocked. 'Do you know who I am?'

'Yes. I do. I need you to step aside and let us conduct the search. We'll need access to every room and Ahmed Shah's devices, phones laptops and tablets.'

'I need to call our solicitor before anyone goes anywhere.'

'I'm afraid that won't be possible. Step aside, please and let my officers in.'

The detectives slid past her, much to her annoyance. She flushed with anger but looked resigned to the situation. She took out her mobile and tried to call her solicitor.

'I need you to put the phone away until we've finished the search, please, Mrs Ahmed.' DS Hill stepped inside and waited until she had ended the call. 'Could you show us where Mr Ahmed keeps his devices, please. It would save us and you a lot of time and inconvenience.'

'What exactly are you looking for?'

'I'm afraid we can't discuss that with you,' Hill replied. 'Does he have a desk?'

'His office is over there, through the kitchen,' Ushna said, folding her arms. 'His desk is never locked, but don't take anything without asking me. I insist on that. We have nothing to hide.'

'Okay, Mrs Shah. Are his devices locked?'

'His password is always 1994. The year I was born.'

'Thank you, search the office, please, any devices are password protected 1994,' Hill ordered. With that, they split into pairs, doggedly searching each room of the house. Time stretched on as the team searched, anticipation mingling with unease. Hill went room to room following the detectives. He moved through the sleek new kitchen, which looked like nothing was ever cooked in there, and into the open living room, where a pristine coffee table held recent magazines and a framed picture of Shah with his wife and kids.

Hill went to the office door, scanning the dark wooden shelves lined with books and awards. His eyes landed on a stack of files on the desk, neatly arranged. He approached and saw several mobile devices in a paperclip tray. He began flipping through them slowly, his instincts heightened.

'Bag these,' he ordered.

In the next room, he could hear the team conversing, their footsteps echoing through the house. It wasn't long before a detective called out from the bedroom upstairs.

'DS Hill! You need to see this!'

Hill hurried upstairs. In the bedroom, he found his colleague holding a phone, the light on and text on the screen. 'We found these messages. They're very explicit, all between Shah and Simmons.'

'You've checked her number?'

'Yes. It's hers.'

'He arranged to pick her up from a bus stop on the day she went missing.'

'Bingo.'

Hill took the phone, his brow furrowing as he scrolled through the evidence. The exchanges were laden with sexual texts, and as he read further, a dark realisation pulled at his gut. There were also mentions of meetings and the flat above the kebab shop, in language that suggested something more than a friendship had happened. It was obvious that Ahmed was a nefarious paedophile.

'Screenshot the messages and bag the phones. We'll need to piece this together before he's interviewed,' Hill instructed, his voice steady but his mind racing with the implications of what they'd uncovered.

As the team continued their search, it was obvious there were layers here—potential betrayal, deception, and perhaps something even more sinister at play. With each passing moment, he became more determined to uncover the truth behind Jennifer Simmons and Ahmed Shah.

Olivia Mann arrived in her own vehicle; professional curiosity had forced her from the station. She wanted to meet the wife and get a feel for their relationship. She stepped into the hallway and saw Ushna standing near the kitchen door. She was watching the officers, horrified and frightened. Olivia approached her with a smile.

'I'm Superintendent Mann,' she said, offering her hand. 'You must be Ushna?'

'Yes.' Ushna looked dumbstruck. 'Are you in charge of this circus?'

'The ringmaster, you mean?' Olivia said, nodding. 'I'm sorry this is happening to you. Unfortunately, the crimes of an individual often affect many others. You look like you could use a cup of tea, I know I could.'

'They haven't searched my kettle yet,' Ushna half smiled. 'Come into the kitchen.' Ushna led the way and put the kettle on. She made two cups of tea and gestured to the stools at a breakfast bar. 'Can you tell me what the fuck is going on?'

'I can try,' Olivia said. 'You're aware of the investigation that's being carried out into the shop owners at the roundabout?'

'I don't live in a box, Superintendent, nor am I blind or stupid,' she said, straightening her dress. 'Some of Ahmed's cousins are scum, chasing young girls around with their dicks in their hands, cheating on their wives at any opportunity. They deny everything of course, but their wives and families talk to me. We're all of the opinion that there's no smoke without fire...'

'But you have to support your husbands, regardless?'

'It's our culture, bullshit, I know but here we are...'

'I understand. I can tell you what we know as fact.'

'Please do.'

'Ahmed was having a relationship with Jennifer Simmons at the time she went missing,' Olivia said. 'We have to investigate where the relationship led him and if he's involved in her death.'

'How old was she?'

'Fifteen.'

'A child.'

'Yes.'

'If there's evidence that he's been having a sexual relationship with a child, he will never step foot in this house again,' Ushna said, wiping a tear away. 'I will divorce him and screw him for every penny we have.' She took a deep breath. 'The girl, Jennifer, was found in Delamere Forest, wasn't she?'

'Yes.'

'With others?'

'Yes. Eight in total, so far.'

'So, whoever murdered her, murdered all of them?'

'Yes.'

'Ahmed is many things and right now, I don't care what you do to him but he's not a serial killer, Superintendent,' Ushna said, sniffling. Tears flowed freely now, the reality that her marriage was over was biting. 'I thought I knew him, but I don't know him at all.' She sipped her tea and composed herself. 'He was in his shop the day she went missing and then we had a dinner party that evening. Your killer is not my husband.'

'I believe you,' Olivia said, smiling. 'Our investigation will uncover the truth but the reason we're here is because of his relationship with teenage girls. I feel for you, I really do.'

'Girls?' Ushna whispered. 'There's more than one, isn't there?'

Olivia nodded but didn't answer. 'Thank you for the tea, Ushna,' Olivia said, standing. 'If there's anything I can do once the investigation is complete, let me know.'

'I will, thank you, Superintendent.' Olivia walked out of the kitchen and met DS Hill at the front door.

'Guv, what are you doing here?'

'Professional curiosity,' she said. 'I wanted to speak to Mrs Shah and get her take on things.' He gestured to go outside.

'Walk me to my car,' Oliva said. 'What have you found?'

'A mobile with text messages on it. Shah arranged to meet Jennifer on the morning she went missing.'

'Okay, that's good. We'll see what he has to say at interview.'

'What do you think, guv?'

'I don't know what to think, but Shah is not Zodiac,' she said.

'Zodiac?' Hill repeated. 'Is that what we're calling him?'

'Everyone else is,' Olivia nodded. 'I'll see you back at the station.'

She got into her BMW and took another look at the house. Ushna and her children were about to have a distressing time, and they would need all their family and friends around them to survive it. Their secrets would soon be laid bare, and the rest of his family would be made fully aware of his despicable behaviour. They would pay a heavy price on his behalf.

Chapter 31

Shah interview

The caged lights burned brightly in the small interrogation room, protected by metal mesh to stop anyone breaking the glass. The bulbs cast an unyielding glare on the metal table that separated DCI Knowles from Ahmed Shah. His brief, Alan Williams was sitting with an air of superiority around him. The atmosphere was thick with tension, a combative standoff waiting to explode. Shah was sweating profusely, an acrid smell emanating from him.

Knowles leaned forward, his expression unreadable, as he reviewed the notes in front of him. DC Clark was sitting next to him, her eyes never moving from Shah.

'Mr. Shah,' Knowles began, his voice steady and composed, 'I want to start with where we found Jennifer's belongings.'

Ahmed sat quietly, his face a mask of anxiety. The shadows beneath his eyes hinted at sleepless nights, and he smoothed his shirt nervously.

'I've been advised to make a no comment interview and I've already spoken to the custody officers about that,' he replied, his voice low. 'I admit I had a friendship with Jennifer Simmons but that is all it was. I have no knowledge of the items you found.'

'You have told the custody sergeant that you won't answer any questions,' Knowles continued, 'but we need to explore this in detail regardless.'

'My client has made it clear he won't be answering questions...'

'He has but we'll be asking the questions anyway...' The brief shrugged and smiled. 'Jennifer Simmons was last seen at the bus stop on her way to school, and her jumper was found in a recycling bin just outside your shop. Can you explain that?'

'No comment.'

'Her training shoes were discovered next to that bin in a carrier bag,' Knowles said. 'Can you explain that?'

'No comment.'

'And a silver ring belonging to her was found in the back of your vehicle. Any explanation?'

'No comment.'

'These are serious associations with a murdered girl that you were having an affair with, Mr. Shah.'

'No comment.'

'We have a mobile phone with text messages to and from Jennifer's number, arranging to meet that morning, with a view to going to the flat above the kebab shop for sex?'

'It wasn't about sex...'

'What was it about?

'No comment.'

'You arranged to meet a fifteen-year-old girl to go to an empty flat, what were you going to do when you got there, Mr Shah?'

'No comment.'

'Watch homes under the hammer and bargain hunt?'

'Please don't be facetious, detective,' Williams said.

'Instruct your client to recognise the facts as we know them,' Knowles countered. 'Let's not fuck about pretending there was no relationship.'

'Okay, okay but I didn't meet her,' Ahmed said, angrily. His brief looked at him, warning him to remain silent. 'When I approached the bus stop, she was talking to a police officer.' He tapped his fingers on the desk to reinforce his statement. 'I drove off, for obvious reasons.'

'Where did you go?'

'What?'

'When you drove off, where did you go?'

'McDonalds,' Ahmed said. 'I bought two lattes and went back but she was gone.'

'Did you pay cash or card?'

'Card,' Ahmed said. His brief whispered in his ear and Ahmed nodded and took a drink of water.

'So, we can verify that?'

'Of course.'

'How long did it take you to buy coffee and return?'

'Ten minutes at most.' Shah shifted in his chair, every movement a sign of discomfort. 'I just want to say, I didn't meet her that morning or take her things. I— I didn't harm her. We were just... friends, that's all.'

'Just friends?'

'Yes.'

'You sent her a message, 'a secret moment away from the prying eyes of the world.' Sounds intimate to me?'

'No comment.' His solicitor whispered in his ear and Shah nodded, eyes closed, breathing deeply. He looked stressed to the limit.

DCI Knowles regarded him thoughtfully.

'Okay. You were friends? How long was the 'friendship' going on?'

'Since the summer,' Ahmed confessed, lowering his eyes. 'We became friends. It started innocently.'

'Mr Shah...' Williams warned.

'They know we were friends,' Shah snapped. 'I'm not saying anything that they don't know...She was just so... different. I could talk to her. She understood me and we laughed all the time.'

'She was fifteen and she understood you?' Knowles scowled.

'Is that a question?' Williams asked. 'Because it sounds like sarcasm to me.'

'Did you have sex with her?' Knowles asked. 'That was a question.'

'No comment. You are making it sound dirty. It wasn't dirty.'

'I understand you may feel like that. But she was fifteen, and you are an adult,' Knowles pointed out, his tone hardening slightly. 'You have to realise it's wrong.'

'I know it seems wrong, but Jennifer was smart. She'd tell me she wanted to find herself, to escape her parents' rules. It was never just about... that. We cared for each other!' His voice was pleading, desperate for understanding. 'I didn't hurt her.'

'Mr Shah!' Williams said, holding up his hand. 'My advice is to say nothing. I must insist...'

'Caring for someone doesn't absolve you of your responsibilities, Mr. Shah,' Knowles replied sternly. 'Did your wife know about your friendship?'

'Of course, not!'

'Did you worry she would find out?'

'Mr Shah, do not answer that question.'

'No comment.'

'Okay, let's discuss your alibi. On the day she disappeared, you said you were at your shop from 11am to 6pm and then went home for a family event.'

'Yes, I was at work all day—' he started, but Knowles interrupted.

'And you have witnesses at the shop, correct?'

'Yes. Chris was working all day. Then I went home, and we had a dinner party, from about six thirty until eleven o'clock.'

'Your wife will be able to confirm that?' Knowles said, already knowing the answer.

'Yes. There were three families there, all of them can confirm I was home after work. I didn't leave.' He tapped the table again. 'I couldn't have harmed her; I didn't even know she was missing until the police came asking about her...' The desperation in his voice was palpable. 'I did not harm Jennifer. The last time I saw her, she was talking to a uniformed police officer.'

'I think it's been established that my client has a cast iron alibi for the day Jennifer Simmons went missing and that the items found at his business were spurious at best. I'm calling an end to this debacle and I suggest you take a long hard look at where your information came from in the first place,' Williams said. 'I want my client released without charge.'

OLIVIA, DCI KNOWLES, DS Hill and DS Clark were sitting around a desk in the operations room. The other detectives were away from their desks, trying to identify their victims and concluding the dig at Delamere.

'Shah's solicitor has demanded he's released without charge,' Knowles noted, his pen tapping rhythmically against the notepad. 'The PVPU are about to charge him for the Debby Barry girl, so this guy is wrong on so many levels. There are still too many questions in my opinion. Why was her ring found in his car?'

Hill hesitated, glancing at the table as if searching for answers within its surface. 'I don't think he killed her... she must have lost it. She took it off one day when they were hanging out.'

'Hanging out?' Knowles scoffed. 'Is that what we call it now?'

'I'm just saying, it's a cheap ring; maybe it simply fell off?'

'And what about the jumper? The training shoes?' Knowles pressed, narrowing his gaze.

'I think the man has his brains in his dick and he's a danger to young girls sexually, but I don't think he's a killer,' Olivia said. 'I spoke to his wife and she's a normal well-balanced businesswoman trying to support her family. She is also a victim in all of this.' Olivia paused. 'We don't know where the tip-off came from, and the journalist you spoke to will protect his source, but we have to assume someone else is involved. Someone else took Jennifer and the other victims, not Ahmed Shah.'

'Are you saying it was all planted?' Knowles asked.

'It's likely,' Olivia said, nodding. 'Which would indicate the killer was aware of their relationship.'

'Then he's familiar to the area and the people in it.'

'I think it's common knowledge that Jennifer was seeing a married man,' Clark said, 'and that it was Shah. Gossip like that spreads far and wide, half the city will know that by now.'

DCI Knowles leaned back, noting the sense in what his boss was saying. For a moment, the hardened stubbornness of the detective faltered, as clarity kicked in. As the weight of truth and acceptance hung heavy between them, DCI Knowles contemplated the gap between Ahmed's words and the evidence before him. He knew that unravelling this web would take more than spurious evidence and an anonymous tip-off. There was no substance behind it.

Chapter 32

2 weeks later-Simmons family

The Simmons household was full of family, friends and well-wishers. There were also some who had a hidden agenda. The downlights illuminated the grief-stricken faces gathered in the living room and multiple conversations were flowing at the same time. Pictures of Jennifer adorned the walls, smiling with an innocence that now felt hauntingly out of place. She looked like a teenage girl with her life in front of her, not a victim of grooming and sexual exploitation.

Her mother, Caroline, sat rigid on the edge of the sofa, her eyes a storm of sorrow and fury. She was dressed in a pink tracksuit and white fake Gucci trainers; her hair and makeup had been rushed. Her eyes were puffy and red from weeks of broken sleep and crying hysterically. She was beyond angry, hatred seeped through her bones. Ahmed Shah was the focus of her hate.

'Okay, everyone,' Caroline said, clapping to silence everyone. 'First of all, I want to thank you all for being here. Some of you have been involved from day one, searching for Jennifer and asking around the area for information.' She paused and her face darkened. 'It pains Dennis and I to admit that Jennifer was having an affair with one of those horrible bastards who run the shops on the roundabout. Paedophiles, every one of them. He's a thirty-year-old married man and Jennifer isn't the only underage girl he's been shagging.' She swallowed hard and wiped away a tear. 'You have all heard the police are investigating a grooming gang operating from there, some of you have daughters who have been violated by those fucking paedophiles and yet nothing is happening.'

'We don't know what's going on behind the scenes, Caroline.' Her mother, Joyce was far more balanced. 'I'm sure they know what they're doing.'

'You're wrong, Joyce. The police are doing fuck all as usual!' a cousin snapped,

'This has been going on for years, Joyce,' another woman said. 'I reported them when our Charlene was thirteen. It would have been her eighteenth birthday last week if it wasn't for the bastard who got her pregnant.' She glared around the gathering. 'We lost our daughter and granddaughter because she couldn't cope with the shame, and she took baby Toni with her.' She pointed towards the shops. 'They have no shame and enough is enough.'

'She's right,' Caroline agreed. 'We can't just sit here and do nothing, year after year!' Caroline's voice broke. 'Our children are being raped, abused and murdered and the police are doing nothing.' The gathering was silent but nodding heads agreed. Through the oppressive silence, her hands clenched into fists. 'That monster is out there, walking free, while our baby is in a box.'

Her husband, Dennis, stood across the room, hands shoved deep in his pockets, his face twisted in agony.

'I can't believe they let him go. The police should've done more. It adds insult to injury.'

'We need to make them stop abusing our daughters,' a cousin said, angrily. He was a steroid-built lump with a shaved head and poor tattoos. A teardrop inked onto his cheek had been done in prison. 'If the police won't stop them raping our kids, I fucking will. Who's with me?' Macca said with venom in his tone.

'Me!' a chorus of voices replied.

'You can't take the law into your own hands,' Joyce protested.

'Shut up, mum,' Caroline said, shaking her head. 'Your granddaughter was sexually exploited and murdered!'

'Don't you tell me to shut up...'

'Shut up! Macca is right,' Caroline insisted, swallowing hard against the wave of emotion. 'I can't let Jennifer's death be brushed aside while that paedo is walking around as if nothing has happened. It's time to take a stand!'

In the corner, Jennifer's older brother, Tom, scrolled through his phone, a glint of dark determination in his eyes. He was in his twenties and loved Jennifer as big brothers do.

'Look here,' he said, raising the device for everyone to see. 'People are angry and they're talking about this online. There's anger out there—people want justice for Jennifer.'

'Justice?' Dennis echoed; the word heavy with disgust. 'What kind of justice can we get by just posting online about it? We need to show them what happens to paedophiles when they harm our children. My daughter was raped. She wasn't old enough to consent to having sex with a man twice her age. If we do nothing, do you think they're going to stop chasing your daughters?'

'There are hundreds online who agree with us,' Tom said. 'We need to go there and fuck them up!'

The room buzzed with a new energy as Tom's idea began to take shape.

'We need a protest. We'll gather everyone who's of the same mind, people who are hurting, people who are feeling betrayed by the system.'

'And what do you propose to do?' Joyce asked, worried about the direction it was going.

'We'll go to that arcade of shops—they're all owned by Shah and his grooming gang. We'll fuck them up!' Dennis said.

'We need to fuck them up,' Tom repeated nodding, his fingers flying over the screen. 'A peaceful protest doesn't cut it. I can set up something much bigger on social media. We can reach out to local groups, who hate men like them and anyone who is interested in standing up to these paedophiles.'

'You mean racists,' someone warned. 'Be careful, Tom. They're a force beyond your control. They're angry at everything.'

'Anger is a good thing. Let's use this anger to our advantage,' Caroline urged, her voice growing stronger with each word. 'They need to see that we're not going to let Jennifer's murder go unpunished. We want them to know that we're watching. That we won't tolerate them touching our kids anymore!'

As the discussion evolved into a planning session, shadows loomed larger within the Simmons family. Paranoia and vengeance replaced the initial grief.

'What about Ahmed Shah?' Tom whispered to his uncles, who were plotting more than a protest. 'We need to fuck him up,' Tom added, his tone lowering to a conspiratorial whisper. 'What if... we took matters into our own hands? Make him pay for what he's done—him and the rest of them.'

Dennis' eyes gleamed. 'And what better way than to hit them where it hurts? If we could create chaos outside their shops as a distraction...give Shah what the bastard deserves.'

Caroline's expression sharpened, caught in the fervour of the moment. 'We could make a real statement. People will notice. They will join us; we just need to ignite the flames of their anger.'

'You do know that if we light this fire, we will not be able to control it,' an uncle said. 'It could get out of control very quickly.'

In hushed voices, the family began discussing the unthinkable.

'I think we burn them down,' Tom said, checking around him for people listening. 'My mates are a dab hand at making petrol bombs.'

'You're looking at serving time for that, Tom.'

'Jennifer had her life taken from her by that paedo.' Tom shrugged. 'He fucked my baby sister and put her in the forest in a hole in the ground. I'm already doing time, we all are...'

'I understand but...'

'If you want out, the front door is there.'

'Okay, okay.'

'If we cause enough destruction, they won't just ignore us anymore. We'll make them fear for their safety,' Tom suggested, the intensity of his words igniting something dark. 'It's payback time.'

'Maybe if we create enough of a scene, someone will get to Shah. He deserves to feel the same fear we're feeling right now,' Dennis said, the bitterness crawling into his tone. 'He should know the pain he's caused our family.'

The sadness of loss filled the shadows of the room, intertwining with an emerging resolve for retribution. They began to formulate their plan, sharing their frustrations while plotting their next steps in the digital space. Caroline and Tom created a social media group, inviting neighbours and like-minded individuals to join their cause of anger and mourning. It grew to over a hundred in less than an hour.

Hours turned into a chaotic blur as the family fuelled each other's resolve, stirring the pot of emotions with fervour. The possibility of a protest swelled into a volatile desire for vengeance, drawing in others who felt similarly over the injustice surrounding Jennifer's death.

Meanwhile, outside, the world continued unaware, the soft whispers of gathering storms brewing beneath the surface of a suburban community, as the funeral of young Jennifer approached. It was a tragic irony that in mourning their loss, they risked losing themselves in the darkness of their own intentions. And as they planned, a once innocent memory of their daughter began to transform into a rallying point for a cause that could spiral completely out of control.

Chapter 33

Bill's past

The living room was tidy for a change and the smell of stew cooking was also a welcome stranger. Bill and Hayley had been making a real effort to be better parents and Rosie and Gary were enjoying being their children for a change. The police and social services had been frequent visitors, which had helped the situation.

The living room was alive with the warmth of the evening sun streaming through the recently cleaned window, but an unmistakable tension hung in the air. The elephant in the room was Aunty Janine, who still hadn't resurfaced. Bill White sat at the edge of the worn-out armchair, his fingers nervously tracing the pattern of the fabric. Across from him, his wife Hayley watched with concern etched on her face, while Rosie and Gary, sat on the floor, absorbed in their mobile phones but aware of the undercurrents of their parents' conversation. They had been talking about Aunty Janine and the men who had bullied her into storing their drugs. It had been a huge talking point at school, alongside the stabbings on the bus. Gary was still being picked on for being a grass, but the teachers and Rosie were protecting him. He seemed to take things in his stride.

The police had no news, and Janine still hadn't been in touch. There had been no activity on her phone or bank account, which was an indication something sinister had happened to her. As time passed, they were more and more concerned, but her name was mentioned in whispers when the kids were out of earshot.

'Dad, are you okay?' Gary finally asked, breaking the silence that had settled around them. 'Are you worried?'

'Yes, son. I'm worried.'

'Do you think she's dead?'

'Gary!' Rosie said, punching his leg. 'What a thing to say...'

'It's okay, Rosie,' Bill said. 'It's what we all think really, isn't it?' No one answered but the silence spoke volumes. 'Even the police think she's dead. I can see it in their eyes when they come asking stupid questions.'

'Why do they keep asking them, if they're stupid?' Gary asked.

'You're the master of asking stupid questions,' Rosie said, laughing.

'You're the queen of Dickheadville,' Gary fired back.

'Behave, you two,' Bill said.

'Seriously, Dad. Why do they keep coming here?'

'Two reasons.' Bill took a deep breath, struggling to find the right words. The weight of his past had become a burden he could no longer keep hidden. 'Firstly, they are hoping she'll turn up here as we're the only family she has got and secondly, they think I know who has her and where she is.'

'Why do they think that?' Rosie asked.

'There's something I need to talk to you all about,' he began, glancing at Hayley, who nodded subtly, urging him to continue. 'You heard the police saying that I knew Bobby Allen?' The kids nodded.

'He is the one who bullied Aunty Janine,' Gary said, nodding.

'Shut up, genius,' Rosie said.

'When I was younger, I made some choices that weren't... well, they weren't the best. I got involved with some people who were bad news,' he admitted, his voice steady but heavy with the weight of his confession. 'Once you do something for these people and take money from them, they own you. Forever. They never let go,' Bill said.

Rosie, with curiosity in her eyes, leaned closer. 'I can't imagine where this is going.'

'So, what did Bobby Allan do?' Gary asked.

'He was a dealer, you know, in drugs and such. I didn't want to be part of it, but...there were pressures. People who didn't take 'no' for an answer.' Bill's memories began to surface, the pressure and fear that had driven him into a world he never intended to join but did. 'I left school with no qualifications and no prospects, and I had no money. Working for them was easy money and I could earn more in a week than the dole paid me in a year.'

'How much did you make?' Gary asked.

'Another stupid question.'

'I'm just asking...'

'Well don't. Dick.'

'Will you two have a day off,' Bill said, shaking his head. 'I'm trying to explain something important to you.'

'Explain why you worked with him if you didn't want to?' Hayley prodded gently, concern for her husband intertwining with the need for understanding for her children.

Bill's gaze dropped to the floor, fidgeting with the hem of his jeans.

'I was intimidated, scared, bullied, all the time.' Bill looked sad as he remembered the young man he had been. 'Bobby wasn't the boss, he worked for other men, Jack Milner and Dixie Dean, who were complete nutters. They still are complete nutters.'

'Wait a minute,' Rosie said standing up, hands on hips. 'Jack Milner and Dixie Dean are Jordan Milner and John Dean's fathers?'

'The guys who died on the bus?' Gary asked.

'Genius.'

'Dick.'

'Yes,' Bill nodded. 'I worked for them when I was young and gullible.'

'Fuck off, no way!' Rosie said, excited. 'You worked for the Diddy Men?'

'Rosie, don't swear, lovely,' Hayley said. 'You know I don't like to hear you swear.'

'You swear all the time,' Gary said.

'I'm an adult.'

'Yes, but fucking hell, mum,' Rosie flapped her arms. 'Dad was a Diddy Man, for fuck's sake.' She slapped Gary on the back. 'Dad was a Diddy Man!'

'Calm down, Rosie,' Bill said. 'Sit down and let me explain why this is relevant today.'

'Dad was a fucking Diddy Man,' she whispered excitedly in Gary's ear, making him laugh. Bill didn't look amused. 'Sorry, Dad.'

'I understand it's a shock,' Bill said, nodding. 'Anyway, I was at the bottom of the pecking order and Jack and Dixie ran the whole operation like tyrants. I knew I was going to end up dead or in jail, but I felt trapped. It went on for a few years, and I had money in my pocket, and nobody bothered me because of who I worked for. It was like being untouchable, no one messed with us. When I finally realised how deep I was in, it was too late.'

'What happened, dad?' Gary asked, his voice quavering as the seriousness of the conversation sunk in.

'I was arrested transporting a kilo of cocaine, but I didn't grass on anyone.' Bill looked at Gary. 'This is why I tell you to keep your mouth shut. They would have killed me, even in prison, so I did time for them. Jack got arrested for battering a rival with a crowbar and he ended up inside with me,' Bill replied, swallowing hard against the unease rising in his throat. 'I was scared for my life in there. Scared of Jack on the inside and Dixie and Bobby on the outside. When I was arrested, the police took the drugs and that meant that now I owed them for the drugs I lost, big time. Fifty thousand pounds big time.'

'You owed them fifty thousand pounds?' Gary said. 'Sick.'

'I worked for them doing shitty jobs when I came out and then I feigned illness, chronic, long-term, making me useless illness. I was unreliable and useless, or that's what I made them think.' Bill taped his temple with his forefinger. 'Eventually, they forgot about me until a few years ago when Bobby approached me.'

'What did he say to you?' Gary asked, with bated breath.

'He told me that they needed properties to store their product, and he reminded me that I owed Jack and Dixie. I told him that it was all in the past now. I have changed, and I'm not that person anymore and he seemed to be listening but a few months later, I found out Janine was storing gear for them and had taken money and drugs from them.' He shrugged. 'I was very young and stupid but even now, I owe them. Whatever I say, the police won't believe that I'm not still involved, even though, I've changed.'

Hayley leaned forward, her hand resting on Bill's knee, providing a touch of comfort.

'Bill, we know that you have changed. We believe you've changed. But... Janine's disappearance... People are talking and the police think those men are involved in her disappearance.'

'I know, and that's what worries me,' he said, his voice strained. 'You need to understand that my past has nothing to do with what's happened to Janine, but they will think it is. She has been missing for days, and it feels like everyone is looking at me as if I had something to do with it or that I know what happened. I would never—' Bill's frustration bubbled to the surface; his emotions raw. 'I would never hurt her...'

'But what if it is connected to them and they have her somewhere?' Rosie asked innocently, her young mind trying to piece together the puzzle. 'If you don't say anything, they will just keep her.'

'We don't know they have her, Rosie,' Bill said.

'What if people think you're involved again?' Gary asked. 'Can I tell my mates you were in the Diddy Men gang?'

'No, Gary,' Hayley said, angrily. 'Don't you dare tell anyone.'

'I don't think it's a huge secret but it's a period of my life that I don't speak about.' He paused. 'People can think what they want,' Bill stated sharply, then softened his tone. 'But I swear to you, I am trying to find Janine.'

'Have you asked Bobby Allen if he has taken her?' Rosie asked.

'Yes. I have.'

'And?'

'He assured me that he hasn't seen her since the explosion and that they didn't lose any product,' Bill explained. 'That means Janine doesn't owe them anything but an apology for causing a nuisance.'

'Then where is she?' Gary asked.

'I don't know but I don't think the police would believe me. I would never hurt her. She means the world to me but proving it to them is impossible.'

The room fell silent, the words settling like a heavy blanket. Hayley sighed; her eyes filled with empathy.

'We just want to protect you, love. The news is swirling with gossip. They don't care about the truth; they only want a story.'

'I'll find her. I have to,' Bill insisted, determination hardening his features. 'I won't let my past define who I am today. I'm your father, your husband, and I love my sister dearly. She deserves better than to be lost like this.'

'Dad,' Gary said softly, 'Maybe you should talk to the police and tell them that Bobby Allen said he hasn't seen her?'

'No.'

'They probably need your help to find her.'

'I've thought about it,' Bill replied, weighing the idea carefully. 'But they're already looking at me too closely. I don't want to give them any reason to suspect that I know anything.'

'But if you have information...' Hayley began cautiously.

'I don't know anything,' Bill interrupted, fear creeping back into his voice. 'I just don't want anything from my past pulling my family into the shit.'

'Do you believe Bobby Allen, dad?' Gary asked.

'No, son.'

'Do you think he's killed Aunty Janine?' Rosie asked. Bill nodded but didn't answer.

In the flickering light of the living room, tension morphed into unspoken fear. Rosie and Gary exchanged worried glances, the reality of their father's history creeping into their hearts. Bill felt their uncertainty, but he also felt the love that connected them all—an anchor in a tide of confusion.

'Promise us you'll do everything you can to find her,' Hayley urged, her voice firm yet soothing.

'I promise,' he vowed, grasping her hand tightly. 'I will not let my past take anyone else from me.'

As the discussion faded into silence again, Bill could only hope that he would find his sister soon. But even as he reassured his family, doubt lingered in the shadows—worries that the past he had fought so hard to escape might still have the power to return and snatch away everything he held dear.

THE SHADOWS OF THE dusk crept through the grimy windows of the warehouse that served as The Diddy Men's base of operations. The air inside was thick with tension, swirling around like smoke. The chaos still lingered from the recent explosion at one of their stash houses and the repercussions. Homemade explosives made the police very nervous. The presence of grenades made the police think a turf war was about to erupt.

Dixie Dean paced back and forth, the sound of his heavy boots echoing against the concrete floor as he clenched his phone tightly in his hand. He waited for Bobby Allen to answer.

'Hello Dixie, what's up?'

'Bobby,' he said, his tone low but edged with fury as the line connected. 'What the hell happened to Janine white?'

A moment of silence hung in the air before Bobby's voice came through, laced with the bravado that had always irked Dixie. 'I don't know, boss. She was taken away by the police at Coppice Hill, and I haven't heard anything from her since. I've been nowhere near her.'

Dixie's patience was wearing thin. 'You saying she just vanished randomly?'

'I don't know, Dixie.'

'You should fucking know,' Dixie snapped. 'Janine White was working for you. A vulnerable adult who could've blown our whole operation to bits if she talks and names people.'

'I told you; I wasn't there, and I haven't touched her!' Bobby barked back defensively. 'You think I'd put myself in a situation like that?'

'Yes, I do because you're a thick twat.' Dixie was becoming increasingly frustrated. 'The police are all over this and we don't need the attention, understand?'

'If she's missing, it's not my fault!'

'Not your fault?' Dixie snapped, stopping mid-pace to glare out at the faded graffiti that marked the walls of their territory. 'You're telling me that you had no idea, you're supposed to keep tabs on our people, Bobby. Do you understand what losing her could mean?'

'I didn't hurt her, Dixie. You know I wouldn't do that. Janine was just—she's not smart, but she's harmless and she won't grass,' Bobby responded, trying to sound more authoritative than nervous. "I wouldn't do anything to attract attention if I could help it.'

Loyalty was a fragile concept in their world, and Dixie felt a knot tighten in his chest.

'You better start being honest because if I find out you've done something stupid, just know that I won't be forgiving,' he warned, letting the implication of his threat linger. 'Now, find her. I want eyes on everywhere, and I want to know who if she has talked and is in witness protection.'

A pause on the other end made Dixie's heart race; the silence felt too long, too suspicious.

'I never thought of that,' Bobby said.

'That's because you're a thick twat, I told you.'

'Okay, okay. I'll get right on it. I swear, I'm not covering anything up... I don't want to end up in your bad books,' Bobby said, his voice now trembling slightly.

'Then prove it. Call everyone in our circle, and I want to hear how they reacted to the blast. There better not be any loose ends, Bobby. And if you see her, you don't let her slip away. Bring her back, we don't need the Dibble looking at us, understand?'

'Yeah, yeah, I understand. I'll find her,' Bobby responded, the urgency sparking in his voice. 'Just... don't go off on me, alright? It wasn't me. I would never—'

'Stop right there, Bobby,' Dixie interrupted, his patience fraying. 'I don't want to hear excuses. Just do your job and make it look like this didn't happen.'

As the call ended, Dixie threw his phone onto a nearby table, causing it to slide precariously close to the edge. He felt the heat of anxiety churn in his gut, knowing Janine's disappearance could spell disaster for The Diddy Men. She may be vulnerable, but she possessed knowledge that could unravel everything they had built. His mind raced as he considered options. If Janine had been taken, it was likely by someone looking to make a statement—someone who knew the game and wanted to exploit the chaos. He couldn't afford to show weakness, not now.

Dixie moved toward the back of the warehouse, where a map of their territory was pinned to the wall, red circles marking locations of their operations. He stared at it, plotting his next steps, calculating risks and assets.

'Bobby better not screw this up,' he muttered to himself, a grim determination hardening in his chest. 'Because if she's talked and is in witness protection, it'll be the last mistake he ever makes.'

Chapter 34

Olivia/ Knowles

Olivia leaned back in her chair. Her desk lamp was illuminating the cluttered surface. Files were scattered everywhere—case notes, photographs, and reports from a grooming investigation into the group of men operating various businesses around the Village Roundabout in Huyton. The low hum of the city outside was pierced only by occasional sirens as vehicles left the car park below, a reminder of the chaos that lurked just beyond her office door. DCI Knowles approached; his expression serious as he held a steaming cup of coffee in his hand.

'The DCI from the Matrix team is on line one.' He shook his head. 'Mark Richards, I think he said. You're going to love this.'

'What do Matrix want?'

She picked up her phone, glancing at the screen. The name "DCI Mark Richards" flashed prominently. He was the head of the Matrix OCG team, a unit she respected but one that always brought its own set of complications. Taking a deep breath, Olivia answered.

'Detective Mann speaking,' she said, her tone professional but slightly cautious. 'How can I help?'

'Olivia, it's Mark Richards from Matrix, we have met before on the Cronton case a few years back,' the voice on the other end was deep and authoritative, yet there was an underlying tension that caught Olivia's attention. 'Do you remember?'

'Lisa Langton,' Olivia said. 'And a very big shotgun. A Mossberg 500, pump action, if I remember rightly.'

'That's the one.'

'What's on your mind?' She twirled a pen between her fingers, her intuition forming a knot in her stomach.

'I need you to pull back on your investigation into the businesses on the Village Roundabout,' he stated firmly. 'Especially Ahmed Shah.'

'Pull back?'

'Yes. All the way back.'

'He was having an affair with a teenage girl who was murdered,' Olivia said. 'How far back do you think I can go?'

'I know why you're looking at him.'

'You know?'

'Yes.'

'We have to investigate it, obviously.' Olivia's brows furrowed. 'You know I can't back off until we're happy he's not the killer.'

'He's not the killer,' Richards said. 'We've been following four of them for six months.'

'What?'

'If he was a serial killer, we would have noticed.'

'Fucking hell,' Olivia said, shocked. 'I'm not sure if I'm pleased about that or not!'

'It saves you wasting your time.'

'Why are Matrix looking at Shah?' Olivia asked.

'Have you seen his house?' Richards asked, laughing. 'You don't get that rich selling mobile phones in Huyton.'

'Well, I'm shocked.'

'The entire family is involved; all the shops are fronts to launder money. These guys aren't just running pizza shops and taxis; we have evidence tying them to a much larger operation in that area'

'That area of the city is run by the Diddy Men, right,' Olivia said, intrigued. 'Are they in cahoots?'

'Absolutely. Olivia, trust me on this,' Mark explained, urgency creeping into his voice. 'We're close to finalising a case against the

Diddy Men gang and Shah and his cronies. Their operation is rooted in those businesses—believe me, there's more going on than meets the eye on that arcade. But we can't have you stepping on our toes while we're finishing up.'

'I think we can withdraw to a degree, but this is part of a wider investigation, as you know.'

'Look, I understand your position,' Mark's voice softened, an effort to bridge the gulf between them. 'But you need to give us space. One wrong move against Shah and we could lose everything.'

'You know he's being charged with impregnating a fourteen-year-old?'

'I've spoken to PVPU,' Richards said. 'They're holding off until we've closed the trap.'

'Wow. Okay,' Olivia said, nodding. 'I had a chat with his wife at their house. I feel for that woman.'

'Ushna Shah?' Richards asked, laughing. 'Don't feel sorry for her.'

'Why not?'

'She's the brains behind it all,' Richards said. 'Ushna is well and truly in charge of the Shah family. She met Milner and Dean through her business connections in the city and they've been in bed together for over five years.'

'You're kidding me?'

'Not at all,' Richards said. 'She's the driving force behind that business. Ahmed Shah is simply a lapdog, and our information tells us she's furious that the grooming that's been going on has put them under the spotlight.'

'Okay, I'll speak to the ACC. No wonder Shah has been so squirrely.' Olivia paused, weighing his words, knowing that it made perfect sense to leave Shah alone. He had the best alibi on the planet. He had been under surveillance for months. 'Do you have a timeframe when you're going to move?'

'Soon, hence the call.'

A silence stretched between them, heavy with the unspoken tension of their respective duties. Olivia could hear the distant thrum of the traffic below and the faint chatter of voices from the operations room.

'We'll leave Ahmed Shah to you.'

'Fair enough, thank you.' Richards replied, a hint of relief evident in his voice. 'I appreciate your understanding. I'll keep you in the loop on developments.'

'Thanks, Mark, and thanks for being so honest about it,' she replied, but the unease still rippled through her. 'Be careful.'

The line disconnected, and Olivia placed her phone down, staring at the files scattered before her. She hoped Richards was right, that they could take down Ahmed Shah and the Diddy Men without risking more lives in the process. But the city was littered with the remnants of stories that ended too soon, the kind of stories birthed from the shadows.

'What do you think of that?' Knowles asked, shaking his head.

'That is a real headfuck,' Olivia said, sighing. 'But it saves us hundreds of man hours.'

'How?'

'They've had Shah under surveillance for six months.'

'No...'

'Yes.'

'What the fuck?' Knowles muttered.

'We need to know where that tip-off came from because the chances are it came from Jennifer's killer or someone close to him,' Olivia said. 'Bring in that journalist and put some pressure on him. We need the source.'

'What if the source is good and Shah is involved along with others?'

'He's been followed for six months,' Olivia reminded him. 'I believe he's got to be looked at, but he's caught up in something far larger than himself and we need to focus our attention elsewhere.'

Chapter 35

The riot. 3-weeks later.

THE AIR WAS THICK WITH tension as crowds gathered in front of the Village Roundabout, a row of shops that was the bustling hub of community life. It was a slow build at first, small groups of people, seemingly going about their business, shopping, chatting and doing no harm. Larger groups of skinheads began to arrive, sporting swastika tee-shirts and 16-hole Dr Martin boots, and their motives were clear. Their arrival triggered the change in atmosphere from a positive protest to violent disorder.

Signs and banners waved high, slogans scrawled in bold letters, demanding 'justice for Jennifer Simmons' and 'paedos out'. The mood shifted violently between genuine protest and an undercurrent of hostility.

The air was electric, charged with the fervour of voices unified in anger and grief. Tom Simmons felt the pulse of the protest around him—honks of support from passing cars, chants echoing off the brick facades of nearby shops, and the palpable tension that simmered in the hearts of those gathered. Dressed in a dark hoodie to blend in with the throng, he stood slightly behind his father, Dennis, whose presence seemed both a shield and a burden. He was completely focused on the mobile phone shop.

Jennifer, Tom's younger sister, had been the light of their family, her laughter ringing like music through their small home. The past few months had been a blur of sorrow and indignation since her murder and the man suspected of committing the heinous act, Ahmed Shah, owned the mobile phone shop just a few steps away from the chaotic demonstration. He could almost taste his hatred for the man, and he was only yards away, within reach.

Every chant calling for justice felt personal; their loss was etched into the fabric of the day, fuelling an inferno within both father and son. Revenge was driving them into blind rage.

'There he is,' Dennis muttered, his voice a low growl as his narrow gaze fixed on the shop window.

'We need to fuck him up!' Tom's heart raced, instinctively glancing at the window framed by garish posters advertising the latest smartphones. Ahmed Shah could be seen moving among the shelves, indifferent to the storm brewing outside. 'Look at him in there as if nothing has happened. Today, you pay,' he shouted.

They waited patiently as the numbers of protesters grew. Hundreds had arrived and the protest enveloped them, a thick crowd swaying under the weight of anger and frustration. But for Tom and Dennis, it was more than a mere protest—it was a chance for reckoning. They weren't there for the slogans on colourful signs; they were there for justice, however twisted their path toward it.

'I say we go now,' Tom said. His uncle and cousins nodded in agreement.

'Stay close,' Dennis ordered, his tone leaving no room for argument. The intensity in his eyes mirrored a plan that they both had kept buried, simmering beneath the surface. Around them, other relatives whispered among themselves, eyes darting towards Tom and Dennis, understanding the unspoken pact forming among them. With a surge of adrenaline, Tom took a deep breath and nodded.

'Let's fuck him up.' They fist-bumped their shared resolve, an unbreakable bond forged in shared tragedy.

'Now!' Dennis barked, the signal barely audible over the rising roar of the crowd.

The men moved as a unit, pushing through the throng toward the shop. Outside, emotions ran high, the air thick with empathy for the Simmons family, but inside, it was a different atmosphere—a quiet oblivion surrounded Ahmed Shah, who seemed blissfully unaware of the storm about to engulf him.

The group burst through the door of the mobile phone shop, the jingle of the bell above scarcely registering against the tumult outside. Customers turned, confusion etched across their faces, morphing into shock as they confronted the intense focus of the Simmons' party.

'Shah! You fucking paedo!' Dennis's voice sliced through the air. 'This man is a paedophile, and he murdered my daughter, but the police let him go!'

A handful of customers left the shop in a hurry.

'I didn't harm Jennifer,' Shah said, frightened. 'I was here all day; the police know it wasn't me!'

'You were abusing my daughter!' Dennis growled, running behind the counter. He punched Shah in the face, knocking him to the ground and followed up with a kick in the ribs. Tom felt the heat of his father's fury and joined in, kicking and punching the man on the ground. Shah found the strength to rise and run towards the rear of the shop, the Simmons men behind him.

Before Shah could reach the back door, Tom dashed forward, tackling Shah to the ground. The other men quickly joined in, dragging the bewildered suspect toward the rear exit. The sound of his protests faded, overtaken by the chants outside, as if the world had no interest in the violence taking place within those walls.

'Paedos out, paedos out, paedos out!' the crowd chanted in unison. The tension reached fever pitch, and a window was smashed with a brick.

'Get his keys,' Dennis said. Tom took them from Shah's pocket and opened the back door. They dragged him outside.

'Please, I didn't hurt her, honestly, I didn't!'

'She was a baby, and you were fucking her, you're a horrible twat,' Tom said. 'You deserve everything coming to you, fucking paedo.'

'She was my friend; I didn't hurt her.' Tom punched him in the face, breaking his nose. A second blow knocked his front teeth out. He spat them onto the ground with a mouthful of blood and phlegm. 'Please, stop...'

'Put him in that,' Tom said, gesturing to a blue wheelie bin. 'Head first.'

In the cramped backyard, they heaved Ahmed into the filthy wheelie bin, the sound of metal against metal reverberating through their minds. Tom's heart raced and a primal fear flickered in the back of his mind, battling against the surge of rage and need for vengeance. Shah struggled but they lifted him easily, tipping him upside down.

'Hold him!' Dennis shouted, his face a mask of fury. Tom struggled but compelled by the shared grief and determination, he pressed forward, forcing Shah's head downward, stuffing him headfirst into the bin. His arms were pinned to his sides. The man's muffled gasps were drowned out by the chants echoing from the streets. He was unable to move his upper body, and he screamed like a child, begging for mercy. His legs kicked like a man possessed, finding nothing but air.

'Are we really doing this?' Tom's uncle screamed, but he was silenced by the look of madness in Tom's eyes, fuelled by the memory of his sister.

'Fucking right we are,' Tom shouted, pouring petrol from a plastic milk carton that he had washed out the night before. The stinging fumes filled the air and Shah's screams reached a new level of desperate, realising that he was being doused in a highly flammable liquid. 'How does that feel, Shah you dirty cunt?' Tom shouted. 'How does it feel to be fucked, Shah?'

'Please.!..Please! Please! Please...'

Dennis stepped forward, pulling a petrol bomb from the depths of his coat; the liquid inside gleamed ominously in the dim light of the yard. He ignited it with a flick of a lighter.

'Justice for Jennifer!' Dennis roared, lifting the bomb high. Tom's stomach twisted; he wanted to object, to run, but the world spun into chaos, adrenaline coursing through him as his father hurled the petrol bomb into the bin.

The explosion of flames erupted, a roar of fire that consumed everything, including their sanity. The acrid smell of smoke filled the alley, mixing with the smell of Shah burning and the screams of agony and horror from him in his dying seconds. The men surrounding the wheelie bin watched, mesmerised. For a fleeting moment, as the fire danced and flickered violently, Tom thought he heard him say sorry, but it was unlikely. The fire burned and spread to other plastic bins and leapt onto the storage shed, which ignited, the roof ablaze, illuminating shadows of regret and dread.

'Run!' Dennis shouted, snapping Tom out of his paralysis.

They bolted back through the shop, tossing another petrol bomb behind the counter. It exploded with a whoosh, and they ran out of the front door into the crowd, into the mass of protesters, weaving through the mass, the cries of those demanding justice acting as their cover. The chaos outside washed over them as they melted into the crowd—a wave of anger and sorrow, each step pulling them further away from the scene of unspeakable horror they had created.

Tom felt a mix of exhilaration and dread. Just beyond the riotous voices, the reality of what they had done began to settle in, gnawing at his conscience. But in that moment, engulfed in the flames of his family's vengeance, he felt only one dictated truth: a terrible justice had been served, no matter the cost.

Bill White stood at the fringes of the crowd, anxiety gnawing at his stomach as he observed the energy bubbling around him. He had come merely to support the grieving Simmons family but felt the mounting pressure seep into his bones. Beside him, Hayley clutched Rosie and Gary close, her eyes wide as she surveyed the escalating situation. The sound of breaking glass and an explosion at the back of the mobile phone shop, silenced the crowd for a second but then a huge cheer erupted.

'Why are they cheering?' Gary asked, frightened. He was being pushed and shoved in the crowd. 'What's happening, Dad?' his young voice barely audible above the shouts and chants.

'I don't know, son. We're here to support the protesters, but this is turning nasty,' Hayley replied, forcing a smile to reassure him, but her heart raced in uncertainty. She was knocked over in a crush.

'Mum!' Gary shouted. He tried to pull her up and Bill helped.

'We need to get out of here!' Bill said. As the crowd surged forward again, the chants morphed into a wild roar. 'Justice for Jennifer!' they shouted, hands waving fervently in the air. The atmosphere, initially charged with resolve, had twisted into something far darker.

Suddenly, a loud crash echoed through the square as a group of protesters pushed their way toward the mobile phone shop. A few figures broke away from the main crowd, and within moments, the glass front of the shop shattered under the weight of their fury. Bill's heart sank as he saw what was happening. Bricks were thrown through the windows of the upstairs flats. The sound of breaking glass filled the air.

'Please, this is not what we came for!' he called out, but his voice was drowned out by the clamour.

Within moments, a line of flames shot up from the interior of the shops, lighting the sky in an orange glow. A gas supply had ignited, creating a plume of dancing flames. The crowd gasped collectively, shock quickly morphing into eerie excitement. They had crossed a line, and Bill watched in horror as the once hopeful protest transformed into something violent and uncontrollable.

'Hayley! Let's get the kids out of here!' he shouted, urgency flashing in his eyes. 'We need to get out of the crowd!'

But it was too late. The chaos spread like wildfire. The off-licence across the pavement was being ravaged, shelves overturned, and bottles smashed as looters rushed inside to seize whatever they could find.

Sirens blared in the distance, the sound of approaching police swirling into the chaos, but as the first units arrived, they were met with an overwhelming scene. Flames danced aggressively from the mobile phone shop, illuminating the faces of those who once stood for justice but now fended off a line between catalyst and criminal. The first fire engine arrived but the flames were climbing higher, and the fire had a hold on the entire row of shops.

'Stand back!' shouted a police officer as he attempted to push the crowd back. 'Move away from the area!'

But the crowd was lost, caught up in the adrenaline of destruction. Some shouted for more chaos; others tried to reason with their fellow protesters, but sanity was a fleeting memory now. More officers arrived, forming a barrier to contain the escalating situation, but the damage had already been done.

Bill felt Hayley's breath quicken beside him as the police officers struggled to gain control.

'We need to go, now!' he insisted, gripping her arm tightly. But before they could move, a burst of flames erupted from the mobile phone shop, forcing everyone to take a step back. The heat radiated against their skin, a reminder of just how easily things could turn dangerous. Rosie clung to Hayley, tears brimming in her eyes, while Gary tugged at his father's sleeve.

'What's happening, Dad?' he quivered.

'It's going to be okay, but we need to move away from here,' Bill assured him, though he was uncertain himself.

Behind them, screams erupted as a group of looters spilled out of the off-licence, arms laden with stolen goods. Shattered glass crunched underfoot, and tensions continued to rise as individuals fought among themselves for perceived scraps of justice. Two Asian men were being kicked like ragdolls on the floor inside. The windows were smashed, and a petrol bomb was tossed into the kebab shop, another into the pizza place. Each explosion received deafening applause as the crowd fed on the madness.

The police moved strategically, deploying multiple units while trying to disperse the growing crowd. Water cannons were prepared as officers shouted commands amidst the chaos that had turned what should have been a moment of mourning into a visceral confrontation with anger and desperation.

Before Bill could make a move, a second wave of flames erupted from the shop, sending a shower of sparks that lit up the early evening sky like fireworks. The sound of smashing glass and shouted obscenities filled the air, weaving together a tapestry of turmoil woven with devastation.

As he held his family close, they began to move away, leaving behind the flames that swallowed the shops and their hopes of a peaceful protest in a roaring inferno. The image of burning buildings and chaos would haunt him, a stark reminder of how grief and despair can twist intentions into nothing but ruin and ashes.

Part two. Chapter 36

12 -months later

GARY WHITE WATCHED from the shadows of a narrow alley, its walls crusted with old posters and graffiti, the remnants of a forgotten world where bands couldn't advertise online, and bill posters were king. He had been told, time and again, to stay away from the partially rebuilt row of shops that loomed just ahead because of a grooming gang that operated in the area before the riots, but curiosity had gotten the better of him. Some of the businesses had reopened but under new owners as the Shah family had been killed or locked up. Three of them had died the day of the riots, one burned to death and two were kicked unconscious and died in hospital from their injuries. No one was ever charged with their murders, but twenty-two men and four women went to jail for rioting, six of them from the Simmons family.

Gary was following Rosie because she was dressed up and looked like she was on the pull. A girl from school, called Suzie had arranged a get together which had become big news on social media, and everyone was talking about it. It was a party on the green by the woods for a sixteenth birthday, so technically there was no alcohol allowed but because it was in the woods, there would be no adults to police the event. Everyone knew the 'get together' would become an outdoor party and there would be underage drinking, smoking and whatever else happened. His older sister, Rosie, was already out of the house on her way there, and when Rosie was involved, things were bound to get interesting.

She had been told not to have anything to do with the men who owned the shops now, but she did what she liked. His dad tried his best to guide her, but she was a wild one and liked to party. If she knew he was following her, she would go bonkers, so he stayed hidden, moving like a shadow from building to building.

As he peeked out of the alleyway, he saw her sitting on a low wall outside one of the shops, her long brown hair cascading down her shoulders, shimmering in the late afternoon sun. Rosie was so pretty and all the lads at school fancied her. Beside her was a girl he didn't instantly recognise — older and with an air of confidence that made Gary's stomach twist in knots. Then he heard someone calling her Amber and the penny dropped. Amber Dean.

He had heard whispers about her in school, tales of her reckless escapades and the social clout she held over the other kids because of who her father was. She was Dixie Dean's younger daughter, and she had been talking to Rosie for months. At first, Amber wanted to hear what had happened to her brother on the bus, that day, but over time they had become friends too. She attracted older boys and young men who had left school, and Gary was worried about Rosie because she looked older than she was. As he watched, Amber stood and started twerking to music coming from her phone. She was sexy. Very sexy.

'Who does she think she is?' Gary muttered under his breath, instinctively fiddling with the hem of his T-shirt to hide his erection. 'She's a cocktease,' he said to himself, but he couldn't take his eyes off her. A group of older lads wolf whistled as they walked by, and her antics became more animated. Rosie was crying with laughter.

He could tell Rosie idolised her; that was worrying enough, and he felt uneasy spying on them. He shouldn't be there at all. He had been forbidden to go there alone, a hangover from that terrible day of the riots. His parents were traumatised by the experience.

As he watched, he wondered what his sister was doing with someone as old as Amber. She seemed to be growing up too quickly. It would only end in tears. He guessed they were probably going to the woods for the party. Just as he thought it, they set off along the parade towards the green and the woods beyond. There were several groups of people gathered on the picnic benches, and the girls sat with some of them for a few minutes until the other girls got up and left, wobbling and giddy from alcohol, leaving Amber and Rosie on the bench.

Suddenly, his attention shifted as he noticed a male figure to his right. It was the uniformed figure of PC Martins approaching them. He would recognise him anywhere as he was a regular visitor to the Whitehouse. In his uniform and shiny boots, he was a handsome sight. Gary got the vibes from Rosie that she fancied him and likewise from the policeman. He was always flirty with her, and it made him feel uncomfortable. Gary had seen the way Martins looked at her, especially her arse. He had seen him looking at her, his eyes lingering too long. She called him George now, so did his mum and dad as if he was a family friend. It did Gary's head in, if he was honest but he didn't like any blokes going near his sister; he was protective of her. He listened to his mates and their older brothers talking about their conquests and he didn't want to think of Rosie being fingered or sucking someone's dick. It made him feel angry at the thought, although he wanted to have sex with other girls, but he didn't want his sister doing it. It didn't make sense, but it did...sort of...

PC Martins walked across the green and headed towards the duo, a friendly smile plastered across his face. Gary's instincts were to dislike him, but he knew everyone else in the family liked him. PC Martins sat down next to the girls, leaving a respectful distance between them while still making himself approachable to anyone passing by. He listened as they chatted, occasionally laughing at something Amber said. Rosie, her laughter ringing out like bell chimes, looked entirely at ease. For a moment, the tension released its grip on Gary, and he knew it was pointless worrying about her. She was big enough to look after herself and PC Martins was a good police officer—always looking out for the kids on the estate.

The laughter faded into a low murmur, and Gary walked further into the shadows between the buildings, but he felt a stirring of unease as if something bad was about to happen. There was something besides his curiosity bothering him, a gnawing fear that he couldn't quite shake off. He wanted to stay and watch but he wanted to go and be at home too, torn between watching Rosie and making sure she was safe and being warm, playing on his PlayStation. He was on unfamiliar terrain, spying on his sister, it was something he shouldn't be doing. Just then, a noise erupted from behind him, and he turned in a panic, to see a group of lads he didn't like.

'Gary White, you little shite!'—the angry call of older teenagers, he knew from school, but they didn't like him either. They moved like a pack of dogs always snapping at people and being dickheads, their abuse and laughter booming along the alleyway. As they turned the corner, the rest of the pack saw him too.

'Look, it's Gary the grass!' one boy yelled, spotting him with eyes gleaming like a shark detecting prey. He started running towards him. 'Let's cut his tongue out!'

Instinct kicked in and Gary ran. He turned, heart pounding, and broke into a sprint. He could almost feel the ground shudder beneath him as the pack raced after him, their jeers echoing in the alleyway. He felt like he was running through treacle, unable to accelerate as fast as he needed to. They were gaining ground quickly.

'Come here, you little grass.'

'Get him!'

Gary White darted through the narrow alleyway, his heart pounding in sync with his hurried footfalls. Dark graffiti-covered walls loomed on either side; the remnants of a once-bustling shopping arcade now turned into a maze of shadows. He could hear them behind him gaining ground all the time, the taunting shouts of the older boys echoing off the brick facades. They were all rough and a lot tougher than he was and they had a reputation for cutting people with penknives. If they caught him, they would hurt him.

'Get back here, Grass!' one of them yelled, the sneer laced with venom. Gary was all too aware of what they meant. He wished he had never picked up the knife on the bus and told the police the name of the lad who dropped it, convinced that it was the right thing to do. Now, he was paying the price.

As he rounded a corner, Gary glanced back. There they were, a pack of eight lads, their faces twisted in anger, gaining on him with each fleeting second. Panic surged, urging him to run faster. His legs burned, but the adrenaline muted the pain. He needed to lose them.

Gary spotted an opening—an old railway track that ran parallel to the alleyways. It was a dangerous choice, but he had no time to think through his options. He veered left, hopping over a pile of debris and landing awkwardly on the rusty tracks. The ground felt stable beneath him, but the air was thick with the scent of rust and decay.

'Don't let him get away!' one of the boys barked, his voice closer now, ringing in Gary's ears like a death knell. The chase was far from over and his lungs were burning.

Gary sprinted along the tracks, the sound of his breath harsh and ragged, his shoes clattering against the weather-worn metal. Old wooden beams lined the sides, partially hidden by tall weeds and broken glass. He eyed a tunnel up ahead, knowing it was a gamble. If he could make it through without being caught, he might slip away. It was like running into the pit of hell. He plunged into the darkness, the walls closing in as he passed beneath the earth. The sounds of the boys' shouts faded slightly, obscured by the echoing walls. In the gloom, desperation flooded his mind. He strained to hear any footfalls behind him, each heartbeat a reminder he was still being pursued.

'Where are you, Gary Shite?' The mocking voice echoed ominously in the tunnel, chilling him to the bone. 'You think you can run forever?'

Suddenly, panic filled him anew as he reached a fork in the tunnel. The roof of one had collapsed and there was no way through, the tunnel was a dead end. He had to act. He spotted a narrow ledge that hugged the side of the wall, the dim light from the end of the tunnel barely illuminating it. With a surge of courage, he scrambled onto it, pressing himself against the damp stone. He could hear the boys approaching, their laughter cruel and sharp, spurring him to silence his terrified breaths.

'Come on, mate! We just want to talk to you!' one boy called out, a sinister undertone in the way he spoke. Gary bit his lip, forcing himself to stay still. If they found him, it would be over. He could already imagine the jibes and taunts, the bruises and beating that would follow.

He heard the boys enter the tunnel, their voices echoing as they split up. Gary's heart raced in a different way now—fear merging with a stubborn hope that they might fuck off and leave him alone. Or were they determined to make him pay for what he had said?

Moments stretched like hours until, at last, he heard their footsteps retreating. They were further down the tunnel now, arguing among themselves, their attention distracted. Adrenaline surged once more. This was his chance. As quietly as he could manage, he slipped back onto the tracks, carefully navigating to the exit of the tunnel. Gary glanced back just in time to see the silhouettes of the boys; their figures illuminated by the faint light from outside as they huddled together.

With a final burst of energy, he bolted toward the end. The tunnel opened to a derelict yard—a vast expanse of weeds and remnants of old train carriages. He skidded to a halt, gauging his surroundings. A fence loomed high on the far side, the only escape route.

He could hear them again, closer now as they regrouped. 'He went this way! Find him!'

Fear erupted into panic once more. Gary dashed toward the fence, the thorns of the underbrush biting at his legs, his breaths coming in ragged gasps. He was nearly at the fence when he heard them again, voices sharp and urgent.

'Don't let him climb!'

A stone whistled past his head, cracking against the fence panel. He leapt, grabbing hold of the rough wood, scrabbling for a foothold. Fingers clawing at the splintered surface, he pulled himself up, launching over the top without looking back. The world fell silent for an agonising heartbeat; then he landed hard on the other side.

Rolling to his feet, Gary took off again, not slowing until the sounds of his pursuers faded completely. He burst out onto a quiet street, the cool air filling his lungs, allowing clarity to seep in. He stumbled into the safety of the interior of a nearby shop, pressing his back against the cool glass door, chest heaving in exhaustion. Gary realised he had escaped, at least for now, but the reality of his choices lurked ominously in the back of his mind. He might have evaded them tonight, but the fear of what would come next weighed heavily on him. The world outside was full of shadows, and he knew they wouldn't stop hunting him that easily. He waited a few minutes and poked his head out of the door. The pack were just across the road.

'There he is, little grass!'

'Don't let him get away!' they shouted, their voices a mix of anger and amusement, the thrill of the chase coursing through their veins.

Adrenaline surged as Gary darted into the open street, dodging past startled pedestrians. He didn't look back. He couldn't. Home was just ahead, safety a few more strides away.

'Keep running to the Shitehouse, Gary, you little grass!'

As he reached his front porch, he used his key to open the door and then slammed it behind him, breathing heavily. The laughter of the boys faded outside, leaving behind a chilling silence that filled the air of his home. Gazing through the window, he peered back into the world he had just escaped, safe for now. The pack retreated, looking for mischief elsewhere. The world outside frightened him, it was a scary place, and Rosie was out there somewhere.

ROSIE COULD SEE HER breath as she stumbled over a tree root. She was struggling to understand where she was and why she was there. The air was cold in the dense woods, a sharp reminder of winter's grip on the weather. Leaves crunched underfoot as Rosie staggered through the underbrush, her heart pounding in rhythm with the frantic thumping of the pulse in her head, which felt like it might explode at any second. Confusion clouded her mind, fogging the memories of the night so far. It had started well but had spiralled out of control quickly. She felt drunker than she had ever been, beyond the dizziness of a few ciders or a small bottle of vodka. Faces flickered at the edges of her thoughts—laughing, dancing, music pulsating, the bassline thumping—then darkness, the kind that seeped into the brain, numbing everything, wiping out all control over her own body.

'Amber!' she called out, her voice trembling. Panic surged as she realised her friend was missing. The last clear memory of the night was the warmth of Amber's hand in hers as they danced around the fire, a circle of shadows and flickering lights. Rosie shivered at the thought of her friend.

Where could she be?

Why did she feel so wasted?

As she wandered deeper into the woods, her vision began to settle into focus for a moment, but the dread in her stomach tightened. She felt the cold dampness on her skin, the rough bark of a tree digging into her bare back, nettles stinging her ankles and shins. There were hints of pain that pulsed through her thighs, reminding her of something distinctly wrong. Very wrong indeed.

She brushed her fingertips against her skin and flinched at the tender bruising, dark stains wrapped around her legs like unwelcome spiders' webs. She felt cramp in her lower stomach and bruised lower down.

WTF was happening.

Flashes of the night crept back—laughter from the party, a drink handed to her, but by who? She couldn't see their face, the memory gone. The way the world had started to tilt was sickening, a spinning mess of sound and nausea. Reality had warped into a melted world, like slow motion sights and sounds.

The taste of something bitter and strange lingered at the back of her throat like an unwanted memory. Panic morphed into dread as she tried to piece together what had happened. It felt surreal, as if she were watching her life unfold in timelapse, a horror film flickering with no beginning, middle or clear ending. Just a relentless blur and sick feeling.

Suddenly, a chill washed over her as she recalled the whispers shared in hushed tones back at school—the rumours about The Zodiac. The serial killer had haunted their city like a dark cloud, speculation swirling around how he chose his victims. Rosie was just a child—fourteen and still innocent in so many ways. Ideas of danger felt foreign until now but now she felt scared, vulnerable, easy prey for a predator.

She stumbled forward, her heart racing with fear, hoping to find someone—anyone—who could help. The trees closed in around her, their gnarled branches stretching like skeletal fingers, grabbing at her. Then, a rustling sound made her freeze. With her breath caught in her throat, she turned, praying it was Amber. But what stood before her cast a shadow darker than the woods themselves. The figure was vague and menacing, blending seamlessly with the darkness. Rosie squinted, trying to make out the details, but dread swallowed her vision, rendering the intruder an indistinct silhouette. Fear bubbled up inside her, and the instinct to flee overpowered her confusion but she couldn't move.

'Amber, help me!' Rosie couldn't get her legs to work. 'Help! Somebody help me!' She managed to shout, her voice cracking with despair.

The figure took a step closer, and Rosie's heart hammered in her chest. She turned and ran a few steps, branches tearing at her skin as she stumbled through the undergrowth. The echoes of laughter that once seemed innocent now haunted her, morphing into sinister cackles chasing her deeper into the trees. Behind her, heavy footsteps thudded against the forest floor, murky shadows lurking in the darker shadows, shifting and merging into one. She thought of Amber and the tight bond they shared, the secrets they shared, the dreams spun of endless fun, now shattered. The figure seemed to hover before her, waiting, enjoying her panic and confusion. Rosie couldn't let this be the end.

She pushed herself harder, adrenaline surging through her veins, but the weight of her desperate situation dragged her down. Finally, she burst into a clearing, moonlight spilling down like a lifeline. Without thinking, she changed direction, eyes scanning for any sign of help. Then she fell. Tripped over something unseen and tumbled to the ground, gasping as pain flared through her limbs. She rolled onto her back, trying to catch her breath, and stared up at the sky. Stars twinkled above, indifferent to her plight.

A noise made her blood run cold. Heavy footsteps approached, slow and deliberate. Rosie struggled to get to her feet, but her legs betrayed her, trembling beneath her. Terror gripped her as a voice, smooth and chilling, sliced through the night.

'You shouldn't have wandered off from me, I haven't finished with you yet,' he whispered into her ear. She felt him lick her cheek, his saliva smelled strange. 'I'm nowhere near done...'

Rosie's heart sank, knowing who this was—her mind turned him into the monster who had imprisoned too many in a web of terror and pain. Was this him?

The stories about The Zodiac were no longer tales spun for fear; they were reality, and she was caught in his grip. Amber's absence clawed at her insides, and as he seemed to smother her. His weight crushed the breath from her lungs. Rosie prepared to fight for herself, refusing to let the darkness claim her. She would not go down without a scream.

'Help! Somebody help me!' she screamed into the night, her voice echoing through the dark, searching for a saviour among the trees. In that moment, within the suffocating fear, something else ignited deep within her—a flicker of resolve to survive. She had to. For herself, for Amber, and for every victim forgotten in the wake of the storm that was The Zodiac. She bit into his cheek, hard but felt pain between her legs. She screamed and felt a blow to her jaw and light exploded in her brain. Then the pain intensified, the world turning black.

Chapter 37

R osie
     The sun had long since dropped and the streetlights were burning yellow, flickering and casting an eerie glow over everything. A hunter's moon was climbing, its silver light beautiful in its splendour. The Sea of Tranquillity was clearly visible to the naked eye. It appeared to be huge that night. There was a knot of concern tightening in Bill White's stomach as he looked for Rosie. He stood at the front porch, squinting at the dark street, the shadows lengthening as he watched the pavements for any signs of her; his heart thumping faster than it should be. Hayley was standing beside him with a furrowed brow, clutching her phone tightly, anxiously refreshing the screen in hopes of a message that hadn't come. She had messaged and called but the phone was switched off.

'Where could she be?' Hayley's voice broke through the stillness of twilight, tinged with fear. The unease that had begun as a whisper earlier in the evening now shouted, 'something is wrong', filling their home with an unsettling silence. 'She knows to be back before nine.'

'She's just out with her friends. She probably lost track of time,' Bill said, trying to inject a note of optimism into the air, but the words tasted bitter on his tongue. Rosie was only fourteen—an age of blossoming independence, yes, but still too young to be wandering around unaccompanied at this hour. The city changed after dark, and she was more vulnerable than she realised. 'Who was she with?'

'She wouldn't say. You know what she's like. I'm worried, it's past ten,' Hayley replied, pushing a strand of hair behind her ear as her eyes darted to the roofline of their neighbourhood. 'She should be home by now. And why hasn't she answered her phone?'

'I don't know, love.'

Bill rubbed his temples, feeling the tension of the day shaping into a palpable headache. 'Maybe her phone died? You know how she can be with that thing.'

'She charges it every night religiously and she never turns it off.'

Hayley shook her head, the frown deepening. She opened her mouth to say something but paused as the screen of her phone lit up once more—a message from a friend of Rosie's that read she had seen Rosie earlier at the park. At a party.

'Great, that's just great,' Bill retorted, crossing his arms. Panic clawed at the corners of his mind, urging him to do something. 'I'll go check the park; maybe she just lost track of time.'

Before he could move, the screen door creaked behind them. Gary emerged from the shadows of the hallway, his demeanour strikingly off-kilter. Gary's expression was unreadable, his eyes darting nervously to the ground as if the carpet might offer some clue about Rosie's whereabouts.

'Gary,' Hayley said softly, kneeling to meet his gaze. 'Have you seen your sister?'

'I saw her earlier, heading towards the park.'

'Who was she with?'

'Amber Dean,' Gary said, shrugging. 'Dixie's daughter. She's much older and all the lads fancy her.'

'What is she doing with her?' Bill asked.

'They've become friends, recently,' Hayley muttered. 'It doesn't matter for now.'

'Do you know where she is?'

'That was ages ago. I... I don't know where she is now,' Gary muttered, his voice barely a whisper. He kicked at a loose pebble on the porch, avoiding their eyes. It was peculiar behaviour for him;

he was usually chatty and boisterous, but tonight he was cloaked in ambiguity, his silence louder than any words. 'The last time I saw her, she was sitting with PC Martins but then I had to run because Mickey Scragg and his mates chased me home.'

'Why are they chasing you?' Hayley asked.

'Because he's a grass,' Bill said, shrugging. 'I've told you what happens when you talk to the police.'

'Shut up, Bill,' Hayley said. Bill exchanged a glance with Hayley. 'Gary, it's important. If you've seen her or know anything, you need to tell us. We're really worried,' she added.

Gary took a hesitant step back, his shoulders hunching as if trying to retreat into himself. 'I didn't see her after that and she hasn't messaged me or anything,' he insisted, though Bill could see a flicker of something in his eyes. Fear, perhaps? Or guilt?

'Gary...' Bill started but hesitated, sensing the fragile thread of trust between them. 'Just... please tell us what you know.'

Gary opened his mouth as if to speak but then clamped it shut again, his small fists balled at his sides. It was the look of a child wrestling with a heavy decision.

'I saw her on the benches with PC Martins, just a couple of hours ago,' Gary said, his voice trembling ever so slightly. He wanted to say what he really thought of the police officer and Rosie. 'Why don't you ring him and ask him?'

'That might be a good idea, to be honest,' Bill said. 'Ring George and ask him if he's seen her since this afternoon.'

'She might be with him,' Gary said, walking up the stairs. 'She fancies him, and I've seen him staring at her arse.'

'What?' Bill said, stunned. 'She's fourteen, for fuck's sake!'

'I'm just saying,' Gary said, going into his bedroom. He slammed the door.

'What is wrong with that boy?' Bill asked. 'He's not right in the head.' He closed the front door and faced Hayley. 'Ring George and ask him if he's seen her.'

Hayley dialled PC Martins on his personal mobile, but he didn't answer. She didn't leave a message.

'He's not answering,' Hayley said. 'I'm going to go to the park to look for her.'

'No, you're not wandering around the woods in the dark,' Bill said. 'I'll go to look for her and when I do, she's getting a kick up the arse for my trouble.'

CYNTHIA DEAN PACED the living room, the soft tap of her slippers against the hardwood floor echoing in the otherwise silent house. Glancing at the clock for the umpteenth time, she felt her heart race. Amber was supposed to be home by now. It was just past ten, and the dusk had long since turned to night with a quickness that shocked; her anxiety tugged at her insides. The dark nights of British winter were long and cold.

'Just a little hangout with my mates, Mum,' Amber had said earlier in the day, her cheeks flushed with excitement as she dashed out the door. Cynthia had smiled, her mind filled with fond memories of similar evenings from her own teenage years. But those memories felt different now, shadows contrasting sharply against the worry that ate at her.

Cynthia picked up her phone again, the screen lighting up with the same message thread, devoid of any new notifications. It was strange for Amber not to text or call, even just to say she was on her way.

What if something had happened?

The thought stirred a cold pit in her stomach. She had raised Amber to be responsible, to communicate, no matter where she was or what she was doing. She'd preached about safety and the importance of being aware of her surroundings. Why wasn't her daughter reaching out to explain why she was late?

She sat down on the edge of the couch, her fingers trembling as she scrolled through her contact list. Should she call? Or would that make things worse? Her heart ached with an urgency she couldn't ignore. Finally, she pressed the call button, holding her breath as the phone rang.

'Come on, Amber. Pick up,' she whispered under her breath.

The call went to voicemail again and she had already left three messages. Cynthia hung up, frustration mingling with dread. She needed to do something—anything. Striding to the door, she pulled on her jacket and trainers, her mind racing with the places Amber could be. The park? The shops? Her friend Mia's house? She messaged her mother to ask is Amber was there. As she stepped outside, the crisp air hit her, but she barely felt it.

Focus, Cynthia. Think.

Maybe her daughter was just caught up chatting with friends, but what if she wasn't? The "what ifs" spiralled around her like a whirlwind, a tempest of anxiety that clouded her judgment. Cynthia walked towards the park, the path lined with shadows and the occasional flicker of streetlights. She squinted into the dimness, hoping to catch a glimpse of Amber's familiar silhouette. Her phone buzzed in her pocket, making her jump.

'Please be her,' she muttered, pulling it out. It was a text from Mia's mother, Helen. Amber wasn't there and Mia hadn't been out because she wasn't feeling well. Fucking hell, she muttered. With hurried steps, she made her way towards the park, ready to confront her daughter. It was a fifteen-minute walk to the Village Roundabout and the woods were a few hundred yards beyond it.

Cynthia's heart raced as she stepped into the park, a chill weaving its way through the damp evening air. Shadows danced under the flickering lights of forgotten candle lanterns, and the smell of stale beer and smoke lingered, heavy and suffocating, tinged with cannabis. The party had left a mark on the park: groups of teenagers sprawled out on the grass, some slumped in tents, laughter mingling with the dull thud of bass from a distant speaker.

'Amber!' she called out, her voice piercing the cacophony of sounds. Panic laced her tone, echoing in the stillness that followed. For a moment, she thought she heard a reply, but it was drowned out by the raucous laughter of a nearby group.

'Has anyone seen Amber Dean?'

She moved cautiously, weaving through the debris: empty bottles, crushed cans, remnants of a celebration that felt foreign to her. It was hard to believe that just hours ago, this had been a vibrant park, full of families and laughter. Now, it felt like a different world entirely—a lawless place where shadows could swallow a person whole.

'Amber! Please, where are you?' She called again, terrified that her daughter would not respond. They had argued before she left the house, the typical teenage defiance flaring between them. She was supposed to stay at a friend's house, but Cynthia had known the invitation to the gathering had included the words "bonfire" and "everyone will be there."

With each passing moment, Cynthia's fear escalated into desperation. She spotted a cluster of tents huddled together, the fabric flapping limply in the breeze. She approached, scanning the faces of those sprawled on the ground, their eyes glazed, their laughter an unnatural cawing cacophony.

'Excuse me, have you seen my daughter? She's about this tall, with curly brown hair—her name's Amber Dean' she asked, her voice trembling.

One boy, his cheeks flushed from drink, squinted in her direction. 'Nah, man. Haven't seen anyone. Go ask over there,' he waved dismissively, pointing to another group. The indifference cut deeper than she expected.

Cynthia's throat tightened. Each passing second stretched painfully, the thrill of hope throbbing and fading. She could feel her stomach somersault as she moved toward the next group, her desperate pleas growing more urgent.

'Amber! Where are you?' This time, it was softer, filled with dread.

As she wandered further, the laughter grew less inviting, turning into mutters and abusive slurs. She caught sight of a couple of girls leaning against a tree, sharing a drink, treating her panic like a silly joke.

'I've lost my daughter, Amber. Have you seen her?'

One of them giggled in reply, the sound mocking. 'Lost? We're all lost, babe!' Cynthia fought against the urge to retort, her resolve crumbling under their careless laughter. 'Get a vodka and chill, lady.'

Her chest tightened as she moved deeper into the park. The shadows deepened, the darkness thickening around her like a shroud. Where were the parents? Where were the other adults? Anger mixed with fear, but that was secondary to the overwhelming need to find her daughter.

Stumbling upon a small clearing, she noticed a fire pit surrounded by a handful of teenagers swaying dangerously, their voices rising and falling like waves. Cynthia felt a ripple of fear as they caught sight of her, their eyes narrowing with intrigue.

'Hey, lady! You looking for someone?' one of them yelled, a smug grin plastered on his face.

'Amber!' she cried again. Her voice cracked under the strain, but she clenched her fists, pushing through the rising tide of despair. She was aware of their stares, measuring her; she felt vulnerable, exposed.

Then she froze, her breath catching. A familiar laughter floated through the air—a sound she knew all too well—strangely carefree but laden with the effect of alcohol. It came from further down the path, where the underbrush closed in like a wall.

Cynthia sprinted toward the sound, her heart pounding in her ears. As she rounded a corner, a shadowy figure caught her eye. There, by the edge of a thicket, a girl sat on the ground, leaning against a tree, her face hidden in her hands.

'Amber!' Cynthia rushed forward, a mixture of anger, relief, and unconditional love coursing through her. As she neared, the girl looked up, her eyes bleary and red, the evidence of the night's escapades clear.

'Are you, her mum?' Rosie White slurred, confusion kicking in.

Cynthia knelt, grabbing Rosie by the arms. 'Where is Amber?'

'I've been looking for her,' Rosie said, wrapping her arms around Cynthia. 'Oh, thank God! I was so worried, I had lost her!' Rosie sniffled. Tears seeped from the corners of her eyes, the fear lifting as she held Amber's mum close. 'Where is she?' Rosie asked.

'Oh, you, stupid girl,' Cynthia snapped. 'When did you last see her?'

'I'm sorry,' Rosie mumbled, her voice muffled against Cynthia's shoulder. 'We didn't mean—'

'We'll talk later,' Cynthia interrupted, pulling back to look at Rosie, her heart still racing. 'When did you last see Amber?'

'I need to get home.' Rosie vomited into the darkness and dropped to her knees. 'I don't know why I'm so drunk, I hardly had anything to drink...'

'Answer me, Rosie,' Cynthia said, angrily. 'When did you last see Amber?'

Rosie was sick again; the acrid smell of her stomach acid reached her. The reality of the night settled around them—chaotic, frightening, and far from over. The shadows of the park seemed more ominous in the darkness surrounding them, every rustle echoing with unspoken threats. Cynthia felt the crippling anxiety return. There was no sign of Amber and Rosie didn't know what day it was.

THE PARK WAS A CHAOTIC scene as Bill White strode through the thick brush, the remnants of the party strewn across the ground like discarded dreams. He glanced up at the black velvet sky, the moon and stars twinkling like jewels, a chill creeping into the night air. With every step, his heart sank deeper into his chest. He hadn't planned on being out this late, and neither had Rosie, she was still a child. Nervousness twisted his mind as he called her name again, hoping the sound would carry through the remnants of laughter and fading music.

'Rosie!' His voice, once steady, now trembled with urgency.

As he made his way past scattered groups of teenagers, he spotted Cynthia amidst the chaos, kneeling beside a teenage girl, who was being sick.

'Is that Rosie?' he asked, shocked. The girl was sprawled on the grass, a look of dazed confusion etched across her features. Bill's pulse quickened. He hurried over, to make sure he wasn't seeing things, to draw some solace, if only for a moment. 'Hello Cynthia! What happened?' he asked, concern etched on his face.

'Amber didn't come home, so I came to look for her. I found Rosie in this state but there's no sign of Amber and she doesn't know when she last saw her.' Cynthia shook her head, her expression a mix of worry and panic.

'Rosie, it's your dad! Wake up.' Rosie lifted her head, blinking slowly as if waking from a dream. 'Where is Amber?' 'Amber? Um...' Her words came out slurred, the cocktail of drinks muddling her thoughts. 'I was ready to leave to get home, so I think she left...like, around quarter to nine.'

Cynthia heart dropped. 'Quarter to nine? Do you know if she was going home?'

Rosie stared into space; her eyes unfocused. 'She said she had to be home for nine, so did I but suddenly, I felt really drunk and then you were here.' She paused, her brow furrowing. 'I haven't seen her since then.'

Bill clenched his jaw, a mix of relief and anxiety flooding through him. Rosie was safe but Amber was missing. At least she hadn't gotten caught up in whatever chaos was left at the park, but the uncertainty hammered against his consciousness. The streets surrounding their estate loomed large in his mind, shadows hiding dangers he couldn't bear to imagine.

'Did you see her leave?' he pressed, his determination rising, desperation creeping in. 'Which way did amber go?'

'I don't know but George was here for a while,' Rosie mumbled.

'Who is George?' Cynthia asked.

'The local bobby,' Bill said. 'He was probably checking on what the kids were up to in here.'

Rosie shook her head slowly, a frown of concentration forming. 'I... I don't really remember anything. Things were too fuzzy. I might have been, like, taking a picture or something.' Bill noticed dark streaks running down her left leg. It looked like black tar in the darkness.

'I think you're bleeding, Rosie,' Bill said. 'I need to get you to a hospital.' Cynthia looked at Rosie concerned. 'She's not due on,' Bill said. He shrugged. 'Everyone in the house knows when Rosie is due on.'

'You don't think...' Cynthia couldn't finish her question.

'Look how drunk she is,' Bill said. 'I think she's been drugged with something. I'm going to get her to Alder Hey to have her checked out. Do you want me to call the police?'

'Oh, my God, what happened here tonight.' Cynthia started sobbing. 'And where is my daughter?'

'Call the police and get them to look around with you,' Bill said. 'She could still be nearby.'

'Of course,' Cynthia replied, urgency mixing with her own fear. 'I'll call them now.'

'I'm going to get an ambulance for Rosie and take her to the hospital,' Bill said. 'I hope you find her...'

He felt bad leaving her, as he picked up Rosie and carried her out of the woods. As the laughter from the party whooped from behind them, he fought to shake off the suffocating sense of dread. Rosie, his bright and spirited daughter, was out of the game and bleeding. It was a father's worst nightmare.

Bill only hoped the park would offer more than just the sounds of drunken revelry, that it would give up the secret of Amber's whereabouts. The cool air bit at his face, echoing the fervent prayer in his heart: that Amber was safe, just on the edge of being lost, waiting to be found safe and sound.

Chapter 38

Olivia Mann

Detective Olivia Mann stepped through the doors of the Major Investigation Team, Canning Place, the heart of the Liverpool police force. The air was thick with urgency, a crackle of tension that buzzed around the bustling precinct. Officers moved purposefully, phones ringing in a steady rhythm, as she made her way toward her desk.

'Olivia!' called a familiar voice. DCI Knowles waved her over, frowning in concern. 'We need to talk before the briefing. This has taken a very different turn. I have called all the senior dicks in on this.'

'What's happening?' Olivia asked, her curiosity peaked instinctively as she sensed the urgency in his tone. She saw George Genesis, Steff Cain and the ACC stepping out of the lift. They were deep in conversation and looked worried. 'Can you please tell me what the fuck is happening, please?'

'My source at the Echo has had an email from the Zodiac,' Knowles said. 'I've sent it to your laptop.' He pointed to the screen. 'Sit down before you read it and then you've got some questions to answer.'

'I have questions to answer,' she muttered. 'Is it from him or is it from a nutcase pretending to be him?'

'Read it and see for yourself.'

Olivia went to her desk and sat down, opening her emails. She clicked on the link from Knowles. As she started to read it, her stomach began to contract.

Zodiac

Friday 13th [Very apt indeed]

To: Detective Superintendent Olivia Mann

My, dear Olivia,

You toil in vain, my dear detective. With every twist and turn, you dance to the rhythm of my game, yet you will never catch me. Your efforts are mere mirages, pulling you deeper into my shadow where I delight in the unfolding chaos.

Watching you dance has been such a pleasure, in more ways than one. I've seen you at work and I've seen you at play. Those gold heels are too high for you, though. You must be careful, or you will twist your heel. I much prefer you in jeans with your grey boots. My grandfather used to call them 'fuck me boots' but he was a cunt. I'm not so keen on your longer coats, the white one especially. Wear the black leather more often for me...

You are one of the most attractive women that I have seen and the fact that you're smart enough to be my adversary is a real turn on. The way you hold a red wine glass in your right hand is almost orgasmic. And I've watched your lips move when you speak, such perfection is rare. And your smell as you walked past me, indescribable...

I feel that there's a meeting of energies on the horizon. We're being drawn together by the universe and that excites me. Being within your aura will be electric. Watching your smile turn into a scream and listening to you beg would be such a scintillating experience, I can hardly contain myself. When we meet, our worlds will collide, and I will rock yours. I will absorb your energy, drink your fluids, eat your solid being and consume you completely. We will be one, with all the others who came before you. Your energy will become mine, a divine union.

I know what you're thinking. Is this really Zodiac or is this a copycat, wannabe nutcase?

Let's play a little game of revelation, shall we? Perhaps these clues will give you the evidence you need. A taste of my artistry.

- **Allison** was a schoolgirl, innocent and bright, snuffed out like a flickering candlelight. Before her soul could fully shine, her meat was sweet with deep red wine.

- **Belinda**, oh sweet Belinda, with her cards and crystals, tried to read the future but could not foresee her own demise.

- **Shelly** sought to communicate with the dead using her Ouija board; little did she know, the only spirit she would encounter is mine. I wonder if she is talking to them now, do you?

- **Candy**, a flower plucked too soon from the garden of life, traded her wares and paid the ultimate price. Her body was her only asset, so I ate it.

- Then we have **Amelia** and **Nigel**, two lost souls living on the streets, consumed by the city's indifference, their cries unheard. Their families didn't stop them leaving home, they ended up drifting all alone. Now they float in the infinite darkness.

- And lastly, **Jennifer Simmons**— oh, the irony is rich. A schoolgirl with her head still resting on her shoulders because you found her too soon; a final twist on a tragic tale.

Each name whispers secrets, and each victim bears the mark of my celestial design. The signs of the Zodiac, engraved in flesh to commemorate their passage and there are only a few places to fill. It won't be long, and my work here will be done and then we can become one.

I have read the nonsense and speculation in the press, and it insults me to be honest. Is it not obvious that my work has been carried out by an absolute master, not a gang of immoral immigrants? I have respect for my victims, they have nothing but disdain. Ahmed Shah and his grooming gang were nothing more than that—let the press speculate all they wish. They grasp at straws. Revenge was the cause of his fiery death, but it was nothing but a fantasy; A family looking for someone to blame, found some peace in his terrible death. I have no sympathy for the vile creature or his torturous end. I am not bound by the constraints of mortality. He is no more than a piece in a game where he has no place. His name should never be mentioned alongside mine.

Continue your pursuit, Olivia. The more you seek, the deeper you will plunge into the abyss and the sooner we shall be together.

With all my love,

Zodiac

The MIT was summoned an it responded immediately. One of their own had been threatened and that wasn't tolerated. The Assistant Chief Constable took the lead, his uniform pristine, grey hair gelled back to his mottled pink scalp.

'You've all read the letter and had chance to analyse it, and we are all agreed this is a genuine communication from the killer we're calling Zodiac?' he asked. The detectives in the room nodded. 'It's clear from the details, he's been watching DS Mann over a period, which we need to establish. This concerns me greatly, as I'm sure it does all of you.' A murmur ran through the gathering. 'Olivia, can you shine some light on where and when he may have seen you wearing the items he's mentioned, please.'

Olivia stood up and looked at the letter which had been loaded onto a screen. 'Okay, let's start at the beginning,' she pointed to the script. 'The last time I went dancing in gold high heels was at Christmas last year. It was a family event, held at Revolution on Bold Street and we eventually went to Concert Square until the small hours.' She shrugged. 'I haven't worn the shoes before or since, but it was a Saturday night, and it was booming everywhere. He could have been standing next to me, and I wouldn't have noticed.'

'Was it a large group of people?'

'About forty people attended and they dwindled down to half that as the night went on,' Olivia said. 'I was drinking red wine that night, so he could have been watching me from anywhere.'

'Did you notice anyone hanging around the group?'

'No.' She shook her head and smiled. 'It was Saturday night in the city and was I was wearing a short black dress and high heels. If I had a pound for every time I was approached and offered a drink...'

A ripple of chatter spread through the team.

'When I'm not at work or going to the gym, I live in jeans and boots, usually knee-length and I love my white overcoat and leather jacket. I can't narrow it down any further.' She shrugged. 'Sorry but it's too vague to be any more specific and I'm sure Zodiac knows that.'

'We have put a marker on your address and ARUs are on standby,' the ACC said. 'We need to double-down on this animal and put him away.'

'Why send the letter to the Echo?' an officer asked. 'Does he have a rapport with them?'

'He wants to put them straight,' Knowles said, nodding. 'This is about the press claiming Ahmed Shah was the Zodiac and that the grooming gang were responsible for the Delamere victims. There have been no victims since he was murdered and the rest of the gang were locked up with Dixie Dean, Jack Milner and their cronies.' Knowles shrugged. 'I think we got closer than he thought we would and stopped killing for a while and he's letting us know he's still here.'

'At least, we haven't found any more of his victims, but I don't think that means he's stopped, not for one minute.' Olivia gestured to the letter. 'Get your team to cross check the information against what we know about the victims.'

'I'm not so sure the timing is a coincidence. I get the feeling it's about Amber Dean,' Knowles said, looking over his shoulder at the screen. 'I'm convinced he's sent this email to distract us from the fact Amber has gone missing.' Olivia frowned and shook her head. 'He wants us to doubt that he's active again, but his ego is demanding he claims the Delamere victims as his own.'

'Amber Dean worries me greatly.' A chill coursed through Olivia as she absorbed the information in the email again, searching for clues in the writing. 'I've scanned the statements made so far and Amber and Rosie went to the woods together, right?'

'Yes. The two girls were last seen talking to a police officer?'

'And we have identified him as PC Martins?' Olivia said, shaking her head. 'What was he doing there?'

'I've checked and there were no calls from that area.'

'Okay, they spoke to Martins, but Rosie can't remember anything after that.' Olivia checked the report from the Sexual Assault Referral Centre at Alder Hey Children's Hospital. 'She was taken to the Rainbow Centre and examined on the night. Her bloods show Rohypnol in her system, and the hospital confirmed she was raped. The bruising indicates a sustained attack. What a bastard.' Olivia shook her head. 'I'm not convinced this is anything but an opportunist stalking the gathering, knowing there would be vulnerable teenagers there. How can we deduce this is anything to do with The Zodiac?'

'I just have a feeling about this.' Knowles shook his head in disagreement.

'I think the timing of the letter is uncanny, granted, but he doesn't mention Amber. Did anyone see anyone else acting suspiciously?'

'Eyewitness statements indicate that Rosie and Amber were seen near the arcade talking to PC Martins on the benches. After that, they went into the woods and vanished,' Knowles explained. 'We've reached out to Martins for his side of the story, but his account is sketchy. He claims he was just chatting with them before he went on his shift.'

'Was he in uniform?'

'Yes.'

'Just chatting to teenage girls in uniform?' Olivia echoed, scepticism lacing her words. 'We also have eyewitnesses who stated that they saw Jennifer Simmons at the bus stop talking to a dark-haired police officer with heavily tattooed arms?'

'He fits that description. We also have a missed call on her phone from an unregistered mobile before she went missing,' Knowles said. 'If we could pin that number on Martins, I'd be seriously concerned.'

'Given everything that's unfolded in the past year, that's not enough detail. We need to dig deeper into what he was doing there

in the first place.' Olivia read the letter again. 'Bring him in. I want
to hear what he has to say and how he reacts under questioning. The
last thing we need is a rogue cop targeting underage girls.'

'Agreed,' Knowles said, determination flickering in his eyes. 'I
want to lead this investigation.'

'You want to look into this as if it's connected to the Zodiac
case?'

'Yes. It's never been closed, officially, I want to rekindle it,'
Knowles said. 'I'll speak with the parents, organise searches, and go
through the tapes from nearby CCTV. We need to find Amber, and
fast.'

As Olivia nodded, a sinking feeling settled in her stomach. The
last time they had experienced such a terrible loss in that community,
Jennifer Simmons, the fallout had been devastating. The uproar, the
fear, and the anger, the riots—it was a cycle she hoped to avoid
repeating.

'I want to know how long Rosie and Amber were together,
before they were separated. Get a hold of the girls' friends too,
anyone who might've seen them leading up to Rosie being found,'
Olivia instructed. 'We need every detail, no matter how small.'

'Yes, boss,' Knowles replied, already formulating a plan in his
mind. 'I'm going to hold the briefing; do you want to sit in?'

'It's your show, crack on with it,' Olivia said. 'I need a drink.'

Olivia walked towards the coffee machine. As she departed the
incident room, she felt the weight of responsibility on her shoulders.
The pressure of finding Amber echoed the past's haunting memories,
threatening to redefine what they had all desperately tried to move
beyond. This was a terrible reminder of what had happened, and
the victims buried in Delamere. When she returned to the desk, a
determined fire fuelled her thoughts. She delved into the CCTV
footage from the area around the roundabout, fast-forwarding
through mundane moments—a world turning normally while the

girls had slipped through the cracks. And then she stopped, eyes narrowing at the grainy image of the arcade entrance.

Two figures appeared: Rosie and Amber, youthful energy radiating from their laughter and dancing, twerking and joking around. Just behind them, a uniformed figure was visible approaching them—PC Martins.

'Keep the focus on him,' Olivia murmured to herself, recognising that old shadows were threatening to reappear. The pieces were falling into place, and it was time to chase down the truth before it slipped away entirely.

Chapter 39

PC Martins interview

PC George Martins sat in the stark, fluorescent-lit interview room, an overwhelming feeling of despair and panic had descended on him. The cold metal table felt heavy beneath his palms as he stared at the plain walls, the silence thick with unspoken accusations. Outside, he could hear the bustle of officers in the precinct, but inside this room, time seemed to stand still and felt like an intruder in his own workspace.

Detective Olivia Mann entered, followed by DCI Knowles. The atmosphere shifted instantly; both detectives carried an air of authority that filled the room. Olivia glanced at the notepad in her hands, and George felt his pulse quicken.

'Thank you for coming in, PC Martins,' Olivia began, her tone neutral but firm. 'We appreciate your cooperation. Are you sure you don't want your union rep here?'

'Of course, I'm fine,' George replied, attempting to sound casual, but the tremor in his voice betrayed him. 'I want to help in any way I can. This should be a formality, shouldn't it?'

'Should be but we have some hard questions to ask.'

'Okay.'

'Let's get straight to the point,' Knowles said, his voice brokering no nonsense. 'You were the last person seen talking to Rosie White and Amber Dean before they were attacked, one of them was raped, the other missing.'

'I'm sure they must have spoken to some of their friends after talking to me.'

'We are not aware of them speaking to anyone else. Can you explain what you said to them?'

'Nothing important.' George swallowed hard, wringing his hands nervously. 'We were just chatting. They seemed fine. I didn't think anything of it. They were on their way to the party in the woods, and I was just doing my rounds before I went on shift. I was in uniform, so I didn't see any problem talking to them. I know them.'

'Let's go back to what you referred to as your rounds,' Olivia noted, her pen poised to capture every detail. 'I'm not sure how your 'rounds' extend to chatting to teenage girls on their way to a party in the park. What exactly were you discussing?'

'Just... harmless stuff,' George stammered, desperate to appear innocent. He blushed, frustrated. 'They were talking about school, their plans for the weekend. Rosie mentioned something about a new PlayStation game they were excited to play. Just chatting...'

'And you didn't think it was strange that two teenage girls were so comfortable chatting with a police officer in uniform, surrounded by other teenagers?' Knowles pressed, leaning forward. 'Most teenagers wouldn't be seen dead with a police officer.......Not given your history?'

'My history?' A flicker of annoyance crossed George's face. 'That's not fair! I'm just doing my job. I've never done anything wrong with any of my colleagues or anyone else.' His defensiveness only seemed to amplify the tension in the room.

'Really?' Olivia asked, her expression cool yet observant. 'Did you just say that?'

'Yes, I'm trying to help you...'

'Your past has raised some red flags.'

'Like what?' George asked.

'Several female colleagues have complained about your behaviour. Words like 'sex pest' have emerged on too many occasions.

You had an affair with a married woman, who had two children. PC Alice Walker—she burned to death in her car.'

'That was over two years ago. I never harmed Alice!' George shot back, his voice rising with indignation. 'She was struggling with her mental health long before I got involved with her. I didn't push her to do anything!'

'But you were involved with her, and now she's dead,' Knowles pointed out bluntly. 'Her death was ruled a suicide, but there are many unanswered questions surrounding it. Which begs the question—how can we take you seriously when you were the last person seen with two young girls, one raped and the other missing?'

'This is ridiculous.'

'One was raped, one is missing,' Olivia said, calmly. 'How ridiculous is that?'

'I didn't do anything to them!' George protested, panic leaking into his words. 'Rosie and Amber were just... just friendly. I was always looking out for them and making sure they were safe...'

'Looking out for them, is quite the phrase, isn't it?' Olivia said, her voice low and steady. 'They are children, and you were in a position of power. How do we know that your interest went beyond being a concerned officer and wasn't sexual, given your history?'

'That's a dreadful accusation with no substance behind it.'

'Did you send them pictures of your penis?' Olivia asked.

'What?'

'Dick-pics,' Olivia said. 'Did you send them Dick-pics because you've sent them to female officers at the station, several times.'

'I haven't sent them anything.'

'You're aware of public sentiment surrounding you?"

George's facade cracked further; sweat began to bead on his forehead. 'I swear, it was innocent. They were just kids, and I know their families! I wouldn't—I'd never touch them!'

'Yet here we are, and those girls are in trouble, Rosie raped, Amber missing,' Knowles said, folding his arms across his chest. 'You chatted to them about computer games and school. What exactly happened after that conversation wrapped up?'

'I walked away!' George exclaimed, desperation spilling into his tone. 'I swear! I had to meet my partner for our shift afterwards. That's all!'

'Your partner?' Olivia noted, swiftly jotting down the detail. 'Can we confirm that?'

'I— I can get you their name and number! Just let me think,' George stammered, glancing at the clock on the wall as if it would provide a way out. 'They must have seen me leave the woods alone!'

'Then let's work on that. But you need to understand this is serious,' Olivia said, her eyes narrowing. 'If you're lying or withholding information, it won't end well for you. If those girls were harmed because of you—'

'I didn't harm them!' George interrupted, his voice breaking. 'I didn't do anything! I'm telling you the truth!'

Olivia picked up her phone and dialled a number. The phone in PC Martins' pocket rang. The colour drained from his face.

'That is the last number to call Jennifer Simmons' phone,' Olivia said. 'The call came from the phone in your pocket.' Martins put his head in his hands. 'Explain that for me?'

'I saw her waiting at the bus stop, but it was way past registration time, so I asked her what she was doing, her name and address and I told her to get on the next bus,' Martins said. 'I called her number so that she had my number,' he added. 'I told her to text me when she arrived at school.'

'You told an underage girl to text you on your personal mobile number?' Olivia asked, shaking her head. 'That concerns me greatly.'

'It was innocent,' he muttered, eyes closed. I can see how it looks...'

'You can?'

'Yes.'

The tension hung heavy in the air, the gravity of the situation crashing down around them. Olivia sensed the cracks beginning to form, the fear radiating from George.

'When did you last speak to Alice Walker?' she pressed, hoping to peel back another layer. 'Did she say anything about feeling threatened? About you?'

'No!' he insisted, his agitation rising. 'I just... I wanted to help her! She was going through a tough time, and I thought I could be there for her. I didn't want things to turn out like they did!'

'What do you mean 'like they did'?' Knowles shot back, leaning in closer. 'Is there something you want to tell us? Because your denial is only raising more questions.'

George let out a shuddering breath, fear in his eyes.

'I'm not saying any more,' George said. 'You're railroading me here because you don't have any other leads.'

'Okay, we'll suspend the interview for now,' Olivia sighed. 'We'll conduct a formal interview at nine o'clock tomorrow morning. I suggest you bring representation.'

Chapter 40

Dixie Dean

The clanging of metal echoed throughout the prison corridor as Dixie Dean sat in his sparsely furnished cell. The stark walls enclosed him, but the ferocity within him was untamed. He knelt on the cold concrete floor, his back pressed against the thin mattress, a newspaper spread open beside him. Each word felt like needles pricking his skin, insignificant in the light of the storm brewing inside him.

Bobby Allen stood outside the bars, nervous energy coursing through him. He took a deep breath before stepping inside, the heavy door creaking ominously shut behind him. Dixie looked up, his sharp gaze penetrating, sensing trouble even before Bobby uttered a word.

'Boss,' Bobby began, his voice shaky. 'We have a situation.'

Dixie's eyes narrowed. 'What now?'

'It's about Amber,' Bobby hesitated, swallowing hard as he gauged Dixie's reaction. 'She's missing.'

Dixie's heart plummeted. The hairs on his neck stood on end. 'What do you mean 'missing'?'

'She went to a party and disappeared...'

'How long has she been gone?'

'Since the night before last,' Bobby replied, shuffling his feet. 'She was with Rosie White, and now... they can't find her.'

A dark rage simmered beneath Dixie's calm facade, but Bobby continued, 'They found Rosie drugged in the woods. She, uh... she was attacked, Boss. Raped.'

'Is this Bill White's daughter?' The word hit Dixie like a punch to the gut. Anguish morphed into a cold, seething fury.

'Yes. She's fourteen.'

'Where is my daughter?' Dixie flushed red with anger. 'I fucking hate nonces. Who did this?'

'Police are trying to figure it out,' Bobby stammered. 'They've interviewed a uniformed Dibble, George Martins. He was the last one seen with them, but they let him go.'

Dixie's expression hardened. 'You're telling me they just let him walk?'

'Yeah, they didn't have enough to hold him. Said he was doing his job, keeping an eye on the girls in that area.'

'Bullshit. The police don't interview their own unless they're sure they're involved,' Dixie spat, the fire in his belly igniting. 'If they pulled him in, Martins is involved, and they're too scared to do anything without enough proof.'

Bobby shifted uneasily under Dixie's gaze. 'What do you want to do?'

'Find Martins,' he ordered, his voice low and dangerous. 'Bring him to the workshop.'

'What?' Bobby's eyes widened. 'We can't kidnap a dibble—'

Dixie cut him off, his voice turning icy. 'If you're too scared to do it, I'll find someone who isn't. My daughter is out there, God knows what's happened to her because of that bastard. I want him—kidnapped and questioned.'

'Kidnapped?' Bobby echoed, incredulity etched in his features.

'Yeah, taken out of the picture until I find out where my daughter is. If he knows something, make him talk.'

'But, Boss, what if it backfires? If the police find out—'

Dixie leaned forward, his face inches from Bobby's. 'I'm not asking for your approval, Bobby. I'm telling you what's going to happen. You get people on it. Tonight.'

Bobby nodded, swallowing his fear, the weight of his boss's demeanour pressing down on him. 'Yeah... I'll make it happen.'

Dixie released a breath as Bobby backed away, the door creaking open and shut behind him. Alone in the confines of his cell, the walls felt suffocating. Beneath the rage was fear—fear for Amber, for Rosie, and the hell they must be enduring right now. He rose from the floor, pacing as he wrestled with the darkness threatening to consume him. His mind raced, navigating through memories of a life spent perpetuating violence. Yet, in this moment, it was his daughter that fuelled the beast within.

Amber was only a teenager, barely skimming the surface of the life he had built—a life of choices that could never protect her from harm. Guilt gnawed at him, the realisation that he was as much a part of the underbelly of crime as those who inflicted pain. If anything happened to her, the regret would eat away at him, as surely as the rust crept into the prison bars. But timing was everything, and the game was one of patience and power. He would play it, and when the pieces fell into place, he would unleash the wrath of Dixie Dean to protect what was left of his family.

He leaned against the cold wall, gaze fixed on the flickering light above. 'I swear, Amber,' he whispered to the emptiness, 'if I have to burn this whole city down, I'll bring you back.'

With that solemn vow echoing in his mind, Dixie Dean began plotting his next move, ready to strike against anyone who stood in the way of finding his daughter and seeking retribution for the horrors inflicted upon her friend. The world outside might have thought him broken, but within these walls, a tempest was brewing—one that promised to spill chaos into the streets of Liverpool.

Chapter 41

P C Martins

A cold wind howled through the cracks of the dilapidated factory, carrying with it the scent of rust and decay. Shadows flickered across the graffiti-scarred walls as PC George Martins regained consciousness, the room spinning around him. He tried to lift his head, but the dull ache radiating through his skull subdued him.

Panic surged within him as the events of the last few hours flooded back. He had been leaving the railway station when he felt the jab of something sharp in his side and warm breath on his neck. Before he knew it, darkness engulfed him. And now, he was here taped to a chair in an abandoned place that felt like the very representation of despair.

The flickering of a single overhead bulb barely illuminated his captors—three men, rough around the edges, their faces obscured by the shadows. They loomed over him, disdain etched into their every feature. Martins recognised them from the whispers around the precinct; they were known associates of Dixie Dean's violent gang.

The sounds of dripping water echoed eerily, creating an unsettling rhythm that only heightened his anxiety. One of the men, tall and muscular with tattoos snaking around his forearms, stepped forward, holding pliers under the dim light.

'PC Martins, I presume?' he taunted, a cruel smile spreading across his face. 'You really should have stayed away from Dixie's daughter.'

'Please......I haven't done anything.......Let me go,' Martins gasped, forcing the words through a throat dry from fear. 'I didn't touch those girls. You've got the wrong guy.'

There was a dreadful stillness, the kind that set the stage for violence. The man lifted the pliers, twirling them menacingly. 'Oh, I think we have the right guy. You see, we're looking for a little information—a missing girl named Amber Dean. You've spoken to the police about her, haven't you? Let's make this easy. Just tell us where she is, and we'll let you go.'

Martins clenched his fists, heart pounding. 'I don't know where she is!'

The man's smile faded, replaced by a grimace of irritation. 'That's too bad.' He motioned to his accomplices, who stepped closer. 'You'll help us find out where she is, soon enough.'

With that, they descended on him, ripping ducts of tape around his wrists, tightening it against his skin until the fibres practically dug into the flesh.

Panic clawed at Martins as he thrashed against the chair, desperate for freedom, but the more he struggled, the tighter the grips of the gang members became.

'I swear, I don't know anything!' he shouted.

His cries fell on deaf ears as one of the men jammed the pliers into his mouth, pinching at the delicate flesh of his gums. 'Time for a little persuasion.'

Martins's heart nearly exploded as he realised what was about to happen. He felt his gums being ripped apart and a tooth cracked into pieces. 'No, please! Don't—'

But it was too late. The man yanked the pliers, a sickening crack resonating through the factory as one of Martins's front teeth dislodged, warm blood spilling into his mouth. The sharp pain tore through him, and dizzying shock muddled his thoughts. He screamed like a child.

'See?' the man said, a twisted sense of satisfaction in his voice. 'Not so hard, is it? Just tell us what we want to know, and this stops now.'

Staring at the broken man before him, he added the pliers to the table beside him, already glistening with the remnants of what they'd just taken. Another man picked up secateurs, the shining metal glinting ominously in the low light. 'Now, let's see those fingers of yours, PC.'

'No, no, no, no, no, please! Don't! I can help you! I swear—I'll get the information!' Tears pricked at the corners of Martins's eyes as panic rooted itself deeper inside him. Blood and saliva trickled down his chin, dripping onto his chest.

'Just tell us where she is,' the man said coldly, and before Martins could say another word, the secateurs were upon him, slicing through the skin at the base of his pinky. Pain exploded in his mind—sharp, unforgiving—as, with a snap, his finger fell away. He screamed, the sound echoing in the emptiness around them, mingling with the cruel laughter of his captors. His sobbing was a dreadful sound.

'Maybe you'll remember that little girl's whereabouts, next time we ask,' the man taunted. He cut another two fingers off.

Snip.

Snip.

Martins let out an ear-splitting noise, high-pitched and wet with phlegm and blood. He babbled incoherently, tears streaming from his eyes, mingling with the blood and snot. Martins fought to stay conscious, the throbbing of his body overwhelming. Desperation clawed at him like barbs. He wanted to shout for help, for someone—anyone—to come and save him. But the factory walls absorbed his cries, and only the darkness answered—the darkness that promised no mercy.

'Listen to me,' he gasped between laboured breaths, each word a struggle. 'I don't know where she is! I swear! You're not going to get anything from me because I don't know where she is...'

'We'll see about that,' another man growled, and the cycle began again. This time he ripped two teeth from his upper jawbone and then another two fingers were cut from his right hand, leaving only the thumb. That was harder to snip, but they managed it eventually. Martins screamed and dribbled and babbled that he didn't know but the questions didn't stop. Martins closed his eyes, summoning every ounce of strength he had left.

As they continued their violent interrogation, the boundaries of his reality began to blur. He lay suspended between torment and hope, clinging to the remnants of his will to survive. Somewhere inside him, a small flicker of resolve sparked to life; he had to endure—he had to hold on. Images of her face flickered in his mind as the pliers tore another molar from his mouth. His brain shut down and he could take any more.

When he woke, PC George Martins sat in darkness, the acrid smell of burnt metal and sweat permeating the air. The cold hard floor pressed against his back, and the bindings around his wrists felt like a vice tightening with every shallow breath. His heart raced, pounding in a frantic rhythm that mirrored the chaos in his mind. The pain he felt was unbearable. His mouth was full of blood, and he spat it out, almost choking.

He couldn't remember where he was until he focused. Before him stood the gang, shadows illuminated by the flickering light of a single bulb, their faces twisted with malice. At their centre was a brutish figure wielding a blowtorch, its fiery tip glowing menacingly, casting a hellish glare across the room.

'Let's get this over with,' one of the men said, his voice dripping with sadistic glee. 'We need to know where Amber Dean is. We don't want to hurt you anymore.'

'I don't know where she, please don't hurt me anymore. I don't know anything!' Martins shouted, desperation threading through his protest. He could feel the heat from the blowtorch even from a distance. 'I swear!'

'Ok, have it your way,' the man replied, a wicked smile forming on his lips as he took a step closer, adjusting the torch. 'You're about to find out just how persistent we can be.'

Martins's body tensed, instincts screaming to fight against the bonds holding him to the chair. He had endured pain before, but this was different. The atmosphere crackled with purpose; the unrelenting pursuit of information bathed in cruelty. The man flicked a switch, and the blowtorch roared to life, the flame dancing menacingly in the air.

'You see this?' he taunted, taking another step closer, the heat now a tangible force. 'This can either be quick or slow, but trust me, it'll definitely happen.'

'Please!' Martins gasped, panic rising like bile in his throat. 'Please, I don't know anything about Amber! She was just a girl—she's missing, I get that, but I'm not involved!'

The man leaned down, heat from the blowtorch making his skin glimmer with sweat.

'Not involved? Then why were you asking questions? Why were you snooping around the park talking to young girls?'

'I was friendly with her...'

'You're a fucking nonce. You'd better start talking before this gets... messy.'

Martins could barely think, the adrenaline flooding his senses. The only thought overriding his own fear was Amber, and what she must be going through right now.

'Didn't you hear me?' the man shouted, his patience thinning. He inched the blowtorch closer, threatening to scorch Martins's skin.

'I don't want to hurt you! I really don't! But you're making this difficult.'

'Just—let me go, please. I'm begging you...' Martins pleaded, though dread coiled tightly in his stomach.

'Someone's lying. All right, let's start with where you think we might find her. You know, just a little flame to loosen those lips.'

The flame flicked towards Martins's arm, and instinctively, he jerked back, the chair squealing in protest.

'No! Please!' he shouted, but the words barely escaped before the man pressed the fiery tip against his arm. The skin blistered and blackened in seconds. The searing pain sliced through him like nothing he had ever felt. It consumed all rational thought, leaving only instinctual responses—fight or flight. But there was no escape. The flesh burned, and he screamed, the sound reverberating off the factory walls, echoing the agony he was in.

'Where is she?' the man hissed, his voice a low grunt.

'I don't know!' Martins gasped, the smell of his own burning flesh filling his senses, adding to the nauseating terror.

The man stepped back, malign satisfaction etched across his face. 'Then let's try something else.'

Without warning, he motioned to another figure who stood nearby, a drill in his hands. The low hum of the machine sent dread creeping up Martins's spine, and he felt every fibre of his being scream in protest.

'Does this make you feel uncomfortable?' the man asked with a twisted grin. 'I'd think so. You should be grateful you don't have much time left to spend with that lovely drill bit.'

Martins shut his eyes, a rush of urgency igniting within him. 'You won't get what you want! I can't help you!' he shouted through gritted teeth, even as fear threatened to overwhelm him.

The drill whirred, its buzzing a grim promise of agony. The man brought it closer, and Martins could feel the vibrations reverberating through his limbs. The world around him faded, leaving only that menacing sound.

'Last chance,' the man said, hovering the drill inches from Martins's leg. 'Tell us where she is, or I'll make sure you regret not speaking.'

Martins's breaths came in frantic gasps, his heart racing against the fear that clawed within him. The drill bit into his thigh, ripping flesh and muscle and drilling into bone. Martins became a gibbering wreck

'No! Just—just stop! Kill me, please, I can't help you!' he gasped, desperation colouring every syllable.

'Where is she?' he echoed, the sound more an ultimatum than a question, as the atmosphere thickened with expectancy. In that haunting silence, time stood still as Martins prepared himself for the torture that awaited him. The darkness of the factory refracted his fears but also held no hope—as the drill hummed back to life, he sought death and peace from the pain...

Chapter 42

Olivia

The early morning mist swept across Crosby Beach, rolling in from the Mersey and shrouding the landscape in an eerie grey veil. The Iron Men were stoic, staring out to sea, a legion of rusting metal, yet forlorn and alone, each one awaiting the relentless tide to swamp them again. Detective Olivia Mann stepped out of her vehicle and walked the long path through the dunes, the chill in the air biting at her skin as waves lapped rhythmically against the statues.

A distant figure on the sands had drawn the attention of the patrol officers stationed nearby, and she could see their tense postures as they cordoned off an area close to the water. Members of the public were curious and approached at a safe distance. Close enough to see the dead body but far enough away to not see the detail of death. When the sea gives up the dead, they're never prettier than before.

As she approached, the commotion faded into the background, her heartbeat quickening with a premonition of what lay ahead. The smell of brine mixed with something far less pleasant assaulted her senses, and her instincts kicked in, warning her to prepare for the worst. She took out her tiger balm and dabbed a blob beneath her nose.

'DS Mann?' one of the uniformed officers greeted her solemnly, his face pale beneath his uniform cap.

'Yes,' she nodded, and approached the cordon.

'We believe the victim is a serving police officer, hence the call,' the officer explained. 'His warrant card is in his wallet, PC George Martins. We didn't expect a superintendent to attend?'

'He's a person of interest,' Olivia said. 'I need to see him for myself, to be sure it's him.' She nodded, steeling herself as she stepped beyond the barricade of tape and into the grim scene. The rising tide had unearthed a sight that churned her stomach—a body half-buried in the sand, grotesque and horrifying.

As she drew closer, her stomach sank. The body was wrapped in wire mesh, giving it a macabre appearance, twisted and deformed. Weighted down by bricks, it had likely been submerged for a long time but had surfaced sooner than the killers would have anticipated. But it was the details that struck her hardest—his eyes were blackened sockets, scorched by an intense flame, the fingers and toes had been gruesomely removed, leaving behind raw stumps. The mouth was swollen, his lips stretched open unnaturally, ripped apart at the corners and the absence of teeth revealed a grim reality of torture and an agonising death—a violent interrogation had claimed this man's life.

'His eyes have been burnt out, never seen that before in fifteen years on the job. He's been tortured,' the uniformed officer said, holding his nose. Olivia looked at him and nodded, wondering why he wasn't a detective with such powers of deduction. 'Obviously...' he added.

'Are CSI on the way?' Olivia asked, her voice steady despite the chaos of emotions surging within her. She crouched low, examining the body more closely. Burns and blisters marred the skin, evidence of terrible torment etched into every inch. It was clear Martins person had not gone quietly; the signs of brutal torture were everywhere. It takes a special kind of lunatic to be able to inflict such damage to another human and listen to them scream and beg for mercy. Even the most hardened criminals employed others to do such specialist work. Someone was desperate for answers, and she knew what the question was. *'Where is Amber Dean...'*

The face was beyond recognition but as she studied the tattoos emblasoned across the victim's arms, recognition rippled through her—his ink told a story of who he had been.

'I think Dixie wanted to know where his daughter is, but you didn't give up the answer easily, did you?' she whispered under her breath, but deep down, she sensed the horrible truth.

'Morning,' DCI Knowles said from behind her. He was wearing his signature black suit and dark overcoat. 'Is it definitely him?'

'Yes.' She stood and looked around the shoreline. 'The last time I was here, I was wearing a uniform. The body of a young sex worker had been washed up just a few hundred yards past the sea wall over there.' She pointed to the spot. 'It turned out her pimp had lost his temper and gone too far. He dumped her in the river near Riverside Drive.'

'By the old festival gardens?' Knowles said, nodding. 'The chances are he was put into the water somewhere near there. The Diddy Men had property on Jamaica Street, didn't they?'

'Yes, they did. Given the tides, volume of the river, the weights in the mesh, probably,' she agreed.

'It looks like he suffered,' Knowles said, grimacing. 'Do you think Dixie Dean was looking for his daughter?'

'That was my first thought,' Olivia grimaced. 'It looks like there was an element of punishment, vindictive injuries like burning his eyes out, inflicted for the sake of it.'

'I'll give Mr Dean a visit, shall I?'

'Good luck with that.' Olivia said. 'Martins was our prime suspect in the rape of Rosie White case... and the Amber Dean disappearance and now he's dead, probably because we let him go.'

'We didn't have enough to hold him,' Knowles said, shrugging. 'Don't beat yourself up about that one.'

Her mind whirled with conflicting emotions. Martins had been under scrutiny, a sordid figure in the investigation of Amber Dean's disappearance. The line between justice and raw vengeance blurred as she felt the sadness of loss from her father's perspective but what if Martins was innocent? His final hours on this planet would have been horrific, regardless of guilt or innocence.

'We need to find out when he was reported missing.' She said to the uniformed officer. 'If he was actually reported missing,' she added.

The officer nodded, taking a step back to relay orders to the team. Olivia turned towards the dunes and forced herself to focus on the scene, the bitter tang of the ocean air filling her lungs. The reality was that Martins, despite being a suspect, was still a police officer—a human being with his own life, now extinguished in the most brutal of ways. No one deserved that level of violence but a father desperately searching for his child might disagree.

She forced her mind to think through the implications. Her thoughts turned to the gang connections, the violent underbelly of the city that had reared its head in recent investigations. There was a message here—one that spoke of danger, retribution, and fear.

As the forensic team arrived, Olivia remained rooted to the spot, her gaze fixated on the body. The wire mesh that encased him reminded her of a prison—one he could not escape, just like the case that had enmeshed them all over the past weeks. She felt constricted by the Zodiac connection, it refused to let go of her. Was it connected to Amber Dean?

'Detective Mann, we're ready for the examination,' a forensic technician called.

'Carry on,' she said. 'We're done.'

Olivia took one last look at PC Martins, a man whose fate had spiralled out of control amid the mistakes he had made. They were his own life choices.

'What are you thinking?'

'He put himself in the frame,' Olivia said, shaking her head. 'Mingling with teenage girls, whatever his motive was, will attract the attention of others. People will watch and analyse behaviour because sexual predators are everywhere, and society is aware of them. He made himself a suspect and that is ultimately how he's ended up here.' She shrugged. 'This isn't all about Amber Dean or the sexual harassment incidents he was accused of at work. This blurs into the zodiac cases too..'

'If Dixie Dean is responsible for this, we'll never know.'

Olivia agreed; this was about a world riddled with violence and revenge, colliding with the desperate needs of a father for searching for his daughter or tough justice.

'Until we find out who attacked Rosie white and took Amber Dean, we'll never find out if what happened here is vigilante justice or a fucking huge case of 'you got the wrong man, guv', Olivia said resolutely, shaking off the malaise that threatened to blanket her resolve. She was not finished—no matter how deep the shadows ran or how unsettling the truth became; she would keep moving forward.

With a determined stride, she prepared to delve deeper into the dark labyrinth that lay ahead, knowing that the answers they sought might just open doors to more unimaginable horrors waiting to be uncovered. The press would put two and two together and come up with six. They would question who Zodiac was and if he was dead, tortured to death by the father of one of his victims. Vigilante justice at its most brutal. Whatever the newspapers made of it, the search for the Zodiac wouldn't stop at the shores of Crosby Beach. It had only become intensified.

Chapter 43

Z odiac

PHIL MOULT KNEW THAT Christmas could be a lonely time, yet here he was having Janine White and Amber Dean for Christmas dinner, literally. Their livers had been pureed into pate, wrapped in bacon and roasted in the oven. They were tasty, Janine's drier and grainy damaged by alcohol; Amber's was moist and juicy, as was the rest of her. Their meat and kidneys were in a festive pie, like Nan used to bake, served with pickled onions and English mustard. The flavours were incredible.

The smell of his pie filled the small living room and there was a thick kind of suffocating silence that became more obvious during the long winter nights, wrapping itself around the house like a thick fog. Outside, the world was dressed in the glimmering joy of Christmas—a blanket of white snow shimmering under the pale moonlight but inside his home, it was dim, a twisted homage to the holiday spirit. The mundane of this world would be stuffing their fat faces with food they didn't need, opening presents they couldn't afford, bought by people they didn't particularly like with money they didn't have.

Sheeple.

'This pie is delicious, Nan,' he said. 'Although, it's not quite as good as yours were. I'm missing something.'

There, next to the cracked leather armchair, sat a withered figure clad in a faded cardigan decorated with little red snowflakes, her skeletal hands resting in her lap, still clutching the kitchen apron she always wore when making her infamous liver pate and meat pies. The scent of roasted meat clung to the air, despite it being months since she last cooked. Her smile, once full of life, was now a line of grinning teeth—no holiday cheer to be found.

At the other end of the dimly lit room, he spoke softly, almost conspiratorially, as though afraid the walls themselves might betray his secret.

The Zodiac Killer—what a title, he considered with sardonic pleasure.

It had a certain ring to it, but today was about nostalgia, not notoriety. Today was about family... sort of...

'Nan, you remember how you used to tell me the stars knew our fates?' he said, leaning closer, watching dust particles dance in the shaft of light filtering through the grimy window. His voice dipped into nostalgia, the words heavy with an eerie kind of fondness. 'You'd sit me on your knee, and we'd look at the night sky together. You'd tell me about Aries and Libra, and how the summer solstice meant I'd be thriving. You said I was destined for greatness, that the universe would shine upon me and that I should embrace it and its beauty. You made me who I am.'

He chuckled dryly, the sound bitter on his lips. 'I embraced it and well, it certainly has embraced me in return.' He paused, searching her face for a flicker of recognition or approval, just a hint of her old warmth. But only coldness stared back.

Killing had been exhilarating, but this—this was surreal. It felt more like poetry than anything else he had ever done.

'You loved the constellations, didn't you, Nan?' he continued, as though the air itself might carry his reverie to her ears. 'I can still hear your voice. You painted them for me with words—the hunter in Orion, the great bear of Ursa Major. But did you ever wonder about the signs that hung around us like ghosts? Those could tell you more than most people ever knew or could learn in ten lifetimes.'

He could practically feel her presence, her strength lingering like a phantom in the vibrating air. He leaned back in the chair opposite her, the creaking leather almost like an echo of their shared past.

'You used to say that each zodiac sign had its own power. A scorpion would sting yet protect, a lion would lead bravely, and Pisces...' He trailed off, contemplating the fish that swam blindly in search of dreams. 'Pisces can drown if they wander too far, can't they? They swim in oceans of emotion, chasing shadows beneath the waves but there are sharks down there too.' He thought about their past and people who were there, back then. 'Like Grandad. He was a shark, well he was a massive fucking paedophile, actually and you knew what he was doing to me, didn't you?' He waited for her answer, but none came. 'Of course, you did. Cunt.'

There was a stillness that clung to the room, as if it held its breath, waiting for him to unravel another thread of conversation, the needle pricked by nostalgia and his growing madness alike.

'I wonder what your horoscope would say about me, Nan. If you could see what I've done—how I've danced among the stars, how I've threaded chaos into this mundane life and given them the most intense experiences of their existence. Would Grandad be proud of what he created, or would he be disappointed?'

His voice trembled slightly, the cracks revealing the façade he wore like armour. He shot a glance at her lifeless eyes—those eyes that once twinkled with warmth and wisdom. Now they held nothing but an echo of silence, a mournful understanding.

'Did you cry when you killed him?' he asked, 'did you?' He shook his head. 'Everyone said he had just up and left you, but we know the truth, don't we?' There was a pause, but Nan didn't speak. 'He wouldn't have stopped interfering with me and my cousins, they never do. You'd had enough and I can understand that.' He smiled at that thought. He could understand people. it was part of his power. 'Did you cry when you cut him up and fed him to the pigs?'

No reply.

'I know you fed him to the pigs because they were shitting bones for weeks and one of them shit his socks out, too.' He nodded to reinforce his point. 'Did you ever cry at all?' He shrugged. 'Scorpio, and that makes you tough on the outside with a sting in your tail.' A chuckle came from his throat. 'Grandad found out the hard way, didn't he?' He took a slice of pie and pickle and chewed it, savouring the flavours. 'I can taste you ladies in every bite. So tasty. So moist...' he swallowed. 'Capricorn, that's me,' he said softly, leaning forward. 'Know what Capricorn means? Ambition. Steadfastness. But damned if it doesn't come with a touch of insanity too, just enough to make life worth living. The stars might have aligned, but I'm the one who chose the way to tear through the fabric of this world into the next. What do you think, Nan?'

He stared at her still form, trying to will her back to life, to a time when her laughter filled the air, and the holiday spirit was alive and dancing.

'They don't show you the darkness when you look at constellations, do they? They make it pretty, image after image, but they forget to paint the shadows in between the beautiful lights. Nan, the shadows are where I thrive, that is where I am.'

As he spoke, he felt as if the whole universe were listening, a cosmic audience hanging on every word, stretching beyond his mundane existence. The light in the room flickered like a gasping breath, and for a moment, he thought he spotted a glimmer of understanding in her vacant gaze.

'Maybe they're right, you know? Maybe I'm just a monster hiding my face behind charming smiles and kind words. Maybe the stars will judge me after all. But I'm no savage killing for fun, and I can still appreciate the beauty of the madness I create. The gifts that I bring are priceless.'

His laughter burst out—a sharp, jagged sound that cut through the thick air, scattering the dust, bringing it back to life. 'Just think of it, Nan. The Zodiac Killer, sitting here, waxing poetic with his dead grandmother. Who would have thought?'

He settled back again, staring at the ceiling, imagining the stars above him twinkling in unison, perhaps even giggling at his morbid joke. 'If only you could answer, Nan,' he sighed, the ghost of a smile creeping across his lips. 'If only those stars held the key to your silence, the magic to bring you back, just for today. If they could, I would snap your scrawny neck and kill you all over again...'

ZODIAC, STOOD AT HIS workbench, wholly absorbed in his macabre craft. Before him lay two human skulls, polished and gleaming under layers of varnish. Each skull had been meticulously engraved with intricate designs of astrological symbols; the twelve signs of the Zodiac entwined with delicate patterns that seemed to pulse with an unholy life of their own. They were art pieces, trophies of his harrowing mastery, positioned atop an ornate wooden effigy shaped like the Zodiac wheel—a grotesque display for the horrific rituals that occupied his mind.

'Ah, my dear Janine,' Phil murmured as he picked up the first skull, turning it in his hands. 'How beautiful you look today, peaceful where no one can use you or mock you anymore. Almost as if you're basking in the glow of your own star sign.' He traced his fingers over the engraving of the Virgin, the delicate lines etched deep enough that they would last for eternity.

He placed it back on the effigy and then lifted Amber's, still envisioning her laughter from the previous world, when she twerked and danced and laughed, so full of energy.

'And sweet Amber, the Libra. Such a beautiful soul you were. But there's no real beauty in this world, is there? Just chaos and death. Everything dies.' He chuckled softly, his voice a chilling mix of tenderness and madness. 'Some take longer than others to die, you know that.'

As he set the skull down on the table, his altar, he stepped back to admire his work. Each skull had been arranged with care, the light reflecting off the polished surfaces as if capturing the last remnants of the victim's humanity. Phil's obsession was a twisted form of reverence—a notion that they were not merely victims, but divine manifestations in his master plan. He chuckled darkly, the sound echoing in the hollow space.

Phil stepped away from the effigy, moving towards a wall plastered with news clippings that chronicled his handiwork. Headlines screamed about missing women, the looming spectre of George Martins, a suspect found tortured to death on a beach, cast in public suspicion. They claimed he was the Zodiac—though they didn't know the truth was far darker and more complex. Poor George had merely become a distraction, a diversion from the grand plan, which had led the authorities away from the real horror.

Zodiac.

As the darkness fell outside, enveloping the old slaughterhouse in shadow, Phil's laughter rose again, chilling and melodic—a haunting symphony mocking the lives he had extinguished. All around him, the Zodiac's signs gleamed fiercely, a promise of more chaos to come within the near future. There was so much more work to be done and so little time to do it.

Chapter 44

Rosie
The sterile scent of antiseptic hung heavy in the air, clinging to the walls of the small examination room like a gloomy shroud. Rosie White sat on the edge of the chair in her consultant's office, anxiety crackling through her as she fidgeted with the hem of her shirt. They had run a DNA test on the foetus a week before and the results were in. Twelve weeks into a pregnancy she never anticipated or even contemplated at her tender age, every second stretched painfully while she waited for the doctor to deliver the results that both terrified and haunted her. How could this have happened to her?

Her mother, Hayley, sat stiffly in the chair next to her, wringing her hands nervously, her eyes puffy from crying. On the other side, her father, Bill, leaned forward, his brow furrowed with concern. He had anger etched into his face. The tension in the room was palpable, a collective breath held in anticipation of a truth they were all desperate to uncover yet equally terrified to face. What parent wants to discover who raped and impregnated their child?

'Rosie, it's going to be okay,' Bill reassured, though the tremor in his voice betrayed the uncertainty they all felt. 'We'll get through this together, whatever happens. I don't want you to feel guilty.'

'I don't feel guilty.' Rosie nodded, but the words barely registered. She felt detached from the world, her mind battling echoes of trauma that threatened to drown her under waves of disbelief and despair. She wished she hadn't gone to the stupid fucking party. As she looked at her parents, their eyes filled with worry, she felt a warmth mixed with sorrow grappling within her. They cared deeply, despite their own issues but they had no idea of the darkness that loomed behind her circumstances or the nightmares she endured. At that moment, the door opened, and Dr Hughes entered, her expression serious but compassionate. Rosie's heart raced, its rhythm quickening in sync with her mounting dread. She could see the doctor held a folder, and in that moment, it seemed to Rosie, the weight of the world rested squarely on those few sheets of paper. Tell me who raped me and made me pregnant...

'Rosie, Hayley, Bill,' the doctor greeted, her voice soft yet firm. 'Thank you for your patience. I know the last few weeks have been incredibly challenging, and under the circumstances, I appreciate your strength in coming forward for the paternity test.'

Rosie felt her stomach twist as she took a deep breath, desperate to remain composed. She searched Dr. Hughes' face for any hint of what was to come, but all she found was a practised professionalism that felt both calming and unnerving. Tell me...

'After conducting the tests, we have identified the biological father of the baby,' Dr Hughes continued, pausing to let the gravity of her words settle. 'The DNA is in the police database. I'm afraid this is extremely difficult for me, as it will be for you, I'm sure.'

In that moment, a chill ran down Rosie's spine as her heart sank. The storm of uncertainty surged within her; a tempest of hate and anger that felt uncontainable.

The memories of being frozen, unable to move or resist while he was on her. Feeling him thrusting inside her, his breath on her neck, his tongue in her mouth, making her gag. She was traumatised by the rape, but nobody seemed to understand the intensity of the damage.

'Hurry up. Who is it?' she managed to ask, her voice barely above a whisper. 'Tell me, for fuck's sake.'

The doctor took a deep breath, softening her gaze. 'The father is George Martins.'

Stunned silence enveloped the room, and Rosie's mind reeled as she processed the name. George Martins, the police officer whose tragic story had gripped the community just weeks earlier was a monster, a paedophile, a rapist.

At first, the press said he was a bright light extinguished too soon, found dead in the river, his body showing signs of having been tortured but that changed when the truth came out. Knowing that he had drugged her, raped her and was the father of her child left her knots of fear and anguish, a whirlwind of emotions that threatened to drown her in hate. It was the ultimate betrayal. He had befriended the family, her especially; she actually had a crush on him at one point. To be drugged and raped by a figure of trust, a police officer charged with working with families was a sick as it was despicable. Why had he done this to her?

Rosie buried her face in her hands, tears springing to her eyes. The revelation felt like additional torment—a cruel twist of fate that connected her suffering to another tragedy, her friend Amber Dean. The implications of her situation began to spiral in her mind, intertwining her with a man who had faced unspeakable horrors during his death, yet he had drugged and raped her, and she felt no sympathy for him. She felt as if the walls were closing in, the burden of her trauma becoming unbearable as the threads of her life tangled further into a web of loss and confusion, betrayal, disbelief and anger like she had never felt before.

The faces of her parents displayed concern morphing into horror as they processed the full implication of the revelation.

'I know you trusted him,' Bill said. 'I'd strangle the bastard if her wasn't...'

'Already dead...'

'You should not feel any guilt...' the doctor began.

'I don't feel any guilt. Why would I? I was drugged and raped,' she interrupted, her voice breaking. 'I didn't have any choice in this, but I have one now. Get it out of me...I want an abortion...'

Rosie took a shuddering breath, still trying to comprehend the reality of everything that had just been unveiled. She looked first at her mother and then her father, their eyes filled with compassion and hurt. The truth was a heavy burden, but perhaps the future wasn't all purely dark. She had a future to look forward to, but her friend Amber was still missing, probably dead. Things could be worse.

Chapter 45

18-months later
Olivia was reading a report from DCI Knowles, who was still scrambling around, trying to identify the victims from Delamere Forest and clarify where they were taken from and why they were targeted. It was like trying to find the beginning of the Sellotape with your eyes closed and gloves on. The common denominator was their precarious attachment to their surroundings. Several had threatened to run away, so when they vanished, assumptions were made. One of the victims had run away from an overbearing father because he had come out and told him he was gay. The homophobic parent had banished his son, and he ended up in a tent on the streets. The homeless are a transient group and if they disappear, no one notices.

Allisson, a young female victim had argued with her foster mother before school, threatened to run away and never arrived. Assumptions were made again. The runaway link prevailed.

They had found a planchet, ornately carved and obviously once loved, beneath the headless body of Michelle Tulley, who had once been called, Donna Walker but had left a stormy marriage behind, run away and changed her name to start again away from her abusive husband. It had taken eight months to get a DNA match on her body and identify her as a woman who made a living from being a sensitive. She advertised her services online and become a victim of Zodiac. They had no clue how or when she was targeted. She was estranged from her family; hence no one had reported her missing. Another runaway.

The pattern repeated itself and if it hadn't been for the rains in Delamere Forest, they would be none the wiser. The big question was, how did the Zodiac know that they were potentially vulnerable? How did he spot his victims?

Zodiac had been an expert at identifying people who would not be missed, with only a couple of exceptions. Was he close enough to know their predicament or was it coincidence?

The discovery of the victims and following investigation had resulted in the questioning of dozens of registered sex offenders, interviews and the elimination of anyone on the radar had taken a mammoth effort. The nets were cast far and wide with no joy. If Zodiac was still out there, he had found another way of disposing of his victims and he had scurried back into the dark shadows where he had dwelled unseen for years.

There was a knock on her door and a face appeared.

'You've had a hand delivered letter, boss,' the detective said. 'Looks suspect according to the front desk.'

'It's not Valentine's Day,' she smiled. 'So, it's not a card...'

'No, ma'am. No roses or chocolates attached to it.'

'Where is it?' Olivia asked.

'They're bringing it upstairs now to check for traces. Do you want forensics informed?'

'Yes please,' she said. 'Who delivered it?'

'Someone dressed in a red coat.'

'A red coat?' she smiled. 'Like a postman.'

'Yes. The temp thought he was a postman, but remembers he was really tall,' the detective laughed. 'The real postman had already delivered to the post room, as usual but the civvy on the desk is an agency temp and hasn't got a Scooby doo how things operate here.'

'Agency staff on the front desk?' Olivia shook her head. 'No wonder things get fucked up...'

She picked up the phone and called Knowles, but he was already aware and on his way to her office. Knowles gathered as many detectives as were available and they met in operations, outside Olivia's office. Fifteen minutes later, they were ready to inspect the mysterious envelope. Two cameras were set up and the images cast to the screens in MIT. There was an air of anticipation in the room, excitement tinged with doubt that it could be an elaborate hoax. Everything was set in motion, poised to be mobilised.

'Are we ready to go?' Olivia asked. Nodding heads gave the green light.

The envelope was brought in, and she cleared a space. A uniformed officer wearing latex gloves placed it on the desk and stepped back as if it might explode.

'It's been checked for explosives,' Knowles shook his head with frustration.

'I know,' the officer said, smiling. 'I checked it, but old habits die hard.'

Another officer was taking photographs of it. Olivia noted it was crafted from coarse brown paper, its surface slightly crinkled and aged, suggesting it has been handled many times before. It was clearly old, finger marks were visible, smudged by time.

'Get images of these finger marks,' Olivia said, pointing. 'He's left these here for a reason. Everything he does, is for a reason.' She donned a pair of her own gloves and inspected it. The texture was rough to the touch, imbued with an air of foreboding. There was a dark teardrop shaped stain, which looked like dried blood. She felt a shiver run down her spine. It was from Zodiac; she could sense it.

'There are too many traces of evidence to look at here,' she mumbled. 'He's been so careful so far. Why leave us all this evidence on one envelope to analyse?'

'Maybe it's not from him...'

'Maybe.' She tilted it in the light. 'Can you see this?'

At the centre of the envelope, a subtle watermark added an eerie detail. It depicted the signs of the Zodiac, embossed into the fibres of the paper, depicting twelve sinister symbols that seemed to shift when viewed from different angles, catching the light, appearing and disappearing as she moved it.

'That is not from Smiths,' Knowles said. 'He's had that made to order.'

'Get someone online to see who can manufacture embossed paper,' she agreed. 'I bet there are only a few. This envelope has been made from a larger piece of embossed paper, maybe A3 in size and then folded down and glued together.'

Wrapped securely around the envelope was a length of old, frayed string, its fibres dulled and discoloured by time, hinting at a history that transcended its current purpose. The knots were tied tightly and there were strands of black curly hair in them, suggesting a strong desire to send a message about whatever secrets lay within.

'This hair looks human to me,' Olivia shook her head. 'He's sent us a letter with traces of his victims in it.'

'Get that hair to the lab. I want it rushed and question one, is it human?'

At the lip of the envelope, a crimson wax seal held it shut, the emblem pressed into the wax leaving an imprint that gave the impression of a bygone era, an ancient symbol from a different time. The seal glinted faintly, its smooth surface contrasting with the roughness of the paper. The seal's design is a scorpion, tail raised in anger, threatening to sting, hinting at the sender's dark intentions, encircled by rune-like script.

'Can we get images of this script sent to our boffins to see if they mean anything or if they're decoration, please.'

She sniffed the air. A strange scent wafted from it—an amalgamation of perfume, one she recognised but didn't wear and something metallic, like blood. This unsettling aroma created an instinctive sense of dread, as if the envelope itself were alive with a sinister energy. Evil oozed from it.

'Okay, this is creepy as shit,' Olivia said, shaking her head. 'This is either from Zodiac or someone doing a fucking great job of pretending to be him.'

The string was removed and bagged and the wax seal, sliced with a scalpel. The letter slid out and they tagged and bagged the envelope, and it was taken away immediately, to be examined. She unfolded the letter and spread it out onto a scanner, so that everyone could read the text. It was handwritten in red ink, or something made to look like blood.

Detective Olivia Mann

Speke Hall Avenue

Liverpool

Darling Olivia Mann,

I hope this letter finds you in high spirits, although with the recent articles circulating through your precious press, I doubt it. The pressure must be on you to get results and quieten them. Cunts.

I have to say you looked gorgeous in your leather pants last week at the wine bar in Lark Lane, sexy but alluring, classy not brassy and your perfume was to die for. I am certain it was Coco Chanel Mademoiselle, my all-time favourite fragrance apart from your underwear. The smell of your underwear is unforgettable.

I'm so glad you don't wash them immediately after you take them off. That dirty washing basket holds some true treasures, only appreciated by yours truly, and trust me, I took my time with them on several occasions.

You are truly stunning and I'm planning to fuck you at some point soon. I'm very much looking forward to it, to be honest. You're drawing too much of my focus away from my plans, so better to fuck you, kill you and absorb you and then I can concentrate on the job in hand. We are so easily distracted, especially those of us with a penis.

Another cycle of the zodiac has run its course since I've spoken, and some people are grating on my nerves, to the point of distraction. Obviously, I am referring to the press. Cunts. And so, I need to clarify some things.

Let me expand. I am writing to you, not out of concern for your wellbeing because you will die soon anyway, but out of fury that you have allowed the liars to continue their speculation without correcting them. It seems the world has intertwined truth with fiction once again, as they declare the Zodiac killer dead, killed by a notorious gangster and his crew in the search for his daughter,

Amber Dean. His search was understandable but in vain. She's with me now, forever at one with the universe.

Some are speculating that she is still alive, held captive in a dungeon somewhere, others are insisting on giving the credit for my work to a mere muppet, constable—George Martins.

How laughable!

PC Martins was a pervert in his own right, no doubt about it and I should know. I'm an expert. I have to say he was unfortunate and must have suffered immensely before he died, which I find amusing. I wonder if they filmed it for Amber's father to watch?

I would love to see that recording. What he did to little Rosie was nothing short of criminal. There was nothing to be gained from it except gratuitous sex. He should have stayed at home and had a wank and maybe he would still be alive. My achievements are far beyond his capabilities. I'm sure you appreciate that, my love...

Perhaps the press should step off their soapboxes and look a little deeper into the shadows for the answers. I know what you're thinking again, is this me or someone else pretending to be me?

It is me, Zodiac, but then I would say that, wouldn't I? Here are some undeniable facts to verify me claims.

I am very much alive, and I have been watching you day and night sometimes both. Your pink nightie is my favourite, although the black one blows my mind too, but seeing you naked is my absolute headfuck. I like the pink nightie best because you leave stains behind, which can be seen as well as inhaled. The black one hides a multitude of sins but looks better on you. Pink makes you look like a Barbie doll. I put both of them over my face and masturbated into your bottle of Baileys four times. That was so much fun. I slept in your bed that night as it was obvious you wouldn't be home for a week. Facebook airport photos are so stupid. I did masturbate into the Baileys again in the morning, but I gave it a good shake before putting it back. The next time I visited, the bottle was nearly empty which made me so hot. Did you taste me alone or did you share it with friends?

You sometimes read naked, your tbr pile is on the bedside table to your left; you've just finished The Child Taker and The Boyfriend, Genesis and Living with a Serial Killer.

Your Rampant Rabbit dildo is in the top drawer to your right, it's blue and smells of you. I spent a while with it, penetrating myself, imagining you being there to watch me; what fun we had in my mind. Sorry, but I didn't give it a wipe when I put it back in the drawer. Did you feel my presence there at all, or smell me on your love toy?

I like watching you fuck yourself with it although when you do it under the covers, it makes me so fucking angry...selfish cunt.

It is best when you take your time on top of the covers with extra lube, (middle drawer), usually on a Sunday morning, isn't it?

We will have such sticky scenes, you and I when the time comes, and I have so much to show you. Things so painful that you could never imagine...

You will be wondering how I have seen such intimate moments and pleasured myself with your rubber friend. You will work it out for yourself.

The clock is ticking and watching you through a lens is no longer satisfying me. A physical connection is nearing.

I often watch you on the cross-trainer at Fitness World and love the shape of your thighs when you wear leggings to the gym. Your muscle tone is to be admired and desired and I look forward to tasting you in more ways than one. I think I will bottle some of your body fluids to remind me of your pain and suffering when you have gone. We can cross that bridge when we reach it.

I must say, I do like your dark friend from Sunday night at the Panam restaurant on Lark Lane. The steak pie and minted peas looked amazing. I liked her so much; I've decided to give her some of my gifts. She has been so much fun, although she's not having as much of a good time as I am, I must say. I'm not sure she has much left in her, but I'll make the most of her while I can. She has begged profusely for death and mentioned your name occasionally, but I can't kill her yet, where is the fun in that?

I've attached some of her hair for you and you may be able to smell her perfume and pussy juice on the envelope. There's a drop of her blood on there too. The pain is exquisite. You will see for yourself soon.

As for your friends at the press, rest assured, the Zodiac will rise from the ashes of their ignorance, and I will remind you and the public of my existence in a most unforgettable way. Once we have shared some quality time together and I've sent some pieces of you to them, my work will continue. I will feed the universe for all of my days.

Over the next twelve months, I will claim a victim for each sign of the Zodiac, carving their symbols into their flesh, etching my legacy deeper into the annals of true crime but not like last time. Attention to detail is crucial. Each victim will be from their own star sign, not random. I missed this important detail last time, but not this time. My table will be perfect, and my plan is set in stone.

Herein lies the list of the Zodiac signs, and the fate that awaits those who fall under their influence:

1. **Aries (March 21 - April 19)**: A fiery beginning. I foresee a victim taken by surprise, just as the first spring blooms.

2. **Taurus (April 20 - May 20)**: Earthy and sturdy; my hand will bring them crashing down. A testament to the stubbornness of the bull.

3. **Gemini (May 21 - June 20)**: Duality will be my theme. A pair, perhaps, entwined in the web of fate, each meeting their end in synchronized despair.

4. **Cancer (June 21 - July 22)**: Comfort will become their curse. In their own sanctuary, they'll discover that the security they cherished was a lie.

5. **Leo (July 23 - August 22)**: A royal decree of death. The lion will learn that its roar cannot save it from the blades of destiny.

6. **Virgo (August 23 - September 22)**: Methodical and precise, just as their nature; they'll be found in a manner that reflects the purity and chaos of life's balance.

7. **Libra (September 23 - October 22)**: Justice will be served, but not in the way they expect. The scales will tip violently, and harmony will vanish.

8. **Scorpio (October 23 - November 21)**: In the dark corners where secrets fester, I will strike swift and sure, embodying the very essence of their depth.

9. **Sagittarius (November 22 - December 21)**: Freedom will be an illusion. As they chase their adventures, I will plot their demise, bringing them back to earth with brutal force.

10. **Capricorn (December 22 - January 19)**: Ambition will be their downfall. I'll infiltrate the halls of their aspirations and leave behind a message carved for the ages.

11. **Aquarius (January 20 - February 18)**: The outcast will face their reckoning; the visionary will see their dreams turned to nightmares.

12. **Pisces (February 19 - March 20)**: In the depths of their imagination, they will drown, lost in a sea of despair without a lifeline in sight.

Let your friend's pain and suffering serve as a warning: do not presume to label me a relic of the past. I will prove to you and to the world that the Zodiac is far from finished. I will be eternal.

The stars have not aligned in favour of your misconceptions. This will be a year to remember—my year with you.

With hungry anticipation to taste you,

Zodiac

P.S. The clock is ticking. Keep your eyes wide open. The countdown has begun.

Olivia felt the bile rise in her throat and vomited where she stood. Several detectives went to her aid, giving her water and helping her to the toilet. A cleaner was brought in to mop up the bile as the stench of puke drifted through the room. A couple of detectives were visibly upset by the letter, their tears hot with the sting of anger in them.

'Take a break,' Knowles ordered the room of officers. 'Have a cigarette, grab a coffee and be back here in fifteen minutes.'

THE GATHERING RECONVENED but was in shock. It was almost silent and long minutes ticked by as the words were read and reread. No one wanted to be the first to speak. Olivia retuned to the room, looking shaken and pale. She was on her phone, hands shaking with concern. The call wasn't answered and Olivia gathered herself.

'Firstly, I'm okay.' She looked at the concerned faces in front of her. 'We need to unpick this sick fucker's words. Priority number one is the reference to Lark Lane on Sunday.' She pointed to the screen. 'On Sunday night I was at an awards event with a friend of mine, Phina Moran,' Olivia typed a message at the same time as making a call. 'She's not called or texted me since Monday night and she's not answering her phone.' She looked around concerned faces. 'Her hair is like the hairs attached and that's her perfume on the envelope. We have to assume that he's telling the truth, and he has Phina.'

'Can I make a suggestion, as well as trying to locate your friend?' Steff Cain asked, taking the lead. 'He has clearly got a camera in your bedroom, so let's work out how he got it there and scan your home for more.'

'Okay. There have been a number of break-ins, starting just over a year ago, the first while I was on holiday, the others when I have been away walking or visiting friends,' Olivia remembered. 'A laptop and tablet were taken, which seemed normal. Some tools and crap from the garage and my bicycle. No mess, no damage, no reason to suspect there was an alternative motive but everything he says in the letter is correct.' Olivia flushed purple with anger. 'This fucker has been in my home, fucking with my dirty laundry, and as for my Baileys....for fuck's sake.' She looked like she was going to throw up again. 'It takes sick to a whole new low...'

'We'll catch him, boss.'

'I suggest we scan everything in your bedroom and living room. We need to do it now and anticipate that he will know we're about to send a search team to your house.' Steff took the lead. 'He may be planning something nasty for us when we get there. Can I have your keys.'

'Absolutely,' Olivia agreed. She picked up her handbag and removed her keys. 'Check my house, inside and out and it would make sense to check over my car too.' Steff took the keys and left the gathering for a small office to the left with three other detectives. 'Do we have the CCTV footage from the front desk yet?'

'Yes, boss,' a detective said. He showed a clear image of the male dropping off the letter at the desk. 'He's at least 6feet-4inches tall, skinny build. His face is covered by the baseball cap and scarf.'

'There were dozens of cameramen at that event on Lark Lane,' Olivia pointed to the image. 'Get hold of the guest list and ask anyone who attended for their images of the night. He's distinctive because of his height. If he was there, he may be in the background somewhere. We may have a clear image of his face just waiting for us to find.'

'Good idea,' Knowles said. 'Check the social media pages for the event and anyone who attended. There will be dozens of images uploaded to them.'

'He said Phina is still alive. Let's find this fucker and take him down.'

'While we gather the images, can we go through the disclosures made in the letter, one by one?' Knowles said. 'Sorry if this is difficult, Olivia. Some of this is very embarrassing.'

'Not for me,' Olivia said, shaking her head. 'There's not a person on this team, male or female who doesn't masturbate, so let's not take things out of perspective. This sick bastard has invaded my home at least once and he's letting me know he can do it again, when he's ready.' She shrugged. 'He has my friend. I'll do whatever it takes to stop him in his tracks.'

'We'll make sure that happens,' Steff said from a side office, on the phone. 'There's a search team on the way to your house. I'll meet them with the keys. You need to find somewhere to stay for a while. Somewhere we can protect you.'

'I want four teams on the CCTV from Sunday and a list of who was there,' Knowles said. 'What was the event for, Olivia?'

'Women in the community,' she answered. 'Nurses, teachers, dentists, support workers, social workers, fire officers, police officers, you know the type of thing.'

'We can rule out the females, obviously but some of the other guests fit what we're looking for,' Knowles said. 'Zodiac has been able to identify runaways, victims, sex offenders, which demonstrates some local knowledge.'

'He said George Martins was a pervert and that he was an expert,' Olivia mused. 'Maybe he is an expert, a support worker, social worker or police officer...'

'That guest list is perfect for our profile.' He picked up his phone. 'Are we on their Facebook page yet?'

'Yes, guv.'

'Good. We need as many images from that night as we can get our hands on.'

Chapter 46

M^{IT} The atmosphere in the Major Investigation Team's briefing room was tense yet methodical. A large screen at the front displayed a collage of images from the recent awards night in Lark Lane, Liverpool. The flickering lights cast shadows on the faces of the detectives as they gathered around, each aware of the urgency behind the investigation.

Detective Superintendent Olivia Mann stood at the forefront, her sharp eyes scanning the room before settling on the screen. There were over sixty detectives extra drafted onto the case. She needed to bring everyone up to speed, quickly.

'Listen up, everyone. We're not just looking for a suspect; we're looking for the Zodiac. The most prolific predator anyone in this room has encountered.' She paused to allow the words to sink in. 'This man has been stalking me, broke into my home and kidnapped my friend. He has killed at least ten people that we know of.' Her words fell hard on the team. 'Our intel suggests he's over six feet seven inches tall. We need to identify and locate him before he kills again.'

She motioned to the first image, highlighting social workers and police officers mingling at the event. 'While it's clear there were many people here, we need to narrow it down to anyone who might fit that description. We have reports of unusual behaviour from a tall male seen lurking outside around the entrance. Witnesses say he clearly knew other attendees there but didn't step inside the venue.

He was socialising with the smokers and others on the pavements outside.'

Detective Harris, known for his unfashionably large stature and constant perspiration, shuffled closer to the projection.

'We need to look for distinguishing features, especially in the background. He might not be in the forefront, but shadows, reflections and mirrors can reveal a lot.'

As the team studied the photographs, Olivia's focus intensified. With every passing moment, the weight of the Zodiac's presence loomed larger in her mind. Her pulse quickened at the thought of the sick bastard being in her home, her bed, her dirty laundry, masturbating in her home. It was vile and made her violently nauseous.

Hours passed as the team meticulously combed through the images, and just when fatigue began to set in, a clear reflection caught Olivia's eye. It was an image of an ornate window, distorted but revealing a figure standing just outside. The individual appeared to be tall, looming over others, just as described in the reports. He was staring at someone inside. Staring at her.

'Look at the reflection there!' Olivia exclaimed, pointing at the screen. The team leaned in closer, recognising the significance of the find. A tall thin male could be seen staring into the window. The body language of the figure spoke volumes—imposing, stalking, predatory.

DS Harris squinted, wiping his brow. 'That's no more than just a reflection... but I'm sure I've seen that face before.' He turned to his colleagues, enthusiasm fuelling the determination in the room. 'Can we zoom in onto the face?'

The image became larger and was brought into focus. As the team focused and gathered around the screens, Harris shouted, 'That's Phil Moult! He's a social worker with the child protection unit in Knowsley. Had a few run-ins with him during my previous investigations in Huyton. Always seemed a bit odd to me.'

Recognition spread across Olivia's face as she recalled the name—Phil Moult had worked with troubled youth, but something about him didn't sit right with her instincts. 'If he's involved in this, we need to act now. He has connections, and he could easily slip out of sight.'

Without wasting another moment, Olivia called for immediate action. 'We need to get his personal details from Huyton HR.'

There were frantic calls and emails made, trying to trace him.

'HR at Huyton said, Phil Moult has been on long-term sick leave for eighteen months,' an officer said. 'Stress apparently following the death of his grandmother.'

'Okay, so we know he has dropped out of work. In the meantime, find out where he is. Track down Phil Moult.'

'Knowsley social services are saying, he lives in an old farm in Tarbock Green, called Blue Duck Corner. The ACC has given the green light for a warrant.'

'I want surveillance on the property and armed response teams ready to mobilise. We're not taking any chances with this fucker.'

The room buzzed with energy as officers sprang into motion. There was an unmistakable urgency in Olivia's tone that resonated with everyone present. Her hatred for this man was clear. Each detective understood the stakes—they were not only chasing a prolific murderer but potentially a murderer who had not finished his mission, had threatened Olivia Mann and eluded justice for far too long.

A few minutes later, the team gathered in the operations room, armed with new intelligence. Dressed in tactical gear, they prepared for deployment. Harris, still sweating, paced back and forth, driven by the increasing adrenaline.

'I know the area well and can give you the directions to the farm. Some of the access roads are not on the maps and there's a deep brook running through the farm. It's secluded and there are half a dozen out buildings and an old slaughterhouse attached to the farmhouse; that's what makes it perfect for someone trying to hide.'

Olivia nodded, her resolve firm. 'Let's keep communication tight. If Moult is indeed the Zodiac, we need to stay one step ahead. Check in continuously.'

As the team divided into squads, Olivia felt a weight lift, yet a new tension formed. Time was of the essence—they were not just chasing a ghost; they were moving toward a confrontation that could endanger lives. With her instincts guiding her, she led the charge, pushing back the fear that urged her to be cautious. In that moment, it was clear—this was more than another arrest for her; it was personal.

Chapter 47

Z odiac
    The air in the old slaughterhouse was thick with the stench of blood, vomit and despair. Shadows danced across the walls, flickering with the dim, buzzing lights of a single bank of fluorescent lights hanging low from the ceiling. In the centre of the room lay Phina, on an old wooden block, her body trembling as Zodiac worked methodically, carving the signs of the zodiac into her back with deliberate precision. She screamed in agony with each movement of the blade. Each incision was a calculated stroke, a grim manifestation of his twisted obsession, a perverse masterpiece he intended to complete. She was becoming weaker and may not survive much longer. She would taste so sweet, the liver strong and savoury, her meat tender like a good pork chop. Maybe apple sauce with her?

Phina had been held captive for days, her spirit nearly vanquished, raped and tortured yet she clung to the flicker of hope that the nightmare would end but it seemed to go on forever. She would welcome death when it came to embrace her. As the sharp blade traced another symbol, her body went rigid, a mixture of pain and defiance coursing through her veins. There was nothing she could do but endure the pain and wait for death.

Suddenly, the heavy metal roller doors of the slaughterhouse burst open. Shouts rang out as armed police stormed in, a unit of heavily armed officers moving like robots with the fluidity of synchronised swimmers, focused on only one thing. Zodiac.

Zodiac froze, his heart pounding in his chest. His sanctuary had been breached and he wasn't pleased about the interruption.

'Aaah Phina, my lovely,' he whispered in her ear. 'They have come too soon. We can finish this another time. I will find you, don't despair.'

Without hesitation, he abandoned his grim task and sprinted toward a narrow staircase that led to the farmhouse next door. Each footfall echoed in the high ceilings, his mind racing. He had planned for this — an escape route, a way to slip into the darkness beyond his killing room. In his mind, he could almost taste Phina, he had been so close. Mundane cunts, ruining the moment.

He reached the top of the stairs and glanced over his shoulder, momentarily relieved. But that relief was short-lived as he found himself face to face with a second armed response unit, blocking his escape. The officers held their weapons steady, their faces hardened with resolve.

'Zodiac! Put down the weapon!' one officer shouted, his voice piercing through the tension like a knife. There was a moment of silence as their eyes locked.

For a heartbeat, the world stopped. Zodiac's fingers tightened around the handle of the meat cleaver gripped in his hand, its blade glinting ominously in the sparse light. He had intended this weapon for Phina, but now it would serve another purpose. Fuelled by desperation and the fear of a cornered animal, he lunged forward, his roar of rage drowning out the commands of the officers. He reached his alarm control panel and pressed the panic button. The noise was ear-piercing, stunning the police officers and the zero vision smoke bombs exploded. Designed to deter burglars from climbing the stairs, they gave him precious minutes to escape in the confusion.

'Step back!' shouted the commanding officer, but it was too late. The cleaver arced through the air, a dark promise of violence, but the officers moved as one, trained and ready. A hail of bullets erupted, filling the air with the deafening sound of gunfire. Zodiac's body jerked as he was struck, the cleaver slipping from his grasp and clattering to the ground. He fell, the fire in his eyes fading, clutching his chest, the pain intense and exciting. The smoke thickened and visibility became zero.

Olivia stood just outside the doorway, her heart racing as she felt the heat of the moment wash over her. She had followed the trail of the Zodiac for too long—a monster that had haunted her every waking thought. She felt a pang of sorrow as she turned her gaze toward the paramedics rushing to Phina's side, her friend barely clinging to life, but the paramedics could hardly breathe. One of them fell to his knees. She ran into the smoke to help them.

'Phina!' Olivia called out, her voice a desperate plea. The shadows inside the old slaughterhouse loomed like dark spectres against the smoke, the air thick with the acrid scent of cordite and adrenaline. The armed police units stormed blindly inside, their tactical lights piercing through the clouds of confusion created by Zodiac's panic alarm and smoke bombs—a cacophonous siren that shrieked like a banshee, disorienting everyone within earshot. Officers stumbled back, clutching their ears, momentarily stunned by the sonic assault, just as the first plumes of thick, swirling smoke engulfed the cramped corridors. Other officers fell to the ground, choked by the fumes, unable to breathe.

Zodiac stood up, his Kevlar vest had done its job and stopped the bullets. The smoke bombs had worked faster than he had anticipated. Vision was snatched away, replaced with a choking darkness that turned the slaughterhouse into a labyrinth of panic and chaos. But within that obscurity, a glimmer of insanity illuminated a dark corner of his mind.

Olivia.

Zodiac had prepared for this moment, knowing the chaos it would unleash. Breathing heavily through his nose, he reached for the gas mask he'd stashed in the shadows of the stairwell—a vital detail that would make all the difference.

With the mask secured, he stepped into the chaos, moving through the smoke like a wraith. The blaring sirens of his alarm had become a cloaking device, making him untouchable again, a thrill igniting the very core of his madness. He had waited years for this; he was not just a predator, but a ghost, a god hunting and his prey was Detective Olivia Mann—the thorn in his side for far too long, the object of his desires and his next victim. He might eat her alive and let her watch as he chewed her.

He navigated the smoke with ease, scanning the shadowy faces of officers who wrestled with their disorientation. Then he spotted her—Olivia, diligently trying to get her bearings and find the ambulance men but she had become separated. He could see the determination in her stance, even amid the chaos, and it fuelled his obsession to devour her.

His movements were deliberate as he waded through the smoke toward her. Olivia, was oblivious to his approach, distracted by the chaos that enveloped the officers around her. He glided past gasping officers, a predator navigating a maze of incapacitated prey. He approached her from behind, the contours of the room bending and shifting like a dream, only Olivia existed.

'Olivia, my darling,' he whispered, his voice smooth and chilling. 'I told you it wouldn't be long before we could be together.'

Before she could react, he seized her wrist and smothered her nose and mouth, pulling her into the dense smoke. The world transformed into a haze of chaotic sounds and frantic movements as he dragged her towards a hidden fire escape, a decaying relic that led downward to the banks of a treacherous brook—his sanctuary as a child and now theirs together. He had her in his grasp and he would never let her go until he had consumed her.

'Let go of me, you bastard!' Olivia shouted, though her voice was swallowed by the alarms and smoke. 'Help me, he's here!'

She struggled, adrenaline surging through her limbs, but his grip was ironclad. He dragged her into the stairwell and kicked the door closed, bolting it from the inside.

'No one can help you now,' he smiled and dragged her by the hair. Olivia was powerless to resist. He was too strong. Down they descended, the metal staircase creaking underfoot and echoing their descent deep into the looming night. Olivia felt as if she was being dragged into hell itself.

The smell in the stairwell was thick with damp and dry rot as Olivia stumbled down the steps, dragged by a total psychopath into the darkness, her breath quickening with each metallic step groaning beneath her weight. The faint light filtering through a filthy window illuminated the cobwebs that hung like veils against the crumbling walls, casting eerie shadows that danced mockingly in air, as they descended to who knows where. Olivia was terrified. Zodiac's grip was ironclad, each finger digging deep into her upper arm, making escape a distant fantasy. Panic clawed at her throat; she writhed, her heart pounding furiously. But he was too strong, an embodiment of evil and malice.

'Let go of me, you bastard!' she screamed and aimed a kick at his genitals. She missed.

With a sudden jolt, he delivered a sharp punch to the back of her head, and the world went momentarily black as pain exploded through her skull. Stars clouded her vision, and she cursed her own weakness as the frantic descent continued.

'Struggling won't help you, my little beauty, but it turns me on,' he taunted, his voice low and sinister, reverberating off the damp walls. Each syllable dripped with mockery. 'Did you enjoy your Baileys?'

'Fuck you! She screamed.

'Oh, you will, beautiful,' he chuckled. 'Alive and dead, you will.'

Tears pricked at her eyes, but Olivia fought them back, focusing on the cold, stinging sensation left by his fist. She had sworn to bring him to justice, to reclaim the souls he had taken and let them have peace. But now, faced with this monster, her resolve fled momentarily as survival instinct surged. She bit into his arm with all her might but a powerful knee to her abdomen knocked the breath out of her lungs and she fell to the ground gasping for air.

'Get up, lovely,' he dragged her by the hair. 'You like to bite?' he laughed. 'Me too...'

He dragged her down the steps until they reached a rusted door at the bottom of the stairwell, its hinges creaking ominously as Zodiac kicked it open. Beyond lay the bank of a deep, murky brook, its waters swirling dangerously, reflecting the grim sky above. Before she could fully assess her surroundings, he unceremoniously threw her onto the damp grass, the impact jarring her senses.

'Welcome to the jungle, my playground as a boy,' he snarled, dragging her by the hair, the sharp pull making her scalp scream in protest. 'My grandfather buggered me for the first time, just over there. Such vivid memories should be kept and learned from, don't you think?'

'You're a fucking freak!' she screamed. 'Get off me!' Oliva tried to break free, but he was holding her hair too tightly.

She could feel the cold, unforgiving earth beneath her as he forced her toward a derelict pier, its splintered wood jutting out over the dark waters like jagged teeth ready to snap shut. There was a small cabin cruiser moored to the bank.

'That little boat holds some memories for me,' he said, as if they were friends, walking together. 'Grandad often took me fishing on it.'

'Let go!

'Shut up,' Zodiac growled, punching her in the head again, stunning her into a confused state. Another blow sent her reeling. Her knees buckled.

'Look at you. The fearless detective, reduced to a scared little girl.' He licked a tear from her face. 'Salty and fear, tastes so good...'

His laughter was a chilling echo that gnawed at her resolve. As they neared the edge of the pier, the smell of decay mixed with the earthy scent of dampness, overwhelming her senses. Though her limbs felt heavy, and her mind swirled with fear, Olivia made a split-second decision: she couldn't let him win. With a burst of desperation, she twisted her body, kicking back with the strength she could muster. For a moment, he faltered, surprise flickering across his face. He was hurt.

'You're feistier than I thought. I like that,' he hissed, regaining his footing, but the moment of resistance only fuelled his rage. He yanked her against him, his breath hot against her ear as he leaned in. 'But all the fire in the world can't save you now. You're mine. Accept it.'

Adrenaline coursed through her veins as she met his gaze, defiance flashing in her eyes.

'You'll never have me, you fucking freak,' she spat in his eyes, her voice steady despite the tremor of fear dancing in her gut. 'They will hunt you down and blow your fucking head off.'

Zodiac's laughter exploded again, dark and unhinged. 'You really believe that? I've played this game for too long. It's your turn to lose. Now, how does it feel to know your fate is in my hands?'

With that declaration, he punched her in the guts and tightened his grip, dragging her closer to the edge of the pier as the brook raged beneath them, darkness swallowed whole the reflections of a moon that no longer shone on this forsaken place. Fear surged anew within her — but alongside it, a flicker of determination endured. As he pulled her closer to the unknown. She would not go quietly into that night.

With a sudden burst of strength, she twisted her body, wrenching her arm free and lunging forward. She collided with Zodiac, sending them both crashing onto the mossy ground at the brook's edge. Water rushed powerfully beside them, swollen from the heavy rains, frothy with the chaos of nature, just as their own conflict swirled tumultuously. In the struggle, the night turned to a blur of splashes and thrashing. She fought against him, desperation fuelling her movements. Their limbs tangled, slippery from the mud, as they rolled precariously close to the churning water. Just as Olivia managed to push him back, the earth shifted beneath her, and she stumbled into the brook. The icy waters surged around her, pulling her under, filling her lungs and wrapping around her like the cold embrace of death.

She drifted for a while like a twig in a tsunami but then her instincts kicked in. She thrashed her arms and legs, breaking the surface with a gasp, lungs burning for the air she craved. She coughed and spluttered, desperate for breath. Water cascaded off her face as she sputtered, but her heart sank at the absence of him.

The Zodiac—her captor—was gone. The swirl of confusion enveloped her surroundings, and she turned frantically, scanning the banks of the brook, but he had vanished into the night, leaving her stranded in a relentless tide of flood water.

A HUNDRED METRES ON, she finally managed to stand and make her way to the bank, scrambling and slipping in the muddy soil. She was freezing, scanning the water all the time for signs of her attacker. He was gone, the water black like oil, flowing fast towards the Mersey.

She made her way back to the slaughterhouse and chaos reigned. Officers were sitting on the floor outside, exhausted and struggling to see, their eyes streaming.

'Olivia!' Knowles shouted. 'Where did you go?'

'He found me,' she coughed. 'We fell into the river but he didn't surface.'

'Fucking hell,' he shouted. 'Paramedic! Get over here and bring a thermal with you.'

The decaying walls of the old slaughterhouse echoed with chaos. Detective Olivia Mann stood soaked and freezing, looking over the aftermath of a failed raid. The Zodiac killer, having just out manoeuvred them, a sense of foreboding filled the air.

Then came the almighty explosion. A sonic boom rattled the structure, sending the floor vibrating beneath her feet. The rear wall erupted in a shower of fire and debris, engulfing the space in an inferno. With a rancid, acrid scent filling her nostrils, Olivia instinctively turned away from the blast, heart racing as the industrial air thickened with toxic gas. Desperate coughing erupted among her fellow officers; their faces contorted in panic. Olivia's instincts screamed at her to intervene, but her body felt heavy with adrenaline, weighed down by the encroaching gas.

'What the fuck was that?' Knowles asked, covered in dust.

'A gas bottle was knocked over, boss. It went off like a rocket.'

'I want that brook watched all the way to the Mersey,' Olivia said. I want that bastard alive or dead and I don't much care which but I want him...'

Chapter 48

3 -months later
   The conference room was filled with the sense of failure. Detective Olivia Mann stood at the head of the room, her expression a mix of frustration and concern as she surveyed her weary colleagues. The raid on the old slaughterhouse had been meticulously planned, but in the blink of an eye, the elusive Zodiac killer had slipped through their fingers like smoke, a leaf disappearing into the turbulent waters of a swollen brook.

'It's been three months since the raid on the Zodiac farm and you all know that we can't throw any more resources at chasing a ghost.' She looked around the concerned faces. 'He may be lying at the bottom of Liverpool Bay, or he could be walking around Benidorm, eying up his next lunch,' Olivia began, her voice cutting through the haze of disappointment. 'Zodiac escaped us. It's that simple. He fell into the brook, but we have no idea where the current carried him and we're at a dead-end.'

Sergeant Mark Lewis leaned forward; his brow furrowed. 'Local farmers all agree that the water was moving fast. If his body was washed away, we might not see him for weeks—if ever.'

'As hard as it is to accept, that's where we are at. 'The positive we can take is that we saved Phina Moran from that bastard.'

Murmurs filled the room as the team processed the name of their survivor. There was an unshakeable silence surrounding her fate—she had been a key target of Zodiac's madness, and now her future lay at the mercy of her doctors and surgeons.

'Our forensic team is working on the evidence we collected at the farm, and answering a lot of questions but for now, the team will be wound down,' Olivia continued, shaking off the ominous thoughts about failure. 'We'll be getting updates on fingerprints and DNA and we'll keep everyone informed if anything crops up. In the meantime, I want to thank you for all your hard work and good luck for the future.'

Chapter 49

Albert Docks
Under the muted rays of the afternoon sun, Zodiac stood inconspicuously at the bustling Albert Docks in Liverpool, a distance away from the police headquarters. He blended in seamlessly with the throngs of tourists wandering the waterfront, the salty breeze tousling his hair as he casually raised a pair of binoculars to study the area. A new beard, glasses and hair colouration made him look different but his height gave him away.

'Perfect,' he muttered to himself, a satisfied glint in his eye. He feigned interest in the picturesque view of the sails upon the water and the vibrant seafood restaurants lining the docks. But his true focus was elsewhere—he was searching for one particular detective inside the police station across the road, Olivia Mann. His desire for her had not diminished, in fact it had grown beyond all recognition. He had been stalking her since the chaos of the slaughterhouse, driven by an intoxicating combination of obsession and admiration.

His heart raced with excitement as he ogled women passing by, sniffing their perfume, tourists unaware of the shadow lurking among them. A man who stared through their clothes, imagining such terrible things, beyond their imagination. Each one offered a brief heartbeat of possibility, a distraction in his quest to locate Olivia. He dissected their movements, the sway of their figures, and the glances they shared with others, wishing he could fuck them, strangle them and taste them. They were all potential victims in his mind, but there was only one he truly desired.

He adjusted the binoculars, narrowing his focus to the police headquarters. There were a few officers moving about, but every time he scanned the crowd, anticipation would surge with the hope of seeing Olivia. A sense of exhilaration coursed through him. He fantasised about the thrill of the hunt, a chill running through him at the thought of what that would mean—to finally have her.

Hours slipped by in a haze of voyeuristic reverie, but just as he began to lose hope, he spotted a flash of familiar features. Her blonde hair glistened in the wind, a smile brighter than the sun itself.

'There you are,' he whispered, a predatory smile creeping onto his lips. Olivia was weaving through the crowds, a determined look etched into her expression. The excitement surged within him, a fire igniting as he adjusted his grip on the binoculars tighter.

Focus, he told himself, feeling the thrill of the chase wash over him in waves.

Chapter 50

H appy Hour

IT WAS A BEAUTIFUL summer's day when Olivia Mann decided
to take a break from the relentless pressures of the investigation and
visit the Albert Docks. The air smelled of fish and chips, mingling
with the briny scent of the nearby river. She wore jeans, boots, and a
simple tee-shirt. It was an outfit meant to allow her to blend in, but
her beauty was rare.

As she walked along the bustling promenade, she caught sight
of a neon sign flashing, "Happy Hour! Double Shots of whisky,
vodka, gin and Baileys—Only £1!" The advertisement twisted in
her stomach. She used to find such things enjoyable, but now, the
thought of drinking Irish Cream was sickening in light of everything
that had transpired. With a slight shudder, she crumpled her
half-eaten sandwich and tossed it into an overflowing bin, the act
feeling like a dismissal of what should have been normalcy. He was
still there at the back of her mind. Always.

Olivia meandered toward the river, each step heavy with the
longing to break away from her thoughts. The laughter of tourists
around her ebbed into the background as she revelled in the
momentary escape. But as the sunlight glinted off the water, a
prickling sensation crept up her spine—a feeling that she was being
watched.

She paused, shielding her eyes from the brightness, scanning the
crowd behind her. It was a busy afternoon, people bustling about,

enjoying the summer air. Yet, among them, she felt an inexplicable weight, a gaze too fixed. Her heart thudded in her chest as she tightened her grip on the bridge railing, forcing herself to breathe.

'Get a hold of yourself,' she murmured. But deep down, she wondered if it was simply paranoia or something far more sinister. The feeling lingered, and she fought against the dread that whispered reminders of the Zodiac, the lingering shadows of terror that had seeped into her everyday life. Determined not to let unease dictate her day, she took a deep breath and turned her attention to the rippling waters before her, trying to shake the sensation that there were eyes on her back. Her mind replayed the blurred image of Phina in the hospital, the fragile strength of attempted recovery, and in that moment, she vowed to drive the bastard from her mind. She wanted to rid herself of the Zodiac but he wouldn't let her go.

Little did she know, hidden amidst the crowd, the very eyes she feared were watching every step she took, every movement she made. The hunt was far from over and she was top of the menu.

Chapter 51

Stalker

The moon hung high in the ink-black sky, its silvery light spilling down onto the quiet suburban street like a ghostly veil. From the shadows of an adjacent alley, Zodiac watched with unwavering focus, a cold thrill shooting through him. He had stalked Olivia for years, and tonight, he felt the darkness surrounding him as his ally. Her house was familiar to him. He had entered it several times, but it had been off limits for a few years, since his face had been plastered all over the news. It was so exciting to be so close to her again. He could almost taste her. Almost.

Peering through the trees, it was the silhouette of Olivia he coveted—not the flashes of her life, but the very essence of her vulnerability. The blinds of her bedroom were closed, but he could see her shadow moving against the fabric. The rhythmic sways of her form sent shivers of anticipation coursing through him. She was utterly unaware of the predator lurking outside, pulse quickening as she shed the weight of the day, shedding layers like the walls she worked so hard to build around herself. Peeling off her clothes and putting them in the washing basket. Her underwear still warm and fragrant. The aromas drifted back to him with a blinding rush, making his head spin.

He could barely contain himself. Tonight, would be different. Tonight, he would claim his prize.

With an eerie calm, he approached her patio door. He used two picks to move the levers and isolate the locks. The lock clicked open under the deftness of his hand. One step across the threshold sent adrenaline surging through him like fire. He moved stealthily through the darkened living room, dimly lit by the streetlight filtering through the curtains—the atmosphere thick with the thrill of impending conquest. His mouth was watering at the thought of fucking her, hurting her so badly, licking her tears. His mind was a maelstrom of devastating evil thoughts.

His heart raced as he turned the lock on the inner side of the door, securing it behind him. He climbed the stairs, savouring the quiet of the house, the creeping silence amplifying his anticipation as he tread lightly toward the bedroom. There would be no one to interrupt him; the shadows were his domain, where he lived and breathed.

As he reached the top of the staircase, prepared to sneak into her sanctuary, an unexpected noise froze him in place. The distinct sound of creaking floorboards drifted through the almost palpable silence. Confusion crackled in his mind. Was Olivia not alone?

As if summoned by his unease, the bedroom door swung open, revealing the darkened interior. He peered inside, the silhouette made sharper against the dim light spilling from the hallway. But instead of the petite figure of Olivia, he was met with a massive form—an imposing young man, covered in tattoos that twisted and turned across his skin like animated shadows.

The man was daunting, the sheer size of him eliciting immediate dread. He brandished a baseball bat wrapped in barbed wire, the flickering light catching glints from the deadly metal. The realization hit Zodiac like a punch to the gut: he had not done his homework. This was not Olivia.

Before he could process or retreat, the young man lunged, wielding the bat with terrifying speed. The blow landed squarely on Zodiac's side, sending him sprawling against the wall. Pain erupted like wildfire, the air leaving his lungs as he tried to scramble to his feet.

'Olivia said you might call,' the giant roared, with a feral intensity that reverberated off the walls. 'You fucking freak. How does that feel?' he struck him again. The bat bruised and cracked a bone, the barbs ripped flesh and muscle. Zodiac cried out in pain and fear.

'You've picked on the wrong house, perverted twat,' another blow stunned him.

Zodiac managed to pierce through the haze of pain, but before he could respond, another brutal hit landed, this time across his back, accompanied by the sickening crunch of flesh against metal. He gasped and crumpled to the ground, darkness creeping in as a barrage of strikes left him battered and broken, each one robbing him of consciousness.

As he slipped away, unconsciousness claimed him. The last thing he registered was the faint echoing of the man's voice, a mixture of rage and confusion, as darkness enveloped him entirely.

WHEN HE WAS JOLTED back to awareness, Zodiac found himself in the cold, sterile confines of an ambulance. Harsh lights stung his eyes, and the steady beeping of medical equipment mixed with muffled voices spoke of chaos all around him. He shifted slightly, pain shooting through him like lances, and then he caught fragments of a conversation from a police officer seated next to him.

"...send a message to Detective Mann. We've got a situation here... someone was breaking into her old house...we think it's Zodiac."

A sense of dread washed over him, a chilling realization that made his heart pound in his chest despite the pain. Olivia had sold the house? The home that had once been a sanctuary for her had now transformed into a trap for him.

He had underestimated every aspect of this night. Pain coursed through him as he mentally kicked himself; he hadn't been careful enough, hadn't been thorough. In his obsession with Olivia, he had allowed the shadows to trick him, and this time—the hunter had become the hunted.

As the ambulance door swung shut, fading lights pulling away from him, a cold certainty settled over Zodiac. He would recover, escape and fuck her brains out. Bitch.

Chapter 52

Kidnap

The blaring sirens of the ambulance drowned out the chaos surrounding it as it weaved through the traffic. Other drivers were completely unaware that inside, the notorious serial killer known as the Zodiac lay on a stretcher, bloodied and beaten, the fight for breath leaving him weak and confused. The paramedics worked swiftly, but the tension in the vehicle was palpable—a harbinger of what lay ahead. They were treating a vicious rapist murderer, a man they would rather kill than save but their vocation denied them that pleasure.

Suddenly, the ambulance came to a screeching halt. Tyres skidded against the asphalt, jolting Zodiac's battered body as the engine nearly stalled. Outside, the muffled sounds of shouting voices echoed through the walls of the vehicle, rising to a crescendo. Confusion and fear flickered in the eyes of the paramedics.

'What the fuck is going on?' one of them asked.

Before anyone could assess the situation, the back doors swung open with a thunderous bang. In rushed four men, clad in black, armed with shotguns, their faces obscured by masks. The police officer guarding Zodiac barely had time to react before they overpowered him, slamming him against the frame of the ambulance. A cacophony of metal clinking echoed as they cuffed him, immobilising him and leaving him at their mercy.

Zodiac's heart raced. An escape? Or a death sentence? The men dragged him from the ambulance with rough hands, tossing him into the back of a waiting white transit van. As the doors slammed shut, one of them leaned in close, a malicious grin evident in his tone. 'Dixie Dean says hello.'

Panic swelled in Zodiac's chest. Dixie Dean—an underworld figure with a reputation for brutality. Whatever fate waited for him, it promised to be far worse than he had ever orchestrated.

THE WAREHOUSE WAS A cavernous, dimly lit space that smelled of rust and decay. Zodiac found himself tied to a grimy workbench, stripped of his clothes and any semblance of dignity. His arms and legs were secured with thick chains; the clanking of metal echoed ominously in the otherwise hushed environment.

Before him stood two men, clad in leather aprons and welding masks, their eyes glinting with a cruel delight. An assortment of tools lay sprawled out on a nearby table: a blowtorch, a jigsaw, a power drill, an array of butcher's knives, and an assortment of hooks and pliers. Each tool seemed to beckon a nightmare that Zodiac had once dished out to his own victims.

'Our boss knows his daughter is dead and that you killed her. He wants to know where her remains are?'

Panic surged as the men advanced closer, their intentions clear. Zodiac's mind raced through memories of his own previous acts of violence, the thrill he once felt now replaced by a primal fear. They began with precision, ripping out his teeth one by one, the searing pain rendering him nearly unconscious. They didn't stop there; fingers and toes followed, knowing that every severed limb brought fresh agony.

But the sadistic rhythm of their ritual was only just beginning. With callous efficiency, they brought forth the blowtorch, using its fierce flame to cauterize the wounds and keep him alive. Each sear of flesh felt like the final farewell to a life he had manipulated so many times.

All the while, the men interrogated him relentlessly. 'Where is Amber Dean buried?' The question was a drumbeat against his consciousness, blurring the line between pain and despair. The agony was more than he could tolerate, and he screamed like a child and begged for mercy, but none was forthcoming.

In moments stretched to feel like hours by agony, he finally gasped out the location— 'In the woods on Water Lane in Tarbock Green. There's a pet cemetery. She's in a grave marked Rocky.' The admission slipped from his lips, a final act of surrender to the nightmare that had ensnared him.

'Please kill me now...'

'Not a chance, Zodiac.' The man smiled. 'We're under contract to make this last a week. Make yourself comfortable because we've only just begun.'

THE MORNING SUN BROKE through the thick canopy of trees, casting slivers of light onto the forest floor. Olivia Mann, leading a focused forensic team, navigated the woods with purpose. They were equipped with the tools necessary to delve into the earth, each step laden with the weight of uncertainty and hope. Their mission was clear: to unearth the remains of Amber Dean, the latest victim linked to the Zodiac, and perhaps even secure the end to his reign of terror.

The air was thick with dampness and the scent of decaying leaves as Olivia manoeuvred further into the heart of the forest. Each step felt like a journey deeper into a realm where time stood still—a place untouched by the mundane world, where shadows lurked behind ancient trees and whispered secrets only the wind could understand. Today, she was on the hunt for a gravestone, one marked simply with the name "Rocky."

A tip from the underworld had led her here, to an obscure pet cemetery shrouded in oak and elm trees. The thick canopy above blocked out most of the sunlight, casting a melancholic gloom on the buried memories of the loved animals that lay within. The delicate crunch of twigs underfoot was the only sound, punctuated by the occasional rustle of branches that echoed unsettlingly.

Olivia's heartbeat quickened as she approached the clearing where the pet cemetery was said to be. A rickety wooden sign bearing the words 'Fred's Bed' leaned awkwardly to one side, as though it too felt the weight of sorrow that enveloped this place. Unkempt grasses and wildflowers choked the paths between the gravestones, each one a testament to a beloved animal lost too soon.

She took a moment to centre herself, focusing back on the reason for being there. Rocky's grave was believed to be the site where Amber Dean's remains were buried. The information could be false but it had to be investigated. It may shine light on the ongoing investigation into the Zodiac killings.

The information had also informed the police that the Zodiac had been interrogated for the location of Amber. She needed answers, and the truth behind Rocky's final resting place which could unravel the mystery of what had happened to Amber, a beautiful young girl, plucked from her world and dragged to hell by the devil himself.

As she moved deeper into the cemetery, her eyes scanned the haphazardly arranged gravestones. Some were adorned with photographs and flowers, while others were simply marked with wooden crosses, fading in the elements. The ominous atmosphere seemed to thicken as she approached the far side of the clearing. Then she spotted it—a gravestone, worn and slightly tilted, etched with the name "Rocky."

A sense of relief washed over her; she had found it. She knelt before the stone, brushing a hand over the mossy surface, feeling the weight of loss that lingered in the air—the love lost, the memories held tightly in the hearts of those who mourned. But as her fingers traced the carving of the dog's name, something caught her eye.

A mere few feet away, on the next grave, hung a pink nightie, fluttering slightly in the soft breeze, its fabric vibrant against the muted hues of the cemetery. Confusion gripped her. It looked eerily familiar.

Olivia's heart sank as she recognised the garment. It was hers. Memories rushed back unbidden—the last time she wore it, a night filled with laughter and warmth, long before darkness crept into her life. She felt as though the air had been sucked from her lungs, her breath catching in her throat as she struggled to process the implications.

'Why is it here, you bastard?' she whispered, dread pooling in her stomach. Had the Zodiac left a taunt, a reminder of his grip on her life even in the most innocuous places? Was this act a cruel joke, or a message directing her straight into his twisted game, that he was playing beyond the grave? He had put it there in the knowledge that only she would recognise it, in the hope she would one day be searching for Amber. The forest around her felt alive as she moved, shadows whispering secrets, as if the ancient trees themselves were bearing witness to her search.

'Let's get to work,' she said. 'If Amber is in there, let's take her home to her mother.'

As they unearthed the soil, the horror of their discovery became evident—Amber's remains, fragile and lost to time, lay shrouded beneath the roots and earth. Scattered among the undergrowth were other remains, a macabre testament to Zodiac's depravity. Overwhelmed by the grim reality before her, Olivia felt tears stream down her face. The nightmare that had engulfed their lives—the agony, the fear, and the endless search—was drawing to a close. The wretched mark of the Zodiac was finally being erased from their collective memory, and with each recovery, the hope of healing emerged from the shadows. As the forensic team carefully documented the findings, Olivia whispered a silent promise to the lost souls: they would not be forgotten. 'We're going to take you all home. Rest in peace now...'

THE END

A request from the author

I hope you have enjoyed my book. If you have, please tell your friends and share online as the market is flooded and being discovered is increasingly difficult! Third party endorsement is the key to the success of any author and makes a huge impact on awareness. There are 35 books across 6 series to enjoy.

The Detective Alec Ramsay series (7 books)

UK: https://amzn.eu/d/07vQ9JGk

USA; https://a.co/d/4cCfu1G

The Anglesey Murders (10 books)

UK; https://amzn.eu/d/02E5RGYq

USA; https://a.co/d/0KWNtHH

The Inspector Braddick series (4 books)

UK; https://amzn.eu/d/0hItuYX2

USA; https://a.co/d/9s2IqCA

The Soft Target series (5 books)

UK; https://amzn.eu/d/0inDPagn

USA; https://a.co/d/eeHM6kf

Cuckoos on the Mersey series (3 books)

UK; https://amzn.eu/d/02fakyFm

USA: https://a.co/d/hDlap59

The Journey series (3 books)

UK: https://amzn.eu/d/00Bs1FkP

USA; https://a.co/d/f2tv5Ar

For all offers and early information on new releases, follow me here;

https://www.facebook.com/conrad.jones.397

https://www.facebook.com/conradjonesauthorpage/

9 781739 406684